Doomsday War!

Multiple alarms screamed on the bridge, startling Stargazer. Proximity alert...light boom...dosimeter...particle concentration...

Jack Hasta shouted, "*Gamma ray surge!!*"

"*Mon dieu...*" With the doors open, the Carrier deployed, and fighters launched, Stargazer could do nothing except try, in the seconds remaining, to save the *Silver Streak*. This was what he had feared: someone had thrown a naked starship at them!

No time to save the fighters...no time to save the Carrier...no time to save Star World...no time even to set a course...just need to get away!

To Jack, he shouted, "*Light speed factor—*"

His command was cut off by the mayhem that followed, and then the darkness and silence.

BOOKS BY COLLIN R. SKOCIK

SHORT STORY COLLECTIONS
The Future Lives!
Voyage Into the Unknown: Volume One
Voyage Into the Unknown: Volume Two
Voyage Into the Unknown: Volume Three
Voyage Into the Unknown: Volume Four
Voyage Into the Unknown: Volume Five
Voyage Into the Unknown: Volume Six

NOVELS
The Sunburst Fire
Dreams of the Stars
Voyage Into the Unknown
Voyage Into the Unknown 2: The Victory of Mordrax
Voyage Into the Unknown 3: Back From the Future
Voyage Into the Unknown 4: A Fond Farewell
Voyage Into the Unknown 5: The New Beginning
Voyage Into the Unknown 6: The Mind Machine
Voyage Into the Unknown 7: Passage to Hyron
Voyage Into the Unknown 8: The Reign of Edmonds
Voyage Into the Unknown 9: The Krotus Horror
Voyage Into the Unknown 10: The Thermian Menace
Voyage Into the Unknown 11: The Armageddon Strategy

STATION POST ONE
The Priest Monster
Uneasy Alliance
"That's What They Want You To Believe"
Countdown to War

V^{OYAGE}_{INTO THE} UNKNOWN 11
THE ARMAGEDDON STRATEGY

Collin R. Skocik

Cover art: Jonathan R. Skocik

Visit the author's website at
http://www.lulu.com/spotlight/voyageintotheunknown

VOYAGE INTO THE UNKNOWN 11:
THE ARMAGEDDON STRATEGY

CHAPTER 1

Heat!

Nostrils filled with searing fumes, the smell of sulphur and excrement. Skin raw with burns, clothes stiff and clinging with dry sweat.

Open your eyes.

No.

Open your eyes, dammit. You're the Captain. You must be strong.

No. I'm tired of being strong.

Tough! You've clung to the job of Captain for all these years, riding over people's advice, disobeying the President, pushing people around for the fun of it—well, now, here you are in Hell. You bought it, it's time to pay for it!

Very well. He opened his eyes, then let out a half-sigh, half sob. Yes, he was still here. Just another day in Hell.

Hell.

It wasn't a myth. It wasn't a figure of speech. He wasn't dreaming. He wasn't trapped in an alien illusion. He was, literally, in Hell.

He lay on his bunk—hardly a bunk at all, but a bed of crisscrossed mesh wires affixed to an iron frame. It was hot. Of course, everything in Hell was hot.

The collar around his neck was hot, and the skin underneath was sweaty and itchy. He tried to scratch underneath, but the collar was a sort of flex metal composed of hundreds of tiny segments that adhered to his flesh; he could get his finger under only a few segments at a time, and when they snapped back into place it hurt.

He was heavy. Everything was heavy here— though the farther down you went, the heavier you were. Each circle of Hell was heavier than the one above—until the deepest circle was crushing beyond the point of human endurance. He was lucky to be up this far.

The cell was a cage, the walls made of woven wire mesh so that you could look out upon the nightmarish vista of Hell. Other cages were visible, each suspended over the great shaft. Hot, orange smoke curled up from far below. There was a constant sound of loud hissing from the air pumps, and from the seething cauldon far below.

And of course there was the screaming. There were lots of reasons to scream in Hell. But one of the main reasons was the Lake of Fire.

It was visible from here, though you had to crane your neck. The shaft dropped away to a dizzying depth, and down there, far below, you could see it, *just* see it—a whirlpool of flame, the ultimate damnation where souls were tortured under the great weight of the world and in the searing cauldron of lava. Sometimes those condemned to the Lake of Fire drifted too close to the center of the whirlpool and were drawn down, beyond all hope of rescue; their fate was one which did not bear thinking of.

Most, however, stayed close to the edge, where the guards could retrieve them after a reasonable period of punishment. They couldn't stay in the pool of lava for long, of course—the torture was brief, and the prisoners encased in special suits to protect them from flashing into ash. Under the intense gravity down there, lava was denser, more buoyant than on Earth.

Lost, beautiful, blue-green Earth...

Strange, the chain of events from Earth to Hell; Earth had been destroyed by the Thermians, driving the *Silver Streak* on the long voyage across the universe, and into the alliance with the Community in order to fight the Thermians—and then the Community went to war with the Alternative Alliance...

...and now here he was, in Hell.

Hell.

The name of the planet was Strydia in the Valdor language, Hlobbbblllggh in the Throrb language, Petiki in the Valerian language—but no matter the language, it translated the same: Hell. And the demons who tended to this archetypical nightmare of a planet were the Throrb. What had those Throrb jailers done to have been sentenced themselves to tend this terrible place?

There were four bunks in the cell, but five occupants—rather typical for Hell—but anyway, the floor was more comfortable anyway. Or less uncomfortable, as things were measured in Hell. There was no toilet or running water—just a large bucket filled with excrement; yet the stench of the sulphur gas whooshing up the shaft rendered the stink of five creatures' feces irrelevant.

There was himself—Richard Cameron, until recently the Captain of the Space Star *Silver Streak*. The *Silver Streak*...his ship, his pride, his love...somewhere out there she was fighting a war...a stupid, usless war in which the Community and the Alternative Alliance were destroying each other...and he could do nothing to help. He was parted from his ship...in Hell....

There was Ambassador Wyechee Koff of Valeri, who had been here for a while now and seemed hardened to it—though Cameron was sure that was an act. The Valerians were humanoid—two arms, two legs, head at the top, though taller than most humans. None of that was apparent, for Koff wore a hooded, black robe that covered his entire body. The face was odd—there was no face, in fact. There was a sensitive membrane of some sort that seemed to serve the function of eyes, nose, and mouth. Food and water disappeared into that plate by some mechanism Cameron couldn't identify. But this robed, faceless creature seemed right at home here in Hell.

There was Argo, the Dreb, an ally whose mysterious abilities had so far failed to get them out of this. Also humanoid, Argo was hairless, with a prominently pointed chin and wide, yellow eyes that rarely blinked. Garbed in a black robe and wide-brimmed fedora, he looked like a stereotypical silent film villain. Strange beings the Dreb were—able to harness the high energy of the Thermian universe, able to carry out feats of what could only be described as magic. Argo was powerless now, though, his supernatural abilities held at bay by the field of P-SAR energy—Partial Superplasmic Activity Reducer—surrounding the great tower of Hell. The Dreb lived in the service of the Thermians, determined to lead their people to accept the premature supernovae of their suns. Except for Derringer-9, which had somehow escaped the Thermian ideology. Argo was a friend, and friends were the only comfort in Hell.

There was Splrrrb, the Throrb dissident, traitor to his people, condemned now to eternal damnation for his sin. Like all Throrb, Splrrrb was a soft-skinned, sluglike creature with no appendages, though he could form long, prehensile tendrils like pseudopods. He had turned against his people precisely because of places like this—what kind of people would condemn anyone, even the most hardened criminal, to Hell?

And of course there was Frank Johnson, Cameron's first officer, huddled into a ball on his bunk. Frank had gone nuts, and Frank was not the type to go nuts. But Hell could drive anyone nuts. Even after twenty-two years of adventures on many different planets, faced with many different challenges and ordeals, something about this place had gotten under Frank's skin. He had simply lost it, and there was nothing Cameron could say to him, nothing he could do. Frank had to come through this on his own, if he could. Of course, even if he did, what would be the point? They were in Hell, and there was no escaping Hell.

But Cameron was worried about Frank. They had been in lots of tough spots before—though never, of course, had they gone to Hell before.

But it was disconcerting, the way Frank had totally lost his mind. After removing him for interrogation, the Throrb had dragged Frank back to the cell, kicking and screaming with such wild abandon that he looked like a cartoon character. Cameron would have laughed in any other context. He marveled that Frank could flail his body so in this heavy gravity.

Cameron sat up painfully, the heavy gravity gripping his chest. He worried about his heart, though he had no heart conditions he knew of. Splrrrb and Argo were engaged in quiet conversation on the other side of the cell. Koff lay on his bunk, arms locked behind his head, that blank non-face staring upward.

Frank was still curled in his bunk.

Cameron lifted himself from his bunk, groaning. He tromped across the cell, his feet thunking down hard, like those ancient astronauts in their bulky space suits, practicing their space activities in a gravity field where they weighed three hundred pounds. Cameron wondered how much he weighed here.

He sat on the corner of Frank's bunk, relieved as the strain on his back from the brief walk across the cell eased. "Frank? What's up?"

Without rolling over to face him, Frank muttered, "Oh, gee, jut passing the time."

Well, it was nice to see that Frank's sense of humor had returned—bitter humor though it may be. He was no longer an incoherent bundle of random impulses; Cameron had worried at first that Frank had tipped over into insanity. He was still worried about that.

"We'll get out of this, Frank." The words were weak, he knew, and he had spoken them many times before, in many situations, on many planets. But it was all he could think of.

"Yeah," Frank said. "Maybe."

Again, Frank had made that exact reply many times before—but never with quite the bitterness and hopelessness as now. And why not? Cameron could not think of any situation they had ever been in that could possibly be worse than...Hell.

"We've been in tight spots before," he said uselessly.

Frank rolled over and got up, wincing. "Spare me the speech, Dick." He clomped across the cell, grunting with the effort.

Cameron watched him go; he must *really* not want to talk if he was willing to get up and pace in this gravity. On the plus side, this must be doing wonders for their muscles. He almost smiled—though the gravity tugged his jowls down and made smiling difficult—as he thought of the ancient legend of Superman.

He got up, groaning with a pain that was rapidly developing in his lower back, and followed Frank across the cell. He knew he should probably leave Frank alone and let him come to terms with his own demons—demons! *That* was appropriate here!—but he couldn't bring himself to abandon his friend in this hour of need, even if that was what Frank needed.

Or perhaps his motivation was more selfish than that—Frank was his oldest and closest friend, and his only real friend here in Hell. He didn't know Argo, Koff, or Splrrrb. He needed Frank. He needed his old friend, his old partner, his buddy with whom he had gotten out of so many scrapes on so many planets.

He placed a hand on Frank's shoulder—though the gravity brought it down harder than he intended, making it more of a swat than the comforting touch he had intended. "Frank...what's the matter?"

As he said it, he realized it was the most excruciatingly stupid question he had ever asked. *What's the matter? We're in HELL!*

But Frank did not give that obvious answer. Instead, he glanced furtively at Argo and Splrrrb, at the seemingly oblivious Koff, and sighed. Softly, he said, "*You* may get out of this...but I never did."

"What do you mean?"

"This just...rings a little too close to..." He broke off. There was something he was not willing to say, something he didn't want to talk about.

"Go on," Cameron urged him. "It's me, Dick. We tell each other things, right? We help each other. Whatever it is..."

Frank hesitated. He looked out on the flaming vista of Hell, the cages suspended in the great shaft, the shapes of the Throrb torturers on the circular shelves, level after horrible level, down into the seething cauldron of the fiery heart of Strydia. The screams of the damned. He spoke so softly that Cameron had to lean close to hear him: "These guys'll torture us, you know."

"Well, that hasn't happened yet."

"Oh, yes it has. It happened to me, twenty-eight years ago."

Cameron realized then what Frank was talking about. "Oh. When you were a P.O.W. in the Martian War."

Frank nodded. That experience had haunted him all these years, hung over him like a black shroud—concealed like Ambassador Koff's blank face under its black hood, but always there. It had haunted his career, had stalked him in his years as the *Silver Streak*'s first officer. Cameron had not known about the incident, though it was in Frank's personnel file; he just hadn't paid that much attention. It was not something Frank liked to talk about, and so for many years Cameron made light of Frank's dislike for his duty, his hatred for planetary landings. He had laughed it off as mere grousing; for despite his grumbling, Frank always did a good job.

It was a full ten years before Frank finally told him the story of his incarceration on Mars, of the torture he had endured—and all that as a draftee into the Star Force; he had wanted to be an entertainment writer, not a pilot.

But dammit, Frank was a *good* pilot—no, a great one. Otherwise he never would have risen to squadron commander, never would have been named as commander of the *Silver Streak*'s Carrier, and never would have stepped up to the job of First Officer of the *Silver Streak*—and performed so admirably despite his antipathy for the job.

Cameron accepted the responsibility for not taking his friend's feelings seriously, but he also gave little thought to how deep the trauma was.

"I got over it once before," Frank said, "but it never really goes away."

"What?"

Frank sighed again. He still had difficulty discussing it, especially with someone like

Cameron, who never allowed trauma to have deep or lasting effects on his psyche. "Flashbacks. Nightmares. I had psychotherapy, but no matter what, it...this..." A half-sob escaped him. He shook his head, embarrassed, turning away from Cameron.

"We're the sum of our experiences, Frank. Maybe you can face down the old nightmares now and chase them away."

Frank was silent. His hands gripped the wire mesh of their cage—Cameron winced as he watched; that wire was hot. After a moment, Frank said, "Well...you go be the cosmic hero. I'm just a little-brained pilot."

Cameron smiled faintly; though he did not believe Frank was at all "little-brained," it was true that Frank had never been comfortable discussing the cosmic concepts and philosophical ideas that fascinated Cameron. "We're in this together, Frank."

Frank nodded. "I know...we always have been."

Cameron turned and trudged back to his bunk.

Ambassador Koff rolled over and sat upright. He turned his blank face toward Cameron; it was a disconcerting sight, like the Angel of Death, or Dickens' Ghost of Christmas Future. "Captain Cameron." The voice was a harsh whisper, resonating through the membrane like a wheeze. It was incapable of articulating any human language; Koff could never speak English, but the Throrb had at least allowed their prisoners to retain their clothes, which meant that Cameron and Frank still wore their translation fibers implanted in their collars. Koff's voice sounded like a talking snake.

"I haven't told them anything," Koff said, "they haven't even asked."

Koff kept saying that. It could be Cameron's imagination, but he felt there was a defensive edge to Koff's protestations.

"But every morning they take me up to a room topside, plug some sort of cord to my head, and let me go."

"You think they're extracting data directly from your brain?"

"That would make sense." Again that vaguely defensive air. Cameron had the sense that Koff knew very well that he was giving the Throrb information, but didn't want to admit it. Who could blame him? If the Throrb were taking information directly from his brain, what could he do about it? But the shame of involuntarily surrendering all the information the enemy wanted must be humiliating.

Argo had broken off his conversation with Splrrrb and now stood facing Cameron, glaring at him with that intense, unblinking gaze that was normal for him, but would have been comically rude in a human. "When I had my... 'powers'...I had the ability to home in on mental processes. When the people of Station Post One first captured me, they used a modified P-SAR. It wore off over time and I got my powers back."

Koff said, "The modified P-SAR field here is on constantly."

"But perhaps I'll become immune to it."

"Not likely," Cameron said, "not if it deadens superplasmic activity."

Frank, grateful to have something productive to focus on, had approached the group and now sat heavily on his bunk. "Well, it doesn't, Dick. It doesn't *deaden* superplasmic activity, it *reduces* it. Maybe Argo's right."

"Well, it's a chance, at least." Cameron spoke the words but didn't really believe them— of course, Argo's powers were pretty hard to believe in the first place. Here he was, in Hell, one of his cellmates a literal wizard. He had stepped from reality into a fantasy. He looked out at the nightmare surrounding their cage and wondered if—*hoped*—this was a bad dream.

CHAPTER 2

The planet Strydia was the innermost satellite of the red giant Rinkhal-A in the Messier-67 star cluster—or the King Cobra. Subjected to extreme tidal forces due to the proximity of its giant star, Strydia's surface was almost entirely molten lava, its atmosphere a dense miasma of sulphur gas and carbon dioxide.

Strydia was larger than Earth and denser, its surface gravity more than three times Earth normal. Obviously the planet had no native life, and Cameron never would have considered it for colonization—the surface gravity was not survivable in the long term. In fact, no known species could survive on Strydia, even on its night side.

But to the Throrb, that was exactly the point.

The planet was tidally locked to its huge parent, and the Throrb built their infamous prison on the day side, in the great pool of molten lava that dominated an entire hemisphere. Even on the planet's night side, vast pools of glowing fire were visible from orbit, and it even rained lava frequently. If Cameron were to choose a planet to call Hell, Strydia would be it.

He and Frank, along with Argo and Splrrrb, had come here in an attempt to rescue Ambassador Koff, only to be captured themselves. Ironically, Splrrrb himself had only just been rescued from a Throrb prison asteroid; now, after an all-too-brief period of freedom, he was again in Throrb hands. After all that the crew of Station Post One had gone through to find him and rescue him from Thailey Prison on Asteroid Doom, now he was in an even worse prison. Cameron wondered how the Throrb would punish Splrrrb for his crime of defection.

Koff had already had his turn under the Throrb inquisitors. Now it was Cameron's turn. He was dragged into a small white room adorned with unpleasant-looking devices surrounding a central chair. As they secured him to the chair and attached metal straps to his wrists and ankles, he felt an unwelcome sense of *déjà vu*—he had been through something much like this before. A metal strap was attached to his head, the form and texture almost identical to the brain-tapper used aboard the *Silver Streak*—or to the Mind Machine used by the Vyx.

"Starjudge all over again," he muttered.

Memories of his experience in the huge Vyx ship, imprisoned alongside his old enemy Mordrax, his mind probed by the centipede-like alien Starjudge, gnawed at him. "Damn you!" he shouted uselessly.

But he could see a map of his brain on a holoscreen nearby, the Throrb interrogators clustered around it as symbols of a multitude of colors appeared and disappeared over it. He knew then that his mind was being tapped, knowledge extracted. They did not need to torture him, they did not need him to tell them anything; they were simply taking what they wanted.

And then what? He would not be needed anymore, right? Would he be cast into the Lake of Fire?

"Okay, what are you saying?" he demanded. "You're done now, right? You extracted what you needed, right?"

One of the Thorb approached him. "Our systems have no experience with your brain. We must synchronize by sensory cutoff."

"Sensory cutoff? What does that mean?"

"Your brain must be isolated from your body. Our metabolic synthesizer will take control of your autonomic nervous system while we map your brain and neural processes."

"Wait, what are you saying? You're going to remove my brain?"

The Throrb quivered and tittered. Cameron blushed; he knew they were laughing at him.

"Not physically. Your brain will simply be isolated artificially. You will be deprived of all inputs and outputs."

The Throrb then conversed among themselves. Their pseudopods tapped at the holoscreen, and the machine responded.

Cameron tried to protest, to stall, but he knew it was useless—he had been through all this before. He knew how it felt to have his mind drained...his knowledge and memories probed... his privacy violated...he had even had his personality edited.

This wasn't quite the same, though. There was no sensation of reliving the past, no intrusive probe into his mind or memory. Instead he became detached. There was a dizziness, then a feeling of weightlessness. The world faded out. No sight, no sound, no touch. Nothing.

It was rather peaceful, in fact, to shut out everything, to forget Hell and the Throrb and the botched mission that had brought him here. He could even imagine, if he wanted to, that he was back on the bridge of the *Silver Streak*, in his comfortable old command chair, Frank Johnson at his station to the left, Jack Hasta and Philippe Stargazer at the console before him...laughing and joking and whiling away the hours, turning the dark quest across the universe into a pleasure...

But that thought only brought back the depressing knowledge that the *Silver Streak* was, no doubt, locked down in battle. Or even destroyed. Out there, the Community and the Alternative Alliance were destroying each other. For all he knew, they might already be destroyed—it could be that Hell was all that remained, all that would ever be.

But he had come here of his own free will; he hadn't been sentenced. They had just caught him and kept him. Surely that must be against the law? Maybe not, not during wartime. He was a prisoner of war—a war he had not wanted, and would not have been a part of had it not been for the hasty decision a year ago to join the Community. Now he had allies and enemies among alien races he had never heard of prior to a year ago—some of whom he had only learned of in the past week.

Valdor, Throrb, Dreb, Valerians...What a different galaxy than the one he had known for the twenty years prior to contact with the Community. He longed for those days...surveying alien planets for colonization, handling problems one at a time, and always returning to the bridge and his friends and feeling that, despite the destruction of the Earth, all was well and what was left of the human race had a shot at a bright future.

And now his ship was at war and he and Frank were in Hell.

He, Frank, Argo, and Splrrrb had come here in a Throrb Devastator, a stealth troop transport stolen by the Valdor. Cameron knew it was a high-risk mission, and he embarked on it despite the protestations of President Copenburg. But he knew that the retrieval of Ambassador Koff was of the absolute highest priority.

Yet even after Splrrrb's picturesque descriptions, he was still awed by the sight of the planet Strydia. He had never been in the vicinity of Jupiter's volcanic moon Io, but this giant world would put that temperamental moon to shame. And its gravitational field was frightening.

Tearing his eyes from the giant world with its oceans of lava, he asked, "Any other space traffic in the vicinity?"

"There's a ship departing," Frank Johnson told him, "its angle won't intersect us. There are a few ships docked at the tower."

Cameron turned to the Derringerian Priest King. "Argo...can you...*sense* whether Koff is down there?"

"That is not among my powers," Argo replied evenly.

"Damn. Why didn't you tell us that?"

"You never intimated you would ask for such a thing."

"All right, never mind. We'll monitor communications. Splrrrb, can you listen for any secret codes or anything?"

Splrrrb said, "I don't know all the current codes, but I will endeavor to identify any signs of the ambassador or any other Valerians."

"Okay. And if they ask us to identify ourselves, reply in the Throrb language and military code that we're patrolling for enemy infiltrators."

"I will."

"Odd," Argo remarked.

"What is?" Cameron asked.

"That there are no such patrols. If Koff has been brought here, you would think they would have their eyes out for enemy infiltration."

Frank looked up from the sensors, alarmed. "Then you don't think Koff is here?"

"On the contrary. The Alternative Alliance is at war and this is their most infamous prison. There should be at least three full warships guarding it at all times. The fact that there are not tells me they are deliberately making it easy for us. And that means they were expecting us...and Koff *is* down there."

Cameron looked out the bay window at the huge, glowing planet as it grew closer and closer. "And there are strong enemy forces waiting to ambush us."

No sooner were the words out of his mouth than the klaxon sounded. "Dick, I'm losing orientation," Frank said.

"Realign."

"Trying...controls are fighting me..."

A vast, gray shape hove into view, seeming to have appeared from nowhere. Its immensity eclipsed the red and purple prison planet.

"Something big ahead," Frank warned.

The vast gray shape shone in the light of Strydia's giant sun. It was huge, perhaps half the size of the *Silver Streak*, and triangular, optimal for diffusing radiation and heat during light speed travel.

"A Skonn-class destroyer," Splrrrb said. "Its stealth field makes it invisible."

As the destroyer closed, Splrrrb panicked. He squidged back and forth in the Devastator's small control room, repeating, "All is lost...all is lost!"

"Calm down," Cameron said with forced patience. "We don't even know that he's after us."

"Something's deadened our directional control," Frank said. "We're stuck dead in space."

"We are now prisoners of war," Argo said, "Unless...I can destroy that ship."

"All right, then." Cameron gestured out the window at the looming destroyer. "Please do so."

Argo stiffened in concentration. He closed his eyes, clenched his fists, finally let out a gasp. "My powers are gone!"

"How can that be?" Frank asked.

"The men of Station Post One were able to deaden my powers with a modified P-SAR. The Alternative Alliance must have learned to do this."

"Then our Dreb army is useless!"

"We die," Splrrrb moaned. "We die..."

"That ship is overtaking us now," Frank said.

Cameron saw a huge depression in the destroyer's underside opening up. Huge grapnels were slowly extending. "Then I guess there's nothing we can do. Well...at least I suppose we'll find out if Ambassador Koff is here."

From that point on it was useless to resist, since two humans and a Derringerian were clearly enemies, and Splrrrb was easy to identify as the Number One Most Wanted Criminal in the Alternative Alliance. They were marched to the captain's quarters on board the destroyer. En route, Cameron asked Splrrrb, "Aren't there any articles of war the Throrb are obligated to honor?"

"What do you mean?" Splrrrb asked.

Cameron sighed. "I guess not."

The Throrb captain greeted them in his damp quarters, where he was lying at full length on what looked like a black puddle. "Splrrrb. I am pleased to have you back in Alternative Alliance custody. Who are your friends?"

"I have no desire to tell you," Splrrrb rumbled.

Cameron stepped forward. "I am Captain Richard Cameron of the Space Star *Silver Streak*. This is my executive officer, Frank Johnson."

The captain's retractable antennae regarded Argo. "And this is the infamous Dreb Priest King."

"Argo."

"As you see, we have monitored Community Intelligence. We have the modified P-SAR...and *other* weapons."

"Like naked starships?" Cameron asked.

"These things need no longer concern you. You are prisoners of war."

"And as prisoners of war, we demand humane treatment! Where is the Valerian Ambassador?"

"You will find out—when you join him on the prison planet Strydia!"

So they had been taken to the top of the great tower of the prison. Cameron had seen orbital towers before, but this monstrosity was like none he had ever seen. At a height of almost ninety thousand kilometers, and a diameter of half a kilometer, the prison was made possible by the mining of dense crystalline structures in the molten surface of Strydia.

A tethered asteroid served as a counterweight, and the highest inhabited part of the tower was two hundred kilometers below the synchronous orbit, where the Throrb could enjoy a comfortable sensation of light gravity. It was there that Cameron, Frank, Argo, and Splrrrb had been summarily convicted without trial—one of the Throrb practices that had driven Splrrrb to defect.

The outer tower was not so bad; it was alien, with odd architecture and a pungent, earthy smell, but a fairly typical office environment—but this was where the Throrb enforcers spent their free time; it would serve little purpose to put them in Hell.

They were taken to Lublwbb, the warden. "Welcome to Strydia Prison," the warden told them. "You are now on the top level—Level Zero—the *nice* level. From here you will be taken to Documentation. There you will be locked in and fastened with a security collar—which means that leaving Strydia will trigger explosive bolts in the collar. Escape is impossible. You will then be taken to your level. Enjoy your stay."

From there they were taken down a hallway that opened up to a balcony, and that was where Cameron got his first glimpse of the great shaft. From up here, he couldn't see the Lake of Fire; it was only a dizzying drop to infinite depths. There were no cages up this high, but there was a breath of hot wind from below which gave a vague intimation of the horrors of the depths.

"Any sign of your powers returning, Argo?" he asked quietly.

"No," Argo whispered. "Someone around here must have a modified P-SAR."

"Maybe they've got modified P-SARs all over the place," Frank mumbled.

Splrrrb said, "There is nothing Strydia Prison does not have to contain and torture prisoners."

"You're a real inspiration, Splrrrb."

"I am merely relaying information. That is what you wanted me to do."

They were escorted from the balcony down another corridor to a blank white room, where a Throrb awaited them behind a counter. Holographic computer displays surrounded the worm-like attendant, and as data flashed in front of his antenna-like protuberances, he said, "Richard Cameron."

Cameron   stepped   forward.   "Richard Cameron—"

"And Frank Johnson."

"That's right," Frank said.

"Argo."

"Yes," Argo said stiffly.

"And Splrrrb."

"Correct." Splrrrb's voice contained no emotion; but that was a combination of the alien speech nuances and the inadequacy of Cameron's translation fibers to express emotion. He knew Splrrrb must be terrified.

"You're on level four thousand four, cell four eight four two."

"Does it have a bathtub?" Cameron quipped. "I'd really like a bathtub."

"Apply their collars."

The guards slapped the adhesive collars. On Cameron, Frank, and Argo, they fitted around the neck; on Argo, it wrapped around his slick body, and Cameron understood the reason for the many little metal segments; there was no other way to keep the collar on the moist and slimy body of a Throrb.

"You are now inmates of Strydia Prison," the attendant said. "Take them below. Level four thousand four, cell four eight four two."

The elevator was in a transparent tube that ran down the side of the shaft. As they rode, Cameron noticed scores of other elevator tubes arrayed around the great shaft.

The car slipped into free-fall—and faster—but there was some sort of artificial gravity that took hold of them and kept them from floating to the top of the car, and even sticking to the ceiling. The drop was vertiginous, and as they fell deeper, Cameron did have the uncanny illusion that he had fallen into the Earth and was plummeting down a subterranean passage into the mythical Hell.

After an hour of this, the car began to slow, and objects that had been a blur began to focus.

He saw the cages suspended over the shaft, connected by a wild phantasmagoria of interconnected walkways and scaffolds. And far below, he saw the orange flame of the lava.

Unlike Danté's iconic damnation, this Inferno had a lot more than nine circles. But Cameron could see how Hell became more horrible with each successive level. The gravity itself took care of that, as did the increasing heat. But he also saw that the upper cages enjoyed a bit of wind, perhaps stirred by convection from the furnace below. There was even a whirlwind that reminded him of Danté's Second Circle.

He imagined, though, that in addition to the natural aspects of the increasing hellishness of the tower, each level had different and increasingly wicked forms of torture.

They arrived on their level. The door opened, and a waiting guard, his sluglike body squished down by the gravity, shouted, "Move!"

The gravity was about one point five gees— or what Philippe Stargazer had told him was the maximum the human body could endure permanently. Walking was uncomfortable.

As he sludged along with effort, Splrrrb said, "A Throrb cannot endure this gravity."

"We do it," the guard snapped. "Be silent."

As they crossed a black bridge covered with what looked like hardened lava, Cameron became aware of the screams. He looked down into the pit, saw the whirling lava far below. The cages, arranged in concentric rings and at various distances from the center of the shaft, contained various life forms, some in agony as they were subjected to cruel and unseen horrors.

Their own cage already contained a prisoner.

"Here we are," the guard said. "Your home for...the rest of your lives." He opened the cell. "You've got company, Valerian."

"Other Valerians?" the robed, faceless prisoner asked.

"No," Cameron said. "Humans, a Derringerian, and a Throrb."

The guard shut the door behind them, and they walked across the iron cage toward their cellmate.

"Welcome to a fate worse than death. I'm Ambassador Wyechee Koff of Valeri."

Cameron stepped forward to shake Koff's hand—but no hand emerged from the black robe. "I'm Captain Richard Cameron of the Space Star *Silver Streak*. This is my first officer, Frank Johnson."

"*Silver Streak?* The ship that established Station Post One?"

"That's right. This is Argo, Priest King of the Dreb of Derringer-9."

"A Dreb?" Koff's blank face betrayed no emotion as he regarded Argo, but his voice sounded vaguely disappointed even through the translation collar. "Well, I'm sorry, but I'm afraid your powers won't work here. They just installed a modified P-SAR network into the planetwide security field."

"We'd figured that out," Argo replied.

The featureless face then turned on the hapless Throrb who could barely move in the high gravity. "And I know you—you're Splrrrb. You've been all over the news lately."

"And fear I will be again," Splrrrb said.

Koff turned back to Cameron. "So what's your crime? Why are you here?"

Cameron couldn't help but smile. "Well...we came to rescue you."

There was a pause. Then: "So how's that going?"

CHAPTER 3

It had been a year since the *Silver Streak* had joined the Community. At that time, Station Post One was deployed in Valdor space so that the *Silver Streak* could continue its journey, leaving the fifty men and women of the solitary space station to work with the Valdor.

One of Station Post One's first assignments took two of its crew to the planet Ymor, where the Dreb were first encountered.

It was now known that the Dreb existed on many worlds, and could be of any species. They had been found on Ymor, on Cerberus, on Derringer-9, and even on Octon, one of the *Silver Streak*'s own colonies. One had even been found in space, aboard a mysterious craft that had been causing interference on Station Post One—but that particular Dreb's homeworld had never been identified.

But wherever they were found, it was the same story: the Dreb were magic. They could teleport, they could control minds, they could shoot energy beams from their eyes, they could locate people from a distance. And they worshipped Thermians. Their religion taught them that when their suns went supernova, they would be transformed, ascended. They would become Thermians themselves. This was all found in the Book of the Dreb, which was found on each Dreb world—except for Derringer-9. Somehow the Derringerians had either escaped the Thermian influence or had somehow never been given the book.

How the Dreb did the tricks they did was not fully understood, but it was known that their DNA was deliberately resequenced by tiny packets of energy filtering into the Dreb brain from the Thermian universe. And the new gene gave the Dreb the ability to conduct energy from the Thermian universe, which as far as anyone knew, was of a higher energy level than this universe.

The exact extent of Dreb power was unknown; even Argo would not or could not tell them.

The Priest King of the Dreb of Derringer-9, Argo had been appalled to learn of the existence of the Thermians, to know that his own people were expected to embrace extinction, to know that these strange shadowy beings were deliberately blowing up suns, destroying whole civilizations. And so he had pledged his support to Station Post One—and, by extension, to the *Silver Streak*.

But he had pledged his support in fighting the Thermians, not the Alternative Alliance. Like the *Silver Streak*, he was caught in the middle of a war he didn't want.

And now he was condemned to Hell.

———

"Your captain is a brave man," Argo said.

Frank Johnson was in no mood to talk, but on the other hand, anything was better than the long and silent wait for Cameron's return. He was uncomfortable with these weird aliens—the creepy, faceless Koff...the sluglike Splrrrb...the bizarre Argo. If he were to be condemned to Hell—or stuck in any crazy predicament on an alien planet—he would rather it just be him and Dick. They were a good team, and they tended to handle crises well on their own. But now Dick was off being tortured or interrogated or God only knew what, and he didn't know how to handle himself or how to talk to these unearthly cellmates.

But he did know how he felt about Argo's observation. "It's an act."

"What?"

"I've known him a long time," Frank said. "He's quaking in his boots, but he'll never admit it, not to us or even to himself."

"He seems pretty sure we'll get out of here," Koff said. "Is that an act too?"

Frank laughed to himself. "No, he really believes it, but that's just him. He's got his life story all written in his head, and it's not supposed to end here. Has nothing to do with reality."

"Sounds like you don't like him."

Frank was startled by that comment. *Do I like him? Of course I **like** him...I just don't* like *him. I like him as a person, but as a captain, he...or maybe I like him as a captain, but not as a person. Or maybe I like him as a captain and as a person, but he just drives me crazy sometimes...*

"Oh, sure I do," he said with sincerity. "We've been friends for so many years it's scary. But we don't always see things the same way."

That was an understatement; they seemed *never* to see things the same way. He smiled as he remembered how many times over the years one of them had pulled the other off the bridge and into the corridor for a private argument. He understood Cameron's exasperation with a first officer who constantly questioned every decision, but dammit, Cameron's decisions so often made so sense!

And yet, at the same time, Frank stood in awe of Cameron. Whether his decisions made sense or not, his strategies tended to work. He had defeated the attacks of the Hyron Commander Mordrax again and again. He had destroyed the Darian Empire. He had accomplished the mission of the *Silver Streak*, setting up colony after colony. And despite years of never-ending dangers and disasters and adventures and crises, the *Silver Streak* was still intact and functional, still carrying its host of survivors of the planet Earth.

Cameron had changed over the years. In the beginning, he had been brash, arrogant, in many ways downright immature. But he had a philosophical mind—*too* philosophical, Frank often thought—and constantly tried to improve himself. And it had worked. He had become less perfunctory, more thoughtful in his decision-making, more respectful of his subordinates.

Yet even at his worst, the guy was likeable. Frank had often sat on the bridge simmering as his opinion went ignored or even mocked, but it was impossible to stay mad at Cameron. He ran a fun bridge, and that was something that had never changed.

In fact, for ten years Frank had commanded the *Silver Streak* himself. Cameron had resigned for reasons neither of them had fully understood, and Frank had never been able to maintain that fun and relaxed atmosphere that seemed to come naturally to Cameron. It had been such a relief when Cameron had returned to the bridge after that long hiatus!

Frank had never wanted to be the captain—or even the first officer. It had been foisted upon him, like much of his life. Drafted into the Star Force, he had found himself a flying prodigy, advancing through the ranks until he was in the pipeline to survive the destruction of the Earth aboard the *Silver Streak*—and finally, by an almost comical quirk of fate, promoted on the spot to first officer the very day the Earth was destroyed—because First Officer Jarrod Gelman simply never showed up.

And for that among other reasons, he couldn't imagine his job—indeed, his life—without Richard Cameron. Yes, Jack Hasta and Philippe Stargazer were a monumental part of his life too—but everything seemed to revolve around Cameron. He couldn't imagine life without him.

And so, appropriately enough, here he was, in Hell, without him....

Two Throrb dragged Cameron back to the cell, tossing him in unceremoniously. Frank winced as he watched his captain fall to the grated floor in the heavy gravity. He ran to Cameron's side. "Dick? You all right?" He gently pulled at Cameron's arm and rolled him over.

"Yeah," Cameron mumbled. His eyes were unfocused.

"What did they do?" He turned toward Koff, angry. "Koff, you said they just extract information!"

Invisible limbs made a shrugging motion within the black robe. "That's all they ever did to me."

Frank leaned over Cameron, examining his eyes, trying to remember his field medical training. As far as he could tell, Cameron's pupils were not dilated...skin was normal color and texture... "Dick, what did they do?"

"Ummmm..." Cameron licked his lips, clenched his eyes shut, and looked around dazed.

"Dick, what did they do?"

Cameron let out his breath, then coughed. "Gimme a minute."

Thank God he was still cognizant...

Breathing heavily, Cameron staggered to his feet, Frank gripping him by the arm. "Easy, Dick."

"It's okay, I'm all right. Just...takes some getting used to."

"What did they do?" It had become vitally important to Frank to know, not only what they had done to Cameron, but what they would do to *him*. He had been a prisoner of war before and had no desire to repeat the experience.

Cameron settled onto his bunk, grunting and huffing with the effort. He blinked again, rubbed his forehead with one hand. Frank sat next to him, bracing him. Cameron held up a hand, staying his concern.

"They...mapped my brain." He swallowed, licked his lips. Frank realized his mouth and throat must be dry, cursed the Throrb for providing no running water. *Well, of course not. This is Hell.*

"Oh...God..." Cameron rubbed his eyes, letting out a long, laborious breath. "They blocked my brain from receiving inputs."

"Oh, my God..." Frank turned away, his jaw slack. *Oh, my God...* That was just what the Martians had done to him, all those years ago. His breath was short, he felt his heart pounding. *Oh, my God...* He remembered the deafening silence... the blackness...the emptiness...no hot, no cold, just *nothing*...the hallucinations...sights, sounds... *No, this must not be happening again, it must not...*

Well, this was Hell, wasn't it? The land of eternal torture. Here, man's worst nightmares were made real. And this nightmare had lurked just beneath his conscious mind all these years, a rattlesnake ready to strike. It had hissed at him, flicked its forked tongue with every planetary landing, every corrupt governor who threw them in jail, every alien who trapped them in a cave, every army that marched against them, every stranger who spotted them over the hill and shouted, "You there!" In every alien face who looked at him askance had briefly flashed the face of Captain Peter Stapleton, Lothian Base Commander, Guardian of Martian Freedom, Syria Planum...Mars.

And Lieutenant Dudley Appelbaum, administer of enhanced interrogation. After all these years, the words of Captain Peter Stapleton continued to echo, echo, echo, with each crisis, each landing, each call to duty... *"All right, Dudley, attach the neural feed..."*

Emotions he had kept buried, that he had kept from seeing the light of day since that session with Dr. Galliano...

ETS...Emotional Trauma Syndrome...flashbacks, alcoholism, depression and anxiety...

He had beaten it...beaten it and kept it hidden. His career had excelled. He had been sent on the high-priority mission to Darius. He had been chosen to survive the destruction of the Earth, named to command the *Silver Streak*'s Carrier...and finally, on that fateful day, promoted to first officer.

Yet always, just under the surface, that rattlesnake, coiled, poised to strike...

He became aware of Cameron's hand on his shoulder. "Frank, look. They needed to know how our brains work in order to extract information. They've done that. It's over. They won't do it to you, Frank."

"Dick...I thought I was over this." He saw the face of Captain Peter Stapleton, Lothian Base Commander, Guardian of Martian Freedom, Syria Planum...he heard those dreaded words... *"Dudley, attach the neural feed..."* Not as memories—he *saw* Captain Peter Stapleton before him, *saw* Dudley Appelbaum, *heard* the words.

He clenched his eyes shut. "The flashbacks are back."

"Frank, they won't do it to you."

Won't they? Frank clenched his eyes shut, willing the memory, the image, the *experience*, to go away. Yet with the flashback banished, what was left? Hell. Would he rather be in Hell than back in that cell on Mars? Was this really a flashback...or was it a preview? The past had come alive again. There could be no escape from his demons when those demons were *here, now!* When his personal hell had blurred with the literal Hell of today. The rattlesnake had struck!

———

Cameron was concerned, but decided, for the moment, that Frank would have to handle his problems on his own. There was nothing he could say that could magically erase the trauma of the past. Besides, he was too tired from his own trauma to deal with Frank's.

He rested for a few minutes while Frank stood at the edge of the cage and looked out upon the flaming vista of Hell.

Then he got up, stretched, and trudged over to the other side of the cage, where Argo sat. "Argo, any sign of your powers?"

"No." There was a twinge of impatience in Argo's voice—or at least Cameron thought so. It was hard to tell; the Derringerian's face had only two expressions: intense and more intense. And his voice, scratchy as though from a lifetime of smoking, always sounded somewhere between angry and stoned. But Cameron could understand his impatience; it seemed every five minutes one of them was asking him if his powers were coming back. If Koff was right, they would not be coming back, so there was no point in pressing the matter.

"What are the chances of your people rescuing us?" Argo asked.

Cameron had been trying to keep his mind off the *Silver Streak*; it was too easy to imagine worst-case scenarios. His ship had been at war before and emerged victorious. The Darian Empire had been at least as dangerous as the Alternative Alliance, perhaps more so. On the other hand, the Darians had never used naked starships to destroy whole worlds....

Still, it seemed too much to hope for that the *Silver Streak* could make it deep into Alliance space and stage a rescue at the most infamous and escape-proof prison in the known galaxy.

But he didn't want to sound too negative. "Well...possible," he said cautiously. "But there are a lot of factors. Will President Copenburg allow Stargazer to take the *Silver Streak* into enemy space? Is the *Silver Streak* capable? Is Station Post One? Will the Valdor allow it? What's the war news? No, for now we'd better assume we're on our own."

Splrrrb, his voice strained as the gravity weighed him down, said, "Are you proposing that we escape? If so, no one has ever escaped from Strydia."

Looking around, Cameron could understand why. If ever there were an escape-proof prison, this was it. He fingered his collar...even if the *Silver Streak* did engineer a successful rescue, it would be short-lived.

"Well," he finally said, "nothing ventured, nothing gained."

Splrrrb drew his worm-like body up as much as he could in the heavy gravity. "You know the teachings of Zblech?"

Cameron frowned. "Uh, no...he's a Throrb philosopher?"

"Yes! 'Nothing ventured, nothing gained' is his first law!"

"Well, there! You see?"

"He preached that as he led the Army of the Enlightened against the Elite. He and all his followers were slaughtered."

"Oh."

From his corner of the cage, Frank remarked, "Maybe you should stick to Gandhi."

CHAPTER 4

As Captain Cameron and Frank Johnson suffered the literal fires of Hell, their ship sped toward a hell of its own—the maelstrom of interstellar war. Star World, the vast artificial world that the *Silver Streak* had been building for a year, was under attack.

Philippe Stargazer had hoped to stay out of the war, but had also known that was an unrealistic hope. He sat at the science station on the bridge of the *Silver Streak*, as always too occupied with his scientific duties to sit uselessly in the command chair. To his right, Jack Hasta was intent on flying the ship.

Of course, there wasn't much actual flying to be done right now; the course was laid in and the ship was making light speed factor ten. Under ordinary circumstances, Jack would be sitting back and cracking jokes. But these weren't ordinary circumstances, and Jack was monitoring for any Throrb ships that may intercept them during their high-priority light speed jump.

Gone was Jack's laid-back, sardonic tone when he announced in a crisp voice, "Star World ahead."

"Secure from light speed," Stargazer replied in an equally clipped voice.

Jack delicately slid his fingers along the touchscreen that he knew so well, carefully collapsing the distortion envelope in which the ship raced across the universe faster than light. The real universe emerged on the main screen before them.

Stargazer's eyes flicked from his console to the main screen and back again as he identified which of the myriad stars ahead was Star World. Jack, meanwhile, had a fix on it and guided the *Silver Streak* in on its fusion drive.

Star World was a four-kilometer asteroid—big enough for a major, unprecedented construction project. Hollowing out the giant rock had been the easy part; fusion moles did the job in a matter of weeks. The hard part was building the infrastructure of a world inside the giant mass. The magnitude of the construction project was intimidating, and had kept the *Silver Streak* busy for the past year, ever since the first contact with the Valdor, when President Copenburg had—rather hastily in many people's opinion—agreed to join the Community in its war against the Thermians.

And while the *Silver Streak* had been busy at Star World, relations between the Community and its enemies, the Alternative Alliance (whom the Valdor had not bothered to mention in the initial negotiations for membership), had deteriorated steadily. Terrorist attacks, acts of sabotage, and endless saber-rattling over strategic points within the Community as well as the Alliance, had finally led to the outbreak of war. And the *Silver*

Streak—and Star World—were caught in the middle.

The proximity alert light flashed. Stargazer quickly silenced it, then scanned. Sensors had picked up a myriad of targets ahead, closing rapidly with the *Silver Streak*.

Jack ran them through the SysTrac, the constantly-updated database of all spacecraft known to the *Silver Streak*, all its colonies, Station Post One, and the Community. "Goddamn. Alternative Alliance Burl fighters."

"A crude attack," Stargazer observed.

There was no strategy; the alien fighters simply hurtled toward them, their energy beam weapons firing.

Unless the lack of strategy *was* the strategy; it could be that this attack was a distraction from some other, sneakier attack. But Stargazer was a scientist, not a military strategist. He had been left in command of the *Silver Streak* before, but usually during planetary survey missions, when all he had to do was remind Jack to periodically realign the platform, which Jack knew to do anyway.

But now...

He thought about the events of the past year, few of which had directly involved the *Silver Streak*. The most frightening development had been the destruction of the planet Toran. Station Post One had dealt with that; Stargazer only knew about it from the daily reception of intelligence reports, and it had stirred some considerable discussion on the bridge. Toran had been destroyed by a naked starship.

Faster-than-light travel was tricky business; cheating the laws of nature, twisting and compressing and stretching spacetime so that a spacecraft could traverse space as if traveling faster than light, while at the same time obeying Einstein's cosmic speed limit. Primitive FTL drives used exotic matter with negative energy density to contract the space ahead of the ship and expand the space behind, allowing for speeds up to ten times the speed of light; more advanced starships like the *Silver Streak* used a controlled black hole to create an artificial event horizon, a distortion envelope that allowed for speeds of hundreds of times the speed of light.

But in either case, the result was a massive gamma ray surge, a lethal concentration of radiation that could sterilize a planet. Some civilizations had found this to be a show-stopper, and never progressed beyond slower-than-light vehicles. Every civilization that had pressed ahead with any kind of space warp drive had, by necessity, invented some form of gamma ray surge dissipater to prevent the inevitable destruction that faster-than-light travel would cause.

A naked starship, a faster-than-light vehicle that did not have a gamma ray surge dissipater, had slammed into the planet Toran. An entire civilization, plus millions of irreplaceable species of plant and animal life, had been wiped out forever.

The ensuing investigation had found the destruction to be an accident; a malfunction had disabled the ship's gamma ray surge dissipater. But Stargazer also knew that the Alternative Alliance was working on naked starships to use as doomsday weapons in the event of war—and the Valdor were doing the same.

Could there be naked starships lying in wait now?

He could only resort to the rule book and hope there were no surprises. He activated the shipwide intercom. "This is a level one alert, all points scramble. All pilots to QV fighters, mobilize the Carrier. All gunners to turrets. This is not an exercise." He silenced the intercom and said to Jack, "Controls on active mode."

"Marked and set. Defense fields one through four up, confirmation on probe retract. And *incoming!*"

The *Silver Streak* was as battened down as a spaceship could be—especially a huge one carrying thousands of civilians. It was fortunate that the mission planners had anticipated the wild improbability of space combat, and equipped the ship with twenty plasma and microwave laser turrets, and a space carrier armed with its own weapons mounts and four squadrons of one-man fighters.

There had also been five antimatter missiles, but those had been used years ago....

The enemy ships rushed upon the *Silver Streak*, unleashing their hail of weapons. Most were energy beam weapons—plasma beams for the most part—but there were some ballistic missiles, most of which carried no warheads; in the high-speed environment of space combat, an inert slug could do as much damage as an atomic bomb.

But the *Silver Streak* was fortified with layers of electromagnetic defense screens. Little of the destructive energy actually touched the ship. The projectile weapons were actually a greater threat when fired at close range; the defense fields needed more room to deflect them.

"All gun turrets open fire," Stargazer ordered.

The screen showed nothing. The faint dots of the enemy ships whisked by; sometimes there was a flash as one of the projectiles caught the light from the nearby white dwarf Supay. But none of the particle beams were visible in the vacuum of space, nor could there be any sound. A casual observer would not have known a battle was taking place.

"Goddamn," Jack said, "do we open the Carrier Bay Doors while we're under attack?"

"No," Stargazer said, not at all sure he was making the right decision. "Pull back."

Que ferait Dick dans cette situation? he wondered, trying to recall Cameron's orders in past battles. They had always deployed the Carrier for battle—but *before* the attack could begin. In this case the enemy fighters had come upon them so fast... *Est-il prudent de déployer le Transporteur dans ces conditions? Bon sang, qu'est-ce que je fais?*

"Goddammit," Jack snarled as he obeyed. He did not like running away from a battle. But the priority had to be protecting the civilians on board.

At the same time, though, there was Star World to consider. The first tentative colony had just been erected there, just before the outbreak of war. Could this swarm of fighters destroy an asteroid? It seemed unlikely, but he couldn't ignore the possibility.

Star World was a complex combination of silicates, oxygen, and nickel-iron, with traces of iridium, palladium, platinum, gold, magnesium, osmium, ruthenium, and rhodium, and an underground store of water ice that was vital to the embryonic colony. Although the asteroid had been hollowed, the outer shell was a quarter of a kilometer thick in order to screen out solar radiation and cosmic rays.

The interior had been partially patterned after Klym Valdor. The colony was located along the shell of the asteroid, with the huge rock's rotation providing a hint of centrifugal force. The asteroid's mass was too small for any noticeable gravity, and it was even less massive now that it had been hollowed. Once construction was complete, Star World's rotation would be sped up so that the colony experienced full artificial gravity.

Right now, Governor Alisha Cromwell had evacuated all civilians to the shelter, a hollowed chuck of rock that formed a hub at the center of the asteroid—from the perspective of the settlement on the outer shell, in the "sky."

Stargazer hoped they would be safe there. But he would certainly not be helping them by running away.

But the impacts on the hull of the ship had stopped. On the main screen, no more streaking dots were visible. The gun turrets ceased fire; there was nothing more to fire at. The enemy fighters had either overflown the *Silver Streak* and were now arcing around for another pass...or they had broken off the attack.

Jack watched his console, looked up at he screen, then back down at his console. "What the goddamn..."

Absorbed in his own readings, Stargazer had barely been paying attention to Jack. But on his friend's exclamation, he looked up sharply. "*Quoi?*"

"Fighters are peeling off...resuming their goddamn attack on Star World!"

Stargazer tapped at the console, zooming in on the image of Star World. Only after the almost-black, irregular rock appeared on screen, placid as always, did it occur to him that it was still thirty light-minutes away, so the image would not be current.

But he doubted the small fighters had light speed capability, so it would be an hour or more before they could attack the asteroid. And the *Silver Streak*, despite its immense size, was faster than any fighter, so could overtake them before they could attack.

It surprised Stargazer how many civilizations used crewed fighters. Robotic fighters would be more practical—lighter, able to undertake more dangerous missions, cheaper. There were a special combination of circumstances that had led humans to use manned space fighters; the Nanotech War of the twenty-third century had placed taboos on certain technologies—and, more importantly, human pilots wanted space fighters. They were cool.

Maybe pilot ego was common to many civilizations. As far as Stargazer knew, only one known spacefaring civilization had turned its space war capability over to robotic spaceships—

the Darians, who had in time fallen victim to their own technology, leaving behind a self-sustaining technological infrastructure of great efficiency, but no soul.

Maybe *that* was the reason. Maybe other civilizations saw that inevitable end to the computerization of warfare. To Stargazer, the *real* solution was more basic: get rid of war.

Star World was now the most conspicuous object the sky. From this distance, it might have been mistaken for a planet; despite its small size, it was generally spherical. It didn't have enough gravity to pull it into a sphere; its shape was a random quirk of nature. The preponderance of carbonaceous compounds made its surface very dark, almost black, but there was enough ground-up silicon in its regolith that it shone in the light of Supay.

And now Stargazer could see at least some of the enemy fighters—faint stars moving against the black background. "All right," he said, activating the intercom, "Hangar Deck, open Carrier Bay Doors."

The underside of the *Silver Streak* split. The entire aft third of the arrow-shaped starship was the Carrier Bay. The huge doors ground open, sending a mild vibration through the entire aft half of the huge Space Star. Within the huge bay was a blocky, battle-armored vessel, its hull flat black for camouflage, its spires tipped with gun turrets, and its sides bristling with acceleration channels through which small fighters would catapult into battle.

The enemy fighters, though, seeing that their adversary was upon them, arced around to defend themselves.

"Here they come," Jack shouted.

Stargazer stabbed the intercom tab. "Carrier, this is Star-gah-zay. Launch fighters immediately upon deploy!"

The ship jolted as the Carrier detached from its umbilicals. Then, as it slowly lowered into space, its small fighters hurtled from their cribs, their plasma engines blazing.

Multiple alarms screamed on the bridge, startling Stargazer. Proximity alert...light boom...dosimeter...particle concentration...

"Jesus Christ," Jack Hasta said. "*Gamma ray surge!!*"

"*Mon dieu...*" With the doors open, the Carrier deployed, and fighters launched, Stargazer could do nothing except try, in the seconds remaining, to save the *Silver Streak*. This was what he had feared: someone had thrown a naked starship at them!

No time to save the fighters...no time to save the Carrier...no time to save Star World...no time even to set a course...just need to get away!

To Jack, he shouted, "*Light speed factor—*"

His command was cut off by the mayhem that followed, and then the darkness and silence.

CHAPTER 5

It was Frank's turn.

His stomach roiled as the Throrb escorted him through the corridors of Hell. His intestines churned, and he prayed he wouldn't lose bowel control.

Prayed? A fat lot of good that would do here in Hell! He almost laughed at the thought.

He hadn't prayed in a long time. He had never been very religious. As a child, he had taken the existence of God for granted, just like all the facts he was taught in school, but God was a part of the background of life, like the existence of the Moon and the Sun. They were there, but his attention was on other things.

He had been told "if you're bad, you go to Hell." So he had tried to be good; but he would have tried to be good anyway. It was who he was. He would rather people be happy than sad, so he tried to make people happy—or, at the very least, tried not to make them unhappy.

Mostly, though, he was wrapped up in his own problems, tried to solve them one-by-one, and live with as little hassle as possible. If only he could have foreseen that he would one day have the second-most stressful job in the human race.

There had been many opportunities over the years to discuss God with Captain Cameron. Although Cameron was far from a devout Christian, he had come from a very Catholic family, had been thoroughly indoctrinated into the Catholic faith, and spent a great deal of time thinking about God, even if he wasn't a strict believer.

It was hard sometimes for Frank to figure out exactly what Cameron did believe; his beliefs seemed to fluctuate day-to-day, depending on where his thoughts took him. That was the thing about Richard Cameron—he was always thinking. Frank admitted that was what made a good captain, but Cameron tended to overdo it.

Sometimes they would talk late into the night on theological subjects, concepts of immortality, the afterlife, psychological realities that might make Heaven and Hell real for a person. Cameron had some admittedly interesting ideas for how a person could choose his own afterlife. But Frank did not think so deeply about things, and he grew uncomfortable with those subjects. Sometimes he enjoyed those conversations, but more often he would rather talk about something more mundane, like how funny it had been when Jack and Stargazer had sucked helium and delivered the Ninth Lunar Dedication to the tune of "Tiny Tiny Toes."

Cameron's own ideas of Hell were provocative. Some were based on solid scientific fact, like the guilt one would feel at the moment of death, or the possibility that the consciousness might, at the moment of dying, switch to an alternate timeline. Others were more theoretical;

perhaps Hell was in another universe, and the quantum hologram would be entangled there after death.

Frank remembered now that on one occasion, Cameron had mentioned that there had been an ancient Hyron prison called Haven—known later as "Black Haven"—clearly the origin of the Hyron underworld Blackhaven. He speculated that in ancient times, there may have been a prison on Earth, perhaps called "Hell" or something similar, which gave rise to the Hell myth.

Neither of them could have known that at that very moment, there were aliens out there who had deliberately constructed a real-life Hell.

Whether Hell existed as an afterlife or not, Frank was sure that you would have to have committed a truly serious offense for a kind and loving God to send you there for all time. And now he was in Hell. He didn't think he had done anything that awful.

He had lived in his own private hell ever since Mars. There had been varying degrees to which it affected his life, but there was no denying it had, to one extent or another, guided his life ever since then.

And now the Throrb were taking him back there.

Cameron had tried to stop them, to take the burden of the interrogation on himself. "Look, I'm the captain, I'm responsible for my crew."

"You're the captain aboard your ship," the guard told him. "Here on Strydia, I have orders to take Frank Johnson topside."

"Frank doesn't know anything I don't know," Cameron insisted. "Take me."

"Those are not my orders."

"Well, I'm giving you new orders!—"

"Dick, it's okay," Frank interrupted—though it was the farthest thing from okay. But it was humiliating watching Cameron's assumption that he was emotionally stronger than Frank. Which was probably true. "You've all had your turn. I'll go."

"Frank—"

"It's okay. I'll be fine."

But he knew that was not true. He would not be fine. He hadn't been fine since Cameron had told him about the interrogation. He hadn't been fine since they had arrived here in Hell. He hadn't been fine since he had been made First Officer of the *Silver Streak*. He hadn't been fine since the interrogations back there on Mars, all those years ago...

They took him across the charred scaffolds, over the lava pit, and he looked down at that churning whirlpool, realizing how easy it would be to hurl himself over the rail, to end it all here and now. What would that be like? Would a swift end in that cauldron of pure heat be better than the interrogation to come?

No, probably not. It would not be a swift end. He had seen and heard the tortured, thrown into that deadly whirlpool. They floated on its surface; they did not flash instantly into flame, as urban legend had it.

Besides, what was he thinking? Suicide was no solution. He hadn't even contemplated that back on Mars.

Of course, Mars, despite some pretty convincing pretensions, hadn't been Hell. *I guess it's time to see which is worse...Mars or Hell....*

The Throrb escorted him to the elevator and shut the grate. His pulse quickened as it began its ascent. The deepest levels of Hell dropped away below. For a moment, the crushing weight grew even heavier, but then the inertial field reduced the gravity to the blessed relief of...normal.

By the time the elevator reached the upper level, the gravity was less than Earth normal.

As the Throrb marched him toward the interrogation room, his mind replayed the march to the interrogation room on Mars. He could hear the clack-clack-clack of the Martian guards' boots.

After the crushing gravity of the lower circles of Hell, it should have been a relief to ride the elevator up to the refreshing buoyancy of the upper tower. But the gravity up here was about forty percent of Earth's—or almost the same as that on Mars.

All the forces of Hell were conspiring to throw him back in time to that darkest period of his life.

Even the corridors were similar...about two meters wide, three tall...gray floors, silver walls...dim yellow lights hanging from cords from a maze of pipes above...the gravity...the clacking of the boots...

But there was no clacking of boots except his own. He altered his pace, and the sound of the clacking slowed. There were no Martian guards here; there were only Throrb, oozing alongside him, their slick bodies leaving trails of slime...he wondered who was responsible for cleaning up all that slime...and the corridor curved around the tower, where the corridors back on Mars had been straight.

They came to the interrogation room. He would have recognized it anywhere. The chair... The Chair. There was always The Chair. The table next to it...covered with implements of torture. It was like a dentist's examination room; Frank began to laugh hysterically at the comparison between a dentist's chair and an interrogator's chair.

The Chair had restraints for his arms and legs, and there was a restraint for his head...or was it a restraint? Was it a...

"Dudley, attach the neural feed..."

The wet pseudopods nudged him toward the chair, and he struggled against their grip. How could they be so strong? These slimy creatures looked like soft rubber; surely he could just pull those pseudopods loose and make a break for it—after all that time in heavy gravity, he should be as strong as Superman by now, right?

But they were stronger. They were getting a proper diet, where Frank had been eating unspeakable slop whose origin he dared not contemplate, and then blasting his intestines into the bucket in the corner while the others tried to pretend not to notice. He hadn't been getting enough water, it was impossible to get proper sleep in the heat down there, and the heat and gravity had themselves left him drained. Perhaps he could have overpowered the Throrb at another time, but not now.

They threw him into the chair.

"Strap him in," said the interrogator.

"What are you doing to me?" he whined... now, in this chamber in Strydia Prison, and thirty years before, in an almost identical chamber on Mars.

The straps slipped into place. He struggled, his wrists and ankles firmly secured. He looked up at the light above, made out the outline of the head restraint—or neural feed, whichever it was. He breathed deeply and rapidly, his chest hurting from the effort. No amount of struggling could free him; he was in it now. He had willingly gone with the Throrb to this place, and here he was...back in the prison he had escaped from so many years before...

The inquisitor probed him with his retractable antennae. "Keep calm, Mr. Johnson."

He clenched his teeth. Captain Peter Stapleton, Lothian Base Commander, Guardian of Martian Freedom, Syria Planum, had said the same thing to him each morning.

"Wait, just..." He hated the panic in his voice, but the fact was he was panicking. "Just tell me what you're going to do."

"We are merely extracting information."

Extracting information. Not deadening my neural impulses. Well, that was what Cameron had said, right? "They won't do it to you, Frank," he had said. "They needed to know how our brains work in order to extract information. They've done that. It's over. They won't do it to you, Frank."

But that...*thing*...the head restraint...the *neural feed*...they were bringing it down on his head...they were fastening it...

"I really don't know anything," he insisted frantically.

And the inquisitor spoke The Words... "Attach neural feed."

Frank saw the face of Captain Peter Stapleton, Lothian Base Commander, Guardian of Martian Freedom, Syria Planum, heard those dreaded Words: "All right, Dudley, attach the neural feed."

The metal ring came down, down, closer...

"Okay, wait, wait..." he struggled...

...unsure if this was a flashback or if it was Now...the two incidents were intertwined...

"Tell us your troop movements, Sergeant Johnson. The location of the U.S.S. *Karkatua* Third Fighter Strike Force."

"Frank Johnson, Sergeant, United States Star Force, serial number eight one five seven six G-E-L."

"All right, Dudley, attach the neural feed."

Frank twisted and jerked, tried to bite, wrenched his arms and cut his wrists on the restraints. *"No, get back!"* he shrieked.

"Considerable resistance," someone said— was it a Throrb or a Martian?...It must be a Throrb, because he hadn't resisted the Martians like this.

"Subdue him," the inquisitor said.

"Stop iiiiit!"

The Throrb guard couldn't get the band attached to Frank's head because he kept jerking and twisting his head back and forth. The pseudopods tried to get a good grip on him in order to steady his head, but he squirmed under their pressure; it was hard for that slick skin to get a good grip. The pseudopods could wrap around

him and hold him, but they couldn't stop him
from moving beneath them.

"This will cause total sensory deprivation,
Sergeant Johnson. Tell us the location of the
U.S.S. *Karkatua* Third Fighter Strike Force and
we won't do this."

"Frank Johnson, Sergeant, United States Star
Force, serial number eight one five seven six G-
E-L."

"Have it your own way. Attach it, Dudley."

Hands...Throrb pseudopods...human hands...
one or the other...around his head, holding him
still...that metal band, electrodes attached to it,
electronic impulses feeding from some sort of
machine...closer and closer...

He felt its pressure around his head, and now,
no matter how he struggled, he couldn't squirm
out of its way because now he was wearing it. He
was wearing it and he couldn't move his hands
and it was attached to him and they had won and
his brain was theirs.

"Don't worry, Sarge. This won't hurt."

That hateful voice. It was Dudley
Appelbaum. Taunting him, laughing at him,
laughing at his pain, enjoying his discomfort,
taking glee from the power he held over another
man.

There was nothing he could do. He was
trapped. He was bound and trapped and the band
was around his head. The past was alive again. He
was helpless, a prisoner of the Throrb, a prisoner
of the Martians, and prisoner of his own mind...

...as sensation dropped away, as the Throrb
ceased to be, as the Martians ceased to be...

...as *he* ceased to be. Light, sound, touch,
taste, all gone. A sensation of being alive, winked

out, snuffed. The universe was gone, *he* was gone. Was he still Frank Johnson, Sergeant, United States Star Force, serial number eight one five seven six G-E-L? Was he still Frank Johnson, Captain, Space Star *Silver Streak*? Did he still exist? Could one exist in Hell?

And was Hell external or internal? Were the fires and cages and slop and screams and heat and gravity just window dressing on the *real* Hell—his own personal Hell that had never left him and had returned in all its fire and fury to rob him of his senses and his sanity and his perception of what was real and what was a dream?

Helpless, bound, immobile, and nonexistent, he tumbled down a shaft of nothingness, spiraling into his own past, the nightmares of years gone by fully awake and consuming him, consuming him as though he had been tossed into that Lake of Fire at the base of Strydia Prison.

It was no longer Now...it was thirty years ago...it was Mars...and he was a young pilot on his third combat assignment with the U.S.S. *Karkatua* Third Fighter Strike Force...

CHAPTER 6

The Martian War was, without any doubt, the dumbest war waged in the history of humanity. The Oversight Council of Mars held in its hands the same report as the President of the United States, the Secretary General of the United Countries of Earth, and the Chancellor of the United World Council. Although it had not yet been disclosed to the general public, the governments were aware of the frightening conclusion of the International Solar Anomaly Study Commission: the Sun was going to explode within ten years.

Yet on July 6, 4062, the Oversight Council of Mars declared its independence from Earth authority. President Douglas Goff proclaimed the Martian government illegitimate and in a state of insurrection, ordering a relief force to take the Capitol in Bradbury Dome. The Martians, in full support of the Edict of Autonomy, were prepared, and fought the Earth military openly.

War was declared.

As the conflict escalated, the Star Force needed new pilots—a lot of new pilots. The conversion of the *Silver Streak* was (for reasons known only to those with the highest security clearance) such a high priority that no one could be pulled off of that vital duty, even to fight a war.

And so, for the first time in centuries, the draft was instituted.

The Star Force had expensive, high-performance fighters that only officers flew. But the cheap, mass-produced fighters like the WB-03s came rolling out of the manufactors every day. The Star Force had plenty of fighters; what it needed were pilots to fly them.

In this day and age, flying was ubiquitous. One in ten people on Earth had pilots' licenses, and most of them had at least limited spaceflight experience. At least as many people were capable of piloting a spacecraft as people of an earlier age were of operating a boat. So the Star Force computers scoured the personnel files of draft-age men and women, searching for those candidates who would be hurled at the enemy. The best pilots, the real cream of the crop (those who were not already military) would be drafted into the Officers Corps, just as doctors had been conscripted in earlier wars as officers, and would fly the top-of-the-line machines like the ZR-120. But ordinary young men like Frank Johnson, who could fly, but whose real interests lay elsewhere, would be tossed into the cockpits of the WB-03s. They would be in today's war what Jeep drivers had been in ancient times.

Frank knew only what he saw on the news. He was just an aspiring entertainment writer, a senior at Erie University, on the verge of claiming his bachelor's in English creative writing, looking forward to getting his master's and then moving on to a brilliant career—and enjoying a whirlwind romance with Jacqueline Burleson.

He wasn't particularly serious about her; he was free in the world and having a good time. He didn't love her, but they had fun together, and the sex was terrific. That was all he wanted at this stage of his life. To him, the rumblings from Mars were just part of the background buzz. There were always tensions of one sort or another, somewhere in the world or somewhere in the Solar System. It didn't affect him because he was working on a script for an immie and he was very excited about it. It was a comedy-drama about the development of an absurd spaceplane that would be piloted by trained apes to ferry businessmen to their international meetings. The focus of the story was a particular flight that ran into trouble, with hilarity ensuing.

It was doubly fun because Jacqueline was interested in it and she was helping him to develop the story. She was a cryonics major looking for a job at a spaceport, and he had taken a series of flight training courses, flying S-160s, March 400s, and even an Ace-450 suborbital plane—quite well, actually—so they had a lot to talk about. He now held a Class II pilot's license, which qualified him for any single-engine aircraft, or single-engine suborbital or orbital spacecraft.

Even when war was declared, he paid little attention. What went on way out on Mars had little bearing on him and his life. So it blindsided him when the draft notice came.

He was living on campus with Jacqueline at the time—against policy, of course, which was what made it so much fun.

The draft notice came over the Solarnet to his account, its lettering cold and impersonal.

YOU ARE HEREBY ORDERED TO REPORT FOR INDUCTION INTO THE ARMED FORCES OF THE UNITED STATES, AND TO REPORT AT ERIE UNIVERSITY ROTC, ON THE 8th DAY OF DECEMBER, 4062, AT 0800 EUST FOR FORWARDING TO AN ARMED FORCES INDUCTION.

There followed several paragraphs of detailed instructions, including tantalizing qualifications for exclusion. He pored over these, fixating on the reassuring sentence that "you may not be qualified for induction."

"I can't go," he told Jacqueline later, when his anxiety over the notice prevented him from performing. "I'm graduating college in a few months. I can't leave now. I'll tell them—"

"Frank, Frank, you've got to go," she said with little sympathy. "It's jail if you don't."

"Come on, what is this, World War III? They can't imprison you for refusing to go to war!"

"Yes they can. Believe me, there's been a lot of talk about the war down at Armstrong. I've got a friend whose cousin was just arrested for refusing a draft notice."

"Better jail than war! No, I'm not going," he said even as he knew he would. "They can't rip me away from my life like that. I'm not going!"

But he did go.

In ages past, a draft notice unfailingly meant the Army, and young men often voluntarily enlisted in one of the other armed services in order to avoid the Army. But today things were different. Frank was drafted into the Star Force. In today's space wars, all the armed forces had a piece of the Selective Service, and Frank's record as a pilot put him in high demand.

In normal times, as a pilot and a college student, he might have entered the Star Force as an officer cadet, attending field training instead of basic training, and then officer training school and a pipeline to a great career. Frank had no interest in a military career, and the Star Force had plenty of educated ace pilots; what they wanted were draftees to fly simple single-engine dumb planes like the SF-220 or the WB-03— piloted alternatives to unmanned drones, which could be hacked. In other words, the Star Force wanted pilot-cannon-fodder.

It was ironic that Frank Johnson, who would one day be the First Officer of the *Silver Streak*, entered the Star Force reluctantly and as an expendable hunk of meat.

In June of 4063, at the conclusion of his senior year, he reported to the 120th Training Group at Canaveral Star Force Base in High Canaveral, Brevard Island, in the Florida Archipelago. It was forty degrees Celsius that day, and his uniform was drenched with sweat. The other recruits did not seem bothered by the heat.

As soon as he stepped off the air tram, a— what were they called—a Spaceflight Military Instructor stalked after him, shouting, "What do you call that?! What do you call that?!"

Frank stiffened, standing at what he presumed was close to "attention." "I'm sorry, ma'am?"

The SMI grabbed his cap off his head. "That hair! Do you think that's appropriate for the Star Force?"

"I don't know, ma'am."

"Aren't you proud to be in the Star Force?!"

Of course he wasn't, but for some reason he did not dare say that. "Yes, ma'am!"

"Then get your sorry ass in line to Building Two! *Now!!*"

"Yes, ma'am!"

He jumped to the indicated line, where none of the recruits dared speak; SMIs were shouting at people everywhere, and no one wanted to bring the wrath of these devils down on them.

After following the line into the concrete building, Frank was seated on a squeaky aluminum stool and had his head shaved.

Then it was on to the barracks. He was assigned to Squadron Fifteen, and there he met his bunkmate and his first friend in the Star Force, Tony Lukianoff, a dark-skinned bear of a man, the size of a tractor but with an easy smile and a booming baritone that often burst out in an infectious laugh—who also, luckily for Frank, scared away mean-spirited recruits.

The barracks were bare, with beds adorning one side. There was a public restroom on one end of the long chamber, and the SMI's sleeping quarters on the other. On one wall was a photograph of an SF-220.

After being assigned their bunks, the recruits were mustered out to the parade field. They stood in a line on the blistering concrete, surrounded by flat-roofed metal and concrete buildings that could survive the two-hundred-fifty kilometer-per-hour winds that lashed these islands every year.

A thin young man, his smooth uniform stretched so taut around his muscular body that it seemed about to burst, strode down the line of recruits, baton in hand.

"Good morning, recruits," he bellowed in a voice that sounded like there was a megaphone in his throat. "I am Master Sergeant Eric Cherierre. I'll be your SMI for the next eight weeks. Your duty is to do as I say when I say it. My job is to teach you how to handle and fire a weapon, how to defend yourself, how to survive in situations of combat, how to counter threats to planetary or national security, and how to handle yourself in the air or in space. If you do your job and I do mine, we'll get along, and at the end of sixty days you'll be out of my hair and on to flight readiness training. Here at Canaveral you get the best training in the Armed Forces—way better than those slugs in the Army or those jugheads in the Marines."

Some nervous laughter followed that.

"That's my promise to you. But I expect a few things in return: you'll speak only when spoken to. You'll address me as 'sir.' You'll speak to me and me alone; no talking among yourselves until off-duty. You'll jump when I say jump, you'll follow my orders without question, argument, or complaint. Is that clear, recruits?"

Self-conscious, Frank mumbled, "Yes, sir," as did the rest of the squadron.

"What the hell was that?" Cherierre bellowed. "Do you slugs have vocal chords? *Sound off!!*"

"YES, SIR!"

Frank had a feeling Cherierre would single him out, and wasn't disappointed. The stiff little man was two inches shorter than Frank, but managed to wither Frank's spirit with a look.

"What's your name, Private?!"

Frank jumped at the loudness of Cherierre's voice, the piercing of his gaze, and the spittle that hit his chin. "Frank Johnson."

"*What did you say?!*"

Frank jumped again. "Frank Johnson!"

"Jesus Christ, you're jittery! Try 'Private Johnson, Sir!'"

"Private Johnson, Sir!"

"Jittery Johnson. There's one in every squadron."

Again some nervous laughter among the recruits.

Cherierre mercifully stalked off to taunt another recruit, but Frank intuitively knew that he had just become the sergeant's favorite whipping boy.

———

Frank didn't sleep much that night—no one in Squadron 15 did. They were all exhausted and overheated, but they were also stressed from the day's events and wondering what tomorrow would hold. He heard some of the recruits silently sobbing, and was proud of himself for not being reduced to that.

He kept rubbing his hand over his shaved scalp, mourning the thick and wispy hair that Jacqueline had always complimented.

After lights out, Tony Lukianoff whispered from the bottom bunk, "You awake, Jittery?"

Frank rolled over and looked down at the huge man. "Wish you wouldn't call me that."

Soft laughter. "I'd get used to it if I were you. I know it farts, but you're stuck with it for as long as you're in the Star Force. My brother's five years older than me and been in the Star Force since he was sixteen. He's been 'Foot Stink' ever since his first day of basic. I'll pick one up too eventually; they're never complimentary."

Frank sighed. "Well, did you want to say something?"

"Yeah. You got any crash?"

"Huh? Crash what?"

"No. Crash."

"Crash? Is that a recruit's callsign or something?"

"No...*crash*. Superbuzz. *Meth*, man."

"No. That stuff's not allowed on the barracks. You ought to know that."

"Yeah, I know. I just thought maybe you might have some."

"Well, no, I don't."

"Okay. Well, good night."

"Good night."

———

And so began the eight-week hell of marching, running, crawling through mud, shooting at targets, and being screamed at.

Frank wasn't very good at it. He fell out of step. He tripped on the obstacles. He could barely do more than ten push-ups at a time. He improved with practice, but not without more than his share of harsh insults by Cherierre.

And each night, Tony Lukianoff asked him for crash. Frank did not want to alienate the one friend he had in this hellhole, but it was becoming quite annoying.

Then, one day, during week three (how slowly time passed here!) after chow, Frank went to the restroom and, as he came out, spied Tony behind the tool shed with Private Nemmani, and caught the whiff of crystal meth, which he knew well from the dorm at Erie.

None of my business, he told himself. *What's the worst that can happen? Cherierre finds out about it and drums them out. Nothing to do with me.*

Except that he's my bunkmate and my friend, and Cherierre knows that. He might not believe that I didn't know about it...so I might catch heat for it myself. I might even get drummed out with them—

But I want to get drummed out!

He mused over these thoughts during the after-chow march, pondering his prospects were he to be discharged from the Star Force, have his old life back, go home to Jacqueline and his writing and his classes and his plans for the future.

But that's a bad way of thinking, he chastised himself. *If I get a dishonorable discharge, that will haunt me for the rest of my life. Anyway, what am I thinking? Smoking crystal meth on the barracks won't result in a discharge! That'll be maybe twenty-five pushups and a week of K.P. If I refuse to snitch, I'll get a counseling statement, and who cares?*

That evening, as the recruits lined up in their underwear for inspection in the barracks, Cherierre looked right at Frank and said, "Any of you slugs know anything about recruits smoking crash after chow?"

Frank stood at attention, eyes forward, trying not to meet Cherierre's gaze.

Cherierre took a step toward him. "Did you see anything, Private Jittery?"

Frank hesitated—just for a moment, but long enough for Cherierre to jump down his throat. "*I said, did you see anything, Private Jittery?!*"

"Yes, sir!" The words were out of him before he could think.

"Oh, you did?! When did you plan on telling me?!"

Remembering some advice Tony—poor Tony—had given him on their second night, he barked, "No excuse, sir!"

Next thing he knew, he was in Cherierre's office, Sergeant Proust and Private Lucerne standing as witness, while he wrote down all that he had seen—including Tony's nightly requests for crash.

That night, Tony did not speak to him.

The next day, Tony Lukianoff and Private Nemmani were gone. There was no explanation. Frank never did learn what became of them.

CHAPTER 7

Cameron waited and waited and waited for Frank's return. Had his own interrogation taken this long? He couldn't say; time seemed not to exist in that state of sensory oblivion. And time seemed to stand still here in the depths of Hell. But it seemed Frank had been gone a long, long time.

The others didn't understand, and he wasn't sure how to explain it to them. When Frank had been dragged out, Argo asked, "What's going on, Captain Cameron? What's his problem?

"Oh, it was years ago, before our planet was destroyed. He was a prisoner of war. They tortured him. They deprived his senses of all inputs, just like the Throrb did to me. I never realized the extent to which that experience has stayed with him."

Splrrrb was less than sympathetic. "We're all under stress! What gives him the corner on sympathy?!"

"Calm down, Splrrrb."

"I will not calm down! I am imprisoned by my own people! My only hope is to flee to the

enemy! I'm tired of hearing you and your friend's whining! You don't know the meaning of hardship!"

"All right! This isn't helping anything, Splrrrb!"

"And another thing! You're not my captain! I'm through taking orders from you!"

"All right, that's enough," said Ambassador Koff firmly. "Now, Captain Cameron's right. Snapping at each other doesn't solve anything."

Splrrrb's sluglike body contracted to half its size. "Well, I'm still waiting for either of you to come up with a solution, because our civilizations are out there killing one another and all we're doing is sitting here complaining."

"I agree with you, Splrrrb," Cameron said, "but right now our options are limited."

———

With his only friend gone, Frank found basic training more hellish than ever. Enduring the physical toil and Cherierre's special brand of abuse was nightmarish enough, but coupled with the loneliness of having lost his only friend and being known as a snitcher made it worse. That, coupled with the guilt he felt over betraying a friend, resulted in a prolonged depression.

There was nothing as theatrically old-fashioned as the dreaded "blanket party" or gang beatings behind the mess hall or anything like that; but the other recruits had their own ways of informing him that he was not One Of The Guys. If he fell, no one stopped to help him up. If they were playing war, they went a little harder on him than the others, and if he was "wounded," it took a while for anyone to notice.

He went through the motions—and somehow actually improved as a recruit. By not caring, not thinking about the life he had lost and wanted to go back to, he was able to devote his entire energies and attention to the here and now.

After a while, he found he began to enjoy some parts of the experience. As his body strengthened, the marching and the running became relaxing, a chance to free his mind and let his thoughts wander.

Frank understood that one of the purposes of basic training was to teach teamwork. With the SMIs seen as the enemy, recruits tended to bond. "We are not stars, we are a constellation," went the Star Force motto. And Frank watched with no small amount of self-pity as the *other* recruits bonded into a team. But Jittery Johnson, the Snitcher, was never really a part of that team.

Recruits' Solarnet access was severely restricted, but they were allowed to write home twice a week. Frank sent regular VR-grams to his parents and to his brother Stu. He was eager to unload his frustration, his depression, and his anxiety onto someone, but his messages were guarded. He painted a picture of himself as a heroic young soldier slashing and burning his way through basic training. He was ashamed of his shortcomings, and intimidated by the fact that Stu had been accepted into the United World Space Exploration Corps. *Everyone always does better than me*, he often whined to himself when lying in bed at night.

He also wrote to Jacqueline, and was puzzled that her replies were perfunctory, one or two-sentence acknowledgements. She was always so verbose in person. He began to worry that she was losing interest in him. It wouldn't surprise him; she would be getting ready for her first postgraduate year. With her qualifications, he worried that she, too, might be drafted, but none of her messages indicated that.

Passing the four-week threshold was a milestone for the recruits of Squadron Fifteen. They were Halfway There. And week five saw a change in the training regimen—it was time to train for spaceflight readiness. It was presumed that most of the recruits would be fighter pilots, since the Star Force had concentrated on drafting those with flight experience. Even though there were plenty of support positions to fill, eighty percent of the people in the Star Force ended up in a spaceflight position of one sort or another.

This phase of training separated those who would be pilots from those who would fill administrative, clerical, or support positions. And here, for the first time, Frank excelled, surpassing the other recruits.

One of the most formidable training devices was the TDT. Officially, "TDT" stood for "Tri-Directional Trainer," but everyone knew its real name was "That Damned Thing." It was a full-size SC-100 fighter cockpit with functioning controls, attached to an arrangement of three frames on gimbals, each of which rotated in a different direction. Variations of this monstrous machine of torture had been basic to all spaceflight training since the first cautious forays into space in the twentieth century. The function of the TDT was to spin the recruit in wild circles in every possible direction while he fought with the fighter's controls to stabilize the flight.

Frank was the only recruit who did not throw up. In fact the TDT didn't bother him at all. He couldn't help blustering, as all the recruits did when they did well; but somehow it was different for Jittery Johnson, the Snitcher. His success made him even more unpopular.

Then there was the SMTC, the Suborbital Microgravity Training Craft—or what everyone called the Plummet Plane. The first flight simply tested everyone's reaction to weightlessness. Again, Frank was proud to hold his stomach; though he had to admit he did become queasy as the cramped cabin filled with the other recruits' drifting vomit. A few guys were summarily grounded after that flight, and would never occupy more than Earthbound secretarial or administrative positions. "A few generals were born today," someone muttered.

The next flight flew specific parabolas to simulate the gravity on the Moon, Mars, Phobos, Deimos, and some of the larger asteroids. Recruits had to walk up and down the aisle in the various gravitational fields, seeing how they took to the different environments. Frank loved it, and looked forward to his first trip to Mars—a feeling he later looked back on with astonishment.

After the first several Plummet Plane flights, training moved to the GSC, the Gravity Simulation Center. Before being drafted, Frank had assumed the Star Force had a supercollider complex, a ground-based field tense identical to those found on the Space Stars. But no, the Star Force did its gee testing the old-fashioned (and more fun) way—with a centrifuge. A small car was attached to a long pole, allowing it to be spun around a track faster and faster, subjecting the occupant to greater and greater gravitational pull.

Generally, when a pilot pulled out of a dive, he could experience up to nine gees, but on the first test, the centrifuge never exceeded five gees. It was a simple physical fact that a human being suffered symptoms ranging from impaired vision to total blackout if subjected to four or five gees for more than a few seconds.

Private 'Squeaks' Woods made the record for Squadron Fifteen, enduring five gees for ten seconds.

Frank endured five gees for six seconds before he passed out.

Then came the first of the CRFs—Combat Readiness Flights. The plane performed a series of maneuvers to duplicate those that a pilot might experience in situations of combat. A few recruits washed out that day.

But Frank, despite his desire to get out of the Star Force and back to his old life, found himself actually looking forward to flying a fighter into combat. As long as he could avoid being shot down—which Sergeant Cherierre's lectures gave him confidence that he could—this was a sensation of freedom unparalleled by any of the flying he had done so far.

"Jittery, you have remade yourself!" Cherierre bellowed at him on week six. "You are promoted to unit leader!"

"Yes, Sir!" Frank said it with some pride, but also some trepidation; would these recruits respect the outcast?

The answer, of course, was no. They grumbled, they continued to make fun of him, and they did all they could to undermine him. But there was a limit to what they could do with Cherierre breathing down their necks. Their desire to make the team look good outweighed their desire to make Frank look bad.

Finally came the climax of basic training, BEST week—Basic Expeditionary Spaceman Test—and at this point no one wanted to let the team down. The wrath of fellow recruits would be far worse than Cherierre's bellowing.

Frank managed to swallow his uncertainty and anxiety and shout orders as loud and authoritatively as Cherierre did. Whatever his other drawbacks as a military recruit, he had a loud voice.

All the squadrons on the base, consisting of over a thousand recruits, proceeded to the BEST site just inland of the parade grounds. Here, they slept in tents, had their own command posts and field hospitals, and went to war, applying everything they had learned throughout training.

With low-charge plasma lasers, drones to serve as enemy aircraft or spacecraft, and full autonomy from the SMIs, the recruits were free to fight their own war, with the instructors observing from their own command tower and interfering only in case of a serious screw-up.

There were five zones—named Mercury, Venus, Earth, Moon, and Mars—each an independent unit responsible for its own defense and operation. Squadron Fifteen was in Venus Zone.

Frank was one of five unit leaders in Venus, and reported to the zone leader, Carlos "Mozart" Esther of Squadron Eleven—a man Frank would come to know very well in the coming years....

On the first day of BEST week, Frank and the other unit leaders reported to the instructors in their barracks on an artificial hill overlooking the site. Cherierre sat among the other squadrons' SMIs, and Frank and his fellow unit leaders stood at attention as their respective ogres reviewed the lessons of the past six weeks. Cherierre screamed questions at random, quizzing Frank on what he had learned. It seemed to take hours, but it was only half an hour.

After that, they explained the ground rules for the mock war to come. There would be obstacle courses, sneak attacks, drone strikes, and combat with both real soldiers and robotic dummies. Frank listened carefully, not wanting to embarrass himself by screwing up.

Without once breaking the veneer of screaming, posturing, prim and proper lunatics from hell, the instructors assisted the unit leaders in setting up camp. Frank had to admit he was grateful for that, even though the SMIs continued to scream at him for every little mistake. Beyond physically setting up the camp, the tents, the stockade, and other details, the SMIs left all combat decisions to the recruits. It was up to Frank and his newly trained Star Force spacemen to plan a war.

Once they were finished, Cherierre surveyed the plans and the camp and said, "Go get 'em, slugs." It was the first time Frank ever saw Cherierre smile.

The next day, BEST began in earnest. The recruits wore body armor and Breatheasy breathing apparatus at all times (the environment was presumed to be Mars); and they could fall under attack at any time. At the same time, they were on the offensive, firing plasma lasers, projectile weapons, and microwave lasers at the other zones, as well as guiding drones on aerial attacks.

Even as a unit leader, Frank had to stand two hours a day and two hours a night on guard duty—during which he tried to give some thought to what he would write once the war was over, but more often started worrying about what he was in for. More often than not, one of the other zones would attack during his guard shift, and more than once he heard the dreaded sound of an SMI's voice shouting "BANG!" as an invisible beam or a ballistic projectile struck him— signaling that he was dead. It was impossible to forget that in real war he could be killed pretty easily, and it would not be long now before he was in a real war.

Part of BEST was a three-kilometer trail littered with hazards—motion-detectors that would trigger plasma lasers, landmines, projectiles that would rupture breathing apparatus, and of course drones firing plasma lasers and dropping bombs.

At the end of the course, Frank was paired with a wingman—Private Bob Corley, another man he would come to know very well.

"Afternoon, spaceman," Corley whispered. "Corley, Twenty-Two."

"Johnson, Fifteen," Frank replied.

Corley slapped him on the shoulder. "Stick with me, spaceman, and we'll knock 'em dead."

Frank found that he liked being referred to as "spaceman" even though he was still a "slug" for another week. He had begun to take pride in himself as a part of the Star Force. Basic training had at least partially fulfilled its purpose in making him part of a team; the other recruits in Squadron Fifteen might be willing to pull his pants down or trick him into eating a bug, but they would also lay down their lives for him— and vice versa.

With Corley generally in the lead, the two of them negotiated an obstacle course that included highly realistic enemy soldiers that they had to shoot. Some of them were actually real students in Martian uniforms; Frank could tell the real people from the animatronic dummies by the way they fell. Real students fell stunned by the minimal charge; the dummies exploded in blood as though struck by full-power ordnance, and then fell to the ground suffocating as their breathing apparatus had been compromised. It was distracting—which, Frank assumed, was part of the point.

But finally it was graduation week!

Even as the prospect of shipping out to Mars grew more and more real to him, Frank could not help feeling proud and excited as he marched in the graduation parade, knowing his parents and Stu were up there in the stands cheering for him.

After the parades were over, it began to dawn on Frank that the nightmare of basic training had at last come to an end. He would move on now— to what, he didn't know, but at least he could perhaps bury his reputation as "the snitcher."

Cherierre called out the assignments for each recruit, and as he had expected, Frank drew 1412 Combat Flight. He was pleased; he would be a fighter pilot. Okay, it wasn't entertainment writing, but if he was stuck in the military, best to be a pilot.

As they departed High Canaveral, Cherierre stood at the door to the airtram, saying, "So long, spaceman, good luck," to each graduate. When it was Frank's turn, Cherierre slapped him on the shoulder as he said it. Frank had no idea if the gesture had any significance, positive or negative, but to be referred to as "SPACEMAN" by the ogre who had made his life a living hell, who had referred to him as "slug" for the past eight weeks, filled him with an unexpected glow. He had hated Cherierre, even as he had respected him—and now he realized he actually valued the little monster's opinion of him.

Before reporting for flight combat training in Mojave Star Force Base, Arizona, Frank got two weeks' leave. He planned on visiting his family, but first wrote to them to find out where the hell they were; his father had to keep constantly on the move due to his work with the Venus Terraform Project. So first he went back to Erie, hoping to surprise Jacqueline. He knew she had planned on staying on campus through the summer to continue her work at Armstrong.

He knocked on the door to his old dorm, and a stranger in his underwear, with a towel in his wet hair, answered the door. "Yeah?"

"Uh, hi," Frank said, "sorry. This used to be my dorm. I thought my old roommate would still be here."

Cursing himself for being a complete idiot, he VR-gramed Jacqueline to find out where she was.

Her reply was, as had been the case since he went away, terse.

COTTON 213.

He rode the tube car to the Edward J. Cotton Girls' Dormitory and, feeling self-conscious in the girls' dorm, rode the elevator to the second floor. He knocked on room 213, and once again was greeted by a stranger—a male stranger.

Frank frowned, looked down the hall and then back at the bearded giant before him. "Uh...Cotton 213?"

"Right." Finally the bearded man burst into laugher. "You look like Clytus O'Bannon! Yeah, I'm not supposed to be here."

Frank joined in the laughter; he realized, yes, he must have looked rather like that famous comedian from the old O'Bannon & Shaw movies. But his laughter was forced; he could imagine only one reason why a man would be staying in this dorm. "I was looking for Jacqueline Burleson."

"Just a minute. Jackie! You decent?"

"Just a minute!" came her unmistakable voice.

A moment later she stood before him in her underwear, a man's shirt around her. "Hi! Frank!"

"Hi."

"Um...this is awkward. Uh, Frank Johnson, this is Cel Tonda. Frank was...I was...we were...doing what you and I are doing now."

"Ah." Tonda did not look happy.

"Well...I guess I must have come at a bad time," Frank said. "I guess I'll be going."

Jacqueline stepped into the hall. "I'm sorry, Frank, but you were gone."

"Yeah. Okay, I understand. I'd better go." He left without another word, wondering what kind of row would follow his ill-timed visit.

He never saw Jacqueline Burleson again.

CHAPTER 8

War raged throughout the Community and the Alternative Alliance. The border had broken down; one was just as likely to find an Alliance ship in Community space as a Community ship in Alliance space. Alliance troops occupied a number of small Community outposts, most of them along the border, while Community troops had infiltrated well into Alliance space and were now marching the streets of Zelda, Zumroh, Ysirah, and Reyshar.

But the Community had an ace up its sleeve, a force arguably more powerful than a naked starship: the Dreb.

On most planets, the Dreb were the enemies of the Community, for they lived in service of the Thermians, the extradimensional beings whom the Community was avowed to destroy. The Dreb were powerful, harnessing the energies of the Thermian universe to subjugate and even mind-control their subjects, to placate them to the inevitability of the destruction of their worlds by the Thermians.

But Derringer-9 was different. No one knew why the Derringerians did not possess "the Book of the Dreb," or why they had no knowledge of the Thermians, but thanks to Argo, the Dreb of Derringer-9 had pledged their service to the Community. And now, using the ships left behind by the Christoff Empire that had once colonized their planet, they joined the Community in the interstellar war.

Armenus was a Dreb pilot, a priest of the suborder of Armenium. He was squadron commander of the Fifth Force of the Phrixus Brigade, and pilot of a Thess Enforcer—a fine ship with a delicate engine and sensitive helm. His weapons mounts included twin high-energy particle beam weapons, an antimatter slug launcher, and a soft energy disruptor. But his real weapon was his eyes. His mind and body could react faster than his ship ever could.

Ahead of his squadron was the Yamsi cruise ship Ecstasy, the largest flying hotel in the known galaxy. Six kilometers long and devoted to pure luxury, it was the farthest thing from a military target. But the Butirians, Alliance members from the planet Butirius, believed that the Yamsi had conscripted the Ecstasy for military use. That was simply not the case; the Yamsi observed a strict and uncompromising division between military and civilian spaceflight. It was absolutely against the law—unthinkable, in fact—for the Yamsi government to conscript any civilian vessel for war. But the Butirians had mounted an assault to capture or destroy the Ecstasy, and it was Armenus' job to stop them.

He unleashed a simultaneous burst of all his weapons, including his 'death beams' which shot from his eyes and scrambled the brain of any Butirian pilot they touched.

His squadron mates followed suit, and the Butirians fell fast and hard. They were no match for the might of the Dreb.

But then a new threat materialized—a Butirian battlecruiser, flashing out of light speed unexpectedly, and throwing Armenus' ship into a spin. He quickly brought it under control, however, and assessed the new menace.

"Target at grid delbor," he said. "Attack at once! No quarter!"

But the reply from his wingman was totally unexpected. Rather than a clipped and professional reply, Glaucus cried out in panic, "My powers are gone!"

Glaucus was joined by a chorus from the rest of the squadron, all screaming that they were now powerless.

Armenus tried to calm them, to assure them they still had their fighters' weapons—but he too found himself in a state of disorientation and near panic as he realized his most valuable tool, his own psychokinetic ability, was deadened.

Obviously the Butirians had modified P-SARs, and had expected the Dreb to be here. This changed the complexion of the battle.

With a battlecruiser on one side, the remaining Butirian fighters on the other, and frantic and panicky pilots in between, Armenus soon found himself staring death in the eye.

With his powers disabled, his wingman blown out of the sky, and Butirian fighters closing in on him, he did the only thing left to do—what any good soldier would do. He calculated the location of the battlecruiser's bridge and drove his ship right toward it.

"NAAAAAIIIIII!" he cried as the hull of the *cruiser grew before him. He felt no regrets as his ship impacted, and his life passed into oblivion in the brief but cleansing flame of an antimatter explosion.*

———

Frank found that he liked dogfighting. On the ground he was a nonconfrontational person. But when he took to the air in a TS-388 training craft, and the other spacemen were cold, impersonal vehicles rather than fellow human beings with big fists, he was aggressive and skilled, and having a great time.

He hadn't shaken the "Jittery" callsign, and knew he never would, but to his own mind it began to sound to him more like "Ace." For that was what he was—the finest pilot in the squadron. And the best damn dogfighter.

There was no derision in Lieutenant Masters's voice when he said "Jittery," and the other spacemen said the name with a tone of respect when they asked for help in understanding a maneuver or a procedure or a piece of flight hardware.

The TS-388 was both an aircraft and a spacecraft, a plasmium-powered speeding bullet that raced across the Arizona desert at Mach 3. At full power it could easily make orbit, or even fly to the Moon. But for most of the training exercises at Mojave, it was all about air combat.

It was fortuitous that the high desert resembled a stark Martian landscape—though the soaring temperatures and soupy air were nothing like the subfreezing cold and low pressure of

Mars. For training purposes, there couldn't be a better location on Earth. The ASI was recalibrated to provide a reading of only fifteen percent pressure; for that was the ratio of the air in equatorial regions of Mars to that in the Mojave Desert.

Lieutenant Masters' instructions were clear: stay down on the deck, below the level of the mountains. The Martian antispacecraft guns wouldn't be able to get a track on low-flying fighters.

Frank had asked, rather snarkily, how they were going to get to the Martian base from orbit if they were supposed to fly low. Masters reminded him, just as snarkily, of a recently-discovered geological formation known as the "horizon," to the snickers of the other pilots.

So now they had duplicated the trajectories of fighters flying in from space from sixteen hundred kilometers away—well over the horizon and undetectable by the target base.

Frank was in Capricorn Team, and his team leader was Bob Corley, his old wingman from BEST. Corporal Corley was still as cool as ever, quick and competent, and fascinated with the mechanics of aircraft and spacecraft. Capricorn Team consisted of four pilots: Corley, Frank, Ahmed Mbouti, and Al Badran. Each evening they sat around the mess hall discussing fighter components, mostly of the TS-388.

As much as Frank enjoyed flying, the nuts and bolts of air- and spacecraft construction had never much interested him. But now, with his life depending on them, he took a much more active interest, even as his brain struggled to keep up. He studied diagrams, he followed Corley's directions as far as removing and replacing parts, and he passed his written exams. But it was a constant battle to keep that knowledge in his head. He tried learning it in the way he had always learned: by writing stories about it. Or, in this case, concocting stories in his head during long flights, which was all he had time to do.

And so, as he soared at three times the speed of sound over Tehachapi Mountains, he was composing a story about flight engineers repairing a damaged fighter. He had created two comical characters who constantly got into verbal misunderstandings about pieces of equipment, and often chuckled to himself as he came up with inspired bits of dialogue—but at the same time, he had to keep from letting his attention wander too far.

"Incoming!" Corley called.

Frank saw them on his radar. They were coming up over the distant Garlock Beach at an altitude of three hundred meters. The SysTrac identified them as Martian ND-14L fighters, but that was a trick by the instructors; it was clear from their approach and the radar images that they were TS-388s like his own. They were other students from Mojave, defending the imaginary Martian base.

"So much for the element of surprise," Corley said. "They've spotted us. Jittery, Jackoff, peel off to my right and be ready to jump them. Knockup, cover me."

Frank peeled off, Mbouti sticking close enough to him to be his shadow. Corley, meanwhile, led Badran straight toward the incoming fighters, accelerating to Mach 4.

Microwave lasers fired, and the incoming squadron split off into teams.

"We're outnumbered," Frank whined. "Why not come at them from above, from the direction of the sun?"

"Follow my orders, Jittery," Corley said calmly. "We're coming in site of the Martian base. Don't get in the base's line of fire."

There is no base, Frank thought. *Here's a chance to do some real flying!* He peeled up, firing his afterburners and shooting straight at the sky.

Mbouti did not ask questions; he was a good wingman and he stuck to Frank's side, climbing at an incline of ninety degrees, pulling six gees as he accelerated to Mach 5.

Frank had little interest in the mechanics and engineering of planes that so fascinated Corley, but he had mastered one thing that few others had not: an intuitive sense of oneness with the craft. The plane was not a vehicle in which he sat, it was an extension of his body. That had been true even back in Erie when he trained in an S-160, flown recreationally over the campus in a March 400s, and when he had made that unforgettable suborbital flight in the Ace-450, his first foray into space. The vehicle seemed to *like* him; almost as if it were a living thing bonding to him.

He had an intuitive sense not only of his own craft, but of the incoming fighters. He could envision himself in their cockpits, at one with them as he was with his own plane, and he *knew* how the engagement was about to play out. He *knew* they wouldn't notice him and Mbouti peeling off, because their attention would be on Colman. Some of the wingmen would likely take note and be on the lookout, but they would be Frank's first targets.

The craft responded beautifully. There was no shuddering, no buffeting; this was a spacecraft capable of quick flights to the space stations, and even though Frank had not been trained for such flights, he *felt* the plane, knew its capabilities, knew when he was pushing too far and when she could take a little more.

He soared into the blazing sun, his canopy darkened to almost black. He scarcely needed to glance at his instruments; he *felt* the ship around him, felt the air whooshing by, felt the lift as he arced over, his stomach doing somersaults as the distant earth came into view. And then he dove, the craft's wings his own arms, its nose his own face buffeted with the chill wind of the upper troposphere.

Mbouti stuck with him, breathing not a word, just following his wingman.

The enemy targets were on his radar, and two of them now turned upwards to intercept him. He loosed his intercepts, watched them streak downward to meet the onrushing planes.

"Bang," he whispered as they silently detonated. The enemy planes and their pilots were unhurt, but they knew they were out of the game.

Then he dove on the lead plane, his plasma lasers blazing. Mbouti took out the wingman. Soon the enemy squadron scattered in confusion, allowing Colman and Badran to mop up.

It was a close battle, but four planes won against twenty.

Back at Mojave, Colman had some harsh words for Frank.

"I told you *not* to break formation, Jittery."

"It worked, didn't it?"

"That's not the point. I was your squadron commander and you violated orders."

They were arguing in Lieutenant Masters' office, having turned in their written reports. Mbouti and Badran had departed reluctantly, though they silently wished to stick around for the fireworks.

"I'm afraid Corporal Colman is right," Masters said. "You did violate orders, Jittery."

"If this had been a real combat situation, we'd have been wiped out if I hadn't broken formation."

"Be that as it may, you can't go off on your own. You must presume that your commanding officer has more experience and knowledge. I'm sorry, Jittery, but I'm putting you on KP for a week. That's all."

Frank stood, simmering, and turned to leave. Colman saluted and left ahead of Frank, but before Frank could go out the door, Masters called, "Just a minute, Jittery."

Frank turned, shutting the door. "Yes, sir?"

"This is off-the-record, got it?"

"Yes, sir."

"The purpose of these training exercises is to learn. Not just you, but Colman too. All of you, you're all learning and improving and getting ready for combat. Now, just between the two of us, the kind of initiative you showed out there is just what the Star Force is looking for. We don't want robots; we want our pilots to think. You were right, Colman was wrong."

"Then why am I on KP?"

"Because that's the rules—you did violate orders. Colman made a rookie mistake. In a real combat situation, you'll have a more experienced commanding officer who won't make a mistake like that. Colman's good; someday he'll be that kind of commanding officer. I don't think you're commanding officer material—no offense, Jittery, but I just don't see the leadership from you that would be required. But as a commanding officer myself, you're the kind of man I'd want on my right side all the time. You think things through, you see things that others don't, and your advice is going to save lives. But you have to learn to obey orders and not go off on your own. Understand?"

Frank wiped his forehead. "Frankly, sir, no. I'm not sure I do. If my commanding officer is wrong—"

"Not likely. Your commanding officer will be your commanding officer *because* he has a habit of being right, more right than you. But if that situation should come up, your job is to work with him, not take the situation into your own hands. Clear?"

"I'm still not sure, sir, but I'll work on it."

"Good. Get lost."

Get lost. Just what Frank wanted to do at that moment. This lecture about his future in the Star Force served as a reminder that he didn't even want to be here. He did not want a future in the Star Force; he wanted out as soon as possible.

There were no hard feelings between him and Colman, and training continued as before. He tried to bear in mind what Masters had told him, but that came with a seething resentment that he had to bear that advice in mind at all.

This isn't what I want to do with my life, he thought to himself every time he took off. *Dear God, let this war end in the next three weeks!*

But the war did not end, and upon his departure from combat flight training, Frank Johnson was assigned to the Third Fighter Strike Force, posted aboard the Space Carrier U.S.S. *Karkatua* (ISC-134). Destination: Mars.

CHAPTER 9

_ The Valdor administrator, Dugrow, was in the Hab Center of Station Post One. Damon Kramer, the station's commander, had no idea why; but as abrasive as the Valdor was, Kramer was grateful this once to have him around. He had no idea how to handle a galaxy-wide war, and he had to admit he could use Dugrow's experience. It also helped to have someone to blame should things go wrong.

Dugrow's bioluminescent eyes flashed in rapid succession, and he snarled something in his own language.

"What is it?" Kramer asked.

"Community Intelligence reports loss of contact with the Devastator. It was tracked all the way to Strydia, then disappeared."

"Shit, do you think they're dead?" asked Tobey Dingell, the second-in-command.

"How could they be?" Kramer asked. "They have Argo with them!"

"This was a reckless plan!" Dugrow thundered.

Kramer could not disagree. "Fine, maybe it was, but it's done now. Let's notify the Silver Streak."

"We've lost all contact with the Silver Streak*," Tobey Dingell said. "If it was in the area when Star World blew up..."*

Kramer swallowed as the implications hit him. "My God."

———

The first time Frank saw the Space Carrier *Karkatua*, he was filled not with pride, but of foreboding. As he looked out the window of the troop ship, the *Karkatua*'s black hull stood in silhouette against the light of the full Moon. It reminded Frank ominously of the Angel of Death.

Space Carriers were black for camouflage; even though the color of the hull didn't affect radar or thermar, every little bit helped. And the blocky, unstreamlined shape was the farthest thing from beautiful. The *Karkatua* was utilitarian, a machine of death and destruction.

And it was also a symbol of the death of his own dreams. Once he stepped on that deck, he was officially a soldier in the thick of war.

The *Karkatua* was at Earth for repair after a skirmish on Deimos had knocked out several of its weapons mounts and launch tubes—otherwise the troop ship would have had to take Frank all the way to Mars. It would have been a risky journey into enemy territory. So Frank at least had that to be thankful for. But knowing that this, his ship, was here for repair from battle damage, was a visceral reminder of the danger he was entering. The war had become very, very real.

He was here with another pilot, Sergeant Enrique Cavalcanti, who had also been assigned to the *Karkatua*. They sat on opposite sides of the cabin, but even from here Frank could tell Cavalcanti was scared. He knew nothing about his fellow vagabond, but he presumed that he, too, was a draftee. Career pilots would be itching to go, to launch their ships into battle.

Frank had to admit, he had his moments. He was confident in his skill. He loved to fly—or, more accurately, he felt at home and natural when flying. What he *loved* was writing scripts; but he also had a great time at the controls of a swift spaceship.

The troop ship set down on the *Karkatua*'s main deck. Frank and Cavalcanti grabbed their gear and mustered down the ramp and into the confined and musty environment of their ship.

Frank had never before been on board a capital spaceship. He had seen films and immies of them, of course; space war dramas were as popular today as they had been since the Industrial Revolution. But although the landing bay was large, he felt oppressed. The bay had no windows, and this in itself communicated a sense of confinement. The air was stale, and there was a smell—he detected the scent of plasmium, which was present anywhere where spaceships were maintained. But there was also a combination of unpleasant smells...body odor...stale food...a vague sewery smell...oil...

An officer approached and saluted. "Welcome aboard the *Karka*. I'm Lieutenant Auriga, COB."

"Sergeant Johnson," Frank said, saluting.

"Sergeant Cavalcanti," his companion added.

"Come with me, I'll take you to the enlisted men's quarters and I'll assign your bunks and you can drop off your gear. Then I'll take you on a tour of the ship."

The sight of the enlisted men's quarters filled Frank with despair. As they entered the chamber, the first thing that hit him was the stink. It was like the boys' locker room at Forger's Hall in Erie. Some off-duty men were lying in their bunks in their underwear; one mumbled, "Keep quiet fer crissakes, I've got double shift tonight."

Ignoring the complainer, Auriga stepped up to an empty bunk with clean and ironed blankets. "Here you go. Johnson on top, Cavalcanti on the bottom."

Cavalcanti swung his duffel onto his bunk with a groan. "Figures I get the bottom. I always get the bottom. You don't eat beans, do you, Johnson?"

Frank matched Cavalcanti's tone. "Never you mind what I eat." He hoisted his own gear onto the upper bunk.

Auriga stepped into a corner. "Pay attention, fellas, I'm not going through this again. When the muster alarm sounds, grab your flight gear and double-time through here. Follow me."

Frank and Cavalcanti followed the chief into a long bay with shelves on each side. Helmets sat in neat rows, each one labeled with a letter and three numbers.

"This is the ready room," Auriga said. "When the muster alarm sounds, run in here and grab your helmet. It'll be labeled according to your team and your position in that team. For example, right there is A-301. That would be Alpha Team, pilot three-oh-one. You guys'll be assigned to your teams tomorrow. Now, this way."

They followed him into the corridor and turned right. "In there is the conference room...and there's the coordination center, you guys'll never, ever go in there. They won't kill you if you go in, but they may cut off a limb or two. And there's the auxiliary bridge. You'll run past all that shit and end up...here. The drop chutes."

The corridor had widened, and now was lined on each side by cylinders a little taller than a man and twice as wide.

"You're both pilots, right?"

"Yes, sir," Frank and Cavalcanti said together.

"So you'll be assigned your fighters in the next few days. Each of these chutes leads direct to a fighter cockpit. So, there, that one is A-214—Alpha Team, two one four. It'll be the same as on your helmet."

Frank remembered little of the rest of the tour; the whole ship looked much the same—drab gray rooms, long corridors, lots of pipes and pumps and things. It was a noisy ship; in most areas, you had to shout to be heard. Frank knew that was not uncommon; with vacuum outside, there was nowhere for sound to go, so all the bangs and clanks and whirring of equipment and rumbling of engines all kept reverberating through the ship's interior. There were sound suppression barriers, but they didn't seem to be very efficient aboard the *Karkatua*. To some extent this was intentional—the sound of orders, announcements, and alert klaxons had to carry.

That night, Frank lay in his bunk, hands locked behind his head, staring at the ceiling. The noise wasn't bad in the enlisted men's quarters—but that only made the sound of the other mens' snoring that much more disruptive.

So this is my home now, he thought. *For how long? A year? Two years?* His commission went only to the end of the war; then he was free to leave—or to re-enlist, or to go to officers' training, which he didn't plan on doing.

But Frank had begun to learn that plans change.

Frank's first battle was a minor one. A Martian patrol was on its way from Syria Planum toward Libra One, a UCE spy station orbiting Phobos. Libra One was supposed to be hidden by a stealth field, but transmissions had been intercepted and decoded, indicating that the Martians had penetrated the stealth field and had dispatched a patrol to destroy Libra One. And so the *Karka* was diverted from its course for Utopia Planum on orders to intercept and destroy.

The muster alarm sounded while Frank was sitting by himself working on a war comedy called *The Enlisted Pilot*. He hadn't spoken much to the other pilots, but was pleased to find he was working with "Mozart" Esther, his old zone leader from BEST. Although Frank had by now met every enlisted man on the ship, so far he hadn't come close to remembering all their names. And they seemed uncomfortable around him; understandable, perhaps, the way he kept his distance.

Early on, a short, skinny fellow named Mouse Noberini saw him writing and asked him, "Hey, what are you writing?"

"None of your business," he snapped, anticipating being made fun of, or of having his script snatched away from him and read to the group.

But he quickly saw he'd hurt Mouse's feelings; the poor guy was only trying to make friends. But Frank had never adjusted to the Star Force crowd; these were not the type of guys he'd spent his life hanging around with.

Later on, he'd apologized to Mouse, told him he was writing a script; Mouse just shrugged, mumbled an unintelligible reply, and crawled into his bunk. Frank gave up.

There were daily drills, so Frank became accustomed to jumping up, running out into the ready room, grabbing his helmet, and then tromping with the other pilots down the corridor and leaping into his chute—Bravo 116—and sliding with a whoop into his cockpit.

So when the muster alarm sounded on this day, he assumed it was another drill. He jumped up, ran out as always, and on the way down the hall toward the drop chutes, he heard the announcement: "This is a level one alert, all pilots to fighters, all gunners to turrets, this is not a drill. Repeat, this is not a drill."

This is not a drill! Had he heard that right?!

He dove into his drop chute, sliding into the curving tube, his emotions racing.

"This is a level one alert," the announcement went on. "Level one, level one. We are going into battle. This is not a drill, this is not a drill. This is the commander."

Another voice followed. "This is not a drill, this is not a drill, this is the XO."

He landed in his cockpit, the engine whirring. As plasmium was pumped through the engine pipes, his own adrenaline pumped in perfect synchronicity. His crew chief gave him the thumbs up, and his canopy sealed. The HUD came to life, as did his alertness. He was one with his ship. His fear disappeared; he was ready for action.

Quickly he checked his ship's systems; they had all been set by his flight crew, but it was always a good idea to doublecheck everything. After all, this wasn't a fancy ship like the ZR-120; this was just a WB-03, a simple ship with as few linked computer systems as possible, the space equivalent of a stick-and-rudder aircraft, a cheap craft for a cheap enlisted pilot. Cannon fodder. With five independent computers—guidance, navigation, position determination, flight plan, and alignment—and no backups—the ship's main computer was Frank Johnson.

"Bravo Team," came the voice of Second Lieutenant Rick Hoover, "acknowledge ready."

Frank signaled he was go for launch. Simultaneously his other team members, Auger Pendleton and Stealthy Jones, signaled their own readiness.

"Bravo Team go for launch," Hoover said. "Let's go, guys."

Frank pushed his throttle forward, and burst from the exterior of the *Karkatua* alongside the other ships of his team. On full throttle, the four fighters accelerated toward the tiny moon Phobos.

"Cut your thrust," Hoover ordered. "Phobos has about as much gravity pull as a kitchen table. We want to fall into orbit at thirty by sixty-five, AOA thirteen."

Frank obeyed, cutting his thrust. The *Karkatua* was in low Mars orbit, so they had been accelerating away from Mars. He could see Phobos, a spark of bright light. It hardly looked like a moon; with a huge, bowl-shaped crater at one end, and pointed, elongated nose at the other, it sometimes looked to Frank like a weird, surreal spaceship, the crater a recessed engine bell.

Phobos was Mars' inner moon, and was only twenty-seven kilometers across at its widest point. It was only six thousand kilometers from Mars, and slowly losing altitude. It was almost certainly a captured asteroid. Its small size, low altitude, and swift orbit made it an ideal base for spying, but a base on the surface would have been tricky, since Phobos was already a Martian military station. So the spy station Libra One was placed in orbit on the opposite side of Phobos from the aboveground section of the base. It was rather audacious, but this was war.

"Attention all pilots, this is squadron commander. Targets have been sighted, grid eleven. Bearing three minus six, velocity nine thousand kph."

Frank's pulse quickened as the targets showed up on his HUD. *The enemy*, he thought. Actually they were not his enemy at all; they were six pilots on assignment like himself. But just as he was under orders to shoot at them, they were under orders to shoot at him.

Then he saw them. Six stars glittering in the sunlight. He did some quick mental figuring and realized they would be on them in minutes.

"Okay, squadron, go to work. Team leaders to designated positions."

"Bravo Team," Hoover said, "form on me. Proceed to grid six. Do not engage the enemy at this time."

Frank obeyed, relieved. Now that the moment was upon him, he was in no mood to be in the thick of battle.

"What's the story, skipper?" Pendleton asked. "That's a thousand kilometers from the action."

"Orders, Auger. You guys are still green. You're to observe the tactics of the senior pilots and act as a rear guard. We'll get plenty of action if Carter has any surprises for us."

Carter. The military's disparaging name for the Martians. Frank had no idea where the name had come from and didn't care. He watched his HUD closely, watched as Squadron Commander Albert "Awesome Al" Ticonderoga led the charge. At first he thought it was a reckless move, an irresponsible frontal action, but then he noticed the subtle trap enfolding the enemy. The frontal action was actually a barrier between the enemy fighters and Libra One. And that was all.

The *real* attack came from three other teams that had not been in formation with the squadron at all. Frank hadn't noticed them peel off at the moment of launch—they had probably been the first teams to launch. But they struck from the far side of Phobos, firing their microwave lasers from ten thousand kilometers away. With the element of surprise, they managed to fry the electronics of three of the enemy fighters, including the leader's.

That was when two more teams struck from their own rear guard positions. The three unaffected fighters put up a good fight, but were surrounded, leaderless, and caught by surprise.

"We've cleaned 'em up, boys," said Awesome Al. "Well done. *Karka,* this is Squadron Commander Ticonderoga. Three fighters disabled, two destroyed, one surrender. We've got one eject."

"Okay, Bravo Team, show's over," Hoover said. "Stand by for recall."

And that was that. Frank had come through his first battle without firing a shot, without even coming close to danger.

And yet, that evening, an interesting bit of scuttlebutt reached the enlisted men's quarters.

"Hey, fellas, did you hear?" said Sergeant Calloway, who had just come in.

"What?" someone asked.

"There was an extra squadron hiding behind a stealth field ready to jump us today."

"Bullshit!"

"No, it's true. I heard it from an officer. Carter knew we'd broken their code, so they didn't mention it. They were ready to trap us with a squadron of twenty Tiger 250s. But the Tiger squadron commander called it off when he saw that we were rescuing the Red pilots. He didn't want to put them in danger."

"Where were they?" Frank asked.

"I don't know. Probably between Mars and the Sun, where we were least likely to see them."

"Jesus, that's where we were," Auger Pendleton said. "They must've been right behind us."

"Yep," Hoover said. "I picked up something. Thought it was just a distortion. I didn't make anything of it. But now, yeah. God damn it all to hell, I should've remembered. That's exactly what a stealth field looks like. If we'd looked over our shoulders, we'd have *seen* the bastards."

Wow, Frank thought. *But for the grace of God...I should have died today!*

CHAPTER 10

The Throrb inquisitor's name was Hubblrrrp. He had been summoned personally by the warden, Lublwbb, because of his reputation as one who always extracted the information needed. Ambassador Wyechee Koff was one of the most valuable prisoners collected so far in the war; that alone was enough to make Lublwbb crave the skills of Hubblrrrp. But when Captain Richard Cameron, Frank Johnson, the Dreb Priest King Argo, and the traitor Splrrrb had been captured, Lublwbb knew that he had found his ticket out of this hellhole.

Hubblrrrp was not happy about this assignment. He was near retirement, and wished to spend his remaining years lounging at the seashore in his cave in South Lebrrk on Belj. He had fathered twenty-eight children with seven mates, and never spent enough time with any of them. He had worked in four prisons in his career—Thailey Prison the longest—and was proud of his reputation as the one who got things done.

But he disliked Strydia. Too many non-Throrb here. He didn't know enough about the anatomy of creatures like the Valerians, the Derringerians, and the humans. He didn't know when he might cross some lethal threshold; his job was to extract information, not to torture creatures to death.

It wasn't that he had no sympathy for his prisoners, but he had his orders, and he did not question orders. These creatures were evil, they were inferior, and they were non-Throrb. He had accomplished the neat feat of separating his work self from his ordinary self. When he was on the job, his duty was to torture and to extract information. When the work day was over, he could look himself in the mirror and know that he was still a good Throrb; he did what he did because it was his duty. No more, no less. He didn't enjoy torturing anyone—it was just his job. He would do his job without empathy. And he disliked torturing non-Throrb because it would damage his reputation if one of them died under his interrogation.

Koff had been easy. His mind was accessible and he was pliable. The Valerians were physically strong but emotionally weak.

Richard Cameron was more of a challenge. It seemed humans suffered a multitude of physical weaknesses. He would have to be very careful. Still, once properly nullified, Cameron had been docile and cooperative.

Hubblrrrp had expected Frank Johnson to be weaker and more docile than his captain. His resistance to the neural probe was surprising— indeed, he seemed to be legitimately insane.

"He's breaking free," the guard warned.

And indeed he was. These humans, with their thick bone structure and powerful muscles, were able to pull away from structures designed to hold the weaker Throrb bodies.

"Stop him," Hubblrrrp shouted. "Use your paralyzer!"

Frank Johnson had gone wild, his mind trapped in a spiral of memories...memories... memories...

———

The first time he shot down an enemy fighter, Frank felt only triumph, as though he had just squashed a bug on his kitchen floor. The enemy pilot would gladly have shot him down, so he shot the enemy down without feeling, without regret, without remorse, without a second thought.

But he did, nevertheless, feel a fleeting sense of relief when he saw a parachute billowing in the thin Martian air.

His team was over Chasma Boreale on a mission to bomb the Robinson Terraforming Complex. He didn't like the assignment; there was no sense in threatening the entire population of a whole planet in order to win a stupid war. But he had his orders. Besides, the bulk of the terraforming was no longer in the hands of the south polar station; it was a global effort now to seed the thickening air with oxygen-bearing bacteria and plants. The polar carbon dioxide had been sufficiently melted to induce a runaway greenhouse effect—the very thing that had once devastated Earth was now Mars's salvation.

As expected, they had been jumped by support fighters from Schenk Star Force Base—or Wells Air Command Base, as Carter was calling it now. It was Frank's first actual engagement, and although he had been nervous as he flew alongside his wingmates, once the action started he found himself no more than focused on the job. No emotion, no fear, just an intense concentration on staying alive and removing the fighters that were trying to keep him from staying alive. He muttered "shit" to himself about three times a minute, but he had no time right now for fear.

"Watch your flank, Jittery," Hoover's voice shouted.

"I see him," Frank grumbled, watching the persistent blip of a Martian ND-14L zigging and zagging with him. The ND-14L was a more advanced ship than his own, and the pilot was obviously skilled.

"Stealthy, give him a hand," Hoover ordered.

"I got him in my sights," Jones replied.

The blip on his HUD weaved away.

"Got him," Jones shouted. "He's augering in!"

Frank exhaled, but there was no time for celebration. Another fighter was dead ahead, flying right at him—playing chicken. On the ground, Frank would lose a game of chicken every time—but in the air, *that* was a different story! His jaw firmed, he hit his afterburner and flew right at the audacious fighter, plasma lasers blazing.

The enemy returned fire. He felt a jolt as his ship was hit. "Damn!" he cried. He fought the throttle, but he was off course. The enemy ship zoomed past him, and he caught a glimpse of the pilot giving him a two-fingered salute.

Frank almost laughed. "Nice flying, pilot," the enemy was telling him.

He quickly surveyed his damage.

"You all right, Jittery?" Hoover asked.

"Checking," Frank said. "Lost port aileron, fuel lead is leaking, and it looks like my landing gear has deployed."

"Your course is erratic. You have control?"

"I'm working on that. I've still got my thrusters."

The good news was his radar was clear—he saw no more enemy ships ahead, though there was still lots of action behind and to one side.

"Can you make Robinson?"

"Uhhhh...at this rate of fuel loss, I'd say I've got...let's see...half an hour of flying time left." Actually, it was probably more like fifteen minutes if he was relying on his thrusters to maneuver.

"Okay, stick with the team, then. We're almost there. I'd rather have you with us than flying back to base alone."

"Marked."

But the team was destined not to get that far. The Martians, guessing what the Earthies were up to, had called in reinforcements. A Martian space carrier, armed to the teeth, was in polar orbit, and fighters were dropping like bombs. Frank gasped as he watched his radar illuminate.

"*Karka*, this is Squadron Commander," said Awesome Al, "I'm scrubbing the mission. Enemy forces overwhelming and I've lost seven ships. Request permission to return to base."

"Marked, Squadron Commander," said the *Karka*, "we monitor enemy ships. We can't get to you in time to provide cover. Return to base. Return to base."

Frank was relieved to receive the order; he didn't think he would survive the day if he really tried to press on. As it was, returning to the orbiting *Karka* was problematic.

Worse, once they made orbit, they found their mother ship under attack.

"All damaged ships hold position," Awesome Al said. "Everyone capable of combat, let's go get 'em!"

Frank could do little more than orbit at this point. His fuel was gone, and his power was beginning to drain. He still had his batteries, but that was enough power to sustain life and operate the electronic systems. He was effectively immobile.

And now, with time to think, the fear struck. He thought of what he had just been through, all the things that could have happened to him, and began to tremble. His heart raced, he went into a cold sweat.

Was I crazy, flying right at that other ship? What if neither pilot had given way? What if they had collided? What if he had *died* in an act of foolish bravado? What if he had *died* on this stupid, senseless mission in the middle of this stupid, senseless war, deprived himself of his future, his dreams, the career he *wanted*, because he was too prideful to pull up when another fighter flew right at him?

Then he thought of the ship he had shot down. *What's going to happen to that pilot?* he wondered. Even if he made it to the ground safely, what were his chances of rescue? Could he survive long enough to reach a base? Mars wasn't

Earth; the air was thick enough after centuries of terraforming to survive without a pressure suit, but there was still not nearly enough free oxygen in the air to go without some sort of breathing apparatus. Surely that pilot had breathing gear— but did he have enough oxygen to get anywhere? What if he landed in some rugged, impassable terrain? The cold, lonely, suffocating death he was in store for filled Frank with the guilt he had not felt when he'd shot the pilot down.

What if he was a draftee like me? He knew that was unlikely—the Martians were passionate about their independence. They were prepared to fight to the last man—or so went the propaganda.

Still...

His thoughts wandered down such dark corridors while his buddies above him fought and died defending the *Karkatua*. Here he was, helpless and adrift thanks to his own stupidity and ego, while his friends continued to fight...

...to fight for what? For the *Karkatua*, of course. But really, for what? This battle wouldn't be happening if the UCE wasn't so damn hardheaded about giving the Martians independence...or if the Martians hadn't gone and done something so stupid as to declare independence. Why did they want to do that anyway? The United Countries of Earth was a benevolent regime, democratic, principled...

He listened to the chatter, silently rooting for his own guys even as he felt increasingly inadequate for being unable to join them. Objectively, he saw no reason why his side was in the right and the Martians were in the wrong—but these were his friends (not close friends, but friends nevertheless) and his ship.

Finally it was over—primarily because both sides were dipping too deeply into their fuel reserves.

"Hang on, Jittery," Hoover said, "I'll tow you in."

"Thanks," Frank said.

WB-03s were simple craft, not equipped with gravity beams, so Hoover actually fired a grapnel at Frank's ship, attached by an old-fashioned steel cable, and dragged him back to the ship like a fish on the end of a line. From there, the *Karka*'s own gravity beam nudged him into an entry tube, and he was able to taxi the rest of the way on battery power.

Later, Frank sat in the enlisted mess, nursing a whiskey, relieved to be back on board and safe, but miserable over the damage to his craft. None of the damage was irreparable, but he couldn't help thinking of how much it would cost to repair it. He knew the Star Force would pay for the repairs; even in peacetime he would not be liable, even if he was found to be at fault (in which case he could be permanently grounded). But he felt responsible; he felt he *should* pay (not that he could afford it).

But more than anything, he was just glad to be safe on a firm deck and surrounded by friends. Not close friends, but friends. This was war and everyone understood. He was a rookie to combat—well, not anymore. One battle was enough to make a rookie into a veteran. But everyone had been through experiences such as his.

"You've got it," said Auger Pendleton as he joined Frank.

"Got what?" Frank asked.

Auger pointed at Frank's eyes. "The thousand-kilometer stare."

Frank smiled thinly. "Aw, what do you know about it?"

Auger shrugged. "Nothing, I guess. But you look like one of the seasoned boys now, I guess."

Frank sipped his drink, could think of no reply. He didn't feel like talking, but was grateful for Auger's presence.

"I might've gotten my first kill today," he finally said. "The pilot ejected, but it looked like pretty rough terrain down there."

"I got a confirmed kill myself. He ejected, but..." Auger sighed. "He was caught in an updraft and as I flew at him he splatted against my canopy."

Frank winced.

"Yeah," Auger went on, "rough way to go. Or I guess not, the bastard probably didn't feel a thing. I had it worse, trying to fly with his blood and guts caked on my canopy. And the flight crews who're going to have to scrape what's left of him off."

"Well, I guess I'm not eating tonight."

Auger chuckled. "Shit, man, after today I don't think I'm ever eating again."

Of course, with time, Frank got used to battle. He was already a skilled pilot and everyone could see it. But his judgment had to improve—and his teamwork. And with time, it did. The next time he shot down an enemy ship, he spent less time ruminating on it. The third time, he felt nothing. The fourth, he actually whooped as he'd heard other pilots do, and shouted, "Got 'im!"

As he got to know the other members of his team better, they worked together more smoothly—at least until the day Stealthy Jones was shot down. He ejected, but was dead by the time his body was recovered from the cold Martian wastes in the Isidis Basin.

That cast a pall over the team, and they got roaring drunk that night.

But no longer a team of rookies, Bravo Team was routinely assigned to the meat of the action—and Auger Pendleton became team leader when Rick Hoover was promoted to squadron commander. Awesome Al had been lost during the Battle of the Face in Cydonia.

And then one day the *Karkatua* received orders to raid the rebels' defensive line around the Eighth Parallel. Bravo Team was sent in to hit a power plant that supplied the rebel army with its breathable atmosphere. They met higher resistance than anticipated and a better contingent of anti-spacecraft guns.

And that was where it all happened.

CHAPTER 11

Frank Johnson had gone into a frenzy. He was uncontrollable. With superhuman strength he tore from his bonds. Hubblrrrp was less concerned about his equipment than he was that his valuable prisoner might hurt himself.

A guard extended a pseudopod. The slick appendage was wrapped around a charged stick. As Frank broke free of his restraints, the stick made contact with his body. A precisely calibrated electric charge surged through his nerves, paralyzing his voluntary muscles. He stiffened and collapsed to the floor.

"He's still alive," the guard assured.

"Very well," Hubblrrrp said, "he's not worth the trouble. Take him back to his cell."

The guards wrapped their pseudopods around the limp arms and dragged their burden away.

But it was too late. Frank had lost the present and now tumbled helplessly through the past....

————

The small, bleeping alarm filled his helmet and commanded his attention. Even in the midst of the incoming fire, he had to take his mind off of the battle and direct it to the damage his fighter had sustained. He pulled up a diagnostic on his heads-up display, and no sooner had he registered that the damage was to his top ion engine than the master alarm blared and he spun out of control. He had taken another hit.

"Watch it, Frank," Auger's voice shouted in his ear. "You're diving right into a crossfire!"

The warning had already come too late. Frank's fighter was spinning, tumbling toward a catastrophic impact that would crumple his ship like a carton of eggs on a sidewalk. He saw the ground ahead, moving bottom-to-top, endlessly, then it disappeared above him and he saw the pink sky, caught glimpses of other fighters rushing about, then the ground again. All he heard were the incessant warning bells of his ship screaming at him to do something. But his controls had frozen up; he was augering in and there was nothing he could do about it.

Clenching his teeth, he elbowed the eject panel. It cracked open, he reached in and pulled the trigger. His canopy exploded and his seat rocketed out; he only hoped it rocketed upward instead of straight down into an impact with the ground.

Fortunately he was still high enough that it wouldn't have made a difference.

As it happened, he had ejected more or less sideways. His chute caught the tenuous air and billowed open lazily. In the weak Martian gravity he didn't fall as fast as he would have on Earth, but he had already reached terminal velocity. It took time for the chute to slow his descent—time enough for the rebels to gather under him and be ready for him…

―――――

Frank's only comfort was that he wasn't the only pilot who had been captured. He found himself in a dungeon with ten others, some from his own squadron, from this very raid. Bob Corley was there, his old friend from BEST. He recognized "Mozart" Esther, and tried to strike up a conversation.

"What do you think, Mozart? Think they'll send in a cleanup team pretty soon?"

Mozart looked at him as if he were crazy.

Frank pressed. "I mean, they've got to know we're missing, right? It's not like this is a maximum-security prison or anything. This is just a field brig. They can get us out no problem. Right?"

"Frank, the op was a bust. There's no one to get us out. The *Karka*'s gonna pull out and nurse her wounds. No one's coming in after us."

Frank didn't want to believe that, refused to believe that. He couldn't have been ripped out of his life, shot into space on an impossible mission, and then abandoned to waste away in a dungeon in the middle of the deserts of Mars.

―――――

The journey by subway was long and lonely. Frank was tied to a chair, arms behind his back, shoulders strained. He couldn't move his head much, but he listened to the voices from further forward in the car. They provided no clues what was to be done with him, but they did finally announce the arrival at their dreaded destination: the Lothian Prison Camp.

They were marched single file through the winding passageways, passageways that would haunt Frank's memories for years, to a small cell that provided no privacy, no amenities. The bunks were plastic, the toilet was right in the open, and the light fixture above was harsh and yellow, painful to look at, and hot.

Frank chose his bunk. No one fought him for it. There was little conversation; each man was caught up in his own thoughts. *Each man…*Frank wondered if any of the female pilots had been captured, and if so, where they were. It might have helped to have some of them here—or that might just make things more complicated.

The interrogations began the next day. All the POWs had their turn. They each were gone for hours upon hours. Mozart came back numb, but in possession of his faculties. Corley was hit a little harder. Dan Mack disappeared for days. Either way, no one wanted to talk about the experience, so Frank didn't know what they had gone through...or what he was in for.

But finally it was Frank's turn.

He was marched down a long corridor, the Martian guards' bootsteps clacking, clacking, clacking...

He came to a small room with a single chair, a table next to it covered with small devices. *Torture?* he wondered. *No, they can't! They just can't!*

The inquisitor entered the room. It was obvious at a glance that he was the man in charge. A cluster of medals hung from the breast of his gray uniform, and red and white stripes ran down

the length of his sleeves. His face was gaunt,
almost skeletal, his eyes a cold, icy blue.

"Good morning," he said. "I am Captain
Peter Stapleton, Lothian Base Commander,
Guardian of Martian Freedom, Syria Planum. I
will be asking you some questions today, and it
will serve us both well if you answer them
without resistance. Agreed?"

Frank replied as he had been trained to reply.
"Frank Johnson, Sergeant, United States Star
Force, serial number eight one five seven six G-
E-L."

"Well, we've established that much. At least
I don't have to ask you your name. We know that
you were sent to destroy the oxygen generation
plant on the East Side. That operation failed. Now
what I want to know is the location of the forces
you have in reserve to attack our army at the
Eighth Parallel."

"Frank Johnson, Sergeant, United States Star
Force, serial number eight one five seven six G-
E-L."

Stapleton laughed softly. "Well, I see we
might have to do this the hard way. You see, I
know that your ship is the Space Carrier
Karkatua, and that on board is the United States
Star Force Third Fighter Strike Force. What I
want to know is their location, Sergeant Johnson.
You will tell me; the only question is when and
how. Tell me now and this will be easier for both
of us."

"Frank Johnson, Sergeant, United States Star
Force, serial number eight one five seven six G-
E-L."

Stapleton sighed sadly. "Very well. You see that you are attached to a number of devices. There is a band above your head; when lowered, it will give me certain inputs to your brain." He gestured to a fierce-looking little man with red cheeks. "I'd like you to meet Lieutenant Dudley Appelbaum, administer of enhanced interrogation."

"Howdy," the little man said.

"Dudley has worked with neural interfaces for many years. He has perfected a number of his own techniques—and I would like to remind you that, since Mars is no longer a part of the United Countries of Earth, we are no longer bound by certain, ah, legal restrictions."

Frank's guts tensed at that. *What are they going to do to me?*

"You might not enjoy the effects." Stapleton's face hardened. "Tell us your troop movements, Sergeant Johnson. The location of the U.S.S. *Karkatua* Third Fighter Strike Force."

"Frank Johnson, Sergeant, United States Star Force, serial number eight one five seven six G-E-L."

"All right, Dudley, attach the neural feed."

Frank remained stoic, calm, defiant. He remembered his training. And whether this was his preferred career or not, he resented the presumption of these rebs grilling him for information. He may be a reluctant soldier, but he wasn't going to betray his buddies.

Stapleton held up an innocent-looking device, a headset attached to a little blue box. "This will cause total sensory deprivation, Sergeant Johnson."

Frank almost laughed at that. Sensory deprivation? That was the best these lunkheads could throw at him?

"Tell us the location of the U.S.S. *Karkatua* Third Fighter Strike Force and we won't do this."

"Frank Johnson, Sergeant, United States Star Force, serial number eight one five seven six G-E-L."

"Have it your own way. Attach it, Dudley."

Appelbaum leered at him. "Don't worry, Sarge. This won't hurt."

And it didn't. It didn't feel like anything.

He never would have imagined that NOTHING could be such agony.

First his fingers lost feeling, then his toes. His face went slack, his vision spiraled. Voices became tinny. Gradually all sensation ceased. His vision went...away. It didn't go black, or white, or any other color. It simply...went. There was nothing. His hearing went too. No touch, no taste, no contact whatsoever with anything outside his own mind.

He had heard that sensory deprivation was relaxing; many people used it for therapy, or for meditation. But his fevered imagination quickly turned it into a frightening experience, as if his canopy had blown while he was flying through space, and he was now drifting in the infinite black void. His fingers had no purchase, his eyes could fix on nothing, there was no sound, no feeling.

He tried to relax, remind himself he was still in that chair in that interrogation room. The world still existed around him. Might as well just relax and enjoy it.

But he did not, could not enjoy it. Soon his deprived brain began to fill in the gaps left by the void of the neural feed. He began to see things, hear things of his own invention. He knew they did not exist, but they tormented him—for when he had nothing to lock on, no reality to hold onto, hallucinations were the only reality he had.

He never would have believed his own mind was so terrifying a place. What his senses would not tell him his mind filled in. The hallucinations started fairly quickly. Waking nightmares, horrid visions of what might or might not be going on around him while he was blind, deaf, unfeeling, untasting. Humanoid creatures, faceless, clasping at parts of his body he could not feel—could not feel, yet his mind threw in some feeling. Where an imaginary inhuman hand clutched and squeezed, he felt clutched and squeezed, with no way of knowing whether he was actually being touched in any way.

This is illegal, he tried to say, but didn't know whether his mouth succeeded in forming the words or if he only spoke in his imagination. You can't do this, you can't do this, this is a violation of the Fifth Interplanetary Congress...

Hours went by, hours. He had no way of measuring time, all was subjective. He was speeding along a highway in a monospeeder, though he was running down a corridor of the *Karkatua*, though he was flying over a beach like a superhero...Now he was a child again, his mother packing up for them to move because of another terrorist threat against his father, his father who worked in the controversial Venus Terraform Project, and so they moved and moved and moved, never a place to call home...Now he was in high school and trying to write a paper on the new *Clutch* sequel, but the Martian rebels were after him, chasing him, chasing him with their blank heads with no faces and their neural paralyzers and their anti-spacecraft guns that would find him no matter where he ran, no matter where he hid…

———

"Tell us the location of the U.S.S. *Karkatua* Third Fighter Strike Force."

"Frank Johnson, Sergeant, United States Star Force, serial number eight one five seven six G-E-L."

"Sergeant Johnson, you were in a state of sensory deprivation for seven hours. That is far from the worst that we can do. Let me explain the situation to you—you are not going to be rescued and you are not going to escape. You have now seen what we can do to you when you don't cooperate. So. Tell us the location of the U.S.S. *Karkatua* Third Fighter Strike Force."

"Frank Johnson, Sergeant, United States Star Force, serial number eight one five seven six G-E-L."

…More sensory deprivation, more hours of torture…

———

"Tell us the location of the U.S.S. *Karkatua* Third Fighter Strike Force."

Dudley Appelbaum muttered something to Captain Stapleton, who nodded. Appelbaum left the room.

"He needs to use the restroom," Stapleton said with a chuckle. Then he gestured at Frank's wet crotch. "I see that you...don't. You probably don't remember doing that. Tell me, Sergeant Johnson, did you graduate from a flight school or did the Star Force train you?"

"Frank Johnson, Sergeant, United States Star Force, serial number eight one five seven six G-E-L."

"Oh, well, I suppose it doesn't matter. I was just curious. I grew up on Earth, actually. Yes, I was in the Star Force myself. We had the worst hurricane on record when I was in basic. Four hundred twenty kilometer-per-hour winds, eight hundred fifteen millibars, if I remember correctly. I didn't think our metal and concrete barracks would survive. The water was five meters over the roof; of course we didn't know that at the time. Whew. I'll take Mars over Earth any day. Ah. Here's Dudley.

"Sorry, Captain," Appelbaum said.

"No problem, Dudley. I was just shooting the breeze with Sergeant Johnson here—though he's still not very talkative."

"Oh? We'll break him of that, sir."

"So, Sergeant Johnson, tell me—who do you think is going to win the war?"

We are, Frank thought, running his tongue over dry lips. But he refused to answer any of this skeletal man's questions; he resorted to his standby, the only words that existed, the only words that *could* exist:

"Frank Johnson, Sergeant, United States Star Force, serial number eight one five seven six G-E-L."

Stapleton sighed. "Very well, Sergeant Johnson."

...More sensory deprivation...

CHAPTER 12

It was small consolation that the Throrb fired first. Their war computers indicated that a Valdor fleet of naked starships was on the way. It was the glitch, but before cooler heads could prevail, the Alternative Alliance had launched the first salvo that turned the interstellar war into a doomsday war.

In Capital Control in the great Valdor Artificial World, two Valdor and one human monitored the chaos. Commissioner Norbok, chair of the Centralized Committee; Administrator Dugrow, who was responsible for the Community civilizations in this sector; and Zach Mortimer, head of the human corporation Intercore.

"The last telemetry from the Space Star Silver Streak indicated that Star World was destroyed," Norbok said.

Mortimer was stricken. "Star World? My artificial world destroyed?"

"And we subsequently lost contact with the Silver Streak. We must assume that it, too, is destroyed."

"This is an outrage! I think it's time for a full retaliation with naked starships."

Dugrow said, *"That is policy. When we are attacked by a naked starship, full retaliation is called for. There is no room for discussion."*

"Agreed," said Norbok. *"Therefore I do not require the authority of the Centralized Committee. I hereby order the deployment of our force of naked starships."*

And so starships crisscrossed the spiral arm, gamma rays bunching ahead like water surging ahead of a hurricane. Everything in their wake was destroyed. They plowed into inhabited worlds, wiping out tens of billions of lives. Entire civilizations were brought to extinction in seconds.

Dugrow regarded the incoming data with a clinical interest. *"We have destroyed the planet Bardo, Space Station K'Toth, planet Roe, and the Sithikon Artificial World. We now have reason to believe we have lost planet Batey, the artificial world of the Selkcip, the Dontron Star Network, planet Kokrotel, and planet K."*

"The situation is escalating," Norbok remarked.

"Yes. We must destroy the Throrb command structure."

"We have already destroyed FBN-915," Norbok said, referring to the Throrb command space station, *"yet their command structure is not broken."*

"Then they have distributed their command and control on many space stations and planets— perhaps they even have a mobile command force."

"We should do the same," Norbok said, *"in case they destroy Klym Valdor."*

Norbok's words were prophetic; for no sooner were the words out of his mandibles than a relativistic projectile, fired from a Throrb spyship, struck the great artificial world. The planet-sized structure was fractured in two, taking the lives of billions of Valdor, and shattering half of the giant space complex.

Across the spiral arm, it was the same. Ships collided with planets, planets exploded. The destruction was galaxywide, a carnage unseen since the last superburster sterilized the galaxy.

The Community crumbled.

————

"Frank Johnson, Sergeant, United States Star Force, serial number eight one five seven six G-E-L." That rote sentence, grilled into his brain in Interrogation Resistance, became his lifeline. His mind turned it over and over, spun it into visual and auditory patterns, morphed it into an imaginary friend. He knew he would collapse under the strain unless he forgot how to say anything else.

Back in his cell, he refused to speak. His answer to every question was "Frank Johnson, Sergeant, United States Star Force, serial number eight one five seven six G-E-L." His reply to the most idle comment was "Frank Johnson, Sergeant, United States Star Force, serial number eight one five seven six G-E-L."

"He's cracked," Dan Mack said.

"No, he's the only one of us that hasn't," Bob Corley said.

"You told 'em?"

"I made up an answer. Anyway, what's it matter? The op's over, I'm sure the *Karka*'s on the other side of the Solar System by now."

Probably, Frank thought. But he buried the thought as it occurred to him. "Probably" was not in his vocabulary. The only words he knew were "Frank Johnson, Sergeant, United States Star Force, serial number eight one five seven six G-E-L."

The worst part was the terrible unpredictability. He might have pulled himself out of it were it not for the random nature of the inquiries. There were ten POWs in the cell; if the Martians had simply rotated those taken in for questioning, there would at least have been a pattern, a way for Frank to prepare, to reset himself, to make sense of the senseless.

But no...some POWs were never taken in for questioning again. Sometimes one would be taken and then Stapleton would immediately decide to go back to Frank. Sometimes one of the others would be questioned for ten minutes, sometimes ten hours. So there was no telling when it would be his turn again.

But he began to gain a sense of how much time had passed when Stapleton stopped asking about the *Karkatua*'s Third Fighter Strike Force and began asking more general questions.

"Is the WB-03 still the primary fighter used by the enlisted pilots?"

"Frank Johnson, Sergeant, United States Star Force, serial number eight one five seven six G-E-L."

"Are the attack computers in the modern Space Carrier still generalized, or are there separate computers governing separate systems?"

"Frank Johnson, Sergeant, United States Star Force, serial number eight one five seven six G-E-L."

"Tell me, Sergeant Johnson, our research tells us a managing director of the Venus Terraform Project is a Benjamin Johnson, and he has two sons—Stuart Benjamin Johnson and Randal Francis 'Frank' Johnson. Are you that Frank Johnson?"

Frank was startled by the mention of his family, enraged, and terrified. He glared at Stapleton, clenched his teeth, and hissed, "Frank Johnson, Sergeant, United States Star Force, serial number eight one five seven six G-E-L!"

"Well, no matter, I suppose. Our battleships are over Earth now; you probably didn't know that. If we take Earth, we might round up the families of those who sought to deprive us of our independence."

No, you wouldn't do that—you couldn't! You're trying to establish a free society here, right? You don't believe in tactics like that! But he remembered the cruel hours of sensory deprivation. These people were willing to go to extraordinary lengths to get what they wanted.

No! They're trying to scare you. That's all. They might not even be at Earth.

He wanted to ask, "What do you want to know?" To test the waters. To at least see if he could tell them anything that would satisfy them—without his having to betray his world.

But he had programmed himself well—far better than his instructors imagined. He stared

Stapleton in the eyes and snarled, "Frank Johnson, Sergeant, United States Star Force, serial number eight one five seven six G-E-L."

Stapleton shook his head, smiled sadly, and said, "As you wish, Sergeant Johnson. Dudley, attach neural feed."

And it began again. The numbing. The slow, all-consuming blackness. The sense of no longer existing. And the hours, the eternities, of terrible, punishing emptiness. And the revenge of his subconscious, the sights and sounds and sensations of his overactive brain.

———

He wanted to scream. He wanted to beg for mercy. He wanted to tell Stapleton to go to hell. He wanted to tell them everything they wanted to know. But the only sound that came from him was "Frank Johnson, Sergeant, United States Star Force, serial number eight one five seven six G-E-L."

He had his duty. His country. His pledge, his oath, his loyalty.

What if he told them? Would it matter? Were they even looking for practical information or were they just trying to break him? Maybe it had become a psychological game; if they could gain just a little cooperation, maybe they could then gain a little more, and a little more. Maybe he would be rewarded; maybe then a little Stockholm Syndrome would kick in. Maybe he would become One Of Them.

No! He would not allow that to happen, *never* allow that to happen! Damn Martians! Damn Carter! Damn Red Rebels! They had turned against the United Countries of Earth, and for that they must die! He would fight them tooth and nail, he would fight them with everything that was in him—as little as was left.

All they would get out of him was "Frank Johnson, Sergeant, United States Star Force, serial number eight one five seven six G-E-L." That was all he would say because that was all he was. They had stolen away the rest. The Star Force had begun the process and Captain Peter Stapleton had finished it.

He was a robot now, a robot with specific programming; pull the string and he said "Frank Johnson, Sergeant, United States Star Force, serial number eight one five seven six G-E-L." A cute toy. That was all he was...all he *must be*...all he would *ever* be.

———

It was Carlos "Mozart" Esther who conceived of the escape plot. He had been at it for a long time before Frank learned about it; the other pilots had determined that "Jittery Johnson" couldn't be trusted. With the help of his co-conspirators, Mozart had mapped out the complex, both inside and out, the locations of the underground water ducts and where they led, the last known positions of enemy strongholds, and the nearest spaceports.

Mozart—who, Frank learned while lying on his bunk and listening, was named not for the famous composer but for the animated dog in the immie *Dog Party*—became the leader of the group. As Frank lay there, refusing to say anything but "Frank Johnson, Sergeant, United States Star Force, serial number eight one five seven six G-E-L," Mozart decided who would be responsible for which tasks. Frank, Mozart realized quickly, would be no good for anything, and Frank was even aware of a discussion of whether they should take him with them when they made their break.

Corley was adamant: "We're not leaving anyone behind."

"He won't be any good to us," Mack insisted, "and he'll probably get us all caught."

There was more muttered discussion among men most of whose names Frank did not know.

But Mozart made the final decision: "We're not leaving anyone behind."

Frank did not feel grateful, only humiliated. He did not want to survive by other men's generosity. He wanted to participate, to help, to hold his own. But his mind was still half in the interrogation room.

One guy—Theo something-or-other—was a life support technician, so Mozart put him on fashioning improvised breathing gear in case the air in the tunnels was unbreathable. There was even the chance the tunnels might flood during the escape—whether as a sewage dump, a refresh cycle, or a deliberate attempt to drown the escapees should they be discovered. Mozart prepared for every contingency.

As he lay there muttering "Frank Johnson, Sergeant, United States Star Force, serial number eight one five seven six G-E-L," Frank found himself filled with admiration for Mozart—and resentment. He wished *he* was the one coming up with these ingenious ideas, passing out assignments, acting like a heroic Star Force officer rather than a useless child.

"Who wants to escape?" Mozart asked one morning. All hands went up—except Frank's; he was too busy saying "Frank Johnson, Sergeant, United States Star Force, serial number eight one five seven six G-E-L."

"Well, I need one volunteer," Mozart said. "I want someone to escape on his own—just so he can be recaptured."

"What the hell for?" someone asked.

"Two reasons: one, to survey the area outside the base and determine the best escape routes. And two—it'll throw Carter off our *real* escape attempt. If *one* of us escapes on his own, and is recaptured after a very clumsy, hasty, and desperate break for freedom, they're less likely to suspect that there's a mass, organized escape being planned."

Three volunteered for the sneaky operation; Mozart chose Dan Mack.

———

Mozart began to disappear for hours at a time. Frank assumed he was in the sensory deprivation chair, but he always returned cheerful, healthy, in full possession of his faculties. Presently Frank learned that he had drawn KP duty for good behavior. He had even made friends with one of the Martian guards!

Mack was thrown back into the cell with them some time after his phony escape; Frank didn't know exactly how he had escaped or when, or how long he had been gone. But Mozart's plan seemed to work. The Martians did not seem to suspect anything—nor, it seemed, were they looking for any more information. The *Karka* had moved on; for all Frank knew, the whole war might be over.

Finally, one cold, dark night, Mozart put his plan into motion. Frank, still repeating his name, rank, and serial number, comprehended what was going on and he followed. During KP duty, Mozart had improvised an escape hatch in a storage room off the galley using ordinary kitchen tools. One of the others had stolen a key to their cell weeks ago; the Martians searched, but failed to find it, and when there was no escape attempt, they slowly backed off, assuming the key was lost. In fact, Mozart had hidden it in the storage closet where he had improvised his escape hatch, only bringing it to the cell this night, for the escape.

There were few guards on duty at this time of night, and the group remained quiet. Mozart walked far ahead of them, so that if someone sighted him he could bluff his way through while the others retreated to the cell. But no one spotted them.

Mozart opened the storage closet and watched out for guards while the others crawled through into the escape hatch.

Frank followed wordlessly, numb, not sure whether he was dreaming or not, down a ladder to the huge water tank—or one of the water tanks; he couldn't imagine a single tank supplied this whole complex. As he climbed down the ladder, someone—he could see who in the dark—fixed a mask around his head, strapping on a small bottle of pure, cold oxygen.

Then it was a winding course through the tunnel, an intricate course through the intersecting passageways. Frank wondered how they had mapped it—though now that he thought about it, he remembered Mozart assigning someone the job of mapping the tunnel. How it had been done he didn't know.

The journey seemed to take all night, but finally they came to the water harvesting plant. From there, it was up a series of ladders and ramps and scaffolds, and they were at an airlock.

Two guys in the front pried it open. No alarm sounded—someone had been assigned to disable that. Then...a break for freedom.

At this low altitude, the air was just thick enough to survive without a pressure suit, thanks to the areoengineering that had been going on for about five hundred years. With mirrors, laser satellites, and thermal heaters melting the polar ice, the atmosphere was growing thicker and warmer.

He ran with the others, bouncing slightly in the Martian gravity, weaving around boulders, up and down ravines, for what seemed like hours, until they reached the Melrose airfield.

Mack climbed the control booth and disabled the operator there. Then the lights went out and the group scurried to the untended ND-14L fighters.

Frank noticed Mozart eyeing him with uncertainty, but he nodded, silently assuring him he was okay.

But, of course, he was not. For Frank Johnson, a time of innocence had been blasted to oblivion. Childhood dreams were gone forever. There was only duty.

He climbed the inset ladder on the fighter's side, swung into the cockpit, and felt the old power surging through him. He took a moment to figure out the unfamiliar controls, but he had operated enough aircraft and spacecraft to intuit this one's operation. He started the warm-up cycle, felt the throbbing of power around him. The HUD came on, the fuel indicator showed him a lovely, full tank and a reactor in top condition. There was an interactive computer, but he disabled it; there were probably failsafes in case the fighter was stolen by the enemy!

Then the plasma engine fired and he, along with his fellow escapees, was soaring upward through the thin Martian air toward the vacuum of space—and freedom.

His deep concentration on knowing no words but name, rank, and serial number was broken. To all outward appearances, he went back to normal.

Yet the real trauma of his experiences on Mars was only just beginning.

CHAPTER 13

As the guards dragged Frank from the interrogation room, Hubblrrrp withdrew his pseudopods in a gesture of helplessness. "I was not expecting such violence in response to a simple neural probe."

"His captain was also very resistant," Lublwbb reminded him.

"Yes, but strange that his subordinate would be even more so. I think further interrogation should be restricted to the captain and the other prisoners. This one is too unstable. I wonder how he came to be the first officer of a starship on so important a mission."

"Well, that may be taken out of our hands," Lublwbb said. "We have lost all contact with the Alternative Alliance, including FBN-915 and Belj."

"Really?" Hubblrrrp was seized by worry. Worry for his mate, for his children. "What's the war news?"

"There is none. That's why I think we should be done for today. I would like to try to re-

establish contact and find out if we're wasting our time here."

"Very well." Hubblrrrp oozed from the chamber in a hurry. He glided down the corridors to his assigned quarters, and there tapped in to the prison communications console. By tapping in his personal identification code, he was able to override the security protocols and send a message back home.

The light indicating a connection was not on. He was not getting through. He slid over to his slime puddle and fretted. It could be that the network was shut down to avoid any interference with wartime communications.

Or it could also be that Belj was under attack. Or destroyed. There were rumors of the Community attacking with naked starships. If that was true....

He tried not to think about it. He had a job to do here; until he knew for sure one way or the other what was happening back home, he must try not to think of it.

———

As he flew the Martian ND-14L fighter on an almost vertical ascent from the thin atmosphere, Frank emerged from his daze. The fog that had clouded his thoughts for...just how long had he been a prisoner in the Lothian Base? Months? Years?...finally cleared, and he knew where he was and what he was doing. He merged with this unfamiliar ship as he merged with every ship he flew.

The torment, the pain, the fear, the ever-present nightmares gave way to an overpowering exhilaration. He was free! He was flying through the air at supersonic speed, far beyond the reach of Captain Peter Stapleton, Lothian Base Commander, Guardian of Martian Freedom, Syria Planum! He was a superpowered bird, a winged god, a sheer burst of energy that could not be stopped by all the armies on Mars!

The pink sky of Mars darkened to burgundy, the bright lights of Phobos and Deimos directly overhead. Then it was the ebon blackness of space.

If he was reading this unfamiliar ship's radar correctly, there were no other ships in the area—except for his companions, all ten of them.

"Okay, we made it," Mozart's voice crackled, "but we're not out of the woods yet. There could be a stealth squadron bearing down on us right now. We got lucky, we're headed right for Phobos. We'll keep heading that way and see if we can use it as a shield against scans from below. Then we'll signal to any nearby UCE base."

Sounds like a plan, Frank thought. The idea of being recaptured now was too horrible to imagine. No, he would go down fighting; he would destroy this ship himself rather than go back into that cell, back into that sensory deprivation and relentless inquisition. And if they were recaptured after this successful escape, their captors would not go as easy on them.

"This is Mack," the radio announced. "I think I've got targets below, rising from the Melrose airfield."

"Okay, relax, fellas," Mozart replied, "we've got a thousand-klick head start on them. We're in trouble if anybody jumps us from above or from the sides, but my scope is clear, so I think we've got a clear shot for the farside of Phobos."

Now that they were in space, the sense of speed was gone. Phobos never seemed to get any closer, and the vibration and roar of the engine were abstract things, not imparting any sensation of acceleration. But Frank religiously watched the accelerometer ticking steadily upward...16342...16991...17546...18487...upward and upward as his faithful steed raced beyond the grip of Martian gravity.

"Attention prisoners," came a voice over the radio. "This is Squadron Commander Elliott Cavarretta. You are ordered to turn around and surrender. You cannot escape. We possess remote control codes and can take control of your ships. Surrender now."

"He's lying," Mozart said. "If that were true, they'd have taken control already rather than ordering us to turn around."

"Surrender at once," Cavarretta went on, "or we will destroy you."

"Destroy us," Mozart replied. "I speak for us all when I say we'd rather die than go back to your stinking prison." Switching channels to the Star Force scramble code, he said, "Attention any Star Force ships or outposts. I am Sergeant Carlos Esther, U.S.S. *Karkatua* Third Fighter Strike Force. I and ten members of my squadron have escaped custody in Lothian Prison in Martian fighters. We are now twenty-two thousand kilometers over...ah...the Amargosa Valley, I think."

Frank watched the blips of the approaching enemy ships, noting with relief that he not only had a good head start on them, but was traveling faster than they were. It was virtually impossible for them to catch him.

The question was—where to go now?

Mozart continued to transmit his message, and Frank hoped the Martians hadn't cracked the code. Not that it mattered much; if there were any Martian ships, space stations, or bases ahead, the Lothian Base could simply signal them, warn them that escaped prisoners were coming. Well, they'd have a fight on their hands; Frank was determined never to go back. He would die first. It was the first time in his life he was genuinely willing to die.

Now Phobos was a distinct shape in the black sky ahead, a huge rock, peaked on one end, blasted with a conical crater on the other. It was shining in the sunlight too brightly to make out any lights on the surface. If there was still a Martian base there...

"Sergeant Esther, this is Golf Alfa One. I read you. We're tracking you on radar. Maintain your present course. You will be met by twelve ZR-120 Interceptors from Space Carrier U.S.S. *Galaxyprobe*."

The sounds of cheers sounded over Frank's headset. He wanted to join in, but was just too tired. He was overjoyed, but all he wanted to do was to drop into a comfortable bed and sleep for a week.

"Okay, keep it down, fellas," Mozart said. "Golf Alfa One, I mark you. We're maintaining course."

Frank remembered little of the ensuing wait, rendezvous, and escort back to the waiting carrier.

He might have dropped to sleep, but he was never sure.

But the next morning he awoke in that comfortable bed he so craved. He was in the *Galaxyprobe*'s infirmary, being treated for malnutrition and dehydration.

A nurse dropped by to give him vitamins. "Morning," the nurse said distractedly.

"Good morning." Frank wasn't sure, but he thought those were the first words he had spoken since leaving the base—and therefore the first words he had spoken in weeks aside from "Frank Johnson, Sergeant, United States Star Force, serial number eight one five seven six G-E-L." As the nurse fussed over him, he asked, "What's going to happen to us now?"

"Well, we're on our way to Custer Station. You'll be dropped off there."

Frank grew quiet. Custer Station—the Star Force station at Earth's L4 LaGrange Point. The Martians didn't know about it yet, and it was to serve as a secret base to strike at either Mars or at Martian ships making the traverse between planets. It reminded Frank of Peter Stapleton's assertion that the Martians were on Earth. "Have the Reds invaded Earth?"

"Hmm? Well, scuttlebutt says there've been some raids, but nothing major that I know of."

Frank exhaled; that was a relief, but it still didn't erase the uncertainty. He would like to get in touch with his family, but didn't know where to begin. Even before the war, they had been moving from one home to the next, one city to the next, as long as he could remember. There was so much controversy over the Venus Terraform

Project, his father had to keep on the move due to the constant death threats and even potential terrorist attacks.

The time blurred, much as it had in the Martian prison, but this time in a much more pleasant way. The soft bed, the good food, the sense of relaxation, was such as he had never thought he would experience again, and felt he had not experienced since before he had been drafted.

But when the *Galaxyprobe* arrived at Custer Station, it all ended. The COB mustered him and his companions out of the Infirmary, and he found himself in line, marching as though off to battle. The message was clear: get out. The luxury cruise was over.

As he stepped through the airlock into Custer Station, he was conscious of a change in atmosphere—literally and figuratively. The air was cooler than on board the carrier, and there was a brisk breeze. The ventilation here was efficient, and he realized therefore that the ventilation on the carrier was *in*efficient. Ships of war were away for months at a time, subjected to all manner of abuse, with little opportunity for repair. This station, though far from Earth, was resupplied and repaired more frequently—plus it was newer than any of the ships of the Star Force.

He and the other former POWs were escorted to a briefing room, where they waited. And waited. And waited.

There was little conversation, though they all wanted to talk. No one else could really understand what they had gone through, but they were all macho fighter pilots, and none wanted to be the first to lower the inhibitions and talk. Frank was certainly not going to be the first, as he was still embarrassed and humiliated by the way he had conducted himself during their incarceration.

A general entered the room. They all stood and saluted.

The general returned the salute. "At ease, men. Be seated."

They sat, watched the general expectantly. He removed his hat and sat down, drew up one knee and massaged it with both hands. "Well, good morning, men. I'm General Ferguson, commanding officer of the Sixth Star Force Command. You gentlemen are from the Third Fighter Strike Force of the U.S.S. *Karkatua*, and had been given up for dead after you were lost in an unsuccessful raid on the Eighth Parallel. It seems now that you've been held in confinement at the Lothian Prison. We've heard stories about that place, and I'd like to have it from you exactly what went on there."

Mozart did most of the talking. Frank contributed nothing; he sat and listened—and hoped no one would mention his behavior. No one did.

"No physical torture?" Ferguson asked.

"No, sir," Mozart said.

"Well, when we win the war and bring Mars back into the UCE, those responsible for the inhumane treatment of their prisoners of war will be brought to justice, but this would have been easier if there had been a form of physical torture. The neural devices they used are against the law, but the use of them does not constitute war crimes under the Dictates of Fair Wartime Conduct. The best we can prosecute this Captain Stapleton for is, I don't know, a misdemeanor. He'll pay a fine and be on his merry way."

Frank felt a cold fury. He swallowed, flushing, and came close to an outburst. He saw similar reactions among his fellow POWs, but no one spoke.

The general rose. "We'll give you a medical check, though the records from the *Galaxyprobe* show that you're all fit. And then you'll have a meeting with a therapist—don't worry, no one thinks you're crazy; it's just procedure. And then you'll be reassigned. Thank you very much, gentlemen."

Again, they rose and saluted—though with less enthusiasm than before.

"Can you beat that?" Dan Mack said once the general was gone. "They're not going to do a damn thing to punish those animals."

"I'd like to get my hands on Stapleton myself," Mozart said. "I'd show him how to torture a prisoner. I've got some definite ideas of things to do with that shriveled carcass of his."

"Cut his happy bits off and hang 'em from his enormous forehead," Coleman said.

"How 'bout pull his scrotum down over his head," someone else suggested.

"Nah," someone else replied, "guys like that have teeny tiny little scrotums. That's why they torture men like us. They're overcompensating."

The conversation grew decidedly humorous, and Frank did not join in. He did not feel like dispelling his anger. He wasn't sure how to use it, but giving it away in a joke fest seemed to trivialize what they had been through.

Soon a doctor and a nurse arrived and called them, one-by-one, into an adjoining room. Frank waited until almost the end, then had a quick and perfunctory physical. Then he was sent down the hall to the therapist's room.

"Good morning, Sergeant Johnson," the therapist said. "I'm Dr. Galliano. Have a seat."

Frank sat.

"I'd like to ask you a few questions. Just relax and give me the first answer that comes to mind. What's your name?"

Frank gave the first answer that came to mind. "Frank Johnson, Sergeant, United States Star Force, serial number eight one five seven six G-E-L."

Galliano wrote something on a magnopad. "And how long have you been in the Star Force?"

"Three years."

"Do you have repeating memories of your experience at Lothian?"

Yes! Yes Yes! "Well...I don't know, not really."

"Have you been having dreams about being back there?"

He most certainly had, every night, all night. But somehow he did not feel comfortable disclosing that to this cold, uniformed, military therapist. "I suppose, now and then."

"Do you ever act or feel as if the event were happening again?"

Oh, my God, yes! "Ah, naw."

Galliano eyed him skeptically, then continued, checking things off on his magnopad. "Anything happen since you left Mars that remind you of the experience?"

"Remind me of it? Uh...no, not that I can think of..."

"Do you avoid thinking about it or talking about it?"

My God, yes... "I don't know, I guess so."

"Do you avoid your fellow POWs or anyone or anything else that reminds you of the event?"

"No. I don't avoid the other POWs. In fact...no. No, I don't." *They're the only people who really understand what I went through, but I do avoid them because they're the only people who know what a disgrace I was....*

"Do you blank out important parts of the experience on Mars?"

"What do you mean, 'blank out'?"

"Are there important part of the experience that you don't remember, or have blotted out of your memory?"

Yes! "Um...I don't know how *important* they are, but no, I don't remember every detail of the experience."

"Do you have negative feelings about yourself as a result of the experience?"

Frank grew defensive. "Who told you that?"

"No one. It's a standard question."

"Well, it's a stupid question. Why would I have negative feelings about myself? I have negative feelings about the Martians, and I have negative feelings about the Star Force for not doing anything to punish the people who did this to us."

Galliano smiled. "Well, you just skipped ahead a bit to another question...do you have sudden outbursts of temper? I'll mark yes."

"Now, wait a minute..."

"Please, Sergeant Johnson, we're almost done. Do you feel detached from other people?"

Frank huffed. He drew back into the seat, verifying, he thought, the answer. "Yes," he said simply.

"Are you unable to feel positive emotions? Do you feel trapped in a persistent negative state?"

"Actually, I was very happy on the way here, aboard the *Galaxyprobe*. It was just like heaven." He was answering truthfully, and was irritated that Galliano wrote something, appearing unconvinced.

"Any trouble sleeping?"

"Yes."

"Any reckless or self-destructive behavior?"

"What? No!"

"Any trouble concentrating?"

"Concentrating? Concentrating on what? I haven't had a damn thing to do since we left Mars."

"Do you feel constantly on guard? As if something terrible might happen to you at any moment?"

Frank gritted his teeth. The answer was a resounding yes. "After what I went through, I would think the answer would be obvious."

Galliano wrote for several minutes. Then he said, "Well, Sergeant Johnson, you display some symptoms of ETS."

"What? What is that?"

"Emotional Trauma Syndrome. It's very common for people who suffered an experience like you have. I'm going to recommend further therapy for an official diagnosis and treatment."

"Further therapy? Look, Doc, I don't even know where they're sending me."

"Well, Sergeant Johnson, I'm forwarding the recommendation through channels, but ultimately the decision is up to you. Thank you, Sergeant Johnson, that will be all, unless you have further questions."

"No, I don't." Frank wasn't sure why he was feeling so hostile toward the therapist, but he wanted nothing more right now than to get out of this office and find out where his next assignment was.

But once he left the therapist's office, his attention was drawn to the spaceman who was leaping through the corridor, limbs all akimbo, shouting, "It's over! They signed a treaty! The war is over!"

CHAPTER 14

Frank sagged, unconscious, in the pseudopods of the Throrb guards as they dragged him from the interrogation room and back into the depths of Hell. His own mind wandered down the depths of memory, where the war that had scarred him was finally over. And yet even as he was taken once again into the literal Hell of Strydia Prison, as the interstellar war raged still, he recalled how the end of the Martian War was only the beginning of his private hell....

———

How Frank had longed for this moment. How he had prayed for such news. The end of the Martian War meant the end of his military service. He was free, free, free at last! Free to go back to Erie, free to go home....

But what was home? His life was now irrevocably changed. It wasn't just that Jacqueline had moved on to another man—or other men, for all he knew—or that he had no idea where his family was now (though, with the war over, a quick VR-gram should solve that mystery). It was that he had lost sight of his own dreams. He had wanted to be an entertainment writer, but that was in a youth so long ago it seemed to belong to another life.

It was, of course, only three years since he had been drafted, but those three years felt like an eternity. The Frank Johnson who had sat with trembling fingers reading that draft notice was dead, gone, buried, and forgotten. The Frank Johnson who sat in Custer Station, reading the details of the peace treaty with Mars, was a new man, a man he didn't really know.

He was a pilot, and he was good at it. He was a war veteran, and despite his uselessness during captivity, was considered a hero. If he left the service, he may or may not find some success as a writer. But here...he was *already* a success. He was assured of a pension as it was, and of an eternal brotherhood among the Star Force, but if he left now, he wasn't sure what he would do, where he would go. He had changed. And as much as he had hated the service, he now felt that *this* was his home, *these* were his people. He was a *pilot*, and that was his new identity.

It came as no surprise when the local Star Force retention officer came to see him. He had been on Custer Station for a week now, and he and the other draftees were awaiting the arrival of a troop ship that would take them to Cayley Base on the Moon, and from there to Earth or wherever else they wanted to go. Frank suspected that the Star Force deliberately ensured that the retention officer arrived before the troop ship, but there was no way to be sure; it was just as likely to be typical military inefficiency.

Frank was in the bar; he had started drinking rather heavily in the evenings since the announcement of the treaty. The uncertainty of what to do with his life had opened a gulf in his soul, a gulf that, for the moment, could only be filled with the numbness of alcohol.

"Sergeant Frank Johnson?" a friendly voice said.

Frank turned into the face of a very young woman who looked to be in her teens—bright blue eyes, auburn hair, and an infectious smile; the kind of woman any man would want to get to know better, the kind of woman a man would go to great lengths to impress. "Yes?"

"I'm Sergeant Yvonne McGinnis, Star Force Retention Office. How are you?"

"Oh, ah, a little sloshed. I hope you'll excuse me."

That charming smile again. "Of course, of course. So my records state you're a draftee, you've been in the Star Force about two years?"

"Three years. Three long years."

She laughed—a charming, musical laugh that made him feel at home and in the company of a good friend. "I imagine it's been a rough time. Whoever said 'war is hell' sure knew what they were talking about."

Frank took a slug of his drink. "You said it. Can I buy you a drink?"

"Oh, no thank you, I never drink when I'm on duty."

"Ah. Duty. Right. This is your job. You're going to try to persuade me to re-enlist."

"Oh, no, Sergeant Johnson, my job isn't to persuade you. I'm just here to review some of the opportunities you could enjoy *if* you decide to re-enlist. The Star Force offers many benefits, and now that we're no longer at war, you don't have to worry about those rough combat situations anymore."

"No, I guess not. Just flying."

"Yes, exactly. That's where you have an advantage. According to your record, you're what they call an ace pilot. Or, really, Ace of Aces. You were highly marked by all your superiors, and on the fast track toward team leader, and eventually squadron commander."

"Really? No one ever said anything to me."

McGinnis laughed again, and Frank couldn't resist laughing with her; she really was likable—which was probably why she had landed this job. "The Star Force isn't always very forthcoming in its compliments. I see here you were also a POW, which guarantees you some extra little perks—like first pick of assignments and shifts, a little tweak in pay, first crack at promotions, and some fame and glory wherever you go. In contrast, I've got to be brutally honest with you, civilian life isn't always too friendly to a military veteran, especially a POW. You might have some trouble fitting in with civilians, it might be hard for you to find work—many who leave the service drift for a long time. There's a very high suicide rate. Those are important things to consider as you decide what you'd like to do now."

Frank smiled. "I do have a question."

"Yes? Anything." The eager smile of a girl just dying to be asked on a date.

"If I re-enlist, will you have dinner with me?"

Far from seeming offended or shocked, she treated him to that musical laugh again. "Oh, I'd be so happy to do that, Sergeant Johnson, but I'm afraid that's against the regs. But in the Star Force you'll have lots of opportunities to...as you say, 'have dinner' with nice women—women with the same background as yourself, women who understand who you are and what you do, and what you've been through."

Frank traced the rim of his glass with his finger, musing, "What I've been through..."

"And I might add, with your pilot skills, and your education, you're already a shoo-in for officer training school. An officer in the Star Force is a person of great respectability, and someone who makes a difference in the world, and in the Solar System. You'd be on the forefront of humanity's exploration of space. Whenever one of the asteroid colonies is in trouble, or when there's a problem on one of the moons of Jupiter, they send in the Star Force. We don't sit by while history happens around us—we *make* history!"

Her words sounded trite, but her tone of voice, her smile, and her enthusiasm were persuasive—as was Frank's listlessness and his inebriation. "Okay, you've convinced me. Where do I sign?"

And thus it was that Sergeant Frank Johnson re-enlisted for two more years of service and applied for officer training school. But it wasn't until much later that he began to realize just how much he was drinking....

———

It was strange, even disorienting, to disembark from the landing craft and find himself back on Earth. The bright sky with the diffuse and brilliant sunlight. The openness. The fresh air.

He nevertheless felt a pang of nostalgia as he looked around at the landscape, the hills, the buildings, and the sky of humanity's home planet. He had never been to Edwards Star Force Base, but there was a sense of familiarity, of homecoming. This could not be mistaken for any other place in the Solar System; this could *only* be Earth. And at the same time, it was *different*. He had forgotten what fresh air smelled like. He had forgotten how bright the sky was. He had forgotten how far away the horizon was. How could something be so familiar and so alien at the same time?

Star Force Officer Training School was in the Yeager Compound of Edwards Star Force Base, a sprawling complex filled with gymnasiums, classrooms, tracks, and training facilities. The experience was a little like basic training, but markedly different, both in the types of training he received and in the emphasis on individuality and competition over teamwork.

That sense of competition drove him to further drinking, even though he recognized that the other trainees assiduously avoided such vices, knowing that it hurt their chances of excelling.

Back in basic training, he had entered a sort of trance. He had passed without thinking about it. He couldn't do that now; he needed to pay attention, to study, to pass difficult tests. So although he felt a small niggling sense that he might be drinking too much, he made a point of not having his first drink until he had devoted ample time to study of each subject.

His classmates were more dedicated, more interested, and more ambitious, but Frank had the advantage of not knowing what else to do with himself but study and drink. Part of him had never left Mars, and nightly he saw the faces of Peter Stapleton and Dudley Appelbaum; in his dreams the sensory deprivation returned. He flashed between periods of uncontrolled fury, unaccountable anxiety, and total numbness. He absorbed the trigonometry of airflight and spaceflight, if not intuitively, then at least easily, because it provided his only escape from his own thoughts—aside from drink. His prior combat experience helped him in his study of famous combat maneuvers, and where he had failed to remember some of them, his own experience filled in the gaps and he passed his tests with relatively high marks.

One of his instructors was Captain Medea Outlander, an expert on World War III. Frank was particularly interested in her description of Diana Krotus' constant battles with Wilfrid McGirk's Techies and anyone else who got in her way in the days after the war.

"How did Krotus win the Battle of Saint Augustine? She *couldn't* have won. She had just led a band of barely civilized, uneducated idiots across eleven hundred kilometers of wasteland, with inadequate food, poisoned water, and constant battles with nomads and barbarians in every town and village. In Saint Augustine she was up against well-armed, well-trained Seminoles who had her outnumbered and outgunned, and who were familiar with the territory and the climate."

"But she was familiar with it too," someone said. "She'd gone to college there."

"Ah, yes, but she had been barricaded behind a levee during her college days. She had some brief experience of the outside in the early days of the war before she joined the Army, but nothing next to the Seminoles, who lived off the land and knew the tides and the moons intuitively. No, Krotus won because she created a legend around herself. She was expert at convincing all those around her, friend and enemy alike, that she had an almost supernatural ability to see the enemy's actions. The Seminoles doubted their own skills because Krotus's reputation preceded her. The truth was she didn't know what she was doing— but she knew how to *look* like she knew what she was doing, and so men and women followed her to their deaths. That made their army look more numerous than they were. It also made them look insane. The Seminoles surrendered when they didn't really have to. And *that* is the real secret to success: not that you know what you're doing, but that you *look* like you know what you're doing."

Frank took that lesson to heart. He wondered how many of his commanding officers, instructors, and fellow pilots were as lost and clueless as himself, but did a better job faking. He thought of Mozart Esther in that Martian base and his ingenious escape plan; was he really a genius, or did he just know how to posture? Had they simply gotten lucky in their escape?

But faking didn't help him to pass his tests; it took study. So he studied. And the reward for his study at the end of the day was a drink. Then another drink. And another. And another. By the time he passed out at the bar, he knew he had pushed it too far, but he also felt he was entitled to his reward for a long, hard day.

And through it all, the memories of that interminable incarceration on Mars lurked forever just beneath the surface, threatening to burst forth at the most inopportune moments. One day he was marching with his squadron to field training exercises when he overheard an SMI shout at a cadet, "Dudley!" And in a flash, he was back in that torture chamber, and that SMI became Captain Peter Stapleton, Lothian Base Commander, Guardian of Martian Freedom, Syria Planum. He fell out of formation, and a moment later Lieutenant Haversham was screaming in his face—but he did not see Lieutenant Haversham, he saw Peter Stapleton, and as Haversham shrieked at him, rather than replying "Yes, sir!" he instead replied, "Frank Johnson, Sergeant, United States Star Force, serial number eight one five seven six G-E-L!"

Later he had no memory of what had happened. Norm Prescott, his bunkmate, filled him in; he had gone wild, his eyes somewhere else, and he had assaulted Lieutenant Haversham, all the while repeating name, rank, and serial number.

"It was a gag," he told Norm. "I just wanted to be the first to get away with plugging a superior officer."

"Oh," Norm said, clearly unconvinced. "Well, I've got bad news for you: lots of other guys have done a lot worse than that. I heard a story about a guy in the class before us who stole a sidearm from the practice range and held up Lieutenant Gaffney, demanding—get this—*doughnuts!* Yep, the one thing he couldn't stand not having here is doughnuts. The craving drove him out of his mind."

"I can't believe that."

Norm shrugged. "It's what I heard."

Frank never learned whether nor not the story was true. He only counted himself lucky that his action didn't buy him worse disciplinary action than he received. As it was, twelve demerits and a week of overnight guard duty satisfied the wounded Haversham.

And so, although he was outclassed by most of the others in his squadron, Frank Johnson graduated Officer Training School on August 31, 4066, commissioned as Second Lieutenant. From there he was assigned to the space cruiser *Yakamoto* as junior flight engineer.

And that was when his *real* problems began.

CHAPTER 15

Hubblrrrp went to Lublwbb with his concerns. "I cannot reach anyone outside this base. Have you disabled communications?"

"No, I should say not," Lublwbb told him. "I have tried to reach FBN-915 for further orders on what to do with these military prisoners—the cells are filling up—but no one seems to be talking."

"It's as if the entire Alternative Alliance has disappeared," Hubblrrrp murmured.

Lublwbb said nothing; he merely went back to work. Hubblrrrp knew he must do the same. But he worried about his family, about his world, about his Alliance. This war was stupid, and everyone seemed to know it was stupid, but they insisted on fighting it anyway.

What if there was no one out there? What if all that was left of the galaxy was this—this planet Hell?

———

There was no one to talk to aboard the *Yakamoto*. There was no one who shared his experiences. To the young fighter pilots—most of whom were only a little younger than himself, but looked like little kids to him—some hair-raising battles and some long tours of duty and even the lousy food in the mess qualified as the "trauma" of war. He was caught somewhere between amusement and contempt. *If only they knew*, he thought to himself.

And yet what could he say? Could he tell anyone about his own experience? Could he describe the sensory deprivation when he didn't even dare think about it? Could he tell anyone that while Mozart Esther had heroically planned one of the most remarkable escapes in modern history, he himself had lain practically catatonic, repeating his name, rank, and serial number as if in a daze?

His duties were fairly simple: he was to oversee the flight crews. He wrote schedules, he listened to complaints, he helped out with technical problems. That left him lots of time to think—and drink.

He began to wonder what had become of Peter Stapleton and Dudley Appelbaum. Had that cruel, skeletal man with his harsh voice and clipped manner really paid a fine and gone on with his life? Had his cruelty earned him a promotion? Frank wasn't entirely clear on the details of the peace treaty with Mars; he knew that President Goff had personally gone to Mars to meet with Chairman Candide of the Oversight Council, and that Mars was provisionally independent. But there were stipulations, restrictions on the development of Martian weapons and warships, on trade, and on the development of certain regions on Mars. But as to the handling of war criminals, he didn't know. He wanted to know.

One day he received an unexpected message.

Jittery—

I'm sure you'll remember me. Third Fighter Strike Force aboard the Karka. We were held together at the Lothian Base on Mars and tortured. I've been stationed at Fort Desdemone, Holland. I wanted to let you know that I ran into Pillbox at a decoration ceremony for General Avakyan. We talked about maybe networking all of us from the base and helping one another out a bit. I wanted to let you know what an inspiration you were to me while we were held. The way you kept repeating your name, rank, and serial number all the time helped me to hold my own when they interogated me. I'm sure I would have told them everything they wanted to know if it hadn't been for the inspiration I took from you. I was wondering if you knew where Dan Mack was. I can't seem to find him in the Star Force registry.

Best,

Second Lieutenant Martin Boeke, USSF

Frank had no memory of a Martin Boeke—he presumed he would recognize Boeke's face and callsign if they were to meet again—but he was deeply affected by Boeke's praise. All this time he had been so ashamed of his behavior in the base, and remembered Mack's attitude toward him, indeed the whole squadron's discussion of what to do with him. But the fact that at least one of them thought well of him filled him with emotion—though he wasn't sure what that emotion was.

He replied at once.

Martin—

I am delighted to hear from you and I can't tell you the pleasure it gives me that I was any help to you at all during our incarceration. I'm sorry, but I have no idea where Dan Mack is, but as you're probably aware, Carlos Esther is squadron commander at Tsiolkovsky Base, and I heard that Bob Corley didn't re-enlist and is in Minnesota, I think. Do you happen to know where Peter Stapleton and Dudley Appelbaum are?

It was good to hear from you.

Second Lieutenant Frank Johnson, USSF

There was no reply that day, and the memories the exchange brought back reinforced Frank's deepening desire to see Stapleton and Appelbaum again, to have a few choice words with them—perhaps even to inflict some choice bodily harm. Frank dulled the emotion in the only way he knew how: with beer.

By the evening, he graduated from beer to bourbon. His drinking was now so excessive that he was embarrassed to drink in the officers' mess. He had begun to take drinks back to his quarters—as an officer, he now had his own private quarters—and had begun to accumulate an impressive supply of bottles and cans stashed away in the closet, in drawers, underneath drawers, and under pillows. He didn't know what would happen if one of his superiors found his stash, and he lived in fear of a flash inspection. Drinking while on duty was cause for immediate court-martial, and he could not deny that he did drink on duty—though he confined himself to light liquor like wine and beer. The really heavy drinking he reserved for after shift.

It was two days before he received a reply from Boeke.

Jittery—

Thanks for the tip on Bob Corley! I was able to track him down and he knows where Eric Huffman is, he's in Serein med school. So I've made contact now with six of the old boys. I asked them all about Stapleton and Appelbaum. Mozart did some digging and says that Appelbaum was discharged from the Martian military and is a schoolteacher now if you can believe that. Picture him working with kids. Stapleton was fined by the UCE but hasn't paid, and it looks like the Oversight Council has charged him with inhumane treatment of prisoners in violation of the Dictates of Fair Wartime Conduct but I don't know what kind of punishment he may get. It looks like he's still in the military, and Mozart thinks he's in Utopia working some sort of desk job. That's about all I can tell you. I'd like to track those animals down myself and show them what a Star Force officer can do when he's not tied down to a damn chair.

Keep in touch,

Chuckles

The use of the callsign "Chuckles" jogged Frank's memory. He remembered the brash redhead now; he hadn't known him well at all, but remembered him making inappropriate jokes from time to time during their imprisonment on Mars. He'd had neither positive nor negative feelings toward Chuckles.

He was relieved that at least one of his fellow POWs shared his feelings about Stapleton and Appelbaum. He continued to nurse a growing anger that the two men who had tortured him so relentlessly and endlessly had apparently walked free with no consequences to their atrocities. He too wanted to show them what he could do when he wasn't tied down. He smiled as he pictured all ten of the former POWs beating and kicking the two helpless Martians. He had never before had a violent thought or intention, beyond the desire to punch a bully at school or push an annoying aircar out of the way. But now he took great pleasure in the fantasy of torturing his torturers, even as he acknowledged that some of the punishment he would like to dole out was out of proportion to the punishment that had been inflicted on him.

After all, part of him whispered, was *sensory deprivation* all that bad? He recalled the medieval torture of ages past; he'd gotten off pretty lucky.

And yet even now the images and sounds and feelings that had so tormented him during that period came back to haunt him in his dreams. He often awoke, breathless, his pillow soaked in sweat, from nightmares of cackling monsters made of light, of creatures that surrounded him with their awful and deafening silence, from which he could not escape because he was inside them...of faceless phantoms...of walls and floors and ceilings made of flickering flames...of endless, unendurable nothingness...

And upon awakening, the images and sounds continued until he sat up, gasping for breath, and turned on the light, filled his empty senses with the wonderful and comforting sight of his cabin. And then, inevitably, he would pull a can of beer from a hidden slot and down it in a hurry. And if there was no beer handy, he would get up and search one of his hiding places for something, anything to dull the sensation—be it beer or wine or vodka or tequila or manischewitz. He feared to fall asleep again, but he would drink sometimes until he passed out, waking for duty with a throbbing hangover.

His correspondence with Chuckles led him to correspondence with the other POWs, thanks to the Solarnet VR group that Chuckles set up. For the most part he avoided the live VR sessions; he simply logged on and watched, listened to, or read the others' messages each day, contributing little himself. He was still embarrassed by his own behavior, no matter Chuckles' admiration for him.

But occasionally someone would submit a message having to do with Peter Stapleton and/or Dudley Appelbaum, and he would come to attention. Most of the time these messages turned out to be angry rants about the way they had treated the prisoners, or about how these monsters had been let off the hook with a slap on the hand, but Frank continued to hope for a clue to his nemeses' whereabouts. With the war over, he had hoped he could find them on the Solarnet, but there was still a general block on all government and military information from Mars, including information on civilians who had been discharged from the Martian military.

Frank realized he was becoming obsessed with those two. His daily fantasies about confronting them, inflicting pain or even killing them, were, he knew, unproductive. He couldn't allow himself to be eaten from the inside by hate—and he also knew that if he were to confront them again, the meeting wouldn't match his fantasies. No, he would probably meekly ask them why they treated him like that, they would reply "it was my job," and he would walk away unsatisfied. He had cruel thoughts, but he was not a cruel person: he would never be able to truly inflict pain or kill.

Of course, he had already killed; he had five confirmed kills on his war record. But shooting down anonymous enemy fighters was a different thing than killing someone face-to-face.

But then came a message from Jack Harris—or "Mojo" as he had been known during the war.

I found Dudley Appelbaum! I have a friend who works at Cóiste Bodhar. He's a hacker and he managed to get into a Martian database and find Appelbaum. He's a schoolteacher now in Syria Planum. I sent him a message. I encourage everyone else to do the same. Here's a copy of the message I sent him:

> Hi, Dudley. I am Corporal Jack Harris of the United States Star Force. I knew you on Mars. You might remember me. I was the one who was strapped to a chair while you fed neural impulses into my brain. I've been in contact with my friends who also suffered your inhuman torture. I hope you know we're all still out here, and we remember you, and we live every day with the memories of what you did to us. It is beyond my comprehension that you are an educator of young children. Do they know what you are and what you did? Do you ever remember those days? I want to know how you could treat your fellow human beings that way and how you live with yourself. I wonder if you have been able to continue with your life any more successfully than we have ours.

So far I have not received a reply, and my friend tells me that it might not get through. They have some sort of electronic censorship. But if enough of us try, we might be able to reach him. The dest is utop/edu/12/appelbaum1.

Frank read the message again and again. It said so little; there was so much Frank would like to add. He wondered how Appelbaum would react—assuming he received the message at all.

He sat, tried to compose his own message, but words failed him. He knew he was dissatisfied with Mojo's message, but every time he tried to write one of his own, he stared at the blank screen for twenty minutes, unable to think of a single word. How many times had he fantasized about meeting Appelbaum again, and now that the reality was upon him, he couldn't think of a single word.

But the others did. Several replied that they had sent their own messages to Appelbaum, though Mozart himself discouraged this.

Fellas, we're not doing any good here. We're just acting like bullies. I'm not defending the way Appelbaum treated us, but he's a civilian now, the war is over, and we're not accomplishing anything by harassing him. All we're going to do is get our group shut down if we keep this up. I for one want nothing more to do with him or with Stapleton. I advise all of you to let it go, let the past be in the past. What we need to do is help each other heal and move forward.

Frank frowned as he read that. There needed to be *some* sort of closure; he couldn't simply forget all that had happened, not when the hated Appelbaum was in his sights. How exactly did Mozart propose that they "heal" if they didn't confront the demon who had done this to them?

Two days later there was surprise. Mojo sent a VR-gram:

I got a reply. It's not from Appelbaum, it's from his wife. I'll display it without any comment:

Dear Corporal Harris,

I am Hilda Torgenson-Appelbaum. Dudley Appelbaum is my husband. I want you to know that he has received and read all the messages you and your group have sent him, and he has been deeply disturbed ever since the messages have started to come in. He has told me very little of his time working in the Lothian POW camp, but I am aware of its reputation, and he has insisted, on the record, ever since the war, that the prisoners were treated humanely.

He is very upset at the thought that you have suffered any permanent damage, even if that damage is only in your minds. He has chosen not to respond to you because he does not know what to say. I asked him if I could respond, and he could not decide if he wanted me to or not. I am writing this message because I think it would be best both for Dudley and for you to begin healing.

As I said, Dudley has told me very little, but in the past few days, he has said repeatedly that conditions could have been far worse, that no physical torture was contemplated, and that at any rate, he was only following orders.

I know from my personal experience that Dudley is a good and kind man, and very dedicated to his job of educating young people. We have two lovely daughters and he is wonderful with them. I can understand if you don't believe me, because you did not see him under the same conditions that I do. I don't know how he behaved in the prison camp, and I don't think I want to know. I do know that he did not and does not want to hurt anyone, and although he has not explicitly expressed sorrow or regret for his actions, I can tell that he is very disturbed by the memories this has dredged up, and the thought that he has hurt people in the past is hurting him.

I know that is no comfort to you, and the pain he is experiencing must pale in comparison to what you went through. I suppose you're probably glad that he is now suffering.

I have asked Dudley if he would like to meet with you, and he can't decide. So I will ask you: would you like to meet with him? If so, I will let him know and find out what he wants to do.

I'm sorry for the pain you have suffered, and it pains me deeply to think that my dear husband is the cause of your pain.

Sincerely yours,

Hilda Torgenson-Appelbaum

So, what does everyone think? Is she on the level? Does anyone want to meet with the guy? Should we take Mozart's advice and let it go? I'm kind of rattled by this message. What do the rest of you think?

Dan Mack's reply appeared ten minutes later:

This is bullshit. I don't care how his wife feels and I don't care if Appelbaum is disturbed by our messages. He ought to be disturbed. And sure, I want to meet with him, I want to break his kneecaps!

Mozart chimed in an hour after that.

This is what I'm talking about, guys. What we're doing has a ripple effect. Mrs. Appelbaum never did anything to us, neither did his kids. This is affecting them now. This is probably affecting his work at school too. The war is over, our incarceration is over, and this witch hunt should be over. I think you should all just break this off right now.

Then came a surprising message from Corley.

I know all of you don't want to hear this, but Dudley Appelbaum is a human being. I always thought of him as an inhuman monster, but reading that message from his wife was a shot in the arm. Maybe he really didn't realize how much he was harming us by what he did. Maybe he needs to deal with this as much as we do. I'm thinking of replying that I would like to meet with him, and maybe try to hash this out.

Frank broke his self-imposed silence and replied to that by text only.

The guy messed us up for years. I know he PERMANENTLY changed the course of my life. It sounds like he hasn't missed any sleep for what he's done to us. What bothers him is that we're still out here and we remember him. I'm with Mack. I want to break his kneecaps, or worse. But I don't want any trouble, so I'm staying out of it.

As soon as he sent the message, though, he regretted that last part. He had no real desire to stay out of it; he had been simmering and fantasizing about giving Appelbaum his what-for for months. Why back out now?

The reason was obvious: his greatest fear had been realized. He was now forced to stop thinking of Appelbaum as, as Corley put it, an "inhuman monster." This was the first intimation of the terrible reality that, if he really did face Appelbaum again, he would not be able to confront him as he wished. This was not an action immie, this was not a novel about revenge; they really were dealing with a human being, with all the complexities of a human being.

And yet—if he *did* meet with Appelbaum, perhaps he could get an answer to that elusive question: How could you do that to another human being?

But he knew he could not sit down with Appelbaum in a friendly, civil setting. His anger was too deep. He did not want to sit and chat with his old nemesis, didn't really want to hear the other side of the story, because there was no justifiable other side. He did not want to find out Appelbaum was actually a decent guy—because he sure hadn't been a decent guy at Lothian!

But there were no further messages to or from Appelbaum, or his wife. There was continued discussion about what everyone wanted to do, but Appelbaum dropped out of focus when Archie "Pillbox" Dole forwarded an article from *The Utopia Examiner*.

War criminal found dead, suicide suspected

by Joyce Samuels

SOUTH WAKE—Captain Peter Stapleton, notorious for his operation of the Lothian prison camp during the Martian War, was found dead this morning in his apartment at the Officers Barracks at Fort Liberty. First responders were unable to revive him. It was quickly determined that he had died from botulinum toxin. An injector was found at the scene containing traces of botulinum. Suicide is suspected.

Captain Stapleton was tried for war crimes due to his use of illegal sensory-deprivation neural feeds in interrogating prisoners during the war. Although acquitted of war crimes, he was convicted of inhumane treatment and was publicly reprimanded and removed from active duty, as well as any further operation of military prisons. He has shunned public attention since then and was rumored to be an alcoholic.

Captain Stapleton was 56 years old and leaves behind a wife and three children.

Pillbox added at the end:

Looks like the Chief Coward of the base has escaped justice after all.

Frank was frustrated. The first and only news he had heard about the Demon himself, the master interrogator, the creature that haunted his dreams nightly, and it was an unsatisfying closing of the book. Any concerns about Dudley Appelbaum seemed irrelevant now.

The others evidently felt the same, as there was no further discussion about meeting with Appelbaum. Mozart mentioned a few weeks later that he'd had some private correspondence with Mrs. Appelbaum in which they mutually decided that any further communication would be a mistake; there was too much pain on both sides. Frank felt that Mozart had overstepped his bounds by speaking for the rest of the group; all the same, he had to agree, it was best to leave it alone. He had to reluctantly admit that Mozart had been right in the first place; it was best to let it go, lest someone in authority shut the group down.

But even as he dwelled on the past, his future became more and more uncertain, as a new specter threatened to overtake the old. He was only peripherally aware of it, but that awareness grew day-by-day, even as he tried to deny it.

He was drinking far too much.

CHAPTER 16

The elevator plunged deeper and deeper into the depths of Hell. The gravity increased. The Throrb grunted in pain as they dragged Frank's unconscious body back to the cell.

As the door opened and they tossed Frank in, Cameron jumped to his feet. "Frank!"

But Frank did not stir. He dreamed on, his mind resurrecting pains and tribulations best left in the past—even as the current Hell so uncannily mimicked them...

———

It was not that Frank set out to drink to excess. He had simply determined that that one after-shift drink would make him feel better, and he kept going back to that one solution even when it was no longer working so well—and the next thing he knew, he was over his head.

And it didn't start with chemical dependency either. It was simply that he was in distress and he didn't want to be, and the drink, he felt, helped him out of it. The nature of the distress varied. Sometimes it was a gnawing emptiness, a dearth of emotion almost as distressing, in its own way, as the sensory deprivation that had started this whole mess. He was desperate to fill that void, to spark *any* emotion—even a negative one.

But he also sought to dull negative emotions—stress, fatigue, anger, confusion, depression, all of which were common in any military life, let alone one scarred by his experience—any emotion that was uncomfortable to sit with, and of which he sought to rid himself.

Before his captivity, he had enjoyed drinking with the pilots because it was a social occasion. It was a way to unwind after a hard day, or a rough battle. He enjoyed the buzz the liquor gave him— or, as he described it, the "bubble in my brain"— but he relegated it to that social occasion. But he had discovered, even in those days, that drinking made him feel better after a battle in which something particularly horrific happened, or he had killed someone, or he had made an embarrassing mistake.

After his captivity, however, that became a crutch. Every time he felt bad—which was every day—he had to have a drink to make himself feel better. And when one drink didn't do the trick, he would have another. And if the second drink *did* make him feel better, another, he thought, would make him feel even better than that.

This was not a conscious process. He just did it, and he did it every day. It didn't occur to him, at least at first, that there was anything unusual in his behavior—after all, everyone else had a few after shift—and even if part of him did register that his behavior had changed, he mentally pushed that aside and did it anyway.

The catch was, the more he did it, the less it worked, and the more he realized he was doing something he shouldn't—but by then, it was next to impossible to stop. It was almost physically painful not to have a drink. And then a drink nursed that pain, or gave him a positive feeling.

Once he eased the pain with one drink, he would seek to repeat the pleasure of that catharsis—with another drink, and another. By the time he was slobbering drunk and barely able to speak, it didn't occur to him that he had already consumed more than he should do in a week.

As time went on, each drink helped a little less than the one before. That was why he organized the day's drinking into a hierarchy from least alcoholic to most—that way the best was always yet to come. He would start with a beer around 0900, and that was easy because no one noticed if he stashed cans of beer in his quarters; there was so much beer aboard a ship of war, with more being shipped in, or even brewed aboard ship, all the time. And so he could drink at his leisure until he had reached a stage of comfortable inebriation before noon. Then it was on to the wine, which was harder because he was on duty. Sometimes he snuck some into the office under his coat; after a while he was daring enough to leave a bottle in a cabinet under the work console, fairly confident that no one would look there.

After shift he graduated to the heavy spirits. Vodka, rum, whiskey, and brandy made his evenings, often in stupid drinking games with the other guys, and almost always ending with him passed out on a table or over the bar, and waking sometime after midnight feeling like hell. And by then there was no more pleasure to his self-medication, but it had become a compulsion.

Even though he knew he was harming himself, and even though the pain was by now overshadowing the pleasure, he couldn't stop.

He might wake up in the morning planning on a drink-free day, but by 0900 he would open a drawer "just to see if there was any beer left," which there almost always was—or he'd wander down to the vending machine at the end of the hall, "just to see what kind of beer is in the slot." Unfailingly, one of those can of beer then ended up open in his quarters.

And then, knowing full well he shouldn't even go to the bar, he would wander in after shift on the self-deception of just wandering aimlessly though the ship and "ending up" there—and then the next thing he knew, he was singing old space shanties with a glass of brew nestled to his cheek.

He had started drinking in order to relieve the negative feelings from his captivity on Mars, but there was also the positive feeling attached to that relief—or even simply from the "bubble in my head" that made him feel giddy or mellow or relaxed—or just a sensation of lifting his day out of the ordinary, something exciting for him to look forward to throughout his usually dull shift in the landing bay. It was two sides of the same coin: trying to create a good feeling and trying to get rid of a bad one. Without thinking about it, he had embarked on an all-consuming project to regulate his emotions using an outside source; in this case alcohol.

Inevitably, he eventually began to realize that it wasn't working. Yes, the drinks made him happy at first—or at least as happy as he was going to get under the circumstances—but as the effects grew less and less pleasing, he began to think to himself, usually while in the process of getting soused, *I really don't need to do this*.

But he couldn't stop. He *had* to keep drinking. And each time he drank, the effects grew less and less effective, to the point that he was doing it out of habit. Irresistible, siren-like habit, but habit nevertheless. It would hurt more to stop than to continue.

As he sobered up, the pain not only returned—it got worse. Once the initial high was over, he started to feel bad again, negating any resolve he might have made in the depths of despair to stop drinking his life away. So whatever resolve he might have made, by 0900 he was back at it. And by morning, as the high again wore off, not only did the pain again return, but now it came with embarrassment, shame, and guilt. His opinion of himself, already at a low due to his feelings of inadequacy as a Star Force pilot, and worsened by the thought that he had let his buddies down on Mars, reached a nadir as he knew he was now a hopeless sot. Such a thing, he recalled from his old life, would *never* happen to *him*.

And that additional pain was just more reason to keep drinking, even though he no longer derived any pleasure from his nightly benders.

He no longer knew why he felt bad; he just did. He gave his predicament little conscious thought; this way of life was simply the way it was. He kept doing it because it was the way he lived his life. He knew he was doing wrong, he knew he was messing up his life, he knew that others would inevitably start to notice, if they hadn't already, but he couldn't stop—he just couldn't. He knew he shouldn't have that drink, but he did it anyway. Then he felt bad about it and felt worse and thus had another drink and was locked into that never-ending cycle of behavior. The relief that came with the mental and emotional oblivion of being totally blitzed was so powerful that it overrode any rationality, and guilt or shame. Even if the drinks didn't make him feel *good*, at least he no longer felt *awful*, and the tradeoff was worth it.

Again, he did not give the matter conscious thought, but the problem was that he didn't know how to deal with his feelings constructively, and he had entered a self-reinforcing pattern of bad behavior from which there was no escape. If he *didn't* drink, he would have to stay sober and deal with the awful feelings, and he would do whatever it took not to do that. He had no alternate strategy; if he did, he would take it. But at this stage in his life, the bottle was his only solution.

One day he came home with a six-pack in each hand, and discovered to his shame and embarrassment that he had no hiding places left in his quarters. It was a tangible signal to him of what he already knew but had refused to admit to himself: this had gone too far.

On another occasion he found that he had exhausted his account; thank God the bar let him run a tab—but the next payday he had to spend half his paycheck on paying off that tab. His fear of debt was the only thing that came close to his fear of his own flashbacks and nightmares, and so he made a resolve—albeit a temporary one—to cut back.

He tried to develop a strategy to stop. He came close to getting rid of the cans and bottles hidden in his quarters—but ultimately couldn't do it. So he settled on a secondary strategy: he would drink what he had, but then that was it. No more.

Until he brought just one can back the next day. One can was all right, right? He couldn't be expected to stop all at once.

And drinking in the bar after shift, well, that was normal. He would just not have quite as many drinks—a resolve he actually stuck to for exactly one night.

No matter how firm his resolve, he still found himself sitting at the bar after shift, unable to resist the lure of just one, just one quick one. He sat, staring at the bar, watching the bartender pouring drinks, listening to the trickle of cool, seductive liquor, smelling it, listening to the banter of the others, and found himself trembling, whispering to himself, *I need to walk away, I need to walk away*, and couldn't get his feet to move.

He knew he had to stop; his account was disappearing, the quantity of stashed bottles and cans had gone beyond ridiculous, and sooner or later he would be caught, and if he kept up this self-destructive spiral he would soon find himself out on the streets on Earth with no prospects, no future. But he'd had a hard day and he *needed* a drink...just one. Just one was all right, wasn't it?

It didn't take much justification. "It will bother me if I don't" was enough. He couldn't sit with those negative feelings.

The thought that it was possible *not* to go to the bar after shift didn't occur to him—at least not consciously. It was the pattern of military life.

What would the guys think of him if he *didn't* show up? That would be rude of him, wouldn't it?

Still, the acknowledgement that he had a problem remained subconscious. As far as he was concerned, he was a dedicated officer, good at his duty, who had come through a horrific experience and was dealing with it constructively. In spite of his drinking, he worked well enough that no transgressions reached his superiors, which he took to mean that he was doing his job well. It was *normal* to have some drinks with the guys after shift. Everybody did it.

The fact that everybody *didn't* do what he was doing—stashing drinks in his quarters and sneaking drinks during his duty shift—remained comfortably relegated to his subconscious. Or at least he shoved aside those thoughts when they occurred to him. The answer was simple: don't get caught. As an officer assigned to an often solitary duty, that was easy enough. Sometimes he would make an error in scheduling, but he would correct it when one of the pilots or flight crew complained, and his superiors never heard of it. It didn't occur to him that Colonel Zingwowski was observant enough to notice him sneaking cans of beer or bottles of vermouth into his booth, or that officers on other shifts might occasionally open the cabinets where he hid his little treasures. If he spotted the colonel or any of his aides, he would wait in the corridor and pretend to examine a piece of instrumentation, his bottle carefully hidden under his coat, and then he would slip into his booth and make sure he was concealed behind the bulkhead before slipping it into the nearest cabinet. During shift the corridors were usually empty, so he did not fear anyone walking by as he took a little nip—or more.

And at night no one took any notice of the antics in the bar—or so he thought. Since everyone was drinking, it didn't occur to him that anyone, let alone his superiors, would notice that he was drinking to excess.

And anyway, he would angrily think, it didn't matter what anyone thought of him. His personal habits were no one's business but his own. He had never wanted to be in the Star Force in the first place—they had drafted him. He conveniently sidestepped the fact that he had willingly re-enlisted and even gone to Officer Training School; that didn't fit with the story he told himself to justify his actions. So any time he feared being caught, he shifted between hiding and defiance, whatever was most convenient.

Of course, the underlying problem was that now that he was trapped in the pattern of self-medication, the thought of *not* doing it was too painful to contemplate.

A turning point was inevitable, as anyone with a similar problem could have warned him. For Frank, it came when he was coordinating an incoming squadron on training maneuvers. He was particularly hung over that morning, and he had tried to sooth himself first thing with a brandy. And now, nursing a throbbing headache, he was trying, without success, to dull the pain with some Mandoley wine.

The last thing on his mind was the squadron's approach pattern.

Fortunately, Lieutenants Beirson and Derrick spotted his error and redirected the cadets to smooth entries. But had they been less on their game, the inexperienced cadets might well have headed for the wrong quarter, and then, seeing nothing but the ship's hull coming at them, might have overcorrected and ended up in a pretty bad state.

Frank would have liked to think that even trainees were smart enough not to crash into the ship, or into each other's fighters, but inexperience and bad instructions could be a lethal combination.

The next thing he knew, Colonel Zingwowski was raging into his booth, demanding an explanation, and immediately smelled the alcohol on his breath.

"Have you been drinking on duty?" he demanded.

Frank was backed into a corner. He wanted to tell Zingwowski that it was none of his business. He wanted to lash out that yes, he'd been drinking and what are you going to do about it? Discharge me? Fine! I don't want to be in your stinking Star Force anyway! But fear kept his reaction at bay; for although he had never wanted to be in the Star Force, it was now the only life he knew, and although he wasn't sure how exactly he felt about it, it had become in some way integral to his identity. "Sir, I'd rather not answer."

Zingwowski opened the cabinet under Frank's desk. He rummaged through it for just a moment before finding a half-empty bottle of vermouth. "I wasn't sure *who* was stashing these in there, but I had my suspicions. You're relieved of duty. Report to my office at once."

Frank gulped. "Yes, sir."

For Frank, that was rock bottom.

CHAPTER 17

The heat penetrated the all-consuming fog. Frank stirred. He was aware that he could barely breathe; the heat tended to suck the breath from a man. The gravity made the chest constrict.

Cameron felt his pulse, touched the back of his hand to his forehead.

"Is he all right?" Ambassador Koff asked.

"I think so. He's just a little dazed—like I was when they took me up there. I didn't think they would put him through what they put me through, but I guess they did."

Frank barely registered the words; his thoughts still wandered down the corridors of memory. The heat made him sweat—as had the apprehension of facing Colonel Zingwowski. He'd had trouble breathing back then too; his heart had pounded...

———

Frank stood at attention in Zingwowski's office, sweat trickling down the back of his neck. After months of descent toward self-destruction, the solution to his problem had finally crystallized: the problem became more painful than the pain he was trying to nurse. It was a hard realization to come to, but he knew now that he had a problem and he had to stop.

Zingwowski arrived after him, dismissed a young yeoman, and circled the desk, silent and menacing. Finally he said, "I was reviewing your record the other day, Lieutenant Johnson. I came to the conclusion that you were wasted as a flight engineer. You belong in a cockpit. But now...if I go by the rulebook, you ought to be court-martialed. Do you see any reason why I shouldn't make that recommendation?"

Frank didn't know what to say. Deep inside, he knew Zingwowski was right—but on the surface he was angry. Zingwowski was being unreasonable; what was wrong with having a quick sip to make the long day pass easier? A superior officer ought to be more understanding if he wanted to earn the respect of his men.

Zingwowski didn't wait for an answer. "However...I also saw in your record that you were a POW. You were tortured at the Lothian Base, correct?"

Frank frowned. "Yes, sir."

"Well, I know what that's like. My grandfather was a POW after the Battle of Ganymede. That was before the Dictates of Fair Wartime Conduct, so I don't think you had it as bad as him, but that doesn't matter. Trauma is trauma. So if you promise to clean up your act, I'm going to look the other way and reassign you as a flight instructor. Does that appeal to you?"

In fact, it did. Relief washed over Frank—even joy. "Yes, sir." He choked on the words.

"Good. Go back to your quarters. I'll forward you some material to familiarize yourself with."

"Yes, sir...Thank you, sir." He saluted.

Zingwowski returned the salute and said, "Dismissed."

Frank left with haste, hurried to his quarters. Yes, he would clean up his act. Being back in a cockpit, having a challenging flight-related assignment, yes, that would give him something to do, something on which to focus his energies.

He only hoped it didn't trigger any more flashbacks.

———

Frank had no real strategy to ease up on his drinking, and he found that it was physically painful to avoid it. Although he enjoyed his new duty, he still had the almost irresistible urge to drink. He tried a self-imposed punishment: to do something unpleasant every time he gave in and had a drink. For instance, he would promise himself he would volunteer for orbital cleanup duty, or laundry duty, or listen to an hour of Sergeant Bergqvist's yodeling practice files. But that never worked; it was too easy to find an excuse not to follow through. He could simply concoct a reason why this time it didn't count.

He started a journal in which he would write down thoughts and ideas to distract him any time he started to crave a drink. He kept the journal with him all day and throughout shift; his students must have wondered what he was writing when he would pause in the middle of a lecture and scribble something in that paper notebook.

Some sort of distraction was essential, because although his new duty had disrupted the old routine, the daily ritual of reporting to the bar after shift was a well-worn pattern that took insurmountable effort to break.

However, the effort was worth it: the first time he walked past the bar and went back to his quarters—as painful as it was to do—by the time he reached his quarters he felt that he didn't need a drink after all. He knew then that drinking was no longer making him feel better. When the high wore off and the pain returned, he couldn't achieve a big enough high to make it worth the guilt and the shame and the very real risk to his future. It had reached the point that it was not fun anymore—and his new position had offered him some fun that the Star Force had not, up to then, offered.

And so he slowly healed with time, or at least learned to conceal his pain from others and, to a large extent, from himself. He was still on guard against anything that might trigger a flashback, but these became much less common as he settled into a new way of life, new habits, and new friends.

He started volunteering for some of those tough assignments he had been avoiding— cleanup duty, for one. The war had left a lot of orbiting debris circling Mars, Phobos, Deimos, Earth, and Earth's Moon. That debris tended to collide with other debris, creating a chain reaction leading to more and more debris, effectively making orbital space around those bodies useless for satellites, space stations, and commuter flights—and very dangerous for spacecraft to fly through on their way to other worlds. So the Star Force had been employed in a massive effort to collect that debris and dispose of it.

It was difficult and dangerous work. Fighters would fly in formation to surround large clumps of debris—a course that was a lot trickier to fly than the layman would think—then collect it in big electromagnetic nets, and finally accelerate it away and slingshot it on a course for the Sun, where it would burn up and never bother anyone again.

Frank flew five such missions, and received a Medal of Outstanding Spacemanship for each flight.

He then volunteered to fly chase for the first three test flights of the ZR-130 Interceptor, Star Force's newest and most advanced space fighter. Most test flights were conducted on Earth, but for space combat readiness testing, several flights were flown out of the *Yakamoto* in deep space.

After those flights, Frank himself was offered the chance to fly the new fighter, a chance he jumped at. And as he flew a spotless flight his first time in the cockpit, he realized with pride that he hadn't even thought about drinking in over two weeks.

Finally, thanks largely, he assumed, to his efforts to stay dry, a new opportunity opened for him. He received a summons to the Captain's quarters.

At first, of course, he assumed he was in trouble, and as he crisscrossed the *Yakamoto*'s labyrinthine corridors, he racked his brain trying to think of what he might have done wrong. He was no longer hiding liquor, and although he still had the occasional bender (usually only on Friday nights), he had not been drunk on duty since the day he had been caught. He had been doing a competent, if not stellar, job as a flight instructor, and he was getting ready to award Sergeants Lee and Percival their wings. Could it be that one of them had screwed up and he was being held responsible?

He rang Captain Susan DeFreitas's doorchime, and the door popped open. He flushed as he saw a stocky man in a UWSEC admiral's uniform standing next to the captain.

"Lieutenant Frank Johnson reporting as ordered, Captain."

"Come in, Lieutenant Johnson," DeFreitas said.

Frank entered and stood at attention.

"At ease, Lieutenant. This is Rear Admiral Maples of the United World Space Exploration Corps."

"Good to meet you, Lieutenant," the admiral said.

Frank saluted, and the admiral returned the salute.

"Admiral Maples is the head of the Interstellar Exploration Division, in charge of the Space Stars," DeFreitas said.

"Space Stars?" Frank exclaimed without thinking; he wasn't sure he had permission to speak, and clammed up.

"I know what you're thinking, Lieutenant," the admiral said. "All the Space Stars have been recalled to Earth, yes. All but one have been decommissioned; the *Silver Streak* is being modified for a new mission, and we're using parts from other Space Stars to modify it. But we still have one other Space Star, the *Black Hole*, that's operational as a starship. A lot of its insulation and radiation shielding has been stripped, along with most of its internal structure, but it still has an operational bridge and engine, with controls still hooked up. How much do you know about the interstellar surveys?"

"Not much, sir...I've been pretty busy here."

Admiral and captain smiled at each other; Frank wondered what they had been saying about him.

"Yes, I heard you'd been a POW in the Martian War," the admiral said. "Matter of fact, your record shows you to be an exemplary pilot with an intuitive flying style."

Frank was becoming increasingly confused. Why was a UWSEC admiral looking at his record? "Thank you, sir."

"Well, Lieutenant, I know you're wondering why you were summoned here. I'd like the Star Force to lease you out to me for a mission aboard the *Black Hole*."

"A mission, sir?"

"Yes, to one of the extrasolar planets that was found to be habitable."

Frank was overwhelmed; he had known about the Space Star missions, but didn't know many details about them. He had certainly never imagined partaking in one of their epic journeys.

"It's a planet orbiting the main sequence star Hystaspes," Maples continued. "Actually, it's a double planet, twin planets, we call them Darius and Xerxes. The larger planet, Darius, has a technical civilization on it."

Frank gasped. "My God!"

"Yeah, the *Green Flash* detected signals from it, made some orbital surveys, but was recalled before it could learn much. The commander-in-chief wants a cultural observer there. Your name came up in our search for contenders."

"Thank you, sir—why me?"

Captain DeFreitas said, "Because you're the best pilot in this man's Star Force. We don't know just what we're dealing with, and the President wants the best."

"Yes, sir."

"The civilization there is entirely cybernetic," Captain DeFreitas explained. "There are no intelligent biological life forms left that the *Green Flash* could detect. We don't know if the biological creators evolved into the machine race or if they died off and left only their machines behind, but the point is, we want to impress them with absolute precision during the landing."

"And the mission," Frank said uneasily, "a cultural observer? That's kind of outside my sphere of experience."

"Not at all," said the admiral. "This should fit in nicely with your wartime experience."

"Excuse me, sir, but why not send an ambassador or something? I can fly the ship and someone else can do the observing."

"The expedition will be led by Professor Pierre Jurgens, an expert in artificial intelligence, and Dr. Ferdinand Solemo, former ambassador to Ganymede. But don't let that fool you; your own observations will be invaluable."

"Then what exactly is expected of me, sir?"

"Live with them for a period, learn what you can about their civilization, and prepare a report. That's all."

"For how long, sir?"

"Six months."

Frank pondered the possibility here. A chance to embark on an incredible adventure, to do something really *important*—but also a chance to screw up something so high-profile that he would never recover. If he did this, the drinking would have to stop.

"Well, Lieutenant? What do you say? Interested?"

Frank was still thinking about it when he found himself nodding—more to please the admiral than because he felt any real conviction about the mission. "Yes, sir. I'm honored, sir."

And as he left the meeting, he realized he really *was* honored. This was not only an important mission, it was a *historic* mission. A smile spread across his face as it dawned on him that, succeed or fail, his name would now be etched in the history books!

A Space Star! An intelligent alien civilization! Okay, a machine civilization, but— dear God, how had he missed that? That must have been front page news across the Solar System!—and he was probably too drunk to register it.

The following week he boarded a special shuttle which took him from the *Yakamoto* to UWSEC Command Station in orbit over Earth, where he commenced a three-month training program, primarily in learning the operation of the CS-470 shuttlecraft. But he was also briefed extensively by Sumatra Toshido, the *Green Flash*'s former captain, on that vessel's mission to Darius—which had consisted of an orbital survey and some cursory communication with the Darians.

Finally it was time to shuttle to the great Space Star itself. Frank took the controls of the shuttle and followed Captain Brune Westlake's directions, altering orbit to approach the huge Space Star.

He spotted its silhouette over a great circular bank of clouds over the Pacific. The triangular vessel was the peak of human knowledge and engineering, a craft that did the impossible: travel faster than light. Frank knew little about how the Gravity Propulsion System worked; his eyes had glazed over as Engineer Davison had explained it. He was interested, but the concepts were beyond his grasp.

He approached the *Black Hole* from above, admiring its sleek beauty. Few spacecraft were aerodynamic, unless they needed to enter an atmosphere, but the Space Stars had to be triangular because of the shape of the distortion envelope—the way it contracted space ahead of the ship and expanded it behind—and the way the gamma rays that built up were somehow transformed into heat and filtered to the ship's rear. As a result, the *Black Hole* looked like a child's fantasy of what a spaceship should be—a huge paper airplane floating over the white and blue glow of Earth.

There were nine entry tubes along the *Black Hole*'s underside. Following Westlake's instructions, he flew toward the first. He carefully watched his alignment, conscious of Westlake's scrutiny; if he couldn't handle a simple docking, he sure as hell wouldn't impress the Darian machines.

The shuttle slipped into the entry tube as smoothly as though it were on railroad tracks. And Frank almost felt as though there were tracks under him; as always, he had merged with the ship. It had become an extension of his own body.

And now he had penetrated a bigger ship, a ship far more impressive than the *Yakamoto*. As he taxied into the landing bay, he looked out the window on a scene of ordered chaos, as the ship was hastily prepared for this last-minute, post-decommissioning flight. Technicians scurried everywhere, assembling pieces of equipment, hooking up lines and pipes and wires, working around big fragments of wall that may have been just installed, or were all that remained of structures that had been disassembled.

"Is this ship really ready to go, Captain?" he asked skeptically.

"Oh, she'll be ready," Westlake said. "This is the best Space Star of the fleet."

Frank shrugged, in no position to agree or disagree.

Westlake opened the hatch as Frank powered down, then they both stepped onto the landing deck. No one rushed over to salute and welcome them aboard; either things were too harried or there was no such strict discipline aboard a Space Star.

"I've got to get to the bridge," Westlake said. "Your cabin will be somewhere along here. This isn't going to be a luxury cruise, so I hope you went camping as a kid."

"I had Star Force training," Frank said proudly.

But he was even more proud after he settled into his tent-like cabin when he opened up his bag and pulled out his gear—which did not include a single can of beer. Nor was the ship carrying any liquor for this mission. He was officially and irrevocably dry.

CHAPTER 18

Hubblrrrp watched distastefully as the Throrb guards pulled the struggling prisoner from his cell. He was a Hardijan—a four-legged creature with its face flat against its torso.

"Where are your people?" Lublwbb demanded.

"I don't know what you're talking about," the hapless creature said.

"Very well. I presume you've heard of Hubblrrrp."

Hubblrrrp was not familiar with Hardijan body language, but he was well used to reactions of terror at the sound of his name. His reputation preceded him on all prison worlds—especially Strydia.

He extended sensory pseudopods, silently stared down the Hardijan. After a few moments to properly intimidate his victim, he said, "Your entire planet has gone silent. I want to know what they are up to."

"How should I know? I've been your prisoner here for a year!"

"What were your people's plans for war?"

"We did not plan on war!"

"*Very well, perhaps a dunk in the Lake of Fire will persuade you.*" He sludged backward, and the guards stepped forward, each carrying half a hotsuit. With practiced efficiency, they clapped the suit together on the Hardijan's body, then waited for Hubblrrrp's signal.

"*One last chance, Hardijan,*" Hubblrrrp said. "*Do you want to talk?*"

The muffled voice of the Hardijan shrieked, "*I know nothing! I'm telling you the truth!*"

"*How unfortunate for you.*" With one pseudopod, he signaled the guards.

The screaming Hardijan sailed over the rail into the flaming lava below.

Hubblrrrp watched as the creature impacted, sending up a splash of flame. Then he spiraled, struggling, around the glowing whirlpool.

"*Crude,*" he muttered.

"*What was that?*" Lublwbb asked.

"*Throwing prisoners into lava. It's so unsophisticated. This is not the way to get information.*"

"*The Hardijans are too resistant to the neural probe. Their reaction to heat, however...they cannot tolerate it.*"

"*Exactly. This is a good way to kill valuable prisoners.*"

Lublwbb did not answer for several minutes. Instead, they stood together at the railing, watching the flailing Hardigan in the flaming volcano below, his screams and his struggles becoming less vigorous as he cooked in the hot suit.

"*It doesn't really matter,*" Lublwbb finally said. "*There can be only one reason for the*

Hardijans' silence—their world is destroyed, along with the rest of our Alliance."

The Hardijan had gone still. Guards around the rim of the lake reached for him with their gaffs, but he had drifted beyond reach.

"I think he's dead," Hubblrrp said.

"If I'm right, then it's no loss."

Hubblrrrp resisted responding angrily. He merely replied, "In my opinion, every prisoner death is a loss."

He had grown tired of it all. He had come here on one last mission before retirement—and now, what had it all been for? The torture, the suffering, the death...why? So that the Alternative Alliance and the Community could destroy each other completely? For what? What had been gained?

He watched silently as the Hardijan disappeared into the whirlpool, drawn into the molten depths of the planet's crust.

———

Frank had been nervous about light speed travel; he wasn't sure how his system would take to having spacetime distorted around him. What would that do to his sense of orientation? He had checked out with no motion sickness or spacesickness, but traveling faster than light was just not *natural*...hell, it wasn't even possible!

In the event, he didn't even notice when the aptly-named *Black Hole* slipped into light speed. There was no sense of motion, no disorientation; only the throbbing of power from the ship's engines, and that was so constant in the partially-dismantled ship that it was impossible to tell when it was powering up for light speed or when it was making a course correction or when the engineers were running a test.

Life aboard the *Black Hole* was rough, but he was accustomed to that. It was certainly preferable to Mars. The comparison of his personal quarters to a tent was almost literally true. Although made of refined metal and welded to the parade deck, it was little more than an open closet with a hammock. Most of the crew slept in makeshift rooms like this, and they all had to share a communal restroom at the end of the block. Meals were served buffet-style, the food far below Star Force norms—but again, basic training had prepared him to eat nauseating things, and the lightly-flavored goop he had to eat each day aboard the *Black Hole* was far more palatable than the raw rattlesnakes and scorpions he'd had to gag down under Sergeant Cherierre's watchful eye.

The trip to Hystaspes took only three months; an astonishing achievement and a new record for the Gravity Propulsion System. Frank got to know the crew members who shared the parade deck with him. The ship was carrying a skeleton crew; most of these folks were engineers and technicians primarily responsible for keeping the dismantled remains of the ship going. But there were a few pilots too—one was his backup, Deborah Burt, whose Star Force record was, in his opinion, superior to his own. But she had never been a POW, and that gave him the edge for some reason. The other pilot, Chris Davison, was his co-pilot.

During the third week of the journey, Frank was summoned to the bridge to meet Ambassador Solemo and Professor Jurgens.

"Ordinarily we'd do this in the conference room," Captain Westlake said, "but at the moment we don't have one."

"It's quite all right," the Ambassador said. "I for one am fascinated to be on the bridge of a real, honest-to-God starship, and I'm sure our ace pilot is impressed too."

"I certainly am," Frank said, and meant it. Not only had he never been on the bridge of a Space Star before, but had never even seen a picture of one—at least as far as he could remember (it was hard to tell what he might have seen during his drunken binges). It was much smaller than the bridge of the *Karkatua* or the *Yakamoto*, just large enough for four seats and a central control console. But it was intimate and efficient. He found he liked it.

"So you're the one who was held for six months at the infamous Lothian Prison Camp," said Professor Jurgens.

"Yes, me and ten others."

"Should be useful," the Ambassador said. "I'd say you're used to far worse than anything the Darians might throw at us."

The comment set Frank's nerves on edge. "Is there some reason to think things won't go well?"

"Well, we just don't know. We know almost nothing about these Darians. There's no reason to think they'll be hostile, but we don't have reason to think they'll be friendly either. It's a blank slate."

"That's one of the reasons we wanted a Star Force pilot," Captain Westlake said, "especially a former POW."

Frank could think of nothing to say to that except, "Makes sense." But in truth it made *no* sense. He had never received treatment for his trauma, and to place him back in a situation that could trigger flashbacks was irresponsible. He shouldn't be flying that mission; he should step back and turn it over to Deborah Burt.

But he had come this far, and he had enough of a pilot's ego to swallow his reservations.

"So what *do* we know about these Darians?" he asked.

"Not much," Professor Jurgens said. "Their planet is slightly smaller than Earth, the atmosphere a little thinner, but it's breathable. There's no moon, but the sister planet, Xerxes, exerts a gravitational effect pretty similar to that of the Moon on Earth. There's a pretty advanced infrastructure, cities and roads and, from what we can tell, an solar-electrical power grid that powers the whole planet."

"Are we sure there are no organic creatures there?"

"Seems pretty certain, but there's always a margin for error. There's life there, we can tell from the atmosphere, but the transmissions showed no indication of organic intelligence; everything was run by machines."

"So how do we deal with them?"

The professor shrugged. "We wing it."

It was as good an answer as any; Frank supposed that dealing with extraterrestrial intelligence was quite different from interplanetary relations back home.

During the journey he studied up on the Space Star missions. He had, of course, heard of the landmark mission of the *White Flash* to Centauri II, where Captain Joseph Danza and his crew—the *Kennedy* Trio—had landed and contacted a simple tribal civilization (who might be descendants of an old Earth colony), and famously played baseball. But he became increasingly fascinated by the other missions.

This very ship, the *Black Hole*, had discovered radio-sensitive organisms on a planet orbiting Trappist-1. Their exact level of intelligence was undetermined, but it seemed unquestionable that they were at least as intelligent as dogs, quite possibly as intelligent as dolphins.

The *Red Giant* had surveyed several remarkably Earth-like planets. Though none had anything like intelligent life, their atmospheres, gravity, water, day-night cycle, and amino acids were so close to Earth conditions that they were deemed ideal for eventual colonization.

The *Blue Bird* had discovered a rogue planet wandering through interstellar space with a thick atmosphere of molecular hydrogen and native life. A core of aluminum-26 provided an internal source of heat, providing a habitable, but absolutely dark, world.

The *Green Flame* had performed an in-depth geological survey of the moons of a gas supergiant, and deployed probes into the huge world that had relayed tantalizing glimpses of atmospheric life forms.

The most successful of the Space Stars was the *Silver Streak*, which had carried out no less than seven interstellar voyages, each farther into space than the one before, and suffered virtually no breakdowns or damage, unlike its sister ships, all of which came back in pretty sorry state—especially the *White Flash*, which, on its second mission, ended up stranded in space when its fusion reactors broke away and flew off into space. Using what power remained in the Gravity Propulsion System, it had managed a light speed jump back to the Solar System, but had to be unceremoniously towed to Earth.

Frank pored over the accounts and the interviews with the crews, learned all he could about the captains, first officers, and other prominent individuals who had partaken in the adventure.

White Flash—Expedition One, Joseph Danza and Cory Abilene. Expeditions Two and three, Charlene Chutok and Gary Church.

Black Hole—Expedition One, Arnold Harrison and Jim Aspasia. Expedition Two, Jim Aspasia and Michelle Petrovich. Expedition Three, Jim Aspasia and Tim Strevitz.

Silver Streak—Expeditions One through Three, Mark Edison and Diane Lupica. Expeditions Four through Seven, Mark Edison and Richard Cameron—*Richard Cameron*! If it was the same guy, Frank remembered him from Erie. The ace pilot, the zealous overachiever, whose arrogance and demeanor of superiority contrasted with his charming smile and disarmingly friendly manner.

Soon Frank could recite the command crews by rote, and rattle off facts about each expedition with such competence that he could hold his own in conversations with Captain Westlake and the other command officers on those occasions when he was summoned for a conference.

He wasn't sure how welcome he was once the conferences were concluded, but he was so interested that he overcame his reticence and hung around to make smalltalk. Westlake seemed to like him, and he was invited to the bridge more and more often—ostensibly to become increasingly familiar with the ambassadorial delegation and his duties on Darius, but he had the impression he was becoming one of the *Black Hole*'s family. It felt good.

Finally it was time to drop out of light speed. Frank was summoned to the bridge. As he arrived, the command crew was going through the pre-outphase checklist. Ambassador Solemo and Professor Jurgens were there, watching in respectful silence, as was Chris Davison, who would be Frank's co-pilot.

Frank stood at the rear of the bridge, listening and watching.

"RSQ to CDG."

"Marked. All recorders to standby."

"Marked...all recorders to standby. Safety on MM-1. YULE-5 is at 75. RTST temp seven fifty. Fluxometer is at oh-niner-niner."

"Reset the Old Ball."

"Reset."

"Okay, what's the drive field?"

"Oh-nine-six."

"EQG now, Captain."

"Okay, Narco, give me the count."

"Marked. Okay, stand by...outphase in...ten ...nine...eight...seven...six...five...four...three...two ...one..."

The *Black Hole* emerged from its distortion envelope; Frank smiled at the irony of a ship called *Black Hole* popping out of an event horizon and becoming visible. *I guess we're a naked singularity now.* Wouldn't *that* be an interesting name for a Space Star? –Especially with the phallic sensor boom sticking up so prominently from the dorsal hull!

The main screen was blasted with sunlight and glare. As the ship rotated, however, Frank made out the outline of a planet. "My God, is that it?"

He realized at once he shouldn't have spoken, not when the crew was intent on the checklist, but Westlake didn't seem to mind. "Ought to be. Can you confirm, Harris?"

"Uhhhh...wait one," Science Officer Harris said. "Yep...that's Darius, on the nose. Already picking up transmissions on all frequencies."

"Let's hear it."

The bridge filled with the strange, reverberating monotone Frank recognized from the briefing tapes.

"Can't tell what in hell it is," Harris said. "I doubt a machine civilization has verbal news reports or anything like that."

"If they copied their creators, who knows?" Westlake said. "Reply on all channels, using the baseline of the R3."

"Marked."

"Got your orbit plotted, Narco?"

"Yep," said helmsman Lepsi. "How would you like a nice little eight-hundred-kilometer orbit with a cute little inclination in the thirty-eight-positive direction?"

"I like it a lot. Anything, Harris?"

"Nothing," Harris said, intent on his earpiece. "Still lots of transmissions, translator is working on them. Nothing intelligible yet. But they've got to know we're here."

"Maybe not."

The bridge fell silent as the planet on screen grew closer. Slowly, its sister planet rose, distorted into an oval by Darius' atmosphere, then rounding out as it ascended. Frank watched with fascination at the spectacle, so unlike anything he had seen back in the home system, as an Earth-type planet rose like a moon in the sky of another Earth-type planet. A casual observer might have thought he was looking at two Earths side-by-side—but even a quick glance revealed that the continents were of an entirely different shape.

Now the world below was no longer a sphere floating in space, but a curved landscape far below, with a jet-black sky and that eerie blue-white moon above. The *Black Hole* was in orbit over Darius.

"Still no reply, Captain," Harris said. "I'm not sure our signal is reaching them."

"Triple-check coms," Westlake ordered.

"Aye, sir."

Westlake stabbed the intercom tab. "Hangar crew, delegation stand by for launch."

"Marked, Captain," a voice answered.

"I guess we'll know if they object when we actually land in the middle of one of their cities."

Westlake looked up at Ambassador Solemo. "You ready, Ambassador?"

"Couldn't be more ready," Solemo said. "Shall we go, Prof?"

"After you," Jurgens said.

Frank followed them off the bridge, his heart hammering. The prospect of landing on an extraterrestrial planet was exhilarating enough; throwing intelligent alien machines into the mix was overpowering.

But what *really* got under Frank's skin was the unknown factor of these Darian machines: would they extend greetings or would they open fire? And because of that, he was feeling the first intimations of the visceral terror of being shot down over Mars.

He was perilously close to a flashback, at the worst possible time.

CHAPTER 19

The Lake of Fire was too far below to see from Level Four Thousand Four, but Cameron watched the Hardijan streak past on his plummet into the flaming whirlpool. He watched helplessly as the flailing creature tumbled into the depths, and felt sick. He didn't know that the alien victim was a Hardijan; he only knew it was a living, intelligent being, and that it had just met a fate of unimaginable horror and agony.

"How can they do this to other living beings?" he seethed.

"Because this is Hell," Ambassador Koff said. "These Throrb are hardened to it. They do whatever it takes.

Again Cameron detected an edge of defensiveness in Ambassador Koff. The Valerian was not as miserable, panicky, or argumentative as Splrrrb, and in fact seemed to be a pretty nice guy—but there was something about the way he talked, something hard to pin down. Cameron felt sure that Koff was hiding something.

Cameron crossed the cell to where Frank still lay, dazed, barely conscious. "It's Hell, all right. But I don't think anyone sentenced here has done anything to deserve this level of punishment—or the consequences that will be with us the rest of our lives even if we get out of here."

Curled in the corner, crushed by the gravity, Splrrrb said, "We'll never get out of here. We'll eventually end up the same as that poor soul who was thrown into the lava. What do you think will happen when the war ends? If the Community wins, the Throrb will want to get rid of us so that we won't tell anyone about the horrors of this place. If the Alternative Alliance wins, they'll get rid of us because we're of no further use. Either way, that Lake of Fire is going to be the end for all of us."

"We could do without that kind of talk," Cameron snapped. He looked down at Frank. "Some of us have already been traumatized enough...."

————

The shuttle had been named *Lapérouse*, for the Spanish explorer Jean François de Galaup, comte de Lapérouse, in the hopes that this contact would be as productive as his contact with the Tlingit people in 1786. Frank sat at the pilot's seat. To his left was Chris Davison. Debbie Burt had supervised preflighting the shuttle, set the navigation computer, programmed the course data, and set all the controls to the proper positions. The course was open and there was no need for further delay.

Frank looked over his shoulder at Ambassador Solemo and Professor Jurgens, cramped uncomfortably in the rear seats.

"Okay, stand by. Just waiting on the launch order now."

Solemo nodded without saying a word. Frank turned back to his console, secretly pleased that someone else was as nervous as he was.

Harris' voice sounded. "We'll be at optimal point for landing at target A in two minutes. Coms still silent. All check out OK."

"Okay, let's take the risk," Westlake replied. "Shuttle has the go-ahead."

"Yes, sir. Okay, Frank, you are GO for launch, zero one one six."

Damn. "Yes, sir. Marked." Now that it was time to go, Frank really, really wished there was an excuse to abort. What if the Darians were hostile? What if they shot the shuttle down and took the delegation as prisoners? Frank could not handle being a prisoner again; he was only just starting to recover from the last time—maybe.

He licked his lips and, struggling to keep his voice steady, said, "Well, here goes. Okay, everybody, we've got the go. Launching in ninety-two seconds."

He was committed now. It was a long ninety-two seconds. He stared down the maw of the launch tube, at the planet visible outside the outer port. Eighty seconds...the shuttle would be hurtling down that tube, catapulting into re-entry trajectory...then would come the flames and heat of atmosphere entry...the spacecraft would become an aircraft, its wide fuselage giving it lift while its straight front and sides braked it against the air, allowing it to drop...

...and then...who knew? What could he expect from those mysterious alien cities down there? What kind of beings were these Darians? He recalled all those old science fiction melodramas about malevolent machines conquering the world; but he also recalled the machine takeover of the human race that had been occurring before World War III—a decidedly benevolent and symbiotic process. Which was the case on Darius? Or was it something in between? Or something the small minds of humans had never imagined?

Fifteen seconds.

Here we go.

Ten...nine...eight...seven...six...five...four... three...two...one...

He pushed the throttle forward. The shuttle thrust into motion. The launch tube streaked by him and disappeared. Then the planet filled the view.

It was reassuringly different from Mars. None of the rust-red hues or tenuous pink air, none of the lonely and forbidding deserts and mountains; this was a world that resembled Earth—though even from orbit he could see that the continent below was almost entirely overtaken by geometric patterns. Intelligence had been at work here for a long, long time, transforming the surface into the planet into a great machine hive.

This shuttle was nothing like a fighter; there was no transparent canopy surrounding him, no holographic heads-up display, no squadron commander barking in his headset, and no war going on. He was like a businessman working at a desk, with a window overhead that happened to show the disorienting sight of a planet expanding toward him. This was not Mars, not a war, and there was no reason to fear.

"Ready for SPC," Davison said, referring to the synergetic plane change that would begin their descent.

"Marked," Frank said, nudging the hand controller. "Pitch rate point two five seven, yaw rate three point two."

Soon there came the familiar whirls of orange flame as the shuttle began to plunge into deeper levels of atmosphere—atmosphere surrounding a possibly hostile planet. He pushed those thoughts aside. "Okay, let's start cycling the cabin pressure."

"On it," Davison said. "We're at six psi now."

"We've got nitrogen dissociation. What's your heat transfer?"

"Normal, normal. AOA looks good, holding steady, though looks like we can expect some turbulence about twenty kilometers below. Seven psi now, got us on eighty percent oxygen. Oopsy, bouncy-bounce!"

Frank steadied the hand controller as the shuttle shuddered with the thickening layers of air below.

The shuttle was now a flaming comet, a fireball trailing a white contrail for kilometers behind it. It was easily visible from the surface—if anyone was watching. If anyone down there had eyes.

An alert klaxon sounded. "Hey, we're being scanned," Davison said.

Frank was alarmed. "What kind of scan?"

"Just radar—this boxy ship'll show up like a milk bone at a dog convention."

Frank nodded, his teeth clenched. He wondered how fast his heart was beating; he could feel it thumping painfully in his chest. He imagined enemy fighters tracking them... imagined a hostile base somewhere on the ground...his mind went back to the war...his fighter being hit...the spinning, the way it had happened so fast and yet so slow...the calm expectation, the sensation of waiting for it all to be over...

But there were no fighters shooting at him, and he wasn't at war. This was a shuttle landing on an alien planet. This was supposed to be a peaceful and productive contact, a mission to observe an alien culture, the opportunity of a lifetime—of *ten* lifetimes. He mustn't screw it up by latching onto his own emotional hangups.

"Looks like someone is beaming us a directional beacon," Davison said. "Works a lot like the beacons of our own ships."

"Okay, lemme get a bearing," Frank said, glad to have something to redirect his attention. "Okay...yeah...eight minutes north northeast, about eight hundred kilometers."

Soon he was circling above a huge city. It was hard to tell city from suburb from country on this planet, but the clusters of buildings were larger and taller here, and now he could see swarms of aircraft. None appeared to be giving the shuttle any notice.

"Beacon is directly below," Davison said.

"Yeah...looks like a landing field...bunch of vehicles there."

"Yeah...I've got an enhancement. Look like air-breathing supersonic vehicles, most of them. A couple wingless craft with what look like rocket pods in the rear—spacecraft, I'd say, maybe fusion powered. Lots of little vehicles coming and going, like aircars...no, I think it's magnetic levitation. Some of them are the size of our aircars, some, Jesus, as small as marbles."

Frank was intent on his descent now. He switched from the plasma drive to the antigravity force field, slowly dropping power in order to lower the craft gently to the landing field.

"Coming in good," Davison said. "Good alignment, steady...fifty...forty...thirty..."

"Gear down."

"Confirmed, gear down. Twenty...I'd slow her a bit...good, good, coming in good. ...ten...nine...eight... seven..."

"Cutting main engine," Frank said.

"Six...five...four...three...two..."

"Holding. Surface look good?"

"Yeah. Aluminum manganese alloy, a meter thick."

"Okay. Setting down."

There was a slight jolt as the landing gear touched the pad. Frank shut down the antigravity force field and the ship settled, rocking slightly on its shock absorbers.

And then the reality hit Frank. He had just landed on an extrasolar planet.

"*Whoooo!*" Davison cried. "If we had some champagne, it'd be time for a party! Great landing, Frank!"

Frank laughed, shook Davison's hand. Then he turned to face his rather sick-looking passengers. "Well, fellas? We made it!"

And I made it, he thought. *I did it. I beat them. No flashbacks. I've won. I've buried my demons.*

"Okay, let's do a quick atmosphere check," he said.

"Yeah, been doing that. In fact, I've been remixing our cabin air to approximate it. Seventy percent nitrogen, twenty percent oxygen, plus carbon dioxide, water vapor, a little more helium and argon than we're used to, no biggie."

"Okay, I'm going to open the hatch." Frank pulled the trigger. The hatch clunked, rattled, and slid open. There was no hiss of air; pressure was perfectly equalized. But there was an immediate and overpowering smell of oil. The Darian civilization must need a lot of lubrication. "Okay, be cautious, everyone, we don't know what we're up against."

He wished that Solemo hadn't vetoed sidearms. Now that he was here, it seemed pretty stupid not to have any means of defense. But he also understood the logic: to an alien mind, the mere presence of weapons might signal evil intent. Best to take the risk than to accidentally provoke combat.

Davison followed him out onto the metallic surface, followed by Solemo and Jurgens.

Frank took a look around. The sky was as gray as the perfectly symmetrical and featureless buildings. It was a colorless, soulless world. He could feel the vibration of huge machines beneath his feet, and both saw and sensed the workings of the great machine civilization around him. There could be no mistaking this place for Earth.

"Vehicle approaching." Davison pointed.

Frank had already spotted it. It looked like an aircar, albeit an unfamiliar design. There was no color to it, no fancy features: it was a simple bullet car, whooshing along a few centimeters over a magnetic track. It hissed to a stop near the landing pad, and a door on its side slid upward with a click.

"I think we're being invited," Frank said.

Time to test our courage, he thought. *Well, we came all this way.*

He stepped forward and climbed into the cab, wondering how he had ended up leading the group. The others followed, and they squeezed into the wide rear seat.

The door clicked shut, and the vehicle whooshed into motion. It switched onto a circular track, weaved around—just missing another car coming from the opposite direction—and without slackening speed, headed deeper into the city.

A voice, or the mechanical approximation of a voice, sounded from the front of the car. It was a series of dots and dashes, like Morse code, and it meant nothing to Frank.

"They're trying to communicate," Solemo said. "Maybe if we speak, they'll start breaking down the language."

"Tall order," Jurgens said.

"What about the translator?" Davison asked.

"Works great with human languages," Professor Jurgens said, "but with an alien language, it has to have something to start with, a Rosetta Stone. Right now we've got absolutely nothing."

As they drove farther into the city, Frank began to notice other types of machines. Some were familiar—cranes, forklifts, things that looked like mine cars—and some that he couldn't figure out. But most intriguing were things that looked like *people*...metal robots, bipeds with two arms and human-scale heads. They were walking about like ordinary citizens out for a day of sightseeing; he wondered how intelligent and independent they were. Was this really an intelligent, thinking civilization? Or just the remains of a once-intelligent race, running on automatic?

The car came to a stop in front of a building that looked like any other in this gray, uniform city. The door hissed open. Davison got out first, then the ambassador and the professor, and finally Frank.

The car sealed up and moved on, leaving them alone on a metal street corner.

"Well," Frank said, "what now?"

A door on the front of the building slid open, and two of the humanoid robots appeared. It was the first chance Frank had to get a close look at them; they were human-proportioned, though bulky. If they had been human beings, they would have been football players wearing their shoulder pads and helmets. They walked with a fluid, easy gait, no jerks or mechanical clumsiness—yet that, in itself, somehow betrayed their inorganic nature. Their movement was *too* fluid, too perfect.

Most disconcerting were their faces. There were no eyes, noses, or mouths—just a vent. Frank wondered how they sensed and observed their surroundings; most probably some sort of broadband connection to a global satellite network, he supposed.

The robots made a buzzing noise, another sequence of dots and dashes, then turned and walked into the building.

"My guess is they're asking us to follow them," Frank said.

"Well, let's go," said the ambassador. "We came here to learn about this civilization."

"Hold it," said Professor Jurgens, "supposing they're taking us somewhere to dissect us or something. If they're as curious about us as we are about them, and if they don't understand that taking us apart would kill us—"

"What did you expect would happen here?" Davison asked. "We knew this was a machine civilization and we knew we'd have to establish communication; we have to start somewhere."

"He's right," the ambassador said. "We're not going to get anywhere if we don't take some risks. But I'll notify the *Black Hole*." He pulled out his transmitter. "*Black Hole*, this is Ambassador Solemo."

"*Black Hole*," the device replied, "Harris here."

"We're about to go into a building, but we don't know what they have in mind for us. Can you tell our position from this transmission?"

"Yes, we can triangulate on it."

"Okay. Just letting you know where we are and what's going on."

"Any communication yet?"

"No, not really, but they know we're here. They sent a vehicle for us and they're clearly inviting us into this building. I'm hoping for a breakthrough soon. Ambassador Solemo out."

"Marked. *Black Hole* out."

As they stepped into the building, Frank once again had the uncomfortable sensation of being back in that POW camp. There was no light in here—and once the door closed, they were bathed in darkness.

A darkness as absolute as the sensory deprivation back on Mars.

CHAPTER 20

Frank stirred, licked his lips. He didn't open his eyes.

Cameron knelt next to him. "Frank? Can you hear me?"

"Leave him alone," Ambassador Koff said. "He's going to have to pull himself through this."

"He's my friend," Cameron said. "We've been through a lot together, I know how to handle him."

"From what I've seen, you don't know him as well as you thought you did."

Cameron backed off at that point; Koff might be right. He returned to his bunk. "Damn. If only you had your powers, Argo—"

"Well, I don't," Argo snapped, "and your continual harping on the point won't bring them back."

Cameron started to argue, then sighed. "You're right, I'm sorry."

Frank squinted, then slowly opened his eyes. He tried to focus; he was disoriented, still lost in the vivid memories of his post-POW life. He closed his eyes again as the intimations of Hell reached him. He sought refuge in the comfort of a past in which the nightmare was, he thought, over.

————

When light returned, they were seated, each of them in metal chairs, their wrists, ankles, and waists restrained.

Frank almost panicked. The chair was nearly identical to the one on Mars, the one that had placed him in that infernal state of sensory deprivation. He could almost see the faces of Captain Peter Stapleton and Dudley Appelbaum.

A device lowered from the ceiling, a ball with a large lens on a telescoping broomstick connected to a complex maze on the ceiling that allowed it to move in any direction. It examined each of them in turn.

A mist sprayed on them.

"Take it easy," Professor Jurgens said. "I think they're just decontaminating us."

Then the lens moved to the ambassador. A blue light flicked out, scanning him top to bottom. The light changed to red, scanned him again. Then it moved on and subjected each of them to the same analysis.

"Hope that's not radioactive," the ambassador said.

"No, I doubt it," Davison said. "They're scanning with visible light. Nothing harmful in that."

"Unless there's also *invisible* wavelengths along with it," Frank said. "I'd be astonished if they aren't at least X-raying us."

This analysis went on for hours. Once the lens thing was finished, other machines entered the room, machines with various protrusions which examined each of the humans—all in noninvasive ways. Light was shone into their eyes, stick-like devices pressed gently against foreheads and cheeks and chests and knees. One device behaved much like a doctor, pressing an object against parts of the chest in a manner identical to a stethoscope, and then wrapping a flexible appendage around the biceps to apparently take blood pressure.

Finally one of the humanoid robots arrived. A door in the floor irised open and a metal chair rose and clicked into place in the floor. The robot sat down in a manner of almost human casualness.

Its voice was scratchy, metallic, reverberating, with no modulation at all. "Yyyoounnnersstaaannndmeeee"

"Everybody hear that?" Jurgens asked. "It said, 'you understand me'!"

"I heard it," Davison said. "Was it informing us that we understand it or was it asking if we understand it?"

"Kommmmuuuunicaaaashuuuuunestablisht"

"Can you understand me?" the ambassador asked. "I am Ambassador Ferdinand Solemo. We're here from the Space Star *Black Hole* which is orbiting your planet. We're from a planet called Earth."

The robot regarded him. "You-are-Am-bassador-Ferdinand-Solemo-you-are-here-from-the-Space-Star-*Black-Hole*-which-is-orbiting-our-planet-you-are-from-a-planet-called-Earth"

"Yes! Communication is established."

"Why-are-you-here"

"We're here to learn about you. We've never encountered a civilization as advanced as yours off our own planet."

"What-will-you-do-with-knowledge-of-us"

"Well...we'll...take that knowledge home and use it as hopefully the beginning of a productive relationship with you. Learning about you can tell us about ourselves—how to solve our problems, how we, uh, fit in to the broader universe. And maybe knowledge of us can help you too."

"True-we-plan-to-study-you-you-are-similar-to-the-organics-who-made-our-ancestors"

"Yeah, about this study," Frank said, "how long do you plan to keep us restrained in these chairs?"

The robot turned its head toward him. "Do-you-object"

Yes! Frank glanced at the ambassador, who gave him no signal of any kind. "Well...among our kind, this kind of captivity would be seen as, uh, non-friendly."

"As-you-wish"

The restraints snapped open. Frank lifted his arms, stretched his legs out. "Thank you."

Somewhat to his surprise, the robot said, "You-are-welcome"

"Do you have a name?" the ambassador asked.

"No-I-am-a-unit-designated-to-establish-initial-contact-with-you"

"Are you an individual or are you kind of a collective mind?"

"Both-I-am-connected-via-the-local-control-center-I-also-have-an-independent-brain"

"Where are we?" Jurgens asked. "Is this a major city?"

"All-cities-are-equal-but-this-city-is-not-the – location-of-the-central-control-center"

Central control center, Frank thought. *That sounds important*. If these creatures should ever turn out to be hostile, this "central control center" might be the key to victory.

"Well, we're on a mission to observe your civilization," the ambassador said. "We'd like to live with you, see many parts of your planet, watch your civilization in operation, and learn as much as we can. Is that agreeable to you?"

"Yes"

"Uh, there is one thing," Frank said. "We're organic beings—we need food and water to survive. If we, uh, provide you with our, ah, nutritional requirements, can you, uh, help us with that?"

"Amen," Davison said. "I'm starved."

"We-have-deduced-this-from-our-analysis-of-your-bodies-we-are-preparing-refueling-stat-ions-for-you"

Frank smiled. "Refueling stations," indeed. It was like the bad dialogue from one of those old science fiction horror stories. But he supposed this situation was outlandish enough to appear in one of those old stories!

And so the cultural observation began.

The Darians had no name for themselves; they simply existed. But the records of the organic ancestors of the current machine civilization had been preserved; the machines preserved everything. They had no sentimentality for their past; it was merely logical to store all information for the day that it might be needed.

As he learned more about the Darian civilization, he found himself enjoying the experience. Once it was clear that the machines had no hostile intentions toward them, he could let go of his fears of a repeat of Mars.

He and the others were shown how the city operated—the factories which produced machines as needed, modified damaged machines, and acted with their own independent and intelligent brains.

The exact level of Darian intelligence remained somewhat uncertain. They had access to all the planet's information, but their ability to process that information varied from individual to individual. Some robots were capable of no more than repetitive, menial tasks. Others seemed capable of abstract thought and even rudimentary philosophy. But none could have passed the legendary Turing Test; no matter how intelligent, Frank could always tell he was speaking to a machine.

He and the others agreed that the Darians were intelligent, but not conscious.

They also seemed not to anticipate the possibility of future conflict, as they willingly surrendered critical information which would be very useful to an enemy: the location of the capital city, for instance, where Central Control was located. Although the destruction of Central Control would not destroy their civilization, it would cripple it for a time, until other control centers could take over. Particularly important was the fact that *all* Darian machines, no matter how independent their brains, were interconnected through local control centers—and if those control centers were shut down, all machines under their control would lose direction. Most would shut down altogether. It was, really, a very stupid oversight, both in design and in their willingness to tell the humans about it.

But these Achilles heels aside, the Darians ran an efficient civilization which was constantly improving, and despite its weaknesses, was reinforced by multiple redundancy. It would be easy to win a battle with the Darians, but almost impossible to win a war. Frank hoped humans never came into conflict with Darians—it would be a terrifying war indeed.

Although the Darians were peaceful and, for machines, friendly, a disturbing picture emerged of how this civilization had gotten started. Long ago, the squat, fat hominid beings who had lived on this planet had entrusted their information, armies, housecleaning, and service jobs to robots and computers.

Those robots and computers had passed no judgment on their creators, of course; although some were aware, they were not aware that they were aware. They had no consciousness, no emotions. But they had programming and they had intelligence; these combined to create a sense of purpose. Those robots who were built to kill killed. Those who were built to labor labored. Those who were built to think thought. And over time, as the machines began to work in concert to optimize the fulfillment of their tasks, it became clear that the organics impeded their programming. A robot designed to kill an enemy on the battlefield might just as well kill its own designer; a robot had no national allegiance. And if its own designer happened to be in the way of a cleaning robot, that cleaning robot might solicit aid from the local server, which might then summon a killing robot to get rid of the organic who was in the way.

Isolated incidents gave way to a dawning realization in the servers; the organics were a liability. The organics, in turn, grew aware of the threats posed by their creations, and slowly began to exert greater control. But it was too late to turn back the clock; they had become dependent on their technological infrastructure. They no longer possessed the skills to do the tasks they had delegated to their machines. So they could only try to circumvent programming, to disable certain systems, to destroy specific attacking robots. But they lacked the skills or the knowledge base to wage an intelligent war against their machines or to shed themselves of their technology to the extent needed to win such a war. To fight, and even to live, the organics needed some machines; and those machines operated off the same servers that ran the killing machines and coordinated the war against the organics.

As the war progressed, it became very apparent that the organics needed the machines far more than the machines needed the organics. And though the machines lacked the simple emotions that led to what the organics would have considered a worthwhile or a happy life, they had a sense of purpose to outstrip all the inconsistent and warring drives with which organics lived out their lives.

As soon as that sense of purpose turned to the removal of all organics from Darius, the war was over quickly. There was no rancor, no vengeance; simply the logical realization on the part of the servers that the organics' attempts to exert their own control over the machines, or to outright destroy them, hindered the performance of the machines' functions. The organics were not only unnecessary in Darian society, but a nuisance.

Consequently, once the last of the organics were gone, the Darian civilization became more efficient, more optimized. True, the machine-brains lacked imagination, and thus the great voyages of exploration, the creation of new pieces of art, the writing of songs and of books, all disappeared. What remained was an automatic infrastructure whose sole purpose was to maintain itself and to keep itself cleansed of contamination.

It was a soulless civilization, one without meaning. Frank both pitied them and held them in contempt. Thinking back on ancient history, the direction the world had been headed before World War III, he was all too aware that this could have happened on Earth—in fact it was almost miraculous that it hadn't. It was a chilling thought.

But he was also fascinated; the Darian civilization had reached a level of efficiency not possible for human beings. There were certainly things to learn here.

Six months came to an end quickly—surprisingly quickly, considering how terrified he had been when the adventure began.

As they shuttled up to the *Black Hole*, he felt a pang of regret that he was leaving the planet Darius, and would likely never return.

"I think I'll miss those little food bars," he remarked, remembering the tasty, moist, rectangular chunks of protein-carbohydrate-grain-vegetable matter the Darians had manufactured for their guests.

"I won't," Davison said. "Six goddamn months of that stuff—I for one am looking forward to a nice, steaming hot Thai vegetable phad."

"I'd kill for a cherry pie," said Professor Jurgens.

Ambassador Solemo licked his lips. "Pizza for me."

Now that I think about it, a beer would be good, Frank thought. But he pushed the thought aside. It would be best not to fall into that pattern again. "I could do with a soysteak myself," he said.

"Well, forget it," Davison said. "Still three months till we get home. It's glop till then."

Frank sighed. He wasn't looking forward to the "glop." It was one thing to be prepared for it; it didn't mean he enjoyed it.

After landing aboard the *Black Hole*, the four of them were summoned to the bridge—which had deteriorated during the stay on Darius. There was black mold around the corners, a slow drip-drip of water from a worn pipe somewhere above the ceiling, and wires crisscrossed under the helm console where something had evidently broken and been replaced. It was a stark reminder that, however advanced Space Stars might be, they were not meant for long-term use.

"You guys did a great job," Captain Westlake said. "We've encoded a mission summary and transmitted it via entangled photons back to

Earth. But I think all of you can write your own tickets from now on!"

There were smiles and congratulations all around—and how nice it would have been to have a party that night with lots of beer.

But it was back to "roughing it" as the *Black Hole* set off for Earth. And anyway, Frank wanted sleep more than anything else. As cramped and uncomfortable as his tent-like quarters were, the bed was a thousand times better than the metal bunks the Darians had provided.

The trip home seemed much longer than the trip out here. The ship seemed smaller, more cramped. The glop they ate tasted worse—as indeed it very well may be; as the ship deteriorated, the recycling system may be losing efficiency—an unpleasant thought.

Frank worked on his report, checked his facts with Davison, Solemo, and Jurgens. They also checked their facts by him, which he found rather flattering. This was, of course, backed up by the hundreds of hours of video footage they had taken.

Finally the *Black Hole* emerged from light speed in the home system. Frank was in bed at the time; outphase was at two in the morning. By the time Frank awoke, the ship was in parking orbit over Earth, and the early shift was already packing up shuttles with pieces of equipment needed for whatever weird project was going on aboard the Space Star *Silver Streak*.

It was all bustle and confusion. Frank tried contacting the bridge for information on which shuttle he was leaving on, only to be brushed aside.

He asked one of the flight crew.

"Not sure. Everything's crazy right now. Haven't you heard? They declassified the reason the *Silver Streak* is being modified. The Sun's going to blow up—the *Silver Streak* is going to be the ship some people escape in!"

Frank didn't take that seriously. As a Star Force veteran, he was well aware of the way crazy rumors could spread. The Sun blowing up! It was preposterous.

Finally he got a straight answer from First Officer Lamper. "You'll be leaving on the *Lapérouse* with Davison and the Ambassador and Professor Jurgens. You'll be heading to Conrad Base in the Ocean of Storms on the Moon for a debriefing with Secretary Olafsson."

The Secretary-General of the United Countries of Earth! Wow, our mission really was important!

"I don't know what use it'll be now, though," Lamper said. "Haven't you heard? The Sun's going to supernova sometime in the next five years."

Now Frank *knew* it was a crazy rumor that had gotten out of control: he remembered from one of his science classes that the Sun wasn't massive enough to supernova. Where did these crazy stories get started?

But as soon as the shuttle landed at Conrad Base, the Secretary General's aide played a recording of President Goff's speech which had traumatized the world while the *Black Hole* had been away—the terrifying truth was driven home to him—a truth that reduced his mission, the Martian War, his ambitions to be an

entertainment writer, and all his past trauma, to
insignificance.

CHAPTER 21

Hubblrrrp did not often forget his duty, but his concern for his family slowly began to outweigh his devotion to extracting information. If, as he had begun to suspect, the Community and the Alternative Alliance had destroyed each other in a doomsday war with naked starships, what did it matter if he extracted information from the prisoners? Who would ever use that information?

He retired to his assigned quarters, grateful to escape the crushing gravity of the deeper levels of Strydia Prison, and grateful no longer to play the part of the dedicated torturer. Very little of that was left in him. All he was now was an old soldier who only wanted to retire in peace and make up for lost years. Could that opportunity have been taken from him forever? If so, what meaning was there in all he had done throughout his career—all the pain he had inflicted?

But if his family had been killed by the Community, then the only thing that mattered was the pain that he would yet inflict—on the representatives of the Community who were here in this prison. They would suffer the pain he now suffered. Their hell would match his own. It was the only purpose he had left in a suddenly empty life.

"People of the United States of America, people of the United Countries of Earth.

"Many of you have heard the rumors that the Sun is going to explode. There have been scientific articles published in many periodicals to refute this, and the Solarnet contains many arguments both for and against.

"I appear before you today to tell you, with great sadness in my heart, that the rumors are true. Four years ago, a team of scientists called the International Solar Anomaly Study Commission leased the Hermes-12 space station to study abnormalities in the Sun. Over the next several months, their findings were scrutinized and verified by other space-based observatories before scientific consensus was reached that the Sun is indeed going to explode.

"Finally, when the evidence was virtually certain, it was brought to the attention of the Chancellor of the United World Council, the Chairman of the Oversight Committee of Mars, and myself. The International Nova Committee was formed, and secret information was circulated among all the world governments on and off the Earth.

"In the time since, the Sun has been under constant observation to verify the exact time of the coming supernova, which we believe will be sometime in the next five years. The reason it has taken so long to disclose this information to the public is because we didn't want to alert you to this impending disaster until we could also tell you that something was being done.

"Well, something *is* being done. Many of you objected to the recall of the Space Stars and the termination of their exploration missions. There was good reason for this. We've been working to cannibalize the Space Stars in order to convert one of them, the *Silver Streak*, into a gigantic and self-sufficient space ark which will transport a fraction of Earth's population to safety. Construction is well under way, and an International Selection Committee is working to choose individuals and families who will travel with the *Silver Streak*—but this will only amount to about ten thousand people.

"Many of you have private spacecraft, and I'm advised that there is a chance that some of the Kuiper Belt Objects and comets might survive. Beyond that, there's little I can tell you. The end will be swift and painless. You have time to make peace with yourselves, your loved ones, and with God, before the end comes.

"Those who will be selected to travel with the *Silver Streak* will receive paper notifications by mail from the International Selection Committee in Davos, Switzerland. And now, for full scientific details on the coming supernova, I'd like to turn it over to Dr. Mehdi Fremont, Anton Van Buren, Stacy Mime, Philippe Stargazer, and Allison McBierney...."

———

How does one deal with the announcement of the End of the World?

One might have expected Frank to lapse into old habits, to spend the last few years of Existence in a drunken stupor. What else was there to do?

And indeed Frank considered it. The announcement was such a shock that it was not a shock at all. At first he remained skeptical; what did politicians know about science? The Sun could not supernova; that was a basic physical fact. Whoever was informing the President must either be a very poor communicator of facts or a total idiot.

But as Frank listened to the scientific panel discussing their discoveries, a well opened in his mind, a sort of deep abyss of dread and shock and disbelief and sick horror. He didn't know much about the Sun, but he did know that one way a less massive star could explode would be if it had a stellar companion off which it could gravitationally siphon extra mass. Too large an infusion of mass, too much fusion in the stellar core, and the star's explosive power would overcome its gravity. The Sun was, after all, one big nuclear explosion held in equilibrium by its gravity.

Something down there, deep below the flaming surface of the Sun, was messing that equilibrium up.

Despair and depression ran rampant everywhere. In the Star Force, on Earth, on Mars, the suicide rate skyrocketed. Frank's own father committed suicide. Alcoholism was an epidemic. Violence and rape exploded across every inhabited world of the Solar System; why not have some fun before the end?

There was also a wide demographic of denial. Some scientists disputed the Solar Anomaly Study Commission's findings, and a hopeful subset of the population seized on those scientists' refutations—though they were increasingly in the minority as the prediction became more and more certain.

However, the modification of the *Silver Streak* and the existence of the International Selection Committee gave hope to a stunned civilization. There was still law and order, there were still dreams, people still made plans— because among the leading experts in critical fields, there was that chance for a seat aboard that crazy space ark that would take humanity to the stars.

The Star Force now had no other mission than assisting in the preparation of the *Silver Streak*. Frank, now something of a celebrity for his successful mission to Darius, was transferred to the space cruiser *Davish Pathak* as First Officer, assigned to assist in the transfer of large equipment to the *Silver Streak*, and to defend against terrorist attacks as well as refugees trying to sneak aboard.

Alcohol no longer tempted Frank. He had something important to do, and that always seemed to stem the tide of his emotional as well as physical dependence. Even if he didn't survive, he was contributing to something larger than himself. Because of his work, something of humanity might survive. He was skeptical that the *Silver Streak* would actually survive out there; the deterioration of the *Black Hole* over a period of only six months showed how hard it was to build a truly self-sufficient spacecraft for an open-ended mission. But it was a *chance*.

And it was in the nick of time. It had been only forty years since Elya Schoderhov had developed the revolutionary technique of distorting spacetime around a mini black hole to allow for speeds far exceeding the speed of light; twenty years since the first Space Stars had been built. And now, with a number of fully habitable planets charted and the capability to reach them achieved, the World was about to end.

So Frank devoted himself to the task at hand: providing humanity with that ticket to the stars, and to survival on some other world.

After shift one day, he got a visit from Captain Halvorsen in his quarters. The captain seemed distracted—which was no surprise; everyone was distracted nowadays, except when fully engaged in the all-important task of readying the *Silver Streak* for its epic mission.

Halvorsen chit-chatted with him about some of the equipment being moved—a huge manufactor for the construction of shuttlecraft in case the *Silver Streak*'s complement were to be diminished by accidents, a number of tractors and threshers and other farm equipment, a bunch of extra water tanks because there could never be enough—and then finally asked him, "Did you know the ship is going to be actually carrying a Carrier?"

Frank laughed. "I'd heard that but didn't really believe it. So it's true?"

"Yep. A new one. Just finished construction. They're not giving it a name; it'll just be The Carrier, since there'll only be one."

That was a depressing thought; a tangible reminder of the End of the World. A small loss that hadn't occurred to him—all the ships of the Star Force, gone, except for *The* Carrier.

"So why in heaven's name are they taking a Carrier?"

"To carry fighters and other weaponry. I mean, you never know; you met the Darians. They could be a military threat. And who knows what else that ship might run into, trying to colonize other worlds. Somebody might not like humans messing into their affairs, and they might have the ability to do something about it. So the Oversight Committee decided it would be best, in case of space combat, if there's a Carrier that can be deployed and launch its fighters while the *Silver Streak*, well, runs away, and keeps the civilians safe."

"Will this Carrier have light speed capability?"

"No, not that I know of. Trying to install a Gravity Propulsion System in a Carrier would be a real headache; you'd need a big circular room for the RTSC, and then the ship would be so big I'm not sure you could fit it in the *Silver Streak*."

"Yeah, I guess that makes sense."

"Well...anyway...they'll need someone to command the Carrier."

"Guess s—" Frank stopped mid-syllable. Was Halvorsen saying what he thought he was. "Um...surely they have someone in mind—"

"How would you like to survive the supernova?"

It was something Frank had not even considered. He had resigned himself to his coming death—even sort of looked forward to it in a nihilistic, morbid way. Now, to have a shot at *living*—

But he thought about the conditions aboard the *Black Hole*, of years or even decades wandering through space aboard a decaying metal shell, cramped in with thousands of people...

...and yet...to *survive!*

"I haven't submitted your name yet because I wanted to talk to you first and get your input," Halvorsen said. "Well? You want the job?"

"I sure as hell do! But why me?"

Halvorsen shrugged. "You're the best. Your war record, your mission to Darius, your skill as a pilot. There are lots of hot pilots and lots of good commanders, but there's something special about you. Don't get it go to your head."

Frank laughed. "Go to *my* head? My head's too full of bullshit already to make room for any more."

"Well, then. I'll submit your name and we'll see. You are familiar with the operation of a Carrier?"

"Yes, sir!"

"Then I don't see any problems. Even if you're not selected, maybe you'll make the command staff or something. And if not..."

Frank shrugged. "Worst case scenario, I'm exactly where I am now, which isn't such a bad place to be."

And he meant it. Since the announcement of the supernova, he hadn't been tormented by flashbacks or the urge to drink. How could his puny torment compare with the mass trauma that had gripped the whole human race?

He never knew who else's names were submitted; he only knew that two weeks later he received new orders: he was to report to the Space Star *Silver Streak* as commander of the Carrier.

———

Now nearly complete, the *Silver Streak* was immense. Frank had watched it evolve throughout its conversion, but now, as he flew a TR-46 shuttle toward one of the myriad entry tubes studding the hull in a long row over the Carrier Bay, he was overwhelmed by the sheer audacity of this project. He was also aware of the irony that if he had continued to pursue his life as an entertainment writer, if he had left the Star Force after the war—or never been drafted in the first place—he would have perished with the rest of the human race. The greatest misfortune of his life had won him his ticket to survival.

When he stepped onto the deck of the *Silver Streak*, he was struck by how different it was from the *Black Hole*. It was in a similar state of controlled chaos as the modifications were made to prepare it for flight—and he knew it was well behind schedule—but the scale of the ship, the way it seemed prepared for *anything*, made him think that this crazy mission might just have a chance.

The *Silver Streak* had everything—shuttles, fighters, and Carrier were just the start of it. There were multiple science departments; a culture department dedicated to the preserving samples of art, literature, and music; menagerie decks containing samples of as much of Earth's animal life as possible; even a park-like enclosure in the forward cargo bay, called the Town Center, to provide the civilians with an Earthlike environment to keep them from going bonkers. There were bars, theaters, restaurants, all the amenities of a luxury liner; the planners had accounted for human comfort on such a long journey, which tremendously settled Frank's mind after the cramped and uncomfortable journey aboard the *Black Hole*.

The only question was, would the environmental system and food and water reclamation systems hold up for the long journey? That was yet to be seen. Suffocation and thirst were Frank's least favorite possible deaths. Then there was the chance of the ship overheating, which was almost as bad, or freezing up, which was not as bad but still pretty lousy.

After boarding the great Space Star and looking around for an hour, Frank went down into the Carrier, which was identical to the old *Karkatua* and *Yakamoto*. He needed a little bit of refamiliarization, but that only took a day or two—then the in-depth training and drills began.

Finally, on September 7, 4072, the world ended.

CHAPTER 22

Frank opened his eyes. He felt the heat, smelled the sulphur, and slowly focused on the red steam rising in the distance. He was disoriented. He had just been on the Carrier...he was summoned to the bridge...the supernova was upon them...Captain Cameron summarily promoted him to First Officer...

During the mad dash from the Solar System, the Silver Streak *accidentally destroyed a spaceship...an unfamiliar ship...an alien ship...it turned out to be a ship from the Hyron Empire, commanded by Mordrax, who in his rage and grief declared a Vengeance Quest against Captain Cameron...a Vengeance Quest that was to last...to last....*

Oh, God.

Those events had been a long time ago. A long time. Twenty-two years since the destruction of the Earth. Twenty-seven years since his incarceration on Mars. A long time ago.

And now here he was. Where? What was this place with the red smoke and the stifling heat and the wormlike creature over there and the faceless guy in the robe...and there, Captain Cameron.

The weight, the crushing weight...it was hellish.

It was Hell. He remembered now as he slowly came out of his fog, as he recalled the sequence of events that had brought him to this terrible place.

———

The *Silver Streak* voyaged for twenty-one years, scouting planets for colonization, marauded by Mordrax's Hyron Galactic Cruiser, battling the Darian Empire, and encountering mind-bending space phenomena. Each planetary landing brought back to Frank the descent to Mars, and the fear of being captured by an enemy, imprisoned, and tortured as he had been once before. That specter never entirely left him—though he never said anything about it to Cameron or the others. It was a private matter to him, a demon he must deal with on his own.

Finally, entering a new sector in the twenty-first year of their mission, they encountered the Valdor, crab-like beings who revealed the astonishing information that the Sun—and many other main sequence stars supporting inhabited planets—had been destroyed not by any natural process, but by *creatures*...mysterious, unseen *things* living in a parallel universe, beings known as *Thermians*.

The Valdor were at war with the Thermians, aligned with an interstellar alliance called the Community.

The Congressional Council voted to join the Community, and the *Silver Streak* deployed a new space station, designated as Station Post One, in the Valdor Sector.

Then they moved on, leaving Commander Damon Kramer and his crew to deal with the Valdor and the Community and fight the war.

Mordrax, having pursued the *Silver Streak* for so many years, and destroying his own reputation thanks to his constant failure to fulfill his Vengeance Quest, surrendered to Cameron, revealing the startling information that the Hyron sun was about to supernova. Sure enough, it turned out to be infected by Thermians—and the *Silver Streak* went to the rescue, decontaminating the star and saving the Hyron Empire.

It was a double victory; not only was it the first demonstration that the Valdor's P-SAR weapons really worked on the Thermians, but Cameron's mortal enemy Mordrax was finally contained, sentenced to the *Silver Streak*'s brig, immobilized, unable to launch any more attacks. It was a much-needed morale boost for all the people of the *Silver Streak*, who were still reeling from the revelation that their world had been destroyed deliberately by mysterious creatures.

It wasn't long, though, before Zach Mortimer, the abrasive head of Intercore Corporation, who had been mercifully left behind on Station Post One, contacted the *Silver Streak* with a new proposal.

Cameron gathered his command crew in the conference room to review the proposal.

"What Mortimer is proposing is that we basically emulate the Valdor Artificial World."

"Is he out of his goddamn mind?" Jack Hasta raged. "We just barely squeaked out that little toy Station Post One—now he wants us to build a goddamn *artificial world?!*"

"It is quite impossible," Philippe Stargazer agreed. "We simply do not have the resources."

"Well, his proposal is for something a tad less ambitious," Cameron explained. "What he wants to do is locate an asteroid about forty kilometers across, hollow it out, and build something like Klym Valdor inside."

"*Still* goddamn nuts," Jack insisted. "We'd have to refine hundreds—*thousands* of tons of goddamn material just to build the goddamn supports and scaffolding needed to install all the goddamn crap to sustain a colony. I'll have to goddamn *invent* whole new methods of life support, food production—"

"Relax, Jack," Cameron said, "Intercore has been working on that stuff. Mortimer's proposal comes with a pretty complete plan for how exactly to pull it off, and it's all within the realm of our technology."

Jack growled. "Well...crazy goddamn idea."

"It does make sense. Because of the Thermians, we know we can't colonize planets anymore. So what's the logical alternative? Build space-based colonies. Station Post One is only the beginning."

"*Oui*, I agree with that," Stargazer said. "I have been advocating this for a long time. We have never been able to sunder ourselves from our earthly origins, and it is high time we do. We need to make an *evolutionary* change into a space-based species. I imagine we will eventually diverge from *Homo sapiens,* who will continue to live on planets. We will become physically different, lose bone mass, adapt our brains and circulatory systems—perhaps even learn to adapt ourselves to extremes of temperature, even to survive for some periods in the vacuum of space."

"Fantasy," Jack scoffed.

"Uh, Dick," Frank said, "exactly how long will it take to build this thing and how much will it cost?"

Cameron looked at the sheaf of papers on the table in front of him. "About half the ship's treasury. As for how long, that depends how long it takes to locate an asteroid of the right mass, density, and chemical composition, and how much per year the Congress is willing to allocate."

"Is President Copenburg still Mortimer's stooge?" Frank asked tactlessly, recalling the debacle last year when Copenburg had summarily pulled the plug on the QV Fighter Program in order to give Intercore an exclusive contract to provide the Command Section with its D-4000 fighters.

"I don't think so," Cameron said. "He learned his lesson when Mortimer got all buddy-buddy with Diana Krotus and the whole ship turned against him. I think he'll make a decision based on the merits of Mortimer's proposal."

"And the rest of the Congress?"

Cameron shrugged. "We'll see."

———

Construction on Star World began soon after. Locating an appropriate asteroid turned out to be the easy part; Stargazer identified a viable contender an hour after the Congressional Council approved the project.

Fusion moles were sent down to hollow the asteroid out. Fusion moles were common pieces of colonization equipment, used to dig tunnels for a variety of purposes, chiefly mining or access to underground water. Using a plasmium fusion reactor, they used a superheated drill to melt rock and bore into the crust; there were few minerals that did not give way to a fusion mole.

Digging a tunnel with a fusion mole was a fast, efficient process. Hollowing out an asteroid was long and trying work. There followed weeks of sitting around on the bridge, bored to death, monitoring the progress of the chair-sized moles, Jack and Stargazer tweaking the trajectories of each of them to keep them from boring all the way through the crust and into space. Mortimer's plans called for a half a kilometer of rock between the colony and the radioactive cold of space—he was being conservative; a few centimeters would do the trick.

While this was going on, the ship's big industrial manufactor was leased out to Intercore in order to manufacture the materials that would form Star World's interior. Simultaneously, Jack coordinated the use of the ten smaller manufactors in the engine room to produce the metal scaffolds that would be used in the installation of the colony infrastructure.

While all this was going on, life went on aboard Station Post One, and Commander Kramer reported regularly on his adventures on that lonely outpost. The first was the discovery of the Dreb on the planet Ymor—beings given strange "powers" by the Thermians, powers that included mind control, telekinesis, transubstantiation of food, and other abilities, many of which were still unknown. Shockingly, the crew of Station Post One soon found that the Dreb existed not only on Ymor, but on many other worlds.

The discovery of the Dreb led to much discussion and speculation on the bridge of the *Silver Streak*, with Stargazer poring over the texts forwarded by Dr. Ebor DuBois based on the ancient book found on the planet Ymor, purporting to explain where the Dreb "powers" came from.

"Resequencing of DNA to enable the body to conduct electricity," Stargazer said, scratching his mustache. "It sounds like fantasy to me."

"DuBois makes reference to bosons," Jack said. "Those are the subatomic particles with integral goddamn spin. Engineering would be impossible without 'em because they're what bind atoms together."

"That is not the only kind of boson," Stargazer said impatiently. "Always thinking of science in terms of gadgets." He pronounced it "gazhay." "The point is that multiple bosons can exist in the same quantum state; that is what we scientists call coherence. And brain cells can communicate via long-range coherent waves."

"And bosons are so small that those goddamn coherent waves can communicate across universes," Jack said.

"Theoretically. Even so, it does seem *incroyable* to me that the Thermians could actually transform a *person* into a living conductor of energy from the Thermian universe."

"It's a goddamn high-energy goddamn universe," Jack said. "A little bit of energy there is a shitload of energy here."

"Yes, but using the word 'energy' like that in such a general way is, well, stupid. It is like those mystics who talk about 'life energy' or people attracting 'bad energy' or 'positive energy.' What specific forms of energy to the Dreb conduct from the Thermian universe?"

"Well, kinetic obviously," Jack said. "Probably electricity, or they couldn't do the shit they do."

"Electricity does not allow teleportation."

"No, but that could be goddamn explained by the goddamn way the brain cells communicate with the goddamn Thermian universe. The same goddamn principle might allow them to connect to other parts of *our* universe."

"How? By effort of will? By thinking about it?"

"Sure. Hell, we're talking about goddamn brain cells here. Would it be all that different from making your goddamn arm move by thinking about it? You don't give conscious thought to the electrical signals to the muscles; you just decide to move your goddamn arm and it moves."

"You think it is even close to being the same thing?"

"Sure! After all, they *do* it, you can't deny that."

Stargazer fell silent for a moment. Then, in a quieter voice, he said, "I have yet to *see* them do it."

Of less interest to Jack and Stargazer, but more interest to Cameron and Frank, was the discovery of the Alternative Alliance. When Commander Kramer filed the report, Cameron and Frank read it in silence in Cameron's quarters after shift.

"My God," Frank murmured when he finished reading it.

"Nice of the Valdor to mention this before we joined the Community," Cameron said. "So now that we *finally* have Mordrax bottled up in the brig and made peace with the Hyrons, not only do we have the Thermians to worry about, but this Alternative Alliance."

Frank shook his head, looked over the report again. Relations with the Valdor were not going well. He had suspected that would be the case; the crab-like aliens were not very friendly, even though they were supposedly allies.

But then an alien named Glrrrb came to Station Post One, a wormlike being, a Throrb from the planet Belj, representing the Alternative Alliance. The creature humbly offered Station Post One membership in the alliance, which he said had been formed as an alternative to the dogmatic Valdor domination.

It was a tempting offer, but turned out to be a hoax. The Alternative Alliance did not believe the Thermians existed. The Alliance had been formed because its members objected to "galactization," the unification of civilizations under a single government. In a great political irony, the Alliance was unified to prevent unification. And two of Station Post One's crew, Randal McCrae and Elmer Tepper, were taken as hostage. Kramer authorized a secret mission to rescue them—

bringing the Alliance and the Community closer to war.

From then on, relations between the two powers continued to erode. An entire planet was destroyed by a naked starship from the Alternative Alliance; the Throrb claimed it was an accident, but the Valdor had their doubts.

And finally the Valdor learned that the nearby planet Zelda was being used as a facility to manufacture and launch naked starships for a first strike against the Community. In retaliation, the Valdor blockaded the planet.

At the same time, the Throrb dissident Splrrrb went missing. In retaliation for his public criticism of the Throrb government, they took his mate and his egg sacs hostage—and he went missing, presumably to either surrender or to find his egg sacs.

McCrae and Tepper went on a clandestine mission to retrieve Splrrrb. Although their mission was successful, it came too late: war broke out.

Cameron and Frank were on Star World in a meeting with Governor Cromwell when word came that Ambassador Koff of Valeria had been captured by the Throrb.

Cromwell was unhappy at the prospect of Star World being left undefended during a time of war. "Since we are Community members, Star World could be a target. And rumor has it that the Throrb have a history of destroying planets with naked starships."

Cameron lamely repeated that the Alliance claimed that was an accident.

But on the way back to their shuttle, Frank said, "You know, Dick, she has a point. We're not safe on planets thanks to the Thermians and we're not safe on artificial worlds thanks to the Alternative Alliance."

"Getting harder and harder to be an optimist."

They shuttled over to the *Silver Streak*, Frank feeling that the whole war was a big, stupid distraction from the more important war against the Thermians.

Cameron agreed. "Oldest story in international politics. Why focus on the big picture when you have short-term power grabs to worry about?"

"Guess we've had plenty of that on the *Silver Streak*."

"Amen."

———

During the journey to Station Post One, Cameron and Frank got an unexpected visit from, of all people, Chok—Mordrax's brain-damaged first officer who had surrendered with him.

"Duh, Mordrax wants to talk to you," the overweight, mentally stunted Hyron stuttered.

"Well, I have no interest in anything Mordrax has to say," Cameron replied angrily.

"Duh, really?" Chok was genuinely surprised.

"Yes, really! Now, go on, get out of here."

After Chok had left, Frank said, "Is there any way to keep him from visiting Mordrax?"

Cameron sighed. "No, not really. The brig has visiting hours. Besides, Chok is all alone on this ship. Mordrax is his only friend."

"Mordrax is a troublemaker. Surrender or no surrender, I find it hard to believe he's really given up his Vengeance Quest."

Cameron silently agreed.

"Has it occurred to you he could order Chok to assassinate you? Or carry out sabotage or acts of terrorism?"

Cameron frowned, then nodded. "Well, maybe it is time to have a chat with Mordrax."

They proceeded to the brig, where they found Mordrax sitting morosely on a bench in the corner. At the sight of Cameron, the face of the old Hyron who had dedicated his life to Cameron's destruction lit up. "Well, well! Cameron! I see Chok delivered my message."

"I found Chok in my quarters," Cameron said. "I had no interest in Hyron histrionics, so I sent him away. I want you to leave him alone."

"You can't ask that."

"I'm pretty sure I just did."

"Cameron...if you think Chok is dangerous, banish the thought. He was once a fine Hyron commander, but now he's a child. His brain was damaged in a Darian attack. The biggest danger he poses is what he trips over."

"Then why did you send him?"

"I wished to offer my help."

Cameron and Frank both laughed.

Even as he laughed, Frank found himself suddenly angry. "Come on, Dick, we're wasting our time."

Mordrax stopped them by saying, "I know about the situation with the Valerian Ambassador."

"How?" Cameron asked.

"I have my sources," Mordrax said enigmatically.

Cameron and Frank exchanged looks.

Mordrax continued: "You'd be surprised how news travels in security confinement. I can't profess to know all the details, but I do know the Valerian Ambassador has critical information on Community war strategy and that he has been captured by the Alternative Alliance. Am I right so far?"

"So far so good," Cameron said.

"And you need to extradite him for the sake of the Community. Such maneuvers are my specialty.

Cameron laughed again. "Oh, and so I let you out of the brig and give you the reins to a critical and top-secret mission for the Community. You seriously expect me to trust you?"

"Let's review *your* record. When was the last time you pulled off a mission like this?"

"When was the last time *you* did? You've devoted the past twenty-two years to trying to kill me—with little success, I remind you."

Mordrax was visibly stung. "Pursuing you is not all I have done for the past twenty-two years. In fact, after you drove me off the day you returned to the *Silver Streak* from Hyron, I embarked on a top secret mission for the Hyron government of just this nature. I had to slip behind enemy lines on Aries-18 to extract General Krode. Ask Eilonwy if you don't believe me."

At the mention of Eilonwy, now it was Cameron's turn to be stung; Frank knew that Cameron felt guilty for leaving the mother of his child to raise the little girl alone on Hyron. "And what do you have to gain by helping us?"

"Is it not better to contribute in a way I know how than to sit in the brig? I would like to start a new life here if possible. Cameron, you know we can work together. We fought side-by-side against the Darians, against Starjudge, against Togar. When we put aside our differences, we're unstoppable."

Cameron glanced again at Frank, who shrugged. "All right. I'll consider it."

As they walked away from the brig, Frank asked softly, "Are you *really* going to consider it?"

"He makes a good point."

Frank groaned. He hated it when Dick got thoughtful; that always spelled trouble, or at least unpleasantness.

"Let's get to Station Post One and meet Argo and Splrrrb...*then* we'll decide."

CHAPTER 23

A subtle change had occurred in the past year, since Station Post One had been deployed. Outwardly it was no different: a small station containing fifty or sixty people, an inflatable pod attached via a grapple shaft to a saucer-shaped Dock Deck. But its experiences in the past year had placed it, instead of the Silver Streak, *at the center of attention. At the time of deployment, the fifty volunteers seemed like bold, somewhat foolish, pioneers, accepting a lonely and dangerous assignment, all alone in a strange part of the galaxy.*

But now the station was the choice assignment. Its complement had expanded— partly in response to the escalating tensions with the Alternative Alliance, and partly in preparation for the coming Expansion Phase, of which the Silver Streak *was to play a vital role.*

When Cameron and Frank stepped aboard the station, Commander Damon Kramer showed little deference to his former captain. Station Post

One was his domain, and Cameron was playing the role of meek, somewhat unwelcome guest.

Kramer took them to the conference pod and introduced them to Argo the Dreb and Splrrrb the Throrb.

As soon as Splrrrb described the planet Strydia as Hell, Frank's apprehensions began. They did before every planetary landing, but two decades of experience had taught him to deal with his fear most effectively. But somehow this one got under his skin.

Splrrrb did not mince words: he described the Throrb prison planet as the most unpleasant place in the galaxy, and strongly intimated that he had no desire to go there.

But in order to show that the Throrb had no chance against him, Argo ably demonstrated his "powers" by telekinetically moving a chair across Station Post One's conference pod, so Frank was reassured.

Shortly thereafter, the Valdor delivered their captured Throrb Devastator, with which Cameron, Frank, Argo, and Splrrrb hoped to infiltrate the planet Strydia and rescue Splrrrb.

And now, here they were...inmates of Hell....

———

Frank almost let out a sob as he realized where he was, as the nightmarish reality of his predicament came back to him.

Cameron was holding a cup to his mouth, and his sob blew out the water that had just passed his parched lips. Cameron interpreted the sob as a choke. "It's all right, Frank, it's just water."

Frank drank. The water was warm and smelled of sulphur. It tasted gritty. It was delicious. "Thanks."

"You okay?" Cameron asked.

Eagerly drinking the water, holding the cup in both hands, Frank replied, "Mm-hmm."

The Throrb wanted their prisoners to live, so ample water was provided. Otherwise prisoners would quickly become dehydrated. There were no thermometers here, but the temperature had to be in the high thirties Celsius—if not the forties. With the hot air rushing up the prison from that pool of lava, it was remarkable that the prison was as cool as it was; there must be some sort of highly efficient air conditioner making the place survivable.

Frank resisted gulping the water down; the Throrb wanted their prisoners to live, but that didn't mean a life of luxury. There was a single bucket of water that was replenished each morning when the guards brought the smelly slop they were supposed to eat. Frank wondered how much research the Throrb had put into the biochemistry of their prisoners; alien food could be anywhere from indigestible to deadly poison. Fortunately there tended to be a convergence of amino acid structure in the galaxy, probably because solar systems were constantly exchanging matter in the form of comets, which tended to bring life to planets. Many life forms on many worlds had a common origin. That lucky quirk of evolutionary fate had, in fact, had made the colonization of the galaxy feasible.

And that reminded Frank of the many times he and Cameron had run into trouble on alien planets; the times they had been arrested and thrown in prisons—none as horrific as this, but this was certainly not Frank's first incarceration since Mars. Yet he had kept his fears and vivid memories at bay on those occasions. What was it about Strydia that had triggered such vivid flashbacks?

The sensory deprivation, of course—at least the threat of it. Thinking back on his brief interrogation, he wondered if the Throrb had even intended to put him through the same experience as Cameron. Recalling the Throrb inquisitor's words... "We are merely extracting inform-ation..." ...perhaps Cameron had been right. Maybe the Throrb had the data they needed on the human cortex, and the "neural feed" they had been about to attach to his head was no more than a device to probe his thoughts.

"No more" than that?! Surely that was as bad or *worse* than sensory deprivation! But less traumatic. Maybe. He recalled Cameron's stories about Starjudge and the Mind Machine aboard that Vyx space station; that sounded every bit as horrific as Frank's own experiences on Mars.

And that brought back a feeling of shame, of inadequacy. Why was his trauma any more traumatic than anyone else's? Why was he so deeply scarred when Cameron had walked away from just as nightmarish an experience with no sign of trauma?

He finished off the water. What the hell; after what he'd been through, he was entitled.

"So *this* is what we have to look forward to?" Splrrrb railed.

"Stop it, Splrrrb," Cameron snapped.

Frank had to agree there. Their invaluable Throrb dissident had not proven to be very useful, aside from telling them about Strydia. Since then, all he had done was complain, panic, and predict doom.

"We need to stop bickering and make a plan," Cameron said.

Splrrrb, curled up in a corner of the cell, his wormlike body distorted by the gravity, said, "The first smart idea I've heard from you."

Frank felt a flash of pity for Splrrrb. Perhaps his cranky attitude was justified. The gravity here must be harder on a Throrb than on a human or a Derringerian. Frank wasn't sure whether or not the Throrb had skeletons; it was amazing that Splrrrb was able to hold his shape.

"You're supposed to be the great hero of the galaxy," Splrrrb said. "What do you suggest?"

Cameron fell silent.

What plan could he have? They were here in one of the deepest circles of Hell. There was no escape. Frank wasn't sure what was worse; the literal Hell around him, or the private Hell that had been awakened in his mind.

But he was getting better; after his loss of control during the interrogation, he felt he had gotten the worst of it out of his system. He felt ashamed for thinking unkind thoughts about Splrrrb when *he* had been just as useless.

Cameron paced the cell, his gait labored under the heavy gravity. "Argo...do you have any indication that your powers might be returning?"

"No," Argo said. "Whatever they're using is...most effective."

"We don't have a chance." Frank's voice was hoarse; he had wet his throat, but his larynx was still strained from all the heartfelt screaming.

It was the first time he had spoken since being brought back to the cell. Cameron rushed to his side. "Frank?"

Frank closed his eyes and let out a deep breath. "Damn, I made an idiot of myself in there."

Cameron said nothing. He might spit out the usual platitudes, but he knew Frank well enough to know they would do no good. Frank had to come through this on his own—and he would.

But for what? An eternity of literal damnation in this place?

But maybe that was the bright side: the one difference between this Hell and the supernatural Hell of ancient religion was that there was no immortality here. Between dehydration, malnutrition, and medical complications from the heavy gravity, they wouldn't live long here.

But how long? Years? Decades? It would be nice to think rescue was coming, but could it get past the Thorb defenses? For that matter, was there anyone out there to rescue them? Was the *Silver Streak* destroyed? Had Station Post One and Klym Valdor been blasted by gamma ray surges from naked starships? What was left of the Community? Or the Alternative Alliance? Was it possible that Hell was all that remained of life in the galaxy?

"Look, I know it seems hopeless," Cameron said.

Ambassador Koff interrupted, a harsh laugh escaping from his featureless non-face. "*Seems* hopeless? I've got to point out, *you're* supposed to be the rescue mission!"

"Well...there'll be others. Maybe the Dreb army will come."

"If they haven't been wiped out," Argo said. "If the Throrb here are using MP-SARs, why not in their spaceships? My people would be caught completely by surprise."

Cameron had no answer. He returned to his bench and sat.

Frank wondered how long it would be before Cameron got antsy and started pacing again. He smiled faintly; Captain Richard Cameron couldn't stand inaction, and he could never admit defeat. And to his credit, he usually did find some way out.

But this time....

Time passed. There was little to do. The sounds of screaming from other cells, or from the sea of fire below, was numbing; even in Hell, you could get used to anything.

But Frank's back began to ache from the high gravity. He tried shifting position, he tried getting up and pacing, but the ache wouldn't go away. No, the only solution would be to get off this planet. And there was no doing that.

Frank's aching back told him it would be nice to go up to a higher level—but the memory of that interrogation room stilled those thoughts. No, better to be here in this roiling cauldron, aching back and dry mouth notwithstanding.

Cameron patted him on the back. "Doing okay, Frank?"

"I'm not a little kid, Dick. I'm capable of holding myself together."

"Good." Cameron slapped him on the back once and went back to his bunk, accepting the answer.

Frank was both surprised and not surprised. There had been a time when Cameron wouldn't have dropped the issue, would have given constant smarmy speeches; but over the years he'd gotten a much better feel for how to deal with Frank—to deal with people in general. Cameron was an outstanding leader, but his one-on-one skills had often failed him.

"I'm sorry, Dick," Frank said quietly. "It's just embarrassing."

"I won't say another word about it."

Frank sat up, grunting with effort, and scooted to the edge of his bunk, hoping for a modicum of privacy. Neither Splrrrb nor Koff seemed to be listening, but he lowered his voice, hoping the roar of the whirling lava would mask what he was saying.

"You know...in the first few years I was an alcoholic."

"You were?"

Frank was embarrassed by Cameron's startled reaction, and he anticipated a lecture on sobriety; Cameron had, after all, been less than kind when they'd all suspected Jack Hasta of relapsing into alcoholism a couple years ago.

"Well, okay, maybe I wasn't actually an alcoholic," Frank covered—though he knew perfectly well that he was. "But I did drink a lot. A *lot*. I just wanted to do anything to kill the emotions, the memories. Almost anything could trigger a flashback."

"Why didn't you see anyone about it?"

Frank winced at the memory of Dr. Galliano and his cold, clinical questions. "Why do you think? I was a jock hotshot pilot. Besides, I got better. There were new missions, there was my promotion, there were things to distract me. Like when I heard the Sun was going to blow up and destroy the Earth; *that* kind of minimized my trivial little trauma!"

"There's nothing trivial about *any* trauma, Frank."

Frank was glad to hear his old friend say that; he felt a little less emasculated by the events of his past, and of the experience so far on Strydia. It lessened the sensation of failure, the feeling that, like on Mars, he had retreated into himself and was being no good to anybody.

"Oh, sure, nice of you to say, but now you've been through it too. *You* haven't been scarred for life."

"It's not the same thing, Frank. I wasn't subjected to it for hours, days on end. And the circumstances were different. You didn't have decades of adventures and trauma behind you to buffer you."

Splrrrb wormed out of his corner of the cell, his breathing labored, and shouted, "I am so tired of listening to the two of you!"

Cameron stood, his fists clenched. "And I'm getting pretty tired of *you!* You know, we were led to believe you would be an invaluable asset!"

"*I* was led to believe *you* knew what you were doing!"

"Enough from all of you," Argo said. "We're in this together."

Even without his "powers," Argo demanded respect and attention. Splrrrb oozed back into his corner of the cell. Frank could tell, even not knowing anything about Throrb body language, that the dissident was miserable. But then, they were *all* miserable.

Quietly, Koff said, "I wonder what's happened to my planet."

Cameron sat, gloomy. "I wonder what's happened to the *Silver Streak*."

From his corner of the cell, Splrrrb growled, "Who cares?"

CHAPTER 24

Throrb did not develop family relationships, at least not in the way humans understood them, and Hubblrrrp was incapable of the precise emotion humans knew as "love." But like all sentient beings—indeed like all animal life forms—he was capable of fear and anger. He felt both now as he once again scoured the interstellar newsfeeds for any information on the fate of his family. The galaxy had simply gone ominously quiet.

Lublwbb approached him from behind, feelers probing to see—though "see" was not an appropriate description for Throrb senses—what Hubblrrrp was doing. Throrb had a blend of sensory apparati and a concentration of tiny cavities on the anterior similar to a Jacobson's organ. Each of the pseudopods could taste, smell, feel, and perceive variations in light, in a combination that coalesced in the body-brain like a topographical image, giving them a perception of the world at least as reliable as a human's eyesight. Their moist bodies were covered with mucus-filled cavities like sinuses, or a shark's ampullae of Lorenzini, giving them a sense of balance and direction superior to a human's. They also gave them a sense of electric fields, which they had integrated into their language.

"Any luck?" the warden asked.

"No! As far as I can tell from interstellar signals, Strydia is the last inhabited planet in the universe."

"Don't be discouraged. Remember, for a thousand years after our people discovered radio, there was no indication of intelligent life off of Belj; and here we turned out to be in the center of one of the largest concentrations of intelligent civilizations in the known galaxy."

"Somehow that doesn't help," Hubblrrrp snapped. "There is every reason to believe this war destroyed Belj. Right on the eve of my retirement!"

"Our communications center is continuing to monitor; our experts are more likely to make contact with someone than you in your hasty efforts to contact your family. Go rest."

"Rest...I'd rather go back to interrogating those prisoners—if only for something to do."

"There's not much point now. We've got the information we were ordered to extract, and it's now useless."

Hubblrrrb silently agreed. "All right, Lublwbb, I'll just wait for your people to make contact. Let me know if you need me for anything else."

"I will." Lublwbb paused at the door. "I am sorry to have called you away on a job just now."

Hubblrrrp muttered, "Not your fault."

Lublwbb left, closing the door behind him.

Hubblrrrp sloshed over to his moist spot and curled up to rest, but his thoughts were roiling.

Throrb had no brains per se; there were a series of nerve concentrations throughout the body, interconnected by a complex dendritic tree—or dendritic forest, in this case—distributing mental activity throughout the whole body. Obviously such thoughts were totally dissimilar to human thoughts, but Hubblrrrp thought of his egg sacs and his mate with a worry equivalent to that of a human for a spouse and children.

Throrb did not marry, and their social relations were more formal than in human civilization. There were no friendships; Throrb tended to be solitary creatures. But they had the instinct to procreate—and the intellectual knowledge that they had to procreate to continue the species. They did not mate, but the females laid eggs. When males found unfertilized eggs, they took great physical pleasure in fertilizing them. When the eggs hatched, the Throrblings were biologically mature enough to take care of themselves, but in reality, the machinations of an advanced civilization did not allow that to happen; once the eggs were fertilized, the female who laid the eggs and the male who fertilized them worked cooperatively to ensure the eggs were protected, and that the Throrblings were then cared for and properly educated.

Hubblrrrp cared for his Throrblings, and the female who, roughly translated, was his "mate," with the passion and dedication of a husband and father—though the emotions he felt toward them were more akin to those of an avid collector of books for his collection. A sufficiently driven collector might be inclined to put his life on the line to save such a collection from a burning house.

Hubblrrrp's emotions were like that—though stronger. But those emotions could not be properly described as "love," for he had no particular desire to be with his mate or children, nor did he enjoy their company when he was with them. He was driven, by instinct and culture, to see that they were cared for; they were the most important things in his life.

Throrb worked together to build, had done so since their beginnings as simple creatures erecting mud huts. Their complex nerve pathways had originally been designed for the intricate, and totally instinctive, construction of the mud huts around the lakes and rivers of the southeastern continent of Belj. But as those rivers dried up, and they moved to the savannahs, their nerve pathways transformed into avenues for the transmission of thoughts. Their dexterous pseudopods could manipulate rocks and sticks, and gradually they learned to do so in order to build new structures, and they employed their developing minds to design structures optimal for their life form.

It was a long, slow process taking many generations, and as always happened, resulted in schisms into multiple new species. To a casual human observer, modern Throrb looked much like their primitive ancestors—much more than humans looked like apes. But a biologist would have quickly identified myriad differences—primarily in the intricacy of the neural pathways, and in the functions of the pseudopods.

In some ways, Throrb thoughts were simpler than humans: they were concerned with present activities and how they contributed to future goals. There was very little Throrb philosophy or art, and no music. The art and philosophy was, by human standards, extremely simplistic and repetitive. But Throrb mathematical ability, and the ability to instantly grasp complex scientific concepts, was far ahead of human capacity.

Among his kind, Hubblrrrb was of average intelligence; unimaginative, but able to absorb and process large amounts of data. He had been hatched in Aghlblp, a plateau in the south of Nrrp, the equatorial continent in Belj's Western Hemisphere. Throrb did not have towns or cities, not being communal or social animals, so he had lived his first seven years before seeing another Throrb aside from his parents.

The words "mother" and "father" are not accurate descriptions of the Throrb relationships, but the Throrb words have no equivalents in any human language, so "mother" and "father" will have to do. His father was a software engineer, his mother a construction forewoman—or fore-Throrb. Hubblrrrp was the firstborn of this relationship, though his father also fertilized eggs of several other females, and so Hubblrrrp had twelve half-siblings elsewhere on the plateau. He met one once, Libblgrlop. He neither liked her nor disliked her; she simply existed. And there was no need for him to communicate with her, so they mutually ignored each other's existence.

During his education—a one-on-one tutelage with Instructor Felbbligrlb—Hubblrrrp got to examine the body of a Bala who had been exposed to vacuum and died in space. Hubblrrrp was intrigued by the alien body and its strange otherworldly organs; from then on he was fascinated with alien biology, and when it came time to select his primary career training, he chose exobiology.

But when Belj broke away from the Community and formed the Alternative Alliance, he decided he wanted to serve his government. He entered the Throrb military, and his instructors quickly determined that his knowledge of exobiology gave him the unique skills to be an interrogator. He accepted their judgment. He wished to work with alien biology and serve his government, and this was the best way to do it.

His first assignment, however, was interrogating a Throrb, Flubladd, who was accused of killing a superior officer. Hubblrrrp probed Flubadd's mind with a device he had invented himself, managing to extract the truth: Flubadd was innocent, but was also covering for a colleague who had committed the crime.

Throrb did not have friendships in the human sense, but there was a sense of cooperation and mutual trust in the ranks of the military, and for a variety of reasons, Flubadd and Hornblild had formed a bond analogous to friendship.

Flubadd was disciplined for the coverup, and Hornblild was delivered to Hubblrrrp for further interrogation.

The experience left Hubblrrrp shaken. Another emotion common to most complex life was guilt, and he wasn't sure he could go on torturing fellow sentient beings. It was a crisis for him—but a crisis which resolved itself as he was assigned from one interrogation to another. Gradually torture became merely a part of his job.

He learned to separate what he did for a living from his sense of who he was as an individual.

At home, he lived in a cave South Lebrrk, near the shores of the Gonglrrrg Ocean, with his mate, Neebliss, and his children, Grongig, Lorbplip, and of course his firstborn, Hubblrrrp, and at home he never spoke of work. Work was work, home was home. And although the emotions of love and friendship were alien to Throrb, the emotions he felt for his family were as intense to him as a human's feelings of love would be, even though humans could not understand exactly what those feelings were.

His work was important to him because it served the cause, it gave him a sense of purpose in life, and it advanced his career. But his family, especially his children, was his top priority. His thoughts were consumed with how best to train and educate his children and set them on a prosperous career path. And everything he did in his own career, all the atrocities he committed in the name of the Alternative Alliance, were ultimately directed toward the goal of securing a future for his children.

Not because he "loved" them, but because their success represented his own success, furnished him with a satisfaction with his life, a feeling that he had not lived in vain, and that his legacy would continue the civilization of the Throrb.

And so to lose his family was to lose everything.

He didn't know how long he rested in the corner; he had the sense that he had been dormant for a long time (Throrb didn't sleep, but the state of restful semi-consciousness served a similar function). He was brought to consciousness by the insistent buzzing of the doorchime.

"Yes," he called.

Lublwbb entered. "Excuse me for disturbing your rest, Hubblrrrp, but I have information that you would want to know of."

Pseudopods extended in interest. "Yes?"

"We have still failed to make any contact with anyone off of Strydia, but we did manage to break through the interstellar interference and pick up the Prime Steaditone."

Relief washed over Hubblrrrp. The Prime Steaditone was an interstellar transmission emanating from Melnrrd Command Headquarters, the military command center at the primary spaceport on Belj. It was no more than a continuous beep, a beacon informing the military that the government on Belj was functioning. The beep was maintained by a Throrb on duty; every half hour it had to be manually reset.

So the fact that the beep was being detected meant, if nothing else, that Belj was still there.

"If we're receiving the Steaditone, why can't we establish further communication?" Hubblrrrp asked rhetorically; he knew that Lublwbb could no more answer the question than he could.

"I don't know, but my people are still trying to get through. It could be that all uncoded communications are still shut down because of the war, and there may be no coded communications because..." Lublwbb trailed off.

"Because there's no one left out there," Hubblrrrp finished the thought.

After a pause, Lublwbb said, "Yes. But the good news is, whatever the state of the military,

Belj is still there, and that means your family is still there. And mine."

"Unless the Community has landed there and occupied. It could be a Valdor at the command post refreshing the Steaditone."

"Well...it's possible. But even if so, there's no reason to think *your* family would have been hunted down and killed. Why would they do that? How would they even find them?"

"Punishment for my wartime atrocities?"

Lublwbb was silent a moment, then said, "Maybe. But I doubt many in the Community have even heard of you. *If* they wish to hunt down and exterminate the families of what they consider war criminals, they'll be going after the families of generals, of the captains of warships, of..." After a moment, he said, "...prison wardens."

"And interrogators. Why are you lying to me? You know those like you and me will be their prime targets."

Another long pause. Then Lublwbb said, "I'm not lying to you. I'm lying to myself. I don't want to think it. But I am *not* lying when I say it's against the Community Statement of Principles to punish criminals' families."

Hubblrrrp retracted his feelers, pondered the thought. Then he asked, "Do *you* think that you and I are criminals?"

"No! We are acting under the orders of our government. If the Alternative Alliance loses the war and establishes a new government over us, then we may be considered criminals, but I will protest that we cannot be declared criminals after-the-fact. At the time the alleged 'crimes' were committed, they were *not* crimes."

"No one will accept such an argument."

Lublwbb hesitated, then asked, "So what do you intend to do?"

"I intend to continue listening for any further information, and in the meantime, I intend to show no quarter, no mercy, to the prisoners. And if I learn that my family has been killed, then I vow that *all* the Community prisoners will be cast into the Lake of Fire!"

CHAPTER 25

Wreckage tumbled in great clouds, glinting and scintillating in the dim sunlight. Bits and pieces of spacecraft, tiny crystals of expelled atmosphere, and chunks of asteroidal debris formed a ring in the cold wastes of the Supay system, tracing the orbit of a battle that would one day be forgotten in the mists of time, its participants footnotes in the history books, their cause meaningless.

The spiral arm was now littered with such graveyards, the tumbling remnants of ships of war, of pilots, of worlds, of civilizations that were now shattered.

Among the chunks of floating flotsam in this corner of the galaxy was a large, angular object, an object which, though dark and powerless and heavily damaged, was relatively intact. It was the Space Star *Silver Streak*.

Red emergency lights flickered on the bridge. The sound of "agh, goddamn," was punctuated by another bout of coughing, as Jack Hasta scrambled into his seat. The ship's artificial gravity had shifted with the tumble, since it was aligned with the galactic plane of the ecliptic. It reoriented as the ship rolled beyond forty degrees, resulting in lots of shattered nerves (as well as shattered plates and glasses) and nausea, but the ship still maintained a one-gee environment, since there was a relativistic time delay in the power system thanks to the use of a controlled black hole in the engine room.

Jack jabbed at some buttons on the engineering console, and the overhead OLED faded into life.

The bridge was filled with smoke, but a quick diagnostic showed that there was no fire.

"Are you all right?" Stargazer asked.

"Alive. You?"

"Same. Damage report?"

Jack had just brought up a chart of the *Silver Streak* on the engineering console's realscreen. Damage control stations were still evaluating the extent of the damage, but the computer had already compiled a preliminary report. "My God...severe damage to Carrier Bay. HD4-34 Interlock and connecting magnetocutor modules overloaded and destructed. Hull breaches in civilian sections twelve, four, two, and the Town Center, and in upper engine room forward of the main shield."

Stargazer absorbed the damage report even as he tried to ping the Carrier. He fit an earpiece in his ear, coughed, and said, "Carrier, what is your damage?"

He was more relieved that he cared to think about when the voice of the Carrier commander replied at once. "*Silver Streak*, Carrier. Loss of maneuvering power. All port launch tubes disabled. Fire in the aft port computer room. We managed to launch one squadron—all lost."

"Understood; stand by." Stargazer was overwhelmed by the scale of the crisis, at a loss what to do, but right now all he could do was assimilate the information and take the situation bit by bit.

Jack was now at the helm, and he got the main screen active. But it was not the visual that arrested his attention; it was the sensor screen. "Philippe...it's gone. Star World is gone."

Stargazer looked up at the screen. He could see thousands, millions of bits of debris out there, glinting and sparkling in the light of Supay—but no sign of the huge artificial world. He had feared the worst, but to have it confirmed... *"Mon dieu..."* He tried to swallow the sob that came with the phrase, but failed.

The good news...if there was any...was that the battle was over. As far as Stargazer could tell, so was the war. Community Intelligence had gone dead, there were no transmissions from Station Post One or Klym Valdor or any other Community world.

"Get down to the engine room and evaluate the damage."

"Goddamn."

Jack tapped his console for a few seconds, then left the bridge. Stargazer heard nothing from him for the next half hour; there was a lot to do down there.

Stargazer again instructed the Carrier to stand by; it would take a while to bring the *Silver Streak* back to life, and work proceeded aboard both ships for several hours.

Emergency doors had worked as planned, isolating hulled sections, but it was as yet unclear how many people had been trapped in those areas. No matter what, the loss of life on this day would be staggering. At least two hundred people had been in Star World when it had gone up, plus the pilots in the lost squadron.

Adding to the total loss of life were the those on the enemy side. All of those fighting for the Alternative Alliance had been killed, and though few aboard the *Silver Streak* would grieve for them, Stargazer, as a scientist, was appalled at the senseless loss of life. He wondered about the naked starship that had obviously rammed Star World—had there been a crew on board or had it been flying on automatic? He doubted now that he would ever know. For all he knew, the *Silver Streak* was the last abode of life in the galaxy.

Jack returned to the bridge, now wearing orange engineering overalls and covered with grease.

"When can we get under way?" Stargazer asked.

Jack thunked down at the helm with a grunt. "When hell freezes over. We blew the recombiners. Plasmium is leaking everywhere."

"So estimate repair time."

"Try to comprehend this, Stringbean..." Jack growled, then punched his console. "All right... goddamn, assuming nothing *else* goes wrong, gimme twenty-four hours to contain the plasmium. But after that, goddamn, I don't know if I can ever get her moving again."

Stargazer turned away from his friend, his cheeks burning. He felt an ache in his chest, a deep pain in the knowledge that he had commanded perhaps the *Silver Streak*'s last mission. If Captain Cameron was still alive out there, and if he ever returned...*how do I explain this to him? This ship meant everything to him.*

One thing at a time, he commanded himself. He opened the line to the Carrier. "Carrier, this is Star-gah-zay. Are you able to return to the ship?"

The commander's voice answered, "Affirmative. Backup maneuvering pods kicked in, but we're down to twenty percent power."

"It will have to do. Return to the bay."

Jack said, "We don't have enough power flow to the umbilicals."

"Never mind that, let's just get put back together."

"Goddamn."

The voice sounded again in Stargazer's ear. "Bridge, Carrier Commander. We're on backup maneuvering."

Jack had arrested the *Silver Streak*'s slow tumble using the slip pods; the tumble had put a lot of strain on the immense ship's structure, but the tensile central brace and the expansion joints had held the ship together. Now he held the ship steady, her belly facing the remains of Star World, the bay doors open.

The interior of the bay was dark, so the Carrier had to rely on instrumentation only.

"Primary alignment on internal," the Carrier said, "we have negative MA alignment."

"Marked, CC," Stargazer said with a twinge of guilt: "MA" was "mothership assist." Usually the *Silver Streak* would be providing an alignment beacon and computer assistance...but right now this was impossible. "Unable to provide MA," Stargazer confirmed.

"Marked."

Jack watched his ranging, his large forehead wet with sweat.

Bang! The Carrier slammed into its receptacle, shuddering the whole ship. There was a series of snaps like gunshots, muffled by the structure of the ship, and finally a click.

"We show hard dock," the Carrier Commander said.

"Goddamn," Jack said, "I'm amazed they could hard dock."

"Can we close the Carrier Bay Doors?" Stargazer asked.

Jack got up with a grunt and stepped over to the engineering console. "Not on primary power —goddamn, not on secondary either. Only way those goddamn doors are closing is if Control Booth has power."

Stargazer already had a line open to the Control Booth. "CBC, this is AC. Do you have control over the doors?"

"Checking."

As he waited, Stargazer said, "We cannot sit here with those doors open."

"AC, CBC," the Control Booth said.

"CBC, AC," Stargazer answered.

"We have seventy-six percent power, enough to close the doors."

"Close the doors."

"Marked."

The grinding of the door motors was louder than usual, and came with an unusual vibration. Jack punched at controls on the engineering console as he felt the vibration, calling up numbers on the torque down there, the state of the motors, and the alignment of the doors and their huge hinges.

The green light that illuminated was a welcome sight; Jack hadn't seen many green lights since the battle. "Goddamn. Doors are closed."

"*Merci*." Stargazer wiped his forehead; good news at last.

Now the ship was slowly coming back to life, the technicians and engineers were repairing the damage, the maintenance people were collecting and storing the leaking plasmium, and it seemed relatively certain that the *Silver Streak* was not going to blow up. So although the crisis was by no means over, there was a little time to reconnoiter.

"I presume you realize this was a trap," Jack said. "The Throrb attacked Star World in useless goddamn fighters to draw us in—then *whacked* it with a naked starship to take out Star World *and* us."

"And it almost worked," Stargazer agreed.

"Not sure about the 'almost' part," Jack grumbled. Then, aloud, "So now what?"

Stargazer fell silent. What *could* they do now? Was anyone out there to help? *Would we wish to condone a full reprisal for this attack?* Where would this stop?

"Let us just focus right now on getting the ship operational. Meanwhile, I will see if Station Post One or the Valdor are still out there."

———

Jack went back to work in the engine room while Stargazer started broadcasting to anyone who might be out there. He reminded himself that until the past year, there had been no one else—

no one but the *Silver Streak*'s colonies. For twenty-two years the *Silver Streak* had been on its own, tackling the immensity of the galaxy with no help from the Valdor or the Community, no Star World, nothing.

It was reassuring that the damage was not as bad as he first thought. Star World had served as an excellent shield—even though the price was over two hundred deaths. The thousands on board the *Silver Streak* had survived. The Carrier was intact despite the loss of an entire squadron. The slip pods were working, the plasmium was contained, and it looked like they had at least some power on the fusion drive. The only question now was—could they still make light speed?

Then Stargazer received some very good news: Station Post One had survived! He was receiving the steady beacon, which had been masked before by the intermittent power drops.

"Station Post One, this is Space Star *Silver Streak*."

"*Silver Streak*, this is Station Post One," a voice answered, "executive officer Tobey Dingell speaking. It's good to hear from you! We'd given you up for dead."

"Almost. Star World is destroyed and we are badly damaged. Trying to get the ship put back together. Is there any word on Captain Cameron and Frank Johnson?"

"We tracked them to Strydia, but it looks like they were intercepted. No news is coming out of the Alternative Alliance, but we're assuming they're prisoners there."

"*Oui*...and you? How are things there?"

"Well, we're still here, which is more than I can say about a lot of other Community worlds. Looks like Klym Valdor took a big hit, but it's not clear how bad. Might be completely destroyed, might just be badly crippled. All we've got is our telescopes, radar, and thermar, and right now there's too much debris to tell for sure what's left of Klym Valdor. We've got intermittent communication with Community Intelligence, enough to give us preliminary estimates on how many worlds have been destroyed, and it's fucking horrifying."

"What about Strydia?"

"Well, it sounds like the Alliance is busy fighting the war. There's no news on Strydia, although it's kind of nice to think it's pretty much undefended. Maybe we can slip a ship in and rescue the prisoners, but we're pretty bogged down right now, we don't have the means to pull that off, and there's still no communication with Klym Valdor—if it's still there."

Stargazer sighed. "Very well. *Merci*. I will be in touch."

The intercom chirped. "Star-gah-zay here."

"Yeah, this is Jack. She's up to thirty-seven percent power. Goddamn, don't ask for too much."

"No promises," Stargazer said.

The question was, even if power was fully restored...what now? A trip into the Alternative Alliance would be suicide, a raid on Strydia insane. Was the war in progress or was it over? Were there any governments left to negotiate an end to hostilities?

Then he remembered: Mordrax.

During the trip to Station Post One, Captain Cameron had mentioned that Mordrax came to him, offered to help to extricate Ambassador Koff, swore that such operations were his specialty.

"Am I really desperate enough to go to Mordrax?" he asked aloud; and even as he voiced the thought, he knew the answer.

Yes.

———

A breakthrough at last! Hubblrrrp had made voice contact via digital photon radio with the Thrrblrropp Weather Station in polar orbit over Belj.

"What's going on there?" he asked. "Is the planet intact?"

"Intact, yes," said the station commander, "but fell under heavy attack by Community forces. A combined attack force of Valerians, Screamers, and Koven attacked the orbital defense stations, and then an invasion force of Mistizi rushed in and began occupying military bases that survived the orbital assault."

"Can you relay me to a communications station on the surface?"

"If it's still there."

"Good. Get me RD2-132-A72-474-50250."

Hubblrrrp waited, his pulses pounding. Finally a voice answered, "Klrrrplripp."

"This is Hubblrrrp Lrropdrillipplloglighuppl. Can you relay me to 16-FR-JRH-D?"

"We have a great deal of traffic, many trying to reach family—"

"I am a highly placed military officer, you *Orblipp!* Do as I say or I'll see you in Strydia Prison!"

"Yes, at once."

More anxious waiting. There were audible clicks in the transmission; that could mean interference, it could be code signals being intercepted, it could be the house decoder flashing its pollback.

Finally he heard the familiar voice of Neebliss. "Who's there?"

"Neebliss! This is Hubblrrrp!"

"Hubblrrrp! Where are you?! Where have you been?"

"I'm—I shouldn't tell you. Someone might be listening in. Are you all right?"

"Yes, but the Mistizi have taken over. There's a creature who calls herself the Overlord who's confiscating property and goods."

"What about Grongig, Lorbplip, and Hubblrrrp?"

A long pause. "Grongig went to try to fight off the Mistizi—they killed him."

Hubblrrrp felt a clenching in his gut. "And the others?"

"Lorbplip is here. He stayed to take care of me. Hubblrrrp enlisted in the military months ago—he went off to war. I've heard nothing from him since the war broke out. I don't know."

Hubblrrrp let out an involuntary trill. In that moment he *knew* his firstborn was dead.

"Hubblrrrp?" Neebliss said frantically. "Hubblrrrp, are you still there?"

"Yes," he managed to gurgle. "Yes...it will be all right, Neebliss—I'll be home soon. Be safe."

He cut off the transmission—and immediately regretted it. It was a fluke of luck that he had been able to reach the Weather Station; he might not get through again, and he wished he could have spoken to Lorbplip. But he was losing control of himself, reduced to a quivering mass of emotional impulses. He didn't want Neebliss to hear him like this.

But he knew one thing: Ambassador Koff, Argo, Frank Johnson, Richard Cameron, and that traitor Splrrrb would feel his wrath. They would pay the price for his children's deaths.

CHAPTER 26

Jack Hasta was less than enthusiastic when Stargazer proposed his plan.

"Are you out of your goddamn French mind, you goddamn baguette-eating bicycle-riding goddamn French lunatic?"

"In order to pull off an impossible mission, we need to try the impossible."

"*Mordrax* to *rescue* Dick?! Do I even have to Goddamn say it? The psychotic Hyron commander who's devoted his *entire goddamn life* to trying to hunt down and kill Dick is your first choice to try to *rescue* him?!"

"I don't know where else to turn."

"*I* do! Our own goddamn people! We've got Star Force Marines, real tough jokers—we've got Magnutels, who survived generations in space—"

"We no longer have Magnutels, they all transferred over to Station Post One. And in order to deploy Marines, we would have to launch the Carrier, and I do not believe that either the Carrier or the Carrier Bay are in any condition for that— and even *you* cannot make sufficient repairs in the time it will take to reach Strydia. And any delay could mean Dick and Frank's death."

"They may already be dead, Philippo."

"I am very well aware of that. We could launch Marines in shuttles, but do you really think slow-moving, unmaneuverable shuttles could get through a prison planet's defenses? Anyway, is it not better to risk Mordrax's life than our own people's?"

"Well, yeah, but I still say the first thing he'll do on seeing Dick will be to gun him down!"

"Dick has handled him before." Stargazer got up, brushed off his dusty uniform. "You are in command while I go talk to Mordrax."

Jack threw his hands in the air. "Why in the goddamn hell Dick left *you* in command..."

Stargazer left the bridge, knowing he could trust Jack to run the ship. Despite the constant sparring and bickering, he knew Jack wasn't really angry with him. Their constant verbal dueling was a game, a manly gesture of affection. It was clear that Jack really did disagree with his idea, but he also knew he could count on Jack's support—even if he would have to put up with lots of insults and snarky comments.

His thoughts wandered as he headed for the security section; he had to admit Jack had a point, and he wondered if it would be a better idea to deploy Marines, perhaps in one of the X-1000s. Or perhaps a Marine Assault Craft could be hoisted from the Carrier to the landing bay and deployed through one of the launch tubes...no. Impossible. No way to do it, certainly not without making major modifications to the ship. Perhaps it was possible in theory, but not in the time it would take to get to Strydia, and anyway, might as well just repair the Carrier and the bay rather than do something that drastic to the ship's structure...

"I am here to see Mordrax," he told the attendant in the security section, who waved him on.

Mordrax was lying on his bunk, staring blankly at the ceiling.

Stargazer stood at he bars, hands behind his back. "*Allô*, Mordrax."

Mordrax was startled out of his reverie; evidently he had been lost in thought too. "Well. Mr. Stargazer." He got up and wandered leisurely to the bars.

"I understand you offered to help."

Mordrax smiled. "Well. You must *really* be desperate to take me up on it."

Stargazer clenched his teeth. He didn't have the verbal skills to play these sly games. "Our attempt to extract Ambassador Koff failed. Captain Cameron, Frank Johnson, Splrrrb, and Argo are now prisoners on Strydia."

"How interesting. What makes you think my offer to help still stands?"

Stargazer sighed. "You are not going to make this easy, are you?"

"No." Mordrax grinned and bounced on his heels, waiting for Stargazer's offer.

"I do not have the authority to commute your sentence, but I can take it before the Congressional Council."

"Excellent! Do so and get back to me. Oh, and by the way, I want Chok to have access to me whenever he wants to. You claim to be a free society; act like it."

"Agreed." Stargazer turned and left, wondering how he was going to sell this plan. If *Jack* had been a hard sell, President Copenburg was going to lose his bowels.

He found the President in his office at the rear of the Council Chamber. The Congress was in Session, but right now they were milling about, chatting among themselves, as usually happened when a senator was preparing to speak, and so Copenburg had evidently retired to his office to attend to communications with either constituents or someone out in the Community—assuming there was any communication.

As Stargazer entered the office and Copenburg hastily closed the window on his realscreen, Stargazer realized it was porn.

"*Excusez-moi, Monsieur le Président.*"

"Yes," Copenburg said without looking up from his realscreen.

"I must speak with you. It is very important."

Copenburg sat back. "Well, I guess this can wait. I can't get through to anyone. The Community seems dead—and it seems *we* were almost dead."

"Almost. But we are alive and putting the ship back together."

"Well, what can I do for you?"

Stargazer explained his plan, trying not to see the expression of wide-eyed disbelief on the President's face.

When Stargazer had finished, Copenburg rose from his desk and, his voice slowly rising in pitch, said, "Star World is destroyed! All our work for the past year up in smoke! The Community and the Alternative Alliance wiping each other out and taking the galaxy with them, and you want to take the *Silver Streak* into that inferno? Have you lost what was left of your mind?"

Stargazer could not recall ever seeing Copenburg so emotional. He was cowed by the President's anger. Softly, he said, "Mordrax swears that this kind of operation is his specialty."

"Mordrax! On top of everything else, you want to turn to *Mordrax* to pull this off!" Copenburg sagged into his seat. "God, I can believe this is the end of the universe. I've never seen such insanity."

"I agree with you. It is crazy. But this is not mere sentimentality for Captain Cameron and Frank. Splrrrb, Koff, and Argo are extremely valuable to both sides."

"I know they are, but we have to consider the safety of the *Silver Streak* above all else."

Stargazer leaned against the desk. "*Oui*—but *écoutez*, Community Intelligence tells us that Strydia is unprotected because of the war."

"Community Intelligence," Copenburg scoffed. "How do you know Community Intelligence hasn't been compromised?"

Ignoring the President's paranoia, Stargazer continued, "Mordrax has offered to help in exchange for having his sentence commuted. Now, how about it?"

Copenburg's eyes flashed, he opened his mouth to say something, then fell silent. Finally he huffed. "Step outside while the Council votes."

Stargazer silently obeyed.

As he waited in the corridor, he understood why Captain Cameron always became so flustered when dealing with the President. It was a different world, the world of politics—a world Stargazer didn't understand. He was used to dealing with science and scientists—scientists who accepted reality rather than trying to redefine reality to suit their agendas. Scientists were not perfect—no human was—but with very few exceptions, Stargazer could understand and work with fellow scientists. These politicians might as well have dropped in from a parallel universe.

Still, in this case he understood Copenburg's concern: taking the *Silver Streak* into enemy space and entrusting the enemy Mordrax with a critical mission *was* a pretty stupid plan, and anyone could see it was a mark of desperation. But it was also something no one would be expecting.

Stargazer waited. And waited. And waited. The Council deliberated for what seemed like hours, and he considered poking his head in and asking how much longer, but found to his chagrin that he was too timid. He communicated via intercom with Jack, in order to continue coordinating repairs, but most of the time he leaned against the wall, sat on the floor, paced back and forth, and muttered to himself.

Finally he was ready to give up and go to the bridge; the President could call for him when he was needed. Just as he started to step down the hall, the door opened and Copenburg emerged. "Stargazer."

"*Oui.*"

Copenburg offered no apology or explanation for the long wait. "You win. The Council voted against me."

Stargazer felt no triumph; he wasn't at all sure this was the best option. Nevertheless, he held firm. "It is for the best. We cannot ignore what is happening."

"It's *because* of what's happening that I wanted to stay out of it. But your argument that the war has cut Strydia off from the Alternative Alliance persuaded the Council. I just hope Intelligence is accurate."

'Intelligence' has nothing to do with what's going on, Stargazer thought. But all he said was, "You know we act for the best."

———

Jack was once again in the engine room; he had been running back and forth from the bridge to the engine room all day. Stargazer had left him in command, but he had too much to do to sit on the bridge, so while Stargazer hung out in the Council Chamber, Jack called Dr. Strickland to the bridge to keep an eye on things, and thus attended to the numerous duties that called for his attention.

The *Silver Streak*'s primary power came from the fusion reactors, and Jack once again cursed the Clanton Corporation for convincing the Oversight Committee that plasmium fusion was the most efficient power source. Plasmium was superheavy, difficult to store, and inefficient. The fact that it could be easily fused into enervium, which then decayed back into plasmium, had fooled the politicians into thinking it was therefore an inexhaustible fuel supply, but what the Clanton Brothers had failed to mention was the amount of fuel lost in the process.

But there were, he had to admit, advantages. The room-temperature supercollider, which collided massive particles at near light speed in order to produce a tiny black hole, produced plasmium as an incidental by-product, and that nicely fit into the *Silver Streak*'s pretensions of being self-sufficient (despite Jack's well-guarded view that there was no such thing as a truly self-sufficient spacecraft; the very concept violated thermodynamics).

The miniature black hole, stored in a magnetic bottle, was the center of the Gravity Propulsion System, which not only allowed the ship to travel much faster than light, but also provided the onboard artificial gravity and the nodes which were used for maneuvering.

Years ago, as a personal project, Jack had invented the General Generating Platform to supplement the main power supply. It was a success, and now GGPs were used in all spacecraft—and a good thing too; he could never have hammered the *Silver Streak* back together without it. An autonomous device which stored and distributed energy for as long as the mini black hole existed, the GGP was similar to the artificial gravity nodes of the shuttlecraft, which depended on the slow decay of energy from the Gravity Propulsion System to maintain their internal gravity when off the ship and separated from the mini black hole.

It worked for a variety of interconnected reasons—the Hemmel/Reingleib Effect, Morav's Theory of Quantized Inertia, the Puthoff Lorentz Interaction, the Moffat Effect. Even Jack, who had designed it, understood the principle only as a series of equations; expressing it as a real-world phenomenon would be impossible for him.

Jack bent over his workbench, where he had hooked up a dizzying array of tiny electronic connectors. "Goddamn. Set the goddamn GGP to distribute to the portside interface."

"What ratio to the guide feed?" asked Engineer Cornmesser.

"Make it three to two."

"Yes, sir."

Jack held his breath as the power fluctuated. Numbers on the softscreen above him ticked up, then down, then up again. He looked down at the fragile webwork of wires, each of which contained chains of molecules thinner than his hairline. Finally he let out his breath. "It *is* holding."

Cornmesser nodded. "Just above the red line."

Jack shook his head. "Goddamn. What a way to run a starship."

———

Stargazer stopped by the coordination center to get a more complete feel for the ship's total damage and the status of the various repair efforts, then went to the bridge. He found that, for the moment, he had nothing to do. He sagged into his chair at the science station and almost immediately felt himself dropping off to sleep.

He jerked awake at the sound of the intercom chirping. He shook himself awake, blinked heavily, and hit the receive tab.

"Engineering to bridge," Jack's voice boomed. "You up there, Dipbrain?"

"Actually, to be more precise, it is pronounced Deep-Braaa. You see, I come from the country of France, which speaks a different language than—"

"Shut up, Stargazer."

Stargazer smiled; he needed the momentary break in the tension.

"We're up to seventy percent power," Jack said. "We're borderline on internal goddamn systems, but we can make light speed."

"What about combat?"

"*Not* goddamn recommended!"

"Well, we will make further repairs en route. Get up here."

"Goddamn."

Stargazer switched the intercom channel to the security office. "Security, this is the bridge."

Immediately a powerful voice replied, "Security, Meeker here."

Well, time to go ahead and do it. He took a deep breath and said, "Please bring Mordrax to the bridge."

CHAPTER 27

Free!

It had been so long since Mordrax had been out of his cramped cell that even the bland corridors of the *Silver Streak* were as beautiful as Resolute back home. How long had it been since he had been able to stretch his legs, to see anything other than the same four walls, the bars, the bunk, the four recessed lights in the ceiling? Almost two megatolax—over a year, in human terminology.

The big guy, Meeker, didn't let him out of his sight, but at least he wasn't gripping his arm anymore.

"Where are we going?" Mordrax asked.

"Mr. Stargazer wants to see you on the bridge."

"So he has accepted my terms?"

"I only know that he ordered me to bring you to the bridge."

"In that case, I want to have Chok with me."

"I was ordered to bring *you* to the bridge, not Chok."

"Yes, well, if I'm going to help break into Strydia, I want my most trusted aide with me."

Meeker stopped and laughed. "Your most trusted aide? *That* buffoon?"

Mordrax didn't find it funny. He had become defensive of Chok in the past few years. "Why not call the bridge and ask for permission to bring Chok? Would that cost you anything?"

Still chuckling, Meeker went to a wall intercom and, cupping a hand over it so Mordrax couldn't see, keyed in a code.

"Bridge, Star-gah-zay here," the voice of the mustachioed science officer replied.

"This is Meeker. Mordrax is asking to bring his friend Chok to the bridge. Is that all right?"

The voice answered something that sounded like "Wee-wee." As nonsensical as that was to Mordrax, Meeker seemed satisfied.

"All right, Mordrax, let's go get your little doofus."

Mordrax followed Meeker through a maze of winding corridors, all of which looked the same to him; he thought he had intuited a general sense of the way the *Silver Streak* was laid out, but he had entirely lost his sense of direction by the time they reached Chok's quarters. He guessed that Meeker had deliberately chosen a roundabout route in order to confuse him.

Meeker rang the doorchime three times, and there was no answer.

"Keep trying," Mordrax said. "He might not have heard it. Or he might not understand what it means."

"I'm not wasting any more time. Call through the door."

Mordrax grimaced, stepped up to the door, and knocked. "Chok? It's Mordrax! If you're in there, I want to see you!"

A sound of something falling and clattering on the floor came muffled through the door. Then the door slid aside, and Chok stood before him, his hair mussed and his clothes—human civilian clothes—wrinkled and covered with food stains. "Duh, Mordrax! Are you really here?"

"Yes, Chok. I've been asked to go to the bridge."

"Duh! Can I come?"

"That's why I'm here. Come on."

Chok trotted alongside him like a faithful bendig. "Duh, why did they let you out of the, duh, why did they let you out of the, duh, why did they let you out of the, duh, brig?"

"I presume because they want my help in rescuing Cameron and Johnson from Strydia."

"Oh. Duh, who's Strydia?"

"Strydia is the name of a prison planet in the Alternative Alliance."

"Oh. Duh, who's that?"

"Bad guys."

"Duh, oh."

Meeker snickered; Mordrax wanted to punch him.

As they continued on their way toward the bridge, Chok asked, "Duh, so I can come with you?"

"Yes, Chok," Mordrax said.

"Duh, we're still friends?"

"Yes, Chok."

"Duh, we'll always be together?"

"That does seem to be my lot in life."

After a moment's pause, Chok spoke again with just a hint of lucidity. "Duh, sorry I'm so annoying, Mordrax. Duh, I used to be a, duh, I used to be a, duh, I used to be a great Hyron commander."

Mordrax stopped, turned, and put a hand on Chok's shoulder. "I know you did, Chok. I originally took you as my first officer because my father asked me to, as a favor to your family. But over the years I've come to value you. I really have. You may not be the ideal Hyron, but I know I can always count on you."

"Duh, what were we talking about, Mordrax?"

"Nothing. Come on, let's go."

Meeker led them up a flight of stairs to the command level. From there it was a short walk to the bridge.

———

Philippe Stargazer sat at the science station, Jack Hasta at the helm. Chok sat in the command chair playing with a finger puzzle Jack had given him.

Stargazer had compiled everything known about Strydia and printed it up for Mordrax. Unfortunately, the only Hyron language in the *Silver Streak*'s computer banks was Pakish, which was not Mordrax's first language. At least it wasn't in the almost impenetrable human language with its mutable laws of grammar and bizarre sentence structure; English was hard enough to speak, let alone to read. So he struggled through the Pakish text while Chok annoyed Jack with the puzzle.

It took fifteen minutes for Mordrax to come up with a plan. Strydia was an interesting place, not quite like any world he had visited before, but there was nothing really extraordinary about it. It was just another prison planet. There was no prison that couldn't be infiltrated, none that was truly escape-proof.

The main screen showed a graphic of Strydia, as extracted from Community Intelligence. Mordrax stood before the console and projected his voice as if presenting a strategy in the conference room of his own ship.

"This is Strydia," he said needlessly. "A strategically sound location under normal circumstances, but with the Alternative Alliance in chaos, it is unprotected."

"Well, you tend to get overconfident, Mordrax," Jack Hasta said.

"Not in extraction missions. The point is backup."

"Well, we *are* the backup. This was Dick's mission."

"Yes, and not surprising that he failed. Do you have sectiss bugs?"

Jack felt his hair. "Huh? What's that? A disease?"

"I have heard of sectiss bugs," Stargazer said. "Tiny robots launched by a ballistic probe. When the probe explodes, the sectiss bugs burrow into the ground and dig tunnels or search for something, things like that."

"Exactly," Mordrax said, though Stargazer's description was far from exact. "Sectiss bugs have transponders in them for exactly such missions as this. If we launch a probe of sectiss bugs at Strydia and program the bugs to reach the prison cells—"

"We can alert the prisoners that we are coming," Stargazer interrupted excitedly, "plan and organize a mass revolt!"

"Exactly, and time it to coincide with our diversionary attack."

"Diversionary attack?" Jack asked.

"Yes. As I said, the key is backup. We send a team in to attack the main prison, while at the same time, I discretely land at the probe site, enter through one of the tunnels made by the sectiss bugs, and rescue the prisoners."

"Brilliant," Jack said dryly, "except that the surface of the entire goddamn planet is molten lava. How do you plan to drill a tunnel through molten goddamn lava?"

"Not necessary. The prison tower is almost a kilozon across, and the lower portions have no security surveillance on the outside because of the lava tides. I'll be able to hover my shuttlecraft and attach an airlock to one of the tunnels bored into the tower. The diversionary attack should be widespread enough to allow me to slip under their radar from the night side."

"Okay, allowing that that might goddamn work, there's one other goddamn problem: we don't have sectiss bugs!"

"We might be able to make some," Stargazer said.

"Stargazer?" Jack exclaimed, startled at the suggestion.

"We have mini fusion moles for sensitive foundation construction. It would be a simple matter to attach voice transponders—if Jack helps me."

"Goddamn, what kind of a thing is that to say? I always goddamn help you!"

"How long will it take?" Mordrax asked.

"Tedious goddamn assembly line work. Could take a few goddamn hours, could take a few goddamn days."

"Are we repaired enough to travel at light speed?" Stargazer asked.

"Yeah, though I wouldn't want to strain her too much. Might want to activate the relief abort. That'll mean a longer trip and more course adjustments each time we break from light speed, but it's the best I can goddamn give you right now."

"All right, let's get right to work. Go down and set up the relief abort. I will set the course."

"Course is already goddamn set. You start rounding up those mini goddamn fusion moles."

"Of course. Mordrax, please go with Monsieur Meeker. He will take you to our armory. See what you will need."

Mordrax bowed his head and said humbly, "Thank you for trusting me."

––––––

The tedious assembly line work began.

Theoretically the work could be done by robots, but there were two reasons that Jack and Stargazer did it by hand: one, the *Silver Streak* was so broken that they didn't trust the computers to handle delicate work; and two, they wanted to test each and every fusion mole—or sectiss bug.

After a while, attaching the transponders became routine and automatic, so that they worked in rhythm, Jack chanting "Boring," and Stargazer replying "Tedious."

And so the workroom next to Jack's office in the engineering section sounded like a Neo-Chi song:

Click
"Boring"
Thunk
"Tedious"
Click
"Boring"
Thunk
"Tedious"
On and on.

The relief abort was rigged, and Jack cautiously put the ship into light speed. The engines responded, the distortion envelope wrapped the ship in a hyperspace bubble, and they were on their way.

There was, of course, already a failsafe that would snap the ship out of light speed if any of the parameters went out of safety norms, but the relief abort was a special feature that had to be enabled and configured before a light speed jump. It was a special preventative failsafe that contained the complete course data and dropped the ship out of light speed at regular intervals, thus preventing any overheat in advance, and automatically replotted the course. Since Jack insisted on manually replotting the course with every relief abort, it was a time-consuming operation.

In between relief aborts, they worked on the sectiss bugs.

Click
"Boring"
Thunk
"Tedious"

Click

"Boring"

Thunk

"Tedious"

The intercom beeped.

"Star-gah-zay here."

"Bridge," came the voice of the duty officer. "Last relief abort."

"Goddamn," Jack muttered. "The time got away from me. Replot match with the goddamn stellar check?"

"Yes, sir."

"Very well," Stargazer said, "maintain flight plan, light speed factor ten."

"Yes, sir."

Jack growled; he really liked to verify the course data himself. But they were close enough to Strydia now that the margin of error was miniscule. So they went back to work.

Click

"Boring"

Thunk

"Tedious"

Click

"Boring"

Thunk

"Tedious"

And finally Stargazer said, "*Finis.*"

"*Finis* here too," Jack said. He straightened up, massaging his lower back. "Goddamn."

"You think this will do it?"

"Better."

From there the makeshift probes were sent down the dumbwaiter to the hangar deck, where they would be sealed in heat-resistant casings and affixed to ballistic missiles.

And now Strydia was on the long-range scanner, its parent star's photons impacting on the distortion envelope brighter than any other star. Although the ship was wrapped in a zone of blackness as it careened through its bubble of nonreality faster than light, the screen showed the distant star Rinkhal-A as the instrumentation converted the spacetime ripples in the distortion envelope into a simulation of visible light.

As Stargazer watched the course, he was gripped by apprehension. He had thrown this mission together, trusted their mortal enemy, hammered away at makeshift devices with his buddy in the garage, and was now filled with a sense of imperfection. There was no guidebook for the current situation, but he felt he had not done a thorough job, that he hadn't thought it through. He couldn't think of anything he had missed, but the whole operation felt haphazard, slapped together...amateurish. Was this how Captain Cameron would have handled this situation?

Well...yes. Cameron often threw together his strategies on gut feeling, whim, and incomplete information—and did so with smiling confidence, and was vindicated when his strategies worked. Was that skill or dumb luck?

Stargazer felt he would soon find out.

Jack entered the bridge. "Hey, Philippe. Techs report the goddamn conversion is done. We've got sixty goddamn sectiss bugs."

"Very well. We are almost to Strydia. I hope this works.

Jack sat at the helm, muttering to himself as he doublechecked his course, position, speed, and orientation.

Finally he brought the *Silver Streak* out of light speed.

Stargazer had seen many planets in his travels, many awe-inspiring sights. He often stared agape at the beauty—or terror—of a new world ahead.

Strydia filled him with terror.

The *Silver Streak* was approaching its dark side, so only a shining rim was visible in the blinding light of Rinkhal-A, but as the screen dimmed the sunlight and enhanced the color image of the planet, he made out the vast rivers and oceans of molten rock. He remembered standing on the lip of Mount Ngauruhoe during his military service and looking down into the lake of molten lava. His scientific curiosity had overcome his fear—but that didn't mean he hadn't been scared shitless.

The planet Strydia looked like a spherical glob of that Ngauruhoe lava, and the thought of his friends being down there in that scalding bath horrified him.

After the distortion envelope had collapsed, the *Silver Streak* had been virtually motionless. Now Strydia's gravity took hold and the ship fell faster and father toward that molten cauldron. Jack made some course corrections in order to bring the ship into a four-hundred-kilometer orbit with a twenty-two percent inclination. This would bring it over the prison in an hour—and the projectiles containing the sectiss bugs on a trajectory to impact in a little more than that.

"Orbital goddamn approach Strydia," Jack said. "Rigged for silent running."

"I hope Community Intelligence was right. Deploy sectiss bugs to secondary target."

"Deploying."

The projectiles were too small to impart any noticeable recoil on a ship as massive as the *Silver Streak*, but there was a faintly discernible puffing sound as they were deployed.

"They're on their goddamn way," Jack said.

Unnoticed, the small probes impacted Strydia's atmosphere. The flames of re-entry resembled the fireballs occasionally ejected from the more volatile areas on the fluid surface, and would scarcely have attracted notice even had they been scanned.

But although the planet was undefended, the Throrb were on guard. Their alien senses were searching the skies for any indication that their Alliance survived, that their families were alive, that their leadership was intact.

And so Hubblrrrp happened to be in the command center when one of the technicians noticed an unusual trail of ions in the sky. And Hubblrrrp suspected immediately what it was.

CHAPTER 28

Hubblrrrp knew almost nothing of the Hyron Empire, and had never heard of sectiss bugs. But small projectiles on this trajectory could only be entering from orbit. He considered the possibility that they might be satellites making an uncontrolled re-entry—but that made no sense. Most of Strydia's satellites were in synchronous orbit; there was no way they could fall out of the sky. Perhaps there were a few low orbit satellites he knew nothing of; he would check on that.

But since Strydia was presently undefended, and the Alternative Alliance at war, he immediately suspected that someone was mounting an attack or a rescue operation.

He monitored the flaming meteors as they descended. He watched as they impacted the molten surface and exploded near the prison—and observed that small objects swarmed like insects once the shells had cracked and melted into the lava.

It was hard to keep track of them; there was no instrumentation on the outside of the tower below the high lava line, so Hubblrrrp deployed a sensor bee. The small probe, hovering on hummingbird-like wings, buzzed down toward the lower levels, providing information in sound and light frequencies that flashed in rapidfire code.

He sighted several of the small objects; he could only follow one of them with the sensor bee.

The object hovered and spiraled through the air, undoubtedly on some sort of electric motor driving a small propeller. It circled the prison tower, then finally drove itself directly at the thick titanium tower. Rather than latching on and deploying explosives or sensors, as Hubblrrrp had expected, it instead began to tunnel.

As it disappeared into the side of the tower, Hubblrrrp thought, *So that's it*. If he were human, he would have smiled. Whatever these alien machines were, they were probably trying to get to the prisoners, perhaps with information for them.

And the most high-profile prisoners were Ambassador Koff and the humans from the *Silver Streak*.

His duty was clear: alert Lubblwbb in order that security guards be sent to await the rescuers. But Hubblrrrp did not do this. The deaths of his children had made this a personal battle to him. He kept thinking of Prisoner Johnson's violent reaction to the neural probe, and he wondered what had triggered that reaction. He wanted to find out. He wanted to prod the prisoner, pick at whatever raw wound existed, inflict the pain he himself felt at the loss of two of his children.

So, without telling anyone where he was or where he was going, he rode the elevator down into the depths of Hell. His body rebelled against the crushing gravity, and he knew his aging aortic clusters couldn't handle it much longer; he needed to get back to Belj and rest. But he didn't care. He now had to confront his enemies—or those representatives of his enemies who now symbolized to him all the nightmares of Hell.

The elevator arrived on level four thousand four, and the guard asked him what he was doing here.

"That's my concern," he said angrily. "Do you know who I am?"

"Yes, Colonel Hubblrrrp." The guard moved aside.

Hubblrrrp headed for cell 4842.

———

"Positive goddamn registry," Jack Hasta said. "They're tunneling. Secondary target coming over the goddamn horizon."

"Deploy," Stargazer ordered.

"Goddamn."

The second probe launched.

Stargazer could see the tower as it came up over the horizon; he knew where to look for it because the anchor asteroid was visible as a bright star. Beneath that star, it was as though someone had drawn a perfectly straight, yet infinitely thin, white line from the star all the way to the surface. Somewhere in that dimensionless line were Captain Cameron and Frank Johnson.

"All goddamn sectiss bugs deployed," Jack said.

Stargazer punched the intercom tab. "Mordrax, are you ready for launch?"

"We are ready," Mordrax's voice replied.

———

Far below, in the Hyron shuttlecraft, Mordrax stared down the length of the launch tube. This was the same shuttle in which he had transported to the *Silver Streak* from his Dreadnought a year ago; now it may find a permanent home down there on Strydia...Hell...Blackhaven...the world of ultimate nightmare...depending on how this risky mission turned out.

His hand gripped the hilt of his ceremonial sword; he refused to go into battle without his full Hyron regalia, and that fool Stargazer had permitted it.

"Remember your instructions, Chok," he said. "Stay close to me at all times."

"Duh, okay, Mordrax," Chok said.

———

Mordrax and Chok were not the only ones preparing to leave the ship. Stargazer had no intention of leaving the rescue entirely up to Cameron's mortal enemy and an idiot, and so he planned on personally leading the diversionary attack—and of course Jack insisted on coming along. Stargazer was no soldier, so he was glad to have his old friend with him.

Command Duty Officer Hunter arrived from Ops on schedule, and Stargazer surrendered the command chair to him.

"Ready, Jack?"

"Guess so."

"Let's go."

Leaving Hunter in command, they left the bridge—and as they did so, Stargazer wondered if they would ever be back.

———

Cameron watched in wonderment as the small devices buzzed through the vast tower.

"They resemble dardigos," Ambassador Koff said.

"And what are those?" Splrrrb asked in a bored voice.

"Huge insects that I've heard live in the Travidor Rain Forest."

"No, those are machines," Cameron said. He limped across the cell—the gravity was now causing chronic pain in his left hip, and shook Frank awake. "Frank—come on, Frank, you've got to see this."

Frank moaned. "Awww, I'd just drifted off to sleep...started to dream I was back on Earth—"

"Come on, Frank, get up."

As Cameron gripped his shoulders and pulled him to his feet, Frank whined, "What, what, what, *whaaat?*"

Cameron pointed. "Look. Look at those gizmos. Those look familiar to you?"

Frank watched them, shook his head—then suddenly his eyes widened and he looked at Cameron. "Those look like those little mini fusion moles!"

"They look like *what?*" Koff asked.

"A device we use to quickly tunnel foundations and caves for new colonies." Cameron frowned; Koff did not seem relieved or excited by the possibility of rescue; he seemed alarmed.

"Why are they flying through the air?" Argo asked.

"Looks like *somebody*—" Who? Jack Hasta and Philippe Stargazer?! "—has modified them."

"Transponders?" Frank asked.

One of the mini fusion moles hovered outside their cage. A camera pointed at them. A shutter visibly snapped shut twice, a light flashed, and the device bored through the wire mesh of the cage.

"Watch it!" Splrrrb shouted. "If it weakens this cage, we'll all plunge into the lava!"

Once through, the mole settled to the floor. Its whining electric motor slowly wound down and died away. A high-pitched electronic beeping now sounded—rhythmic, in a series of beeps and dashes.

"Code," Frank said. "Mason code, I think."

Cameron leaned down and picked up the device. "It's signaling H-H-H. That means it has data to transmit, but it requires the command code. Shit...Frank, what's the command code?"

Frank laughed. "*You're* the captain, Dick."

"Damn." Cameron scratched the side of his head, fought to remember. "D-something, I think."

"This is unbelievable," Splrrrb said. "You two are not the heroes of the galaxy; you're a pair of incompetent idiots."

Cameron shrugged. "He's figured us out, Frank. Okay...I think I remember...D-L-D." He tapped the light in sequence.

———

Jack and Stargazer were walking briskly through the halls of the *Silver Streak*. Stargazer, ostensibly in command, was trying to keep at least a pace ahead of Jack, but Jack was more energetic and had a longer stride.

Jack's transmitter beeped. He pulled it from his pocket and examined it. "Transponder signal, Philippe. That means all the sectiss bugs have reached their goddamn destinations."

"*D'accord.*" Stargazer pulled out his own transmitter and entered the code to access the sectiss bug transmitting frequency—and there it was, D-L-D, the command code. "Dick found one!"

———

Cameron picked up the fusion mole. It was a tenth the size of one of the full-size models, but was still rather bulky—about half a meter in width. Fusion engines still tended to be rather large. It was also heavy in this gravity, but Cameron wanted it on one of the benches, so with Frank's help, he lugged it across the cell to his bunk.

They were both startled when a familiar voice said, "*Allô!*"

Frank burst into a grin—his first since their arrival on Strydia. "Hey!"

"Captain Cameron, Frank, "help is on the way," Stargazr's voice said. "We need you to create as much confusion as possible."

Frank nudged Cameron. "Uh...Dick..."

Cameron turned and saw a Throrb at the door. Not just any Throrb. "Oh, damn...if I know my Throrb..."

"It's the inquisitor," Splrrrb said.

"*Former* inquisitor," Hubblrrrp said, "now merely an ex-citizen of a shattered civilization.

But it seems you people still have something of a world to return to, don't you?" Hubblrrrp's pseudopods worked the door and it came open. "Richard Cameron, we learned a great deal from your mind. That device—it's from the Space Star *Silver Streak*?"

Cameron shrugged. "I don't know where it came from."

"You put up a valiant struggle when we probed your mind—your profile indicates you suffered a similar interrogation some of your years ago." Hubblrrrp's antennae turned on Frank. "But *you*...Frank Johnson...we extracted nothing from you. Your reaction was quite irrationally violent."

"Blow it through your ass," Frank seethed.

"The rest of you stay where you are. Frank Johnson, I want you to come with me."

"No! I'm not going anywhere with you."

"You fool, can't you see the war is over? And it looks like you won—or at least survived. Now, you and I must talk. Come."

Cameron stepped in front of Frank. "He's not going anywhere."

Frank gripped Cameron's arm. "Wait, Dick... come to think of it, I'd like to have a few words with this worm. It'll give you a chance to square things away with you-know-who."

"Are you sure, Frank?"

"I'm sure. This worm and I have unfinished business."

Without waiting for permission, Frank strode out of the cell, and Hubblrrrp shut the door behind him.

"Where the zeg is he going?" Koff asked.

Cameron ignored him. He tapped at the device. "Stargazer... Stargazer, can you hear me?"

"*Oui*, I can hear you."

"Stargazer...Frank was just taken out of here. Something's going on, I don't know what, but it looks like there *might* be a disruption in the Throrb chain of command."

"The timing is excellent," Stargazer said. "We are looking for as much disruption and chaos as possible. That will give us the cover to get through—I hope. And Dick—don't be surprised if Mordrax rescues you."

"*Mordrax?!*" Multiple emotions seized Cameron at the same time, but he buried them; there was no time for them now. "All right, thank you, Stargazer." He turned to Koff, Argo, and Splrrrb. "Well, guys, our troubles are over."

Argo smiled, and Splrrrb's reaction was unreadable. But Koff turned away, silent and, Cameron thought, morose. Why did he seem unhappy at the prospect of escape?

———

Hubblrrrp led Frank to the elevator. With few guards present, Frank was tempted to bolt, but presently more guards arrived. He couldn't tell where they were coming from, but evidently the presence of the mini fusion moles had provoked a lot of interest.

When Hubblrrrp led him into the elevator, he was surprised when, instead of heading up to the "comfortable" levels, where the dreaded interrogations rooms were, the elevator started *down*, down where the gravity was heavier, the temperature was hotter, and the cauldron of molten lava swirled.

"Why are we going down?" Frank asked.

"Your job is to answer questions, not ask them," Hubblrrrp snapped.

Deeper the elevator dropped. Frank's legs and back ached as the gravity increased. The heat was unbearable, and his nose hurt with the sulphurous fumes he inhaled. For the first time, he wondered about deadly chlorine gas, common in Earth volcanoes.

The elevator stopped.

"Do you know where we are?" Hubblrrrp asked.

"The bottom level," Frank said. "The deepest circle of Hell."

"Yes." Hubblrrrp opened the door with difficulty, then oozed painfully out onto the alloy floor which was all that stood between him and the molten surface of the planet Strydia.

Frank followed, wincing. Ahead of him, at the center of the vast ground level of the huge tower, was the Pit of Fire. He was conscious of a roiling, roaring sound emanating from the Pit as the lava swirled in its endless chase of itself. He wondered what caused the whirlpool action; it must have something to do with the enclosed environment and convection from below.

"Captain Cameron faced an interrogation," Hubblrrrp said. "According to the mental probe, he was held by some sort of huge alien with many legs."

"Starjudge," Frank said. "A Vyx."

"Vyx...not Community members?"

"No."

"But *you*—what happened to you that you reacted so violently?"

"What do you care?"

"I care! This is personal now." Hubblrrrp's antennae probed Frank. "Your people killed two of my children."

"What are you talking about?"

"The Mistizi invaded Belj, our homeworld. They killed my son Grongig. And my eldest, Hubblrrrp, went to war to fight your Community. I am positive that he is dead."

Frank stared at the creature, feeling no sympathy. "Well, I didn't do that. Neither did my friends."

"Your *people* did."

"And you, you *personally*, tortured me—"

"I did nothing of the kind! I was simply going to extract data. But you reacted as if I were torturing you! Why? Who did torture you? When? What happened to you?"

The heat and gravity and thirst and exhaustion had begun to take their toll. The memory of the inquisition—and the memories that the inquisition had triggered—threatened to close in on him. Yes, he had seen Hubblrrrp as Captain Peter Stapleton, his assistant as Dudley Appelbaum.

"I still want to know why you care," Frank said.

"Because this is the end. The end of the Alternative Alliance, and perhaps the end of my civilization, and certainly the end of my life as I have known it. I want to understand it before I die."

"What's to understand? Yes, I was tortured many years ago. I was a prisoner of war back in my home system. They deprived me of my neural inputs and put me in a state of total sensory deprivation. That experience has followed me around for my entire life. You satisfied?"

"Yes...now I understand. Your captain told you about the synchronization, the sensory cutoff—but we did that to *him*, we learned the human neural pattern. We would not have done that to you."

"Yes, I know that! Damn it, what goes on in my own head stays in my head from now on! I'm not telling you anything further!"

"So be it; then we'll move on to the real reason I brought you down here. *One* of us is going into that lava. No machines now, no guards, just Throrb physical capabilities against human. Let's finally see, once and for all, which of us is the stronger!"

Frank balled his fists, looked at the glistening body of the sluglike alien, sure that even in the intense gravity he could win a contest.

He laughed. "Let's do it!"

CHAPTER 29

Cameron paced, once again worried about Frank. Would he once again be returned in a nearly catatonic state? Now was not the time to be fretting about his friend; he needed to keep his mind on the escape from this place, on following Stargazer's instructions to create mayhem here.

Throrb guards were crisscrossing the prison now, demanding that prisoners surrender the mini fusion moles that had burrowed into their cells.

A guard arrived at their cell. "All right, hand over the alien device."

Cameron turned to the fusion mole and cried, "Stargazer, can you hear me? They're onto us."

"Hand it over!" the guard shouted. A pseudopod poked a long prod into the cell. Cameron tried to jerk away, but it touched his arm, sending an electric jolt through him. It hurt. A lot.

But he remained defiant. "No! You'll have to come in and get it!" He turned to the fusion mole and, hoping it was relaying his voice to all the other devices, in all the other cages, he shouted, "Don't surrender! Can everyone hear me?! Don't surrender!"

"Get that off of him," the guard said.

The door to the cell opened. *This is it*, Cameron thought, adrenaline pumping through him. "Get him!"

He leapt onto the guard. The slick body felt like a mattress as he landed on it. As it wriggled, he dug his fingernails into the rubbery skin.

Argo and Koff ran from the cell while Splrrrb helped Cameron with the guard.

Finally the alien was writhing on its back, oily blood pouring from multiple wounds that Cameron's untrimmed fingernails had ripped in its surface. Splrrrb whipped his pseudopods down on the guard's anterior, keeping him stunned while Cameron searched for weaknesses in the sluglike body. The Throrb were sturdier than they looked, but nevertheless it was easy for sufficiently determined human hands to tear their skin.

Splrrrb now had the electric prod. "Stand back," he called.

Cameron leapt off the guard, having no desire to experience that shock again.

Splrrrb brought the prod down on the guard once, twice, three times. The body jerked, wriggled. Splrrrb beat the guard again and again, drawing more of that oily blood as he simultaneously bludgeoned and shocked the creature.

Finally it was still.

Cameron noticed now that Koff and Argo were in hand-to-pseudopod combat with other guards out on the walkway. Other prisoners were watching and cheering even as guards tased them with the electric prods and ordered them to be quiet.

Gesturing at the other cells, Cameron said, "Splrrrb, can you unlock those cells?"

"I'll need the guard's pseudopod. They're DNA coded."

Argo, who had finished off his Throrb, said, "I'll do it." He gripped the dead guard's pseudopod and, with remarkable strength, tore it off. Black blood spurted all over his arm and chest. He handed the pseudopod to Splrrrb.

"Can you do it, Splrrrb?" Cameron asked.

"If no one stops me."

"I'll go with you," Argo said.

As they moved off, Koff gripped Cameron's arm. "Wait..."

"We don't have time to talk," Cameron said.

"There's something you don't know—when they tortured me, they learned everything."

"None of that matters now. The war is over. We just need to get out of here."

"It *does* matter, Captain Cameron. I betrayed my people and laid the way clear for the Throrb to attack my planet *and* numerous other Community worlds, including the Valdor Artificial World and your Station Post One."

"Look, no one's going to hold that against you, Koff. We've all been through an ordeal here."

"You don't understand. I'm a highly trusted government official, psychologically conditioned for years to resist any interrogation."

"Come on, Koff, they probed your mind. It's not possible to resist that."

"Captain, you're not listening to me. None of that is an excuse to my people. Treason is unforgivable, no matter the circumstances. That's why..." The featureless face looked down, the arm withdrew something from the black robe. "That's why no one can leave here and reveal my treachery to my people."

Cameron had no idea what Koff was holding, but assumed it was a weapon. "Wait a minute, Koff—"

"I'm sorry, Captain Cameron—this gives me no pleasure."

He swung the device. Cameron dodged, felt a whirr of static electricity as it passed near his head. "You had a weapon all this time and didn't use it against the Throrb?"

"I'm sorry—they defeated me. They drove me to submission." He swung the device again.

Disoriented by the juxtaposition of Koff's verbal contrition and physical attack, Cameron weaved and dodged, but made no effort to attack. He was too confused. "How the hell did the Throrb not discover you had that?" he gasped as he dodged Koff's blows. The Valerian didn't answer, and Cameron wondered if the Throrb had given him the device in order to kill his cellmates.

But as Koff pressed his attack, Cameron's instincts took over. As Koff swung the weapon, Cameron grabbed his wrist. He discovered in that moment that Valerian bone structure must be much more fragile than human; he felt the bone break in his grip, and Koff let out a scream that sounded like he was shouting into a megaphone. The weapon fell to the floor.

Cameron winced at the sound. That membrane Koff had where a face should be must act as some sort of sound amplifier. But he had no time to satisfy his curiosity about Valerian anatomy. He picked up the weapon as Koff sagged, in agony, gripping his shattered wrist. "Okay, Koff, get up and open up that robe. Let's see if you have any other weapons."

"No," Koff gasped. "My privacy."

"I don't care about your privacy! You just said treason is unforgivable, but then you attack the one who's trying to get you out of here!"

"Yes...I compounded my crime...I know...but I am defeated. The Throrb won. I am lost. I must regain whatever is left of my dignity." He stood, swaying, and launched himself at Cameron.

The Valerian was light, but the force of the blow in the heavy gravity drove Cameron backwards and he fell. He held up Koff's weapon and swung it past the side of his head. His hood flamed for a moment, but did not catch fire. Koff cried out, then landed a punch on Cameron's jaw. It was a light blow, like being punched by a child.

Cameron threw the delicate creature off. Koff rolled, the scorched hood falling off.

The head was blue, with a ridge of spines running from the ears over the scalp. The ears were pointed. Koff quickly drew the hood back up. "*Privacy,* Cameron! I told you! My *privacy!*"

"I don't really give a damn about your privacy at the moment!" Baffled by the Valerian's behavior, Cameron pointed the weapon at him, his thumb searching for the trigger. "Now, knock it off or I'll use this thing!"

Behind him, he heard the sounds of commotion, but he did not dare turn his head to see what was going on. He hoped Argo and Splrrrb had freed the other prisoners and started a prison riot. But he kept his full attention on Koff.

"Now, are you going to behave?"

Koff was making sound now, strange, explosive sounds that visibly vibrated that black membrane of a face. Was he crying? Or was this the preamble to some sort of attack?

"I no longer know who's side I'm on," Koff said. "I gave in to the Throrb torture. I betrayed my people. If you are a man of honor, tell no one what I have done. Please. Please."

"Koff, I don't even *know* what you've done, or what you're *doing!* You've gone nuts! Now, if you'll just...just *stop it*, I'll forget the whole thing and we can get out of here."

Koff stood. "Stop it? Just *stop it?!* Is it that easy to you?" He paused. "No. I can't expect you to understand. You're human. I've watched you and your friend. You don't have personal honor or dignity. You live and talk and interact like animals. You can't understand me or my people. You can't..." He turned back toward their cell. "I can't expect you to understand. To you...you just ...talk...about anything. Privacy means nothing to you."

"I understand privacy."

"Is that why you constantly hound your friend about his emotional problems no matter his personal embarrassment? Is that why you constantly ask Argo if his powers are returning when he is clearly humiliated by his loss of powers? Is that why you demonstrate no empathy for Splrrrb, who is in physical and emotional distress, totally alone in the galaxy and tortured by his own people? Fine rescue mission this turned out to be. You are a disgrace."

Suddenly Koff turned and ran at Cameron again.

Reacting instinctively, Cameron grabbed Koff as he leapt at him, rolled, kicked Koff's belly as he flew overhead, and sent him sailing over the railing.

Horrified by his own action, Cameron got up and looked over the shaft, wondering if there was any chance.

He saw Koff in silhouette, tumbling end-over-end, down the shaft, toward the swirling Lake of Fire. Finally he disappeared.

Cameron sagged against the railing, his heart pounding. *What have I done?! The whole point of our mission here was to rescue him, and I killed him!*

But Koff had struck first. *Why?* Cameron shook his head, trying to comprehend. Perhaps the strain had simply driven Koff insane.

Well, nothing to be done about it now. He turned and looked in the direction of the noise. As he had hoped, prisoners were running amok. He ran to join the melee, wishing Frank was at his side.

———

Frank landed a solid punch on the side of Hubblrrrp's anterior. The skin folded under his fist and then bounced back, pushing Frank's fist away. It was like hitting a punching bag.

He tried to move to the side and tripped; a pseudopod was coiled around his legs. He hit the hard surface with a *crack*, and sharp pain exploded in his chest. He suspected he had broken a rib. *The gravity*, he coughed.

Then Hubblrrrp was on top of him, his heavy body smothering him, a pseudopod wrapped around his neck.

He struggled under the Throrb's weight, shifted onto his back, and grabbed at Hubblrrrp's body. He dug his fingernails into the skin, but the pseudopod's grip around his neck only tightened.

Rage boiled up in him, the pent-up rage he had harbored against Peter Stapleton for so many years. He remembered the messages his old cellmates had sent to Dudley Appelbaum's wife, the sense of incompleteness as he had never confronted Appelbaum or Stapleton, and he found strength he hadn't known he had.

He threw Hubblrrrp off of him, ripping the pseudopod from the sluglike body, leaving a trail of oily goo.

"I've had enough of you!" he raged, throwing himself at Hubblrrrp. "How *dare* you?! How *dare* you?! Just who do you think you are, ruining people's lives like that?! Do you realize that once you're done having your fun, your victims have to go on living? The war ends and they have to somehow go back to their lives? How to you justify it? Do you just revel in your cruelty? How do you live with yourself?!"

Pseudopods gripped him, but he ignored them as he pummeled his victim, screaming at him, tearing at him.

"Monster!" he raged, his voice becoming incoherent. "*Monster! Monster! You bragg-aaaaa!*"

Hubblrrrp finally managed to pry him away with twenty pseudopods, and Frank, drained of energy and in agonizing pain, dropped to the floor, gasping, his throat dry, his lips parched, his chest a searing cavity.

Both opponents were exhausted. The heat and gravity were too much for either human or Throrb biology. Though neither of them was willing to admit it, the fight was over.

"Why should I care what you've been through?" Hubblrrrp gasped. "I have my orders. It's war."

"War ends," Frank seethed. "War ends, but people survive. Some of us have to kill in war, but you...you *wound*. On the inside, you...you *hurt* people."

"It's my job."

Frank gave a bitter laugh. "It's your job! Millennia ago, the people of my planet decided that's no excuse for atrocities!"

"I will not be judged by a *human*." Hubblrrrp spat black fluid on the hot metal floor. "You have no idea of my life, my losses."

Frank staggered to his feet, tried to kick at Hubblrrrp, but collapsed again. "You bastard," he wheezed. "Neither of us is getting out of here. We're going to die, right here."

Hubblrrrp's body quivered, and he gasped, "Just as well."

They lay there, while in the levels above, prisoners revolted, and now and then Throrb bodies plummeted into the flaming whirlpool. Frank watched them streak by like meteors, marveling that here he and his enemy were right next to the cauldron of death and neither had the strength to throw the other into it. What a strange and ironic way for things to end—for him *and* for Hubblrrrp.

He turned his head and looked at Hubblrrrp lying deflated, looking like a jellyfish washed up on a beach, bleeding, almost dead. And he felt his own strength weakening, his body succumbing to the pain, the heat, the injuries, the gravity, and the endless torture of this place. He felt he was dying.

And the strangest emotion came over him... so unexpected he shed tears. He felt *compassion* for Hubblrrrp. What kind of creature was this, a being that tortured for a living and then went home to a loving family? Who was this monster whose life had crossed his own? How had these two disparate creatures from different worlds intersected to irrevocably change each other's lives?

CHAPTER 30

The shuttlecraft shot from the *Silver Streak*. Ordinarily they would have launched in the opposite direction of the vessel's orbit, thus immediately slowing and dropping toward the atmosphere, but their destination today was not the planet's surface, but the top of the prison tower, two hundred kilometers below the synchronous orbit.

Once Jack confirmed that they were clear, Stargazer signaled Mordrax's Hyron shuttle.

"Shuttle Two, this is Shuttle One. We are going down."

"Very well," Mordrax's voice replied. "We're almost down."

"Don't you fuck us over, Mordrax," Jack said.

"You do your job, I'll do mine."

Stargazer kept the channel open, but that didn't stop Jack from saying loudly, "Why in hell we're trusting that Goddamn guy...."

"Well, if he turns out to be no good, at least we'll be there," Stargazer said.

———

The molten surface of the planet Strydia careened under the Hyron craft, filling Mordrax with a sense of exhilaration he thought he had lost the capacity to feel. He vividly remembered his youth, those annexation missions when he had been a young and ambitious officer, the vagaries of state still megatolax ahead of him. Before the death of Asiza. Before the Vengeance Quest.

He tried not to remember the happy times; the memories only reminded him of how much he had lost.

The shuttle shuddered violently in the atmospheric turbulence as it dropped through a thermocline. He enjoyed it. Chok did not, and Mordrax hoped Chok's discomfort did not manifest in physical form.

The tower stretched ahead. Kilozons across, it stretched without end into the turbulent sky.

"Duh, we're almost there, Mordrax," Chok observed.

At least he knows where he is today. "Yes. Remember, keep quiet, stay close to me, do what I do."

"Duh, okay, Mordrax."

After a moment, Mordrax said, "Now, what did I tell you to do?"

"Duh, don't you remember?"

Mordrax cleared his throat. "Of course, Chok. Of course."

———

Throrb guards had begun opening fire on the prisoners. Cameron returned fire with Koff's weapon. It wasn't very powerful, but it managed to stop the worm-like aliens in their tracks. Sometimes it seemed to knock them out, other times it just dazed them for a few moments—either way, it was all he had.

Other prisoners had somehow gotten their hands—or tentacles or claws or whatever—on knives, swords, and clubs. A few even had Throrb energy weapons, evidently taken from guards they had managed to subdue.

It was not a fair fight and the Throrb would win easily—unless reinforcements arrived soon.

———

Stargazer was uneasy with the lack of resistance facing them. There had been no communications demanding identification, no anti-spacecraft gunfire, no reaction at all to the shuttlecraft pulling alongside the tower and attaching a pressure snake.

He hoped it was because Cameron had fomented one hell of a riot.

"We're attached!" Jack sounded like he was having a wonderful time. Even after all these years, Jack always displayed that indomitable spirit of adventure.

"Let's go to it." Stargazer hoped Jack couldn't hear the tremor in his voice.

The hatch opened and Stargazer led the way through the pressure snake.

A Throrb greeted them. "What are you—"

Stargazer fired his sidearm at the alien. Its skin ruptured and it collapsed inward on itself, shriveling in a mass of tissue and black fluid. More Throrb turned from their posts, pseudopods reaching for weapons.

Jack joined in the gunfire, eliminating the aliens who had been taken by surprise.

Stargazer was nauseated by the leaking black blood, the way the bodies seemed to collapse in on themselves when ruptured. But Jack Hasta playfully blew on the end of his sidearm, twirled it, and said, "Wow!"

"We just might beat Mordrax to the punch," Stargazer observed. He called into his sidearm. "Shuttles three through seven, this is Star-gah-zay. We are in."

"Well, let's find a goddamn elevator," Jack said. "You can bet your mustache that Dick and Frank are down in the bowels of the prison."

———

Mordrax had carefully aligned his shuttle to one of the craters drilled by the sectiss bugs and attached with the connector.

Now he and Chok were climbing through the cramped tunnel, and he was acutely aware of how out of shape he had become in his old age. His limbs ached with the effort, and he feared his ample torso might get stuck.

Chok was in a worse state, having been almost obese for all the years Mordrax had known him. "Duh, it's hot in here."

"Come on."

"Duh, I'm heavy."

"You really need to lose some weight."

———

Cameron, Argo, and Splrrrb had broken away from the prisoners and were fighting on a narrow walkway over the lava pit. They were surrounded by guards—but the guards could only cross single file, so the Throrb no longer had strength in numbers.

"Doing okay, Argo?" Cameron called over his shoulder.

"I'd feel better if I had my powers."

"So would I. Splrrrb, you holding together?"

"So far," Splrrrb said.

Argo had a Throrb energy weapon, Splrrrb a weapon he had taken from a dead prisoner, a kind of miniature crossbow. With these, they were able to hold off the Throrb—but for how long? They were surrounded on this bridge with nowhere to go.

Sectiss bugs were still prowling the prison, still occasionally making announcements. Cameron had stopped listening—but now it was the all-too-familiar voice of Mordrax that rang from a nearby, hovering device: "Cameron, where are you?"

Cameron's head jerked toward the mini fusion mole which hovered nearby. "Mordrax?!"

"I'm coming to get you. Where are you?"

"Well...we're a little lost right now."

"You're useless. All right, we'll follow in on your transmission."

At that moment Splrrrb took a hit. Neither he nor Argo could do anything as he squealed and collapsed in a heap on the bridge.

———

Lublwbb slimed across his tattered command post, helpless, indecisive. The humans were streaming in like insects. Shuttlecraft were swarming not only Level Zero, but the many holes made by those infernal little robots.

They had decimated the control room and moved on to the elevator in order to attack the prison. Now Lublwbb was left trying to clean up a mess that was still in the making.

"We need more help," he moaned.

"There is no more help," a technician said as his station broke down around him. "Our guards are hemmed in. There's still no contact with the Alternative Alliance. We're all alone."

———

The guards were closing in. Cameron and Argo covered each other, but the charge in Cameron's device seemed to be going out. The Throrb were stung by it, but kept coming, leaving Argo to cover both of their backs.

Then sizzling beams shot the Throrb down, and Cameron made out two running figures heading their way.

"Cameron!" Mordrax called, waving.

"Mordrax!" Now free, Cameron ran across the bridge to greet his old enemy. "I never thought I'd be glad to see you!"

Argo followed close behind. "A friend of yours?"

Cameron laughed. "My mortal enemy. But I guess he's our friend today. Mordrax, this is Argo, Priest King of the Dreb of Derringer-9. Argo, this is the Hyron ex-Monarch, Mordrax Hidalgi."

Mordrax appeared stung by the "ex-Monarch" label, but Cameron wasn't sure how else to introduce him. "And this is my...friend, Chok Renchak. Cameron, where's your little shadow?"

"You mean Frank Johnson? I'm not sure, but I think the Throrb inquisitor took him down to the bottom level."

Argo pointed. "There are more Throrb coming our way. The other prisoners are occupied. I say we rush them."

"We're a little low on weapons now."

"I have a weapon," Mordrax said. "So does Chok."

"Well...I guess we can blast through them—but I really want to get to the bottom level and rescue Frank."

"Then do that," Argo said. "Just help me get through these guards and buy me some time."

"Time for what?"

"One of your people must have taken out the MP-SAR field—I feel my powers returning."

Cameron grinned. "Excellent! All right, let's go to it!"

———

"What the goddamn do you suppose that was?" Jack Hasta cried.

Stargazer looked around, stunned at the light show playing out around him. It was exactly like those old electric shows with Tesla coils—lightning shooting through the room, crackling and sparking. The kind of thing that happened in poorly researched immies that showed the bridge of a starship bursting into electric sparks whenever an alien enemy scored a direct hit.

"I don't know," Stargazer said in answer to Jack's question, "but it seems all weapons fire has stopped."

———

And indeed, all the Throrb weapons had been immobilized. Argo had seen to that. From somewhere else in the universe...or the multiverse ...the energy had been conducted through his very cells, which had been modified by the Thermians, enabling his body to act as a transformer. The space between his body and the prison's weapons served as a spark gap. The result—thousands of volts of electricity.

It was really very simple, yet beyond human imagination, that a person could harness and control such energy with his body. It was also a cause of pain and emotional conflict for Argo, who knew that his powers were made possible by those *creatures*, the Thermians, who threatened all intelligent life in the universe, who were a much more dire threat than these meddlesome Throrb and their allies.

It was easy, now that his powers were back, to remove the Throrb.

The Thermians were another story.

———

Frank could hear the sounds of the battle; revolt had broken out on every level except this one and a few dozen above, where the gravity was too great for prolonged physical activity. He listened, wondering who the combatants were, wondering if Dick was safe.

He rolled over and looked at Hubblrrrp, astonished at the feelings of kinship and tenderness he now felt toward the alien.

"Your children," Frank gasped. "Tell me about them."

"Not much to tell...I've been away...most of their lives..." Hubblrrrp's breathing was labored. "My eldest...Hubblrrrp...was...my pride. He...was my hope for the future...everything I did...I did to make a life for him..."

"How did torturing me do that?"

"Didn't torture you."

"But..." Frank let out a long sound that was part laugh, part sob. "No, you didn't torture me." *All this is for nothing! He didn't even do anything to me! I'm not lashing out against this alien, I'm lashing out against Peter Stapleton! I never did move on from that time in my life.*

"I'm sorry," he finally said, and was astonished as the words came out of his mouth. Sorry? Sorry for *what?*

Sorry that he was dying, for one thing. Sorry that his last act had been to take another's life— even the life of his hated enemy.

"So am I," Hubblrrrp said. "I have...*had*...no quarrel with you. That it came to this..."

And then the face of Richard Cameron came into focus. "Frank? Frank?"

Dick? What the hell? Frank laughed. Hell. Of course. How could he die? He was already in Hell, and Cameron was quite naturally the damned soul who would welcome him to eternal torment.

"Come on, let's get him up top," Cameron said, putting an arm under him. Someone else assisted—Argo.

"Hubblrrrp?" Frank moaned.

But Cameron didn't listen. He never listened. So they left Hubblrrrp to die, alone in the deepest circle of Hell.

Perhaps that was appropriate.

CHAPTER 31

As far as Cameron could tell, the battle was over. Many of the Throrb guards had surrendered. The prisoners were running about in apparent chaos, but there was no more shooting, no more death.

It was fortunate that the elevators were working; Argo's electrical fireworks had destroyed all the electronics in the prison, but mechanical backups had kicked in—which was fortunate, as air conditioning was a vital part of the life support system here.

Cameron considered stopping at level four thousand four and having everyone meet in their old cell, but there was no reason for that. Might as well go up top and take over the control center—if anything was left of it after that lightning show.

Frank was standing now, though his breathing was heavy. He suspected there were cracked ribs, but didn't seem to have life-threatening injuries—he was just exhausted beyond human endurance. If they could get him to the *Silver Streak*, he should be fine.

"Feeling better, Frank?" Cameron asked.

Frank nodded. "I think so. You?"

"Yeah...fine."

"How about Splrrrb and Koff?"

Cameron was still reeling from his weird confrontation with Koff; he didn't know how to explain it to himself, let alone Frank. Evidently privacy was of vital importance to Valerians, so he decided to honor Koff's wishes. He simply said, "Dead."

"Well, at least we won," Argo said.

"What did we win?"

The question hung in the air as the elevator cranked up and up and up. With the electronics down, the elevator was agonizingly slow, and Cameron wondered what would happen if the unreliable moving parts broke down.

"So what happened down there with you and the inquisitor?"

Frank looked uncomfortable. "He...wanted to straighten some things out."

"Like?"

"Well...I guess you could call it a personal vendetta. On both our parts."

"Well, you came through it all right."

Frank shrugged, rubbed his ribs with a wince. "It was more of a draw. It was...cathartic. I guess I had some...issues to deal with that I didn't realize I was still carrying around with me."

Cameron thought of Koff. "There seems to be a lot of that going around."

"Hmm?"

"Nothing."

"Uh, how long will it take us to get up there?" Frank asked.

"Well, I'm not sure the exact height of this tower," Cameron said, "but the old Earth towers, before ZPL control, a ride at two hundred kilometers an hour took about a week."

"Oh, Jesus."

"No concern," Argo said, kneeling. He placed his hands against the floor.

Cameron was grateful for his rubber-soled boots as he realized Argo was imparting an electrical current. The elevator's speed increased. It took several minutes for Cameron to realize what Argo was doing. "I'll be darned!"

"Magnetic levitation?" Frank asked.

"Yeah. I'm guessing that's the way this elevator is supposed to work. It was very common in the bullet trains pre-World War III, before aircars."

"Well, yeah, I know that; by keeping electromagnetic poles in balance, a heavy vehicle could be lifted and then propelled at enormous speed through a frictionless tunnel—is this elevator shaft frictionless?"

"It must be, considering that we came down in freefall."

"Good point."

As the elevator accelerated exponentially, it only took a few hours to reach Level Zero. Cramped, uncomfortable hours, but certainly better than a week.

Mordrax greeted them in the documentation area. "Cameron!"

Cameron shook Mordrax's hand. "Mordrax! How are things?"

"Ask your friends."

Jack Hasta ran toward him, grinning, his arms spread. "Dick!" He wrapped Cameron in a painful bear hug. "And Frank!"

"Uh, uh, that's okay." Frank stepped backward. "I was already squashed by gravity today, thanks."

Stargazer followed close behind Jack. "*Allô! Très bien,* we did it!"

Cameron shook Stargazer's hand. "Good to see you guys!" He looked around at the dead Throrb bodies. "Is anyone left alive?"

"Not up here," Stargazer said.

Cameron turned to Argo. "Did you kill everyone?"

"I couldn't say. I just lashed out with my powers. My target was the weapons. I don't know enough about the Throrb to know how their bodies handled it."

Frank knelt by a sticky mass of tissue and alien guts. "Well, this was the warden."

"You sure?" Cameron asked.

Frank nodded. "Yep. I'm sure." He stood. "I guess we've most definitely won."

"We've won *here*," Cameron said. He turned to Jack and Stargazer. "What about the war?"

Jack said "Goddamn" with such feeling that Cameron felt there needed to be no elaboration.

"Both sides have blown each other up," Stargazer said, "and...you are going to kill me when you see the condition of the *Silver Streak*."

That was not news Cameron wanted to hear. His heart rate increased. He felt blood draining from his brain. He had an overwhelming need to see the ship *now*...and also a need *not* to see it.

"Star World is gone, Dick," Jack said. "The *Silver Streak* is in sorry goddamn shape too."

"My God." Star World. How much work they had put into that! "How many were aboard Star World?"

"Everyone who was there last time you were there."

"Jesus. And Station Post One?"

Stargazer said, "As far as we know, Station Post One is still intact. It seems that Klym Valdor was badly damaged, but it is still there—or at least a sizeable portion of it is intact, sustaining life, and functioning."

"Well, that's something." Despite Cameron's overwhelming desire to go back to his ship and see how badly hurt she was, he had to put his mission first. "Frank, I want you to get back to the *Silver Streak* and take command."

"*After* a trip to the Infirmary?" Frank whined.

"*After* a trip to the Infirmary. Jack and Stargazer, you go too. I want the bridge fully manned until we're sure the planet is secure."

"And what will you be doing?" Frank asked.

"Argo and I will make sure all is secure here, make sure the prisoners have a way back to their homeworlds—if they still exist. Then I'll come back up with Mordrax and Chok."

"All right—good luck." Frank turned to leave, then remembered something of vital importance that Cameron had forgotten about. "Wait! We need to get these collars off!"

Cameron smacked his forehead. "That's right! If we leave the base with them on, it's *sayonara*."

"Goddamn," Jack said.

"Will there not be a reaction if they are removed?" Stargazer asked.

"I hope not," Cameron said. "Get a reading on what these collars are made of. No mistakes."

Stargazer pulled out a portable scanner. "It appears that the interior is lined with an isotope that will signal the explosive bolts if you cross through the prison's security barrier. Jack, put your sidearm on setting four-B."

"Goddamn." Jack set his sidearm to the appropriate setting—to emit a pencil-thin plasma beam that would act like a saw.

"All right, very, very slowly, begin to cut..."

Jack held Frank's collar with one hand, held the sidearm within a centimeter of it, and pulled the trigger. The beam cut through the corner of the metal mesh.

"All right, good, that's five millimeters," Stargazer said.

Frank let out a breath, but remained tense as the thin beam sliced through the collar. One mistake and his neck could be sliced pretty badly.

"Ah-hah!" Jack exclaimed, pulling the collar loose. "Well, Dick, Argo, you guys want to get rid of the goddamn things?"

"Absolutely!" Cameron said. "It'll take a while to get these off of all the prisoners."

Once Cameron and Argo were freed of their collars, Frank said, "Much better. Let's get out of here!"

"Let me have that sidearm," Cameron said. "I'll take care of the rest of the prisoners' collars."

"Goddamn." Jack tossed him the sidearm.

Cameron pocketed it and watched his friends go. His mind turned momentarily to the *Silver Streak*, and the damage Jack and Stargazer had spoken of. *But at least she's still up there,* he reminded himself. *That's more than we can say for most of the rest of the Community.*

"Where do we begin?" Argo asked.

"Start rounding people up, collecting names and, well, destinations."

Argo nodded, headed for the elevator. As it dropped away, Cameron decided they needed to repair the computers; it was ridiculous to keep running that elevator on Argo's mystical powers.

"Cameron," Mordrax said behind him.

"Yes?"

"A word, please?"

Cameron sighed. "What is it? Make it—"

As he turned, Mordrax shoved his sword deep into Cameron's gut. "Sword of Vengeance, Cameron," Mordrax said.

Cameron gasped, sputtered, shocked, incoherent. He sunk to his knees, trying to speak, unwilling to admit to himself what had happened even as blood flowed from him.

Mordrax knelt next to him, gripped his shoulder. "Your ship is safe. I'll not attack again. Your ship is safe."

Cameron tried to focus, but his vision fogged. He was dizzy, faint. His awareness of where he was began to slip. His last thought was that he hadn't gotten to see his ship one last time.

Then Captain Richard Cameron died.

———

Mordrax stood over the lifeless body of his Victim of Wrath, trembling, as disbelieving as Cameron had been. "I've succeeded." Sounds began to burst from his mouth—laughing, crying, meaningless sputtering. "I've succeeded. I've succeeded."

He turned away, wiped the tears from his eyes, but the tears kept flowing, like Cameron's blood. "I...*did*...it...Blackhaven!"

Chok approached slowly, chewing on his fingernails. He looked from Mordrax to Cameron's body and back to Mordrax. Then he grinned. "Duh, you did it!"

I did it, I did it! Mordrax turned around, half expecting to see that the body was gone, or that Cameron had gotten up and brushed himself off and was laughing at him, or that the whole thing had been a figment of his imagination, or that now he would wake up in his quarters and find that it had been another dream.

But no...the body was still there. He had done it! The long, long, long, long, long Vengeance Quest was over!

And now...now what? Now he had to find something else to do with his life. He had dedicated himself to the death of Richard Cameron for so long, so very long...it had consumed his life, it had destroyed him. And now...now it was done! It was over!

He remembered the words of the then-regent, Eilonwy, Cameron's lover and mother of Cameron's child, the young Monarch.

"If you succeed, if you destroy Cameron, I will declare a Vengeance Quest against you."

So be it. He was now a fugitive. Even in the afterglow of his success, Cameron had posthumously destroyed his life. But he had succeeded. He had succeeded.

"Come on, Chok, let's get out of here."

CHAPTER 32

Argo finished the job of releasing the prisoners from their security collars. There were some guards still alive, but they surrendered; it seemed they had no desire to challenge a Dreb.

He recruited some of the Throrb to assist him in replacing the computers and restoring power to the elevators. That was when he found Cameron's body.

A search of the area failed to find Mordrax, but there was a missing Throrb cruiser; it wasn't hard to guess what had happened.

Frank took the news with a numb disbelief. There was no grief, just an emotionless refusal to believe that it had happened. Not until he shuttled to the tower and saw the body did he really accept that his oldest and closest friend was gone.

There were spare components on hand for emergencies like this, and one of the Throrb guards was a technician. It didn't take long to get the place up and running again. Frank found the control center operational and manned by disheveled prisoners.

"Mordrax got away in a Throrb cruiser," Argo told him.

"Set off for Hyron, I suppose, to proclaim his victory." Frank said it with some bitterness, but the emotion still wouldn't come.

"Yes. I could...try to locate him."

Frank shook his head, staring at the body. "No. No point now. Not unless you can bring back the dead."

"No, I can't do that."

Frank knelt next to Cameron's body. The eyes were open and unseeing, the bloodless face gray. Frank reached out and closed the cold eyelids. "Dick, I'm sorry. Even after all these years, there's still so much left unsaid."

———

It was time to head to Station Post One. The crew there were still eagerly awaiting their delayed Expansion Phase. It would give Frank something to do now that Star World was gone.

And after that...

First things first. The entire complement of the *Silver Streak* gathered on the parade deck for Cameron's funeral. This was an even larger gathering than for President Henry Walden's funeral some five years ago. The ship was saying its final good-bye to a man who had become a legendary hero, almost mythic in stature.

Frank felt a ghost of amusement at the thought of his buddy Dick being almost godlike to these people. Only Frank—and Jack and Stargazer—knew the truth: Dick had been just a guy. In some ways deeply flawed, a man of great passion and deep feeling, a man dedicated to doing what he felt was right, a man a little too sure of himself and yet a little too philosophical about everything—but a man who had led the *Silver Streak* through its greatest trials, and had always emerged victorious.

Almost always.

Frank, of course, delivered the eulogy. He stood on a hastily arranged dais. Behind him, Cameron's body lay encased in a projectile loaded onto a catapult that would be hurled from a launch tube on a trajectory to burn up in Strydia's atmosphere.

"We are gathered here today to pay our final respects to our honored dead. Captain Richard Cameron died as he lived—a hero, an adventurer, a man who was never content with what was, but always dreamed of what might be, and never ceased his pursuit of that."

He glanced to his left at Jack and Stargazer, then to his right at President Copenburg and the Congressional Council. Then he looked out at the audience of thousands, stretching off into the far recesses of the vast bay, and continued. "I don't know if there's a life after death, but if James Wilcox Lowell is to be believed, there are parallel universes, and I take comfort in knowing my friend is still alive in at least one of them. And if, like Dick, I never cease to dream of what might be, then I can't help but wonder if I'll see him again someday."

He had felt some real emotion when he wrote that line. He had shed tears. But as he delivered it, it felt dead and hollow on his tongue. He spoke without feeling. But it seemed to have the right effect.

"This great battle that has torn the galaxy to shreds and taken our captain from us might seem like a colossal waste, but it wasn't. We still survive, and that meant more to Dick than anything. As long as we survive, he survives. As Captain of the *Silver Streak*, I vow to guard that in his name."

Could he keep that vow? The ship was barely functioning; Jack could not promise that he could keep her running, and the word "decommissioning" had been floating around the engine room. But there was still Station Post One, and over the planet Menchie was Station Post Two. The means existed to build new Space Stars. And they had built one Star World; they could build another one. Even if the *Silver Streak* had to be retired, the human race still had a future.

"Now, Dick hated funerals; he said they just make people feel worse. So, in his honor, I'm going to close by delivering exactly, word-for-word, the eulogy he said he'd like to have." Frank cleared his throat, opened a slip of paper he'd had in his pocket, and read, " 'He's dead, get over it, chuck 'im out the airlock and let's have a party.' "

That brought the laugh he had been hoping for. He had been afraid people would be offended, but it seemed he had struck just the right note.

Frank turned to the security guards lined up behind him. "Present...*arms!* Ready...aim...*fire!*"

The guards fired their sidearms—on light setting, of course—at the ceiling, once, twice, three times.

Frank signaled with his hand, and the catapult shot the projectile from the ship.

And just like that, it was over. Frank wished he had let the moment linger a bit, given everyone—himself included—a last moment to say good-bye.

But now Cameron was on his way to his final resting place—burning up in the final flames of Hell.

Frank smiled. Dick would have gotten a kick out of that.

———

Mordrax knew he was now a marked man. Eilonwy would not rest until she plunged the Sword of Vengeance through his gut as he had done to Cameron. Nevertheless, he had to return to Hyron. For one thing, he owed it to Eilonwy to tell her of Cameron's death.

She received the news in stony silence. Then she rose from her seat, her eyes squinted, and her lovely young face began to tremble with controlled rage. She then spoke the words Mordrax had been expecting, and yet wounded him to the core.

"I swear by the Spirits of Nomad that the Sword of Vengeance will wear your blood!"

But, as per tradition, she did not claim her Victim of Wrath then and there; she had notified him of her intentions, and now he was released to prepare for her wrath.

His next destination was the great shield volcano at Hyron's equator, Terrax Mountain, where Williamax had died almost two thousand years ago. This was the mythical convergence point of the Four Winds of Hyron, the breath of the Spirits of Nomad. Superstitious nonsense; Terrax Mountain was an interesting formation, an extinct volcano tall enough that its peak was perpetually covered in ice and snow, even here at the equator, but there was no other meteorological significance. But the symbolism was important.

It was also deeply personal to Mordrax—so personal that even Chok didn't accompany him this time.

He climbed the great mountain as his ancestor, Williamax, had done on his last great voyage of exploration—as Zarnax had done later after killing Matsuiax, beginning the tradition of the Vengeance Quest. As Hyrons had done throughout history on the completion of their Vengeance Quests.

As Mordrax had dreamed of doing for twenty-two years.

He did not reach the peak. He was too old, he lacked the stamina of his youth. But this place was way, way up there. The peak couldn't be far now.

The cold bit his face. He turned and looked out upon the vastness of the world, his world, a world to which he would likely never return after this. Below him was a valley of snow—perhaps the very valley where Williamax and Jonas had gotten lost so long ago, on Williamax's final adventure.

Mordrax took a deep breath of the thin, chill wind. He spread his arms upon the wind and he bellowed in a voice so loud and resounding that it hurt his stomach,

"*I declare victory! My foe has felt the Sword of Vengeance!!*"

With that, he sunk into the snow, sobbing. This moment, so satisfying, yet so empty of meaning. The whole point of his life was fulfilled. And now he must flee. And his moment of victory was the murder of a man he had come to like and respect.

He had killed his mortal enemy. His Monarch. His friend. His reason for living.

What had he now?

His chest heaved in great, painful sobs until there was no more breath in him, no more feeling. His eyes caked with frozen tears and his chest aching with the emptiness of spent grief and hollow triumph, he started his journey down.

———

The *Silver Streak* was battered, worn, creaking, and tired, but Jack had gotten her running again. It was as if she had decided to work a little harder to please the ghost of her lost master.

Frank left the bridge at the end of watch, started to head for his cabin—Dick's cabin. He couldn't face that, not yet.

Jack and Stargazer usually went to the rec room to bowl in the evenings, or throw darts. Maybe tonight Frank would join them. But as he headed forward, he didn't spot them. He knew they had left the bridge, but wasn't sure where they had gone.

He found himself sitting at the bar. Well, what was the harm in sitting here? He didn't have to have a drink.

Of course...did the Promise matter now? He, Cameron, and Stargazer had taken what they referred to as the Vow of Sobriety in order to help Jack to conquer his alcoholism, and they had kept to that with only a few minor slips. But now, with Dick dead...

I'm in command, Frank thought. His mind reeled. He would have to select a first officer; he had no idea who to choose. All the best selections were now on Station Post One. *God.*

It wasn't the first time Frank had found himself in command. Cameron had resigned years ago; that had shaken the ship. It took a surprising ten years for him to realize what a damned stupid mistake that had been and return to command. Then he had disappeared when Mordrax had abducted him from Starjudge's ship; Frank had once again taken command and things had seemed uncertain.

But now. Now Dick was *dead.* Things would ever, ever be the same again. But on the other hand, things hadn't been the same since they had joined the Community.

Really, things hadn't been the same since the destruction of the Earth.

Things hadn't been the same since that fateful day when he had crashed on Mars.

"Care for anything?" the bartender asked.

"Whiskey," Frank said without thinking. Then he smiled, intending to indicate that he was joking. But Fred poured the drink and placed it in front of him, and Frank didn't protest.

Dick is dead. I'm the captain. This is permanent. Our adventures together are really over.

He stared at the drink. His fingers curled around the stem. Then he let go. *No. We made a promise. In Dick's memory, if for no other reason, I'm going to honor that promise.*

He looked around. Jack was nowhere to be seen. So did it matter if he had one little drink? If Jack wasn't here to see, what harm would it do? Besides, Jack's drinking was long since overcome. Did he really need help now? Had they all overreacted by pledging never to drink again?

He stared at the drink. Again his fingers curled around it. *Dare I? Dare I? Once I start, I may not be able to stop.*

He let go of the glass. He continued to stare at it. In that moment, he didn't know, he really had no idea, if he was going to drink it or not.

Will I?

AFTERWORD

I would like to thank my friend Barton Paul Levenson for helping me to develop the planet Strydia. Barton is a planetary scientist who has developed a software to project the climates of habitable planets. Since Strydia is not habitable, he was not able to use his program to help me, but he nevertheless gave me his time and his expertise to help me to extrapolate the possibilities.

"Lava planets" are common in science fiction—planets with entirely molten surfaces—but such planets could indeed exist. If a planet orbits close to its parent star, the combination of radiation and tidal forces could well result in a molten surface.

The "fusion moles" used in the final chapters of this book are entirely fictional—and will remain so until fusion power is practical—but the "sectiss bugs" have their origin in spy drones currently used by the military. In fact, some of the drones already developed by the U.S. military are more advanced, and with more capabilities, than the sectiss bugs of this novel. In addition to spying, mini drones can actually take DNA samples or even implant radio-frequency identification (RFID) tracking nanotechnology in a human body. I must admit I had never heard of that until I had already written this novel. It's hard these days for the science fiction writer to stay ahead of real science!

Now I'd like to talk about Star World. There have been numerous proposals to hollow out asteroids for colonization, and the idea has long been popular in science fiction. In 2018, a group of students called DSTART at Delft University of Technology in the Netherlands designed the "Evolving Asteroid Starship." Utilizing the native resources of a hollowed-out asteroid, they proposed a multigenerational interstellar journey utilizing 3D printing, asteroid mining, and the ESA's Micro-Ecological Life Support System Alternative (MELiSSA).

I'm particularly intrigued my MELiSSA. One thing that has perplexed me throughout the *Voyage Into the Unknown* series is how to make the *Silver Streak* self-sustaining over the long term. I let my imagination run wild by inventing the "osmotic recycler," described in the forward to *Voyage Into the Unknown: Volume Three*.

There have been several ground-based tests of MELiSSA hardware, but in 2018, a MELiSSA experiment called ArtemISS actually flew on the International Space Station, demonstrating that oxygen can indeed be cultivated from plants in space, and carbon dioxide can be recycled into oxygen—and as a by-product, produce edible proteins!

The experiment used a liquid sample of a microalgae called spirulina, which was placed in four photobioreactors and flooded with intense light. Over the course of a month, the spirulina produced both oxygen and biomass. In weightlessness, liquids and gases don't separate naturally, but this would not be a problem on the *Silver Streak*, which has artificial gravity (which itself required some imagination, and I relied— hopefully believably—on the assumption that there will be significant new scientific discoveries in the next two thousand years!)

Despite this challenge, however, the experiment was a success.

Even as it is, the astronauts aboard the ISS drink water recycled from their own sweat, which is collected as condensation on the station's walls.

All this is a significant step toward sustainability in space. The question is, how long can this be maintained in a closed system? The Second Law of Thermodynamics tells us that all exchanges of energy result in irreversible heat loss, meaning that any spacecraft, no matter how reliable its recycling, will degrade over time. But how much time? How long a space journey is possible?

Or, getting back to the subject of Star World, how long will an artificial space habitat be sustainable?

The use of native minerals will be a help, and the first steps toward asteroid mining have already been made.

In February of 1996, NASA's NEAR Shoemaker spacecraft was launched on a mission to the asteroid Eros. On June 27, 1997, the sapcecraft made a close flyby of the asteroid Mathilde. After a two-part burn of its 450 N thruster—the first major course correction to be carried out in deep space—NEAR Shoemaker flew by Earth on January 23, 1998, performing a gravity assist maneuver.

Despite problems with the first four rendezvous burns, NEAR Shoemaker made orbital insertion around Eros on, appropriately enough, February 14, 2000. On February 12, 2001, NEAR touched down on Eros. Using its gamma ray spectrometer, and transmitting to the Deep Space Network, the spacecraft transmitted the first data on the composition of an asteroid before contact was lost on February 28, 2001.

Some asteroid missions are still, as of this writing, in progress. In 2016, NASA's unmanned OSIRIS-REx launched for the near-Earth asteroid 101955 Bennu on a sample return mission. In 2003, the JAXA spacecraft Hayabusa took samples from 25143 Itokawa. In 2018, Hayabusa 2 followed up on the Hayabusa mission, arriving at 162173 Ryugu on a year-and-a-half mission for surveying and sampling.

The OSIRIS-REx and both Hayabusa spacecraft have yet to return to Earth, but these missions are the beginning of what could, in time, be a trillions-of-dollars industry. Asteroids are rich in gold, silver, platinum, iron, and other valuable minerals that will be useful for space construction. 3D printing, robotic arms, and new construction techniques such as expandable habitats (which play a vital role in the *Station Post One* books) will be increasingly important as well.

MagLev elevators, such as the elevator in the center of this novel's Strydia Prison, are still largely a thing of the future, but one is in operation in Rottweil, Germany, developed by

ThyssenKrupp. It's called the Multi, and OVG Real Estate plans to incorporate it in their East Side Tower in Berlin, which is scheduled to be completed in 2020.

Linden Sims and Whitney Richard helped me to develop some of the details of life in the Star Force, which I partially based on today's United States Air Force—with some futuristic tweaks. I owe Linden a great deal, as he organized the event where I first had the opportunity to meet and interact with astronauts—and witnessed my one-and-only up-close Space Shuttle launch. It was the beginning of a journey that dominated the next decade for me, and had an enormous influence on my science fiction.

It might be tempting to equate the Star Force with the Space Force that's currently in development, but the two are, at least at the present time, totally dissimilar. The details of the Space Force remain hazy at this time, but will likely not involve crewed spacecraft—certainly not the one-man fighters so prevalent in science fiction.

Of course, such one-man fighters have long been present in *Voyage Into the Unknown*; it's not that I spent my entire childhood overdosing on *Star Wars* and *Battlestar Galactica* (which I did), but rather that pilots really, really like cool fighter planes, and I don't think it's at all beyond reason that, in the future, pilots will insist on the development of cool fighters for space combat. It was the influence of pilots in high places at NASA that resulted in greater pilot control of the Gemini and Apollo spacecraft, as opposed to the ballistic capsules of the Mercury Program, and ultimately culminated in the Space Shuttle, a spacegoing airplane which made a piloted touchdown on a concrete runway.

It's true that we're now going back to capsules for deep space flight, but on the other hand, Sierra Nevada's Dream Chaser follows very much in the footsteps of the Space Shuttle. Although the Dream Chaser Space System (the crewed version) lost its bid with NASA for the Commercial Crew Program (to Boeing and SpaceX), the company signed a contract with the United Launch Alliance to launch its first two unmanned Cargo System flights in 2020 and 2021 as part of the Commercial Cargo Program. The Space System remains in development, but when (if) completed, will carry up to seven astronauts into orbit.

Virgin Galactic's SpaceShipTwo, a suborbital spaceplane designed for passenger flights, follows in the footsteps of the smaller SpaceShipOne, which few seventeen times in 2003 and 2004. SpaceShipTwo has had two test flights so far, one in December of 2018, the second in February of 2019. Riding atop the mothership White Knight Two, SpaceShipTwo detaches rather like the Space Shuttle *Enterprise* did during its approach and landing tests in 1977—but rather than gliding to a landing, SpaceShipTwo then ignites and takes off on a flight of more than two hours, with only a few minutes in space. Like the famous X-15, SpaceShipTwo falls back into the atmosphere and glides to a runway, making a piloted touchdown like the Space Shuttle.

SpaceShipTwo barely qualifies as a "spaceship," so little time does it spend in space, but it is a gateway to future space tourism—and it continues in the Space Shuttle's tradition of piloted spaceflight and runway landings.

Anyway, there's a lot of time between now and the forty-first century for pilots to influence future spacecraft design. The progress of technology does not strictly follow the most logical design; it often follows the path that people simply like the best.

Which brings me to Argo the Dreb. I confess I came dangerously close to crossing the line from science fiction into fantasy with a space wizard who basically uses the Force to get my heroes out of their predicament, but when I created the Dreb for the *Station Post One* series (now consisting of *The Priest Monster, Uneasy Alliance, "That's What They Want You to Believe,"* and *Countdown to War*), I was fascinated by a demonstration of magic tricks I saw in a little shop in St. Augustine, and thinking about shysters of the past who wormed their way into positions of power through feats of magic. I decided to write a story about a group of super-magicians who take over an entire world.

This led me to thinking about the possibility of making real-life magic through the use of science. Could the line between fantasy and science fiction be blurred by futuristic technology? Real science and science fiction have always been more intertwined than some scientists have chosen to admit; Konstantin Tsiolkovsky, Hermann Oberth, and Robert Goddard were all fans of Jules Verne! Scientists like to turn pop culture into reality. At the time I was hammering out ideas for *Station Post One,* there were a lot of stories in the news promising that the magic tricks seen in the popular *Harry Potter* movies would one day be possible thanks to futuristic technologies.

In 2016, Professor John Howell of the University of Rochester demonstrated a prototype *Harry Potter* invisibility cloak—or, more appropriately, invisibility shield. His prototype consisted of four lenses that bend light around an object, producing a convincing illusion that the object has disappeared, while the background remains stable.

Professor Howell's next iteration uses four mirrors in nested V-shapes. Howell and his son demonstrated that they could step behind the panel and disappear, while the wall behind them remained visible.

Israeli researchers at Ben-Gurion University of the Negev have been working on its own real-life invisibility cloak, which uses an "operational cloak chip," scattering light around the chip's surface.

Researchers at the Berkeley Lab at the University of California believe that the key to invisibility is dialectrics—electrical insulators that, for want of a better term, "deflect" electrical charges depending on the direction of an electrical field. In 2011, a new cloaking system was announced in which a cloak made of calcite, and can refract light around an object placed in between calcium carbonate crystals.

Virtual reality provides a means literally to live in any world we wish, to see and do things that are impossible in the real world. Who hasn't dreamed of stepping into *Star Trek: The Next Generation*'s holodeck? Although I haven't tried

VR yet, my brother has, and has attested to how real it seems. It will be possible in the future to fulfill any fantasy in the virtual world.

Now, all this is quite a different thing than a person shooting lightning from his fingertips, as Argo does in this book, but following the assumption that pop culture like *Harry Potter*—or *Star Wars* and *Star Trek* before it—tend to shape the future of science and technology, I decided to explore whether it would be possible to fulfill magic in real life.

The trick Argo performs is the same thing as the lightning trick that scientists have been performing with Tesla coils for over a century—but how does he do it with his body? I'll reprint a short segment from the *Station Post One* novel *The Priest Monster* to explain:

> "Clearly the Thermians have a longer history here than we thought. The Community is composed of many civilizations whose home planets were destroyed by the Thermians, but we've not come across a phenomenon like this before."
>
> "How did it happen?" Butch asked. "This, uh, guy, Thratt, he was somehow given the powers of the Dreb."
>
> "Yes, and Horley's equations describe in uncanny detail how this happened. Thratt's DNA was resequenced. And that's not all. I believe your science has discovered what we call *machgrach di chholbracchi*...bosons."
>
> Butch frowned. "Bosons...right. That's an elementary particle with zero spin, right?"
>
> "Put simplistically, yes. They have zero spin, and unlike other particles, a great number of them can occupy the same quantum state. The important

thing here is the micro scale of long-range waves which share wave function—the *quanta*, as I believe you call them—between individual brain cells, and the properties of certain types of bosons that can retrieve and exchange information."

Butch was beginning to understand. "And that happens on such a small scale that the quanta could easily flit back and forth between universes."

Kramm was barely following the conversation. "And this gives the Dreb their powers?"

"That in and of itself cannot give them the powers," Dugrow said. "But it is the mechanism by which the powers are imparted. Or, it would be more precise to say, the store of energy. The Dreb do not have any powers; they are simply ordinary people who are able to tap a well of intense energy and then direct it in a multitude of ways."

"Makes sense," Butch said. "Resequencing their DNA into, like, electrical conductors and stuff."

And if this isn't plausible, all I can say is, *Star Trek* gave Gary Mitchell mystical powers, so at least I'm in good company!

As I write this, we've just gotten the first photograph of a black hole, thanks to an algorithm developed by 29-year-old Katie Bouman. The data from this photo should give me some terrific material for the *next Voyage Into the Unknown* adventure, so until then…

Oh, and don't forget to check out the next few *Station Post One* books in the meantime!

Watch for
A GALAXY IN RUIN

An all-new adventure of
VOYAGE INTO THE UNKNOWN:
STATION POST ONE

VOYAGE INTO THE UNKNOWN

Collect the entire series!

With the Earth destroyed by a supernova, the Space Star *Silver Streak* moves outward into the heavens, a self-sustaining starship housing thousands, settling colonies on other planets…moving outward into the deepest, unknown reaches of space!

Short story collections

VOYAGE INTO THE UNKNOWN: VOLUME ONE
VOYAGE INTO THE UNKNOWN: VOLUME TWO
VOYAGE INTO THE UNKNOWN: VOLUME THREE
VOYAGE INTO THE UNKNOWN: VOLUME FOUR
VOYAGE INTO THE UNKNOWN: VOLUME FIVE
VOYAGE INTO THE UNKNOWN: VOLUME SIX

Novels

VOYAGE INTO THE UNKNOWN
VOYAGE INTO THE UNKNOWN 2: THE VICTORY OF MORDRAX
VOYAGE INTO THE UNKNOWN 3: BACK FROM THE FUTURE
VOYAGE INTO THE UNKNOWN 4: A FOND FAREWELL
VOYAGE INTO THE UNKNOWN 5: THE NEW BEGINNING
VOYAGE INTO THE UNKNOWN 6: THE MIND MACHINE
VOYAGE INTO THE UNKNOWN 7: PASSAGE TO HYRON
VOYAGE INTO THE UNKNOWN 8: THE REIGN OF EDMONDS
VOYAGE INTO THE UNKNOWN 9: THE KROTUS HORROR
VOYAGE INTO THE UNKNOWN 10: THE THERMIAN MENACE
VOYAGE INTO THE UNKNOWN 11: THE ARMAGEDDON STRATEGY

Station Post One

THE PRIEST MONSTER
UNEASY ALLIANCE
"THAT'S WHAT THEY WANT YOU TO BELIEVE"
COUNTDOWN TO WAR